THE ALIEN REGARDED THEM WITH HEAVY LIDDED EYES

"Do not attempt deceit, Captain Graham," it said. "Your technology is generally inferior, but I know your capabilities exactly. Call Mr. Mason and give the necessary orders to move the ship into a higher orbit."

"I will not." Arlene set her jaw, though Wyckoff could tell she was trembling.

"Captain, I am quite sure that you believe I am helpless, and perhaps I would be if you did not have a substantial colony on the surface. They serve me as hostages. I am prepared to sacrifice them all if that is necessary to gain your cooperation. Do you want a demonstration, *barbarian?*"

At that moment the bridge communicator chimed. "Captain," Mason's voice said, "I've been trying to reach you ... I can't raise the colony...."

JOSEPH H. DELANEY

LORDS TEMPORAL

BAEN BOOKS

LORDS TEMPORAL

A Baen Books Original

Baen Publishing Enterprises
260 Fifth Avenue
New York, N.Y. 10001

First printing, January 1987

ISBN: 0-671-65613-9

Cover art by Alan Gutierrez

Printed in the United States of America

Distributed by
SIMON & SCHUSTER
1230 Avenue of the Americas
New York, N.Y. 10020

Chapter One

There is nothing quite so terrible as a big city on a cold night. By day at least there are people to panhandle, vehicles to dodge, cops to avoid, chances to duck inside store foyers and warm up a bit. It is a shade less lonely.

These distractions flee with the sun, leaving streets so silent that the crunch of a foot on dirty gray snow sounds like thunder. The people leave for warm, comfortable homes elsewhere in the sprawling city and lock the doorways of their stores with collapsible steel gates studded with padlocks. They trust to luck that when the sun comes up again the show windows will still be intact; that out of dim shadows will come no thief with the determination to break in, or that if one does he will be quickly caught by vigilant police on patrol.

This was Wyckoff's world. New York City, 2069 A.D. He shared it with perhaps half a million others as unfortunate as himself, who had no homes, no jobs, and who lacked the capability to get out of the north when the frost came.

For most of the year the street was not too bad. Wyckoff knew his jungle well. Every season was unique, bringing both new rules and new opportunities. He liked winter the least, because it was physically the

1

hardest and the pickings so abysmally slim. Some days it was all he could do to get enough to eat. And seldom in the dead of winter could he accumulate enough coins to buy a flop. The flophouse operators knew the desperation the cold bred in their customers and raised the rates as the temperature fell.

So, those who could pay, did. The others just kept going all night or, if they were really badly off, descended into the subways or the Mission hostels.

Wyckoff huddled out of the wind, standing in a darkened doorway half a block from the nearest light, and tried to make up his mind what to do with the rest of the evening. It had not yet gotten really cold—the temperature was still in the high twenties—but a look up at the sky told him this would not last long. The night was comparatively clear, and stars could be seen even through the heavy smoke and haze. There were no clouds to hold the planet's heat.

He felt in his pocket with fingers stiffened by the cold, counting coins gathered during the day. There were so few of them; no chance of getting in anywhere warm with what he could afford to pay.

Not so long ago he had been lucky enough to have a hole beneath a demolished building, where a couple of small, dank basement rooms were still habitable, if the occupant possessed the determination. For a while Wyckoff had exercised that determination, leaving each day just before dawn and returning after dark, lest he be seen entering or leaving.

Then the cold had come, and he'd taken to building fires in a makeshift stove fashioned from an old oil drum. It worked fine until the ruins caught fire, and on that night he escaped with his life only by the sheerest luck.

Now, until he found another such redoubt, he was at the mercy of the elements or the flophouse operators, and he couldn't make up his mind which he detested more.

Suddenly these dismal reminiscences fled, replaced by another, more immediate problem. Lights caught his eye, arcing through the night with that curious languid pause peculiar to roving police patrols. With practiced skill, Wyckoff froze and huddled deeper into the shadows. This was a neighborhood of commercial shops in which, during the day, labored printers, shoe finders, cutlers, hardware wholesalers, electrical and plumbing jobbers, and the like. Here was no score, unless a man happened to be a burglar. Wyckoff was not, though to the approaching police patrol that might be a distinction without a difference. He decided he didn't want to chance it.

The patrol edged closer, having stopped at an alley a little farther down, while a cop inside the car shined his spotlight on the rows of locked doors. Cops didn't do that very often; these must have found a break-in somewhere nearby.

That changed everything, and Wyckoff's street savvy told him that this doorway was no place for him to be. Though it would be comparatively warmer, he preferred not to be in jail, even in winter. Some street people did, and routinely provoked some incident at the first frost. These were usually the older dudes, who'd lost that stamina Wyckoff still possessed and weren't good candidates for the press gangs, who sold their dignity for three months out of each year.

Wyckoff knew some of them well. There was a guy called Silky, a giant black dude who claimed to have been a prominent pimp in his younger days and who told endless stories about how things had been then. Jails, he said, had been palaces, with clean cells and decent food, where an inmate could lie around and do his time watching TV. Nobody worked on the roads, or cleaned public buildings, or was shipped off to algae farms or sludge plants. The con's life was an easy life then.

Whose wasn't? To hear the old geezers talk—and Wyckoff had, from the day he'd been old enough to understand—the quality of life had worsened with every generation. His own grandfather hadn't been employable the last thirty years of his life, and he'd let the world know he didn't like that. His endless complaints about the system constituted some of Wyckoff's earliest and most vivid memories.

Everybody knew the story—how the so-called Cold War between the United States and Russia had ruined the economy of the whole world. It was history, rapidly becoming ancient history at that; but its effects continued to be felt with undiminished severity almost a century after the fact.

The SDI, they called it: Strategic Defense Initiative, Star Wars. America said she wanted it, though many of her most illustrious scientists argued ably and at length that it wouldn't work.

They were wrong. To a man they were wrong. The SDI, though it failed technically for scientific reasons, nevertheless worked perfectly and devastatingly, precisely as western economists intended.

Because the only possible way to stop U.S. development of the system was to have the devastating nuclear war it was meant to avoid, and because they were unwilling to trust their enemy to share the technology as he said he would, the Russians had no choice. They had to try to match the effort—and thereby tumbled neatly into the economic trap.

They did not at first understand this trap—or, more likely, did not appreciate that worldwide realities operated upon their fiscal system the same as on any other. And so by the time the situation's true character was apparent, they were lost; they had spent too much of a national wealth that never had matched that of their adversaries' to begin with. The result was economic chaos and political collapse.

In the United States the reaction had been joyous. A hundred years of nuclear bondage had come to an end at last. Better yet, there now existed, thanks to the effort, a well-developed space technology. In near-Earth orbit, satellite factories and cities had sprung up. At the LaGrange points, vast laboratories and workshops had been constructed, and a young mathematical physicist named Eric Aschenbrenner was busy trying to prove that there was a way around the light-speed barrier. It was about this time that Wyckoff's grandfather had left his prostrate Russian homeland and emigrated to the United States, now unquestionably the dominant power on Earth.

Grandfather Wyckoff was a farmer of sorts. Raised and trained under the Russian system, he had understood the theory of large-scale agriculture better than most—well enough, in fact, to move steadily upward within the country's foremost agricorp.

But it was a long way down from the top. Grandfather Wyckoff did not understand the reasons, while it was happening, but he figured them out afterward, and spent the remainder of his life explaining them to anyone he could persuade to listen.

Being a child, young Stanislaus had little choice in the matter. Grandfather was around constantly, with nothing to do, and he was often lonely. Worse, there was a bitterness in him that his double portion of calamity could only fortify. He had emerged from one decaying economy just in time to witness the collapse of another; this time, that of the entire world.

He told his story often. With each telling it was embellished, and details were added that had not been apparent before. It was the story of the little bank in Singapore whose wild speculations in overvalued real estate had created a Frankenstein's monster of tiered credit in Eurodollars and brought about the collapse of the entire worldwide banking system. "Deflation," Grandfather had called it, as though he understood what that meant.

And maybe he had; Wyckoff didn't know. But he did know that there was one thing all the old-timers agreed upon: the Great Depression of 2028 made all prior economic upheavals pale by comparison. More than a quarter-century later it still exerted its effects.

Because young Stanislaus had grown up during those

years and had known nothing else, his approach to his
lifestyle had been a great deal more philosophical than
that of his elders. What they lamented he endured
without a murmur, because he knew no better. As a
child, he had not been aware he was poor, because
everyone around him had been poor, and he was the
same as they.

Only when he had grown a little did he learn that
there dwelt on Earth people who did not sleep a dozen
to a room or eat porridge with their fingers from a
common pot, who wore shoes in summer when they
were not needed. Wisdom arrived about the time his
first whiskers appeared, when a sanctimonious social
worker appeared at their flat accompanied by a re-
cruiter from the Conservation Corps. The Corps, they
said, was just the thing to make a man of him.

The Corps, Wyckoff mused—it still existed. He and
his contemporaries called it the "Corpse." It was the
principal reason he avoided the Mission hostels like the
plague. Too many people he had known had checked
into these—and into the arms of a press gang.

Wyckoff crept out of the doorway just as another car
was passing the police cruiser, and while the spotlight
was trained on another doorway farther up the block.
He hoped the cops inside would be distracted enough
so that they wouldn't notice him.

It was a hope soon dashed, and he knew as soon as he
ducked around the corner that they would be after him.
Reason told him not to run; he'd done nothing and he
had nothing to hide. Impulse argued differently. At the
very least it meant detention here on the street, a
search, perhaps a beating, while they tried to learn his
true identity. As a fugitive from the Corps, Wyckoff
didn't carry an I.D. That would have made it too easy
for the police to check his background if they ever
stopped him. This way was safer.

He took off down the alley, sprinting over the hard-
packed snow, which in places had already started to
glaciate into cloudy ice—the kind that would still coat

patches of the alley in June. He reached the end of the alley and took a turn to the right, so that he could come up behind the squadron. In this neighborhood the police always kept one man in the car, and though the man in the car might move it, he would not be likely to join his companion in a foot search.

Wyckoff reached the right-angle street and raced across a bare sidewalk to the other side. Behind him, he could hear curses echoing through the stillness of the night, and he knew the pursuing cop had fallen on the ice. That assured his getaway, since he could now easily put two or three blocks between them.

Even when he knew it was no longer necessary, Wyckoff continued at a slow trot. The exertion was warming his body, and he was reluctant to let that feeling go. He'd have to be careful not to sweat, though, since that would aggravate his problems with the cold. He ran on through the silence.

The run ended at the next intersection, where two arterial streets met in chilled, forsaken emptiness. One side of the intersection was blind. There a huge truck had apparently broken down, and now sat with five feet of its length protruding into the crosswalk. In the morning, when traffic swelled to its daytime proportions, it would have caused a snarl which would have had every cop on the force here. But in the dark, nighttime emptiness it was safe, serene, and unnoticed—until now.

Notice arrived late to the driver of the low-slung Mallory Electric who whipped around the corner just as Wyckoff was stepping off the curb. The idiot! He didn't have lights on, and electrics made almost no noise. The car missed Wyckoff by only a hair, as he frantically leapt back up on the curb, shaking his fist in the air.

The Mallory's driver must have first seen him at that instant. He must also have been greatly startled at what had almost happened. He turned sharply away from the curb. Then he tried to correct.

But by that time he was out of the intersection. There, the driver made a second mistake and laid his foot heavily on the brake. Lacking friction on the frozen slush, the brakes could lock, but they could do nothing else, and natural laws sent the car onward in the direction of its present motion. That motion was toward the next corner—the one where, down the street, the lone cop sat in his cruiser.

Wyckoff watched. The car slid onward, its momentum undiminished either by the driver's frantic braking or his erratic steering. Nothing he did would stop the car. A fireplug slowed it, though its upper casting broke off instantly as the car plunged on.

A torrent of water rose high into the air, where it was caught by the icy wind. Wyckoff's clothing was saturated with freezing droplets before he could take a step. His chance to survive the night outside vanished, though he quickly moved out of the worst of it.

Already the numbing cold was seeping into him. He knew he'd have to go with the police now; he'd die if he didn't. If he was lucky they might not bother to check his fingerprints against the files. Wyckoff knew that doing that was a lot of trouble, and that as a bum he wouldn't rate close attention. If they learned he was a deserter from the Corps he would be in real trouble, but the odds were that these guys would understand and hold him only long enough to dry him off.

He started to turn to find the foot cop, intending to surrender and be marched off to jail. The cop could hardly have failed to hear the crash and should be coming around the corner any moment.

Wyckoff waited patiently, glancing behind nervously. He was growing colder by the instant, and still there was no cop. He was about to start walking to the squad car and give himself up when he heard wheels squealing behind him. He looked at the Mallory, now stationary with its nose against a building and its back wheels turning frictionlessly in a snowbank. The driver couldn't be conscious; not unless he was so stupid or drunk that he planned to drive through that wall.

Wyckoff despaired of finding the cop. The cop, too,

must be unconscious from his fall, or else they had
received another call with a higher priority than this
and left—left Wyckoff here to freeze to death.

Well, Wyckoff would see about that. Though he was
even now starting to shiver uncontrollably, he struggled
through the drift of snow toward the trapped car. Its
rear wheels were still spinning.

He reached it and grasped the handle to the driver's
door, hoping it would not be locked. It came open with
a crunch that told Wyckoff the hood had been forced
back against its leading edge.

Inside, the driver lay against the wheel, out like a
light but moaning softly. He smelled heavily of the
sauce and was bleeding from the nose. Its bridge looked
curiously and unnaturally flattened, and it was starting
to swell. Blood was trickling from the corner of the
driver's mouth, which made his injuries look more serious than they actually were. Wyckoff had seen enough
battered mugs in his time to know the difference.

Wyckoff noticed something else. The car was warm
inside. Somewhere below the dash a catalytic heater
filled the interior with the characteristic odor of burning alcohol.

Not by any means a man to disdain comfort, Wyckoff
slammed the driver's door and raced around to the
passenger's side. He slid in gratefully and began soaking up heat. After a moment he felt the edge of the chill
leave him, and he stopped shivering. Then he reached
down and pulled the driver's foot off the accelerator
pedal. The squealing stopped.

Wyckoff took a look out the back window, wondering
how long it would be before somebody noticed the
ruined hydrant, connected its condition to this car, and
threw both him and the driver in a cell. Certainly this
would happen long before Wyckoff's clothing was dry.
Wyckoff liked being warm so well that he decided to
take the car somewhere where he could cozy out the
night next to the heater. The driver wouldn't know;
drunk as he was, he wouldn't care, either.

Besides, he owed Wyckoff—he was the reason for Wyckoff's predicament, and it was only right that he pay for his transgression in coin of Wyckoff's choosing. Though the driver obviously had money, and therefore clout, Wyckoff doubted the city would look kindly at the damage he'd done. Getting him away from the scene of his crime might be the biggest favor Wyckoff could do him. He might even be grateful enough when he sobered up to reward Wyckoff for his trouble.

That possibility was the kicker. Though reluctant to leave the heat, even for an instant, Wyckoff stepped out and dragged the driver over to the passenger's side.

A minute later he was behind the blood-slippery wheel, carefully backing the car out along the tracks it had made coming in. Wyckoff wasn't a very good driver—he'd never had much practice—but the car's controls were simple and he took his time.

Fifteen minutes later, with the driver now sleeping uncomfortably and noisily, he parked on a deserted residential street on the east side. He sat there, waiting for his clothes to dry, and thought about tomorrow.

Tomorrow, now that it looked like he would still have his freedom when it came, would still find Wyckoff with his usual problems: no money, no dinner, and no place to sleep but on the street.

That is, he told himself, unless this dude is carrying some real green on him—some "pocket money," out of which a reward could be gained. He didn't look like the kind who would. The typical individual affluent enough to drive a car of any kind generally carried only credit cards, if he carried anything at all. In many instances voiceprint verification was all that was needed to buy almost anything, anywhere in the country.

Wyckoff checked him over anyway, noting that they were about the same size and build and that the dude was sporting a really fine set of threads. To Wyckoff, even in the dim light on the instrument panel, the cloth looked polyinsulated. Polyinsulated clothing was very new. It had been developed for astronauts, but the civilian market included many of the affluent, and Wyckoff had seen lots of it down around Wall Street this winter.

Pockets, let's see; where were the pockets? He fumbled around on the sleeping body until he found a ridge, which indicated a seam.

Awkwardly, he managed to pry an opening with a thumbnail. It had nothing in it.

He gave his companion a roll, so that he could get at the one on the other side, and was rewarded by a blast of stale whiskey-breath in his face. He pushed the other's head aside and dived into that pocket. This one held a slim leather case, which Wyckoff extracted and held under the dash to read.

He found an I.D. card, examined it carefully, then dug underneath the plastic flap and pulled it out. The plastic laminate card had an elaborately scrolled green border and a white and yellow striped interior. Printed in the margin in bold type were the words UNITED STATES AERONAUTICS and SPACE ADMINISTRATION. Below that was a long number, separated into four groups of three digits each: some kind of I.D. code for the card's owner, Emory Knowles. And underneath that were the words, "This certifies that the bearer hereof is a member in good standing of the Brotherhood of Masters, Mates, and Spacemen." It bore countersignatures of the Space Administrator and of the Union Secretary.

So: his benefactor was a spaceman. Wyckoff wondered briefly just what kind of spacehand he was. He had never, of course, met one before. Few people had. When planetbound, they stayed aloof from the rest of the population. They were an elite, well-paid group, who commanded the best company in the best accommodations. They were a new nobility.

"What's a bird like him doing in the neighborhood I found him in?" Wyckoff asked himself. He got no answer, of course, and the man was obviously not in any shape to ask. He'd certainly sleep the night, perhaps part of the next day, and he'd be reasonably comfortable until his alcohol tank ran dry.

Wyckoff fished around some more in the pocket. He found nothing except a thin, barely readable copy of some kind of rental receipt which listed Knowles' local address as the Carlton Arms Motel, but he did notice how warm his hand had become. That polyinsulated fabric was all right, he thought. With a suit of that, he could be comfortable anywhere, all winter.

Well, why not? Would the chance ever come again? Certainly not. Would its owner miss it? Not until he sobered up, and besides, dudes like him had money all the time. He could just buy himself another one.

In that instant Wyckoff realized that he would be foolish to count on generosity from a stranger, that he risked all by being squeamish, that the only sure way was to take: as the rest of the world took, as this Knowles must have taken to get where he had gotten.

Wyckoff stuck the cardcase back into the pocket. Then he found the fastener rings and peeled the suit off the drunken Knowles. The man shivered a little with the shock, but went on snoring. With the heater going, he'd be all right.

Wyckoff pulled off his own soiled clothing and stacked it on the back seat, remembering to retrieve his little hoard of coins and the packet containing his comb and razor. Then he slid into the coverall.

He was astonished. It felt just as if he were sitting nude in a flawlessly temperature-controlled building. Wyckoff had heard that this garment alone would keep a person's skin temperature perfectly at optimum at the equator or at the pole. Now he believed it.

This accomplished, he turned the key and drove the car from the curb. He wanted to be long gone when Knowles awoke, and now that he had the suit he didn't need the heater anymore. He drove the car downtown and parked it in a place sure to infuriate the first traffic cop to spot it the next morning. Tossing the key onto the pile of clothing on the back seat, he strolled nonchalantly away. He spent the night perched high on a fire escape behind an apartment house, resting comfortably in a place where normally a polar bear would have frozen to death.

Chapter Two

Wyckoff arose at sunup, and was cautiously descending the snow-encrusted steps when he saw the ambulance rush by. Curious, he watched, and noted its destination.

The ambulance stopped a block and a half away, where several police cars had already congregated. He arrived in time to see ambulance attendants lifting a stiff figure onto a stretcher. The figure was covered with frozen blood, but there was no question about who it was: Knowles.

Wyckoff could have kicked himself. Thanks to his stupidity, a man was dead. He'd left the car doors unlocked, thinking Knowles would soon be found. He was right about that. Somebody had found him, only it was the wrong person—one of the street crazies, no doubt, who'd taken the car and cut Knowles' throat before throwing him out in the snow. Wyckoff had spent nearly half his thirty years out on these streets, and in that time had managed to avoid committing any really serious crime. Now, in one fell swoop, he had made up for this with the most serious of all. He had killed Knowles as surely as if he had cut the man's throat himself.

Panic then struck Wyckoff like a battering ram. That

might be exactly what the police would think if they happened to notice him here and question him. He had to run. He was wearing the dead man's suit, and it probably had a personalized brand in it somewhere; most expensive property did. If he was stopped for any reason that might result in a check, they'd have him cold. It was all very well for him to experience guilt and remorse—these he deserved. But society's chastisement would be an altogether different thing—he did not deserve that.

Wyckoff turned and walked away at the safest, yet fastest pace he could manage. He intended to put as much distance as possible between himself and the scene of the crime. Already police were swarming into the area, and most were heading from there toward the south side, which direction it was Wyckoff's natural inclination to go. That was territory he knew, where he ordinarily felt safe.

It was not safe now. Down there, every derelict the police encountered would be thrown across the hood of a car, searched, and questioned, especially if he were dressed a little bit out of his class. The south side wouldn't do. Enough cops down here knew him by sight to make that risky. He'd be better off to head for a neighborhood where that couldn't happen, and wait for things to cool off. He knew how these things worked—a fresh crime, a furious initial effort to find a suspect, then gradual abandonment and indifference as soon as the hopelessness of the quest was apparent. The cops were like a pack of hounds—eager, but helpless without a scent and thus easily distracted in favor of the next possible chase. He would retreat and wait for that to happen.

Wyckoff felt in his pocket, silently counted the coins. Yes, there was enough—just barely enough. Though it would mean nothing to eat for a while longer, it was the only way out. He took the coins out and hailed the oncoming northbound bus.

*   *   *

The marquee said "Hotel von Steuben." It looked old, but it was well maintained, and there was a lot of traffic in and out its doors. From the looks of it, there was some sort of convention going on. Good. That'd mean all the employees would be fairly busy. They'd be unlikely to notice another unkempt stranger, especially as the suit's hood concealed the worst of his straggly hair and beard. He could duck into an upstairs washroom and clean up, maybe even shave.

The hotel was busy. Wyckoff stepped onto an elevator with a porter bearing a rack of loose clothing who seemed to be preoccupied with searching through his keys. Wyckoff waited until the porter got off, then stopped the elevator at the next floor.

There was soap in the washroom. He quickly lathered up and shaved, then trimmed his wild locks as best he could, camouflaging the worst of the rest by turning up the collars of the garment. This was how he found the hidden pockets.

There was a slight bulge under each lapel. They weren't large but they were obviously meant to hide valuable things. Wyckoff pried each of them open and examined the contents.

One item was a flimsy—a lightweight but very durable type of paper much favored by government agencies. Wyckoff unfolded it and read it.

Knowles, it seems, had been promoted and assigned to a new ship, the *Corona*. Wyckoff did not know what a chief storekeeper did, precisely, but the name was itself suggestive of the duties.

He checked the other pocket. There were two items in it. One was hard metal; the other was paper, folded tightly.

With fumbling fingers he dug them out. He thought at first that the metal object was a coin. It wasn't. It was an I.D. medallion for the *USSS Corona*. Interesting. Wyckoff thought this might have street value. If he could sell it, it should bring a good price, because it would get its bearer on board one of the huge colonial ships that left Earth once a month.

He slipped the medallion back into the pocket and looked at the other object. It was a 500 CR. note. Wyckoff couldn't believe it. This was more money than he had ever before seen in all his life.

He gazed into the mirror, surveyed the face that smiled back at him, and was pleased. The smile became less a smile than a grimace, but this seemed tempered by the earnest look of his ice-blue eyes, and on the whole, the effect was impish instead of wicked, as he meant it. With his whiskers gone, and the wildest of his wavy brown locks trimmed and pasted into place with warm water, Wyckoff decided he looked like a man who would wear a polyinsulated suit. The appearance, in turn, begat the proper mood. He took a towel and removed what few flecks of blood had managed to adhere to the material, slipped the flimsy and the medallion into one hip pocket and his razor and comb in the other, then strode off down the corridor to the elevator.

Reaching it, he pushed the button and waited. While he was there a young woman came along and stood waiting beside him. Wyckoff could feel her eyes on him, and for an instant he thought there was something wrong. But when the elevator arrived and he stepped aside for her to enter, she gave him a warm smile.

He instantly relaxed. The gaze had been one of curious admiration—something he was definitely not used to getting, though that was largely the fault of his lifestyle. Clothes, he observed, definitely do make the man.

The realization struck him like a poleax. All these years he'd been doing things wrong, hiding out down on bedbug row. The real scores were up here, and now the door was open. He had the means to mingle among the affluent. In this suit, he would be accepted on sight. And with the money, he might share what they had—buy his way into a legitimate business, or parlay an influential acquaintance into a real job.

Wyckoff entered the lobby and stood there amidst the throng of bodies and stacks of luggage, looking around. This, he decided, would be the place to break that big bill. In the rush, who would notice? Travelers could be expected to carry big money.

He consulted the lobby directory, located the dining room, and went in to order breakfast. Though it, too, was crowded, he was quickly seated, thanks to his appearance. He ordered eggs Benedict, the most expensive thing on the menu, and told the waitress to bring him the latest news printout.

Breakfast arrived first, and it was all he could do not to simply wolf it down. He had never before in his life eaten like this. Afterwards he sat there, leisurely sipping coffee and scanning through the fanfolded news printout.

At the end was the crime news. There was so much violent crime in the city these days that the news sheets didn't give it special attention, unless it involved a public figure. They listed murders, for instance, by location, date, and name, if known. Knowing the location, Wyckoff found Knowles quickly. He was described only as an unidentified Caucasian male.

Wyckoff felt better. He would not be hunted as Knowles' murderer. The police never bothered with John Doe stiffs. These were carted off to the crematory and forgotten. Perhaps the killer had done Wyckoff a bigger favor than he realized, running off with the man's car. Wyckoff wondered briefly about that—could he be traced through the car?

He relaxed. No, the car had been rented, so the police would have no way of associating the body with the car, because Wyckoff had all Knowles' papers and his I.D. If the car ever did turn up, the rental agency would simply bill Knowles for the use, and that wasn't Wyckoff's worry. By the time it happened, the ship— what was the name? *Corona*—would be light years away, hauling a load of colonists to a new and uncrowded world.

Long ago, when he was a child, and when the colonization program had been just getting under way, Wyckoff had dreamed of getting into it. People had talked about it endlessly, as the answer to the overcrowding and the poverty here on Earth. It hadn't been, though, any more than the ability to reach other worlds had solved the economic problems with which Earth was fraught.

The capital had simply gone out into space with the ships, creating a new ruling class of affluents, and preserving below the same grinding poverty that had always existed among the masses. Space glittered in newness and innovation; Old Earth languished below and rotted. There wasn't a municipal sewer or water system on the planet that hadn't been built in the previous century. The golden age promised by the fiction writers had passed this old world by. It had become instead a living, functioning museum, albeit a creaky one.

Wyckoff knew that there was pressure on governments to do away with the colonies, which promised not to be profitable for centuries to come, if ever, and whose meager demands for people made not the slightest dent in Earth's seething hordes. For every colonist who left, two more were quickly bred, and it was estimated that the world's population now numbered ten billion.

Wyckoff's attitudes toward social questions were frankly fatalistic, except when he had been touched as personally by them as he had by this one. He favored the continuation of the colonization program, whatever its cost, over the alternative—the Corpse—which he knew for certain was both evil and ineffectual.

Perhaps, in reality, it need be neither. Wyckoff didn't know, and didn't particularly care, whether the underlying theory was sound, while he did know and did care that what had come of it was corrupt. He had seen that with his own eyes, and knew that the stories that circulated were not "just rumors propagated by the

shiftless lower classes," as some politicos claimed. They
were real.

So Wyckoff did favor the colonial program, which at
least was a new start with a new chance for a fortunate
few, whereas cleaning up the poisoned areas of the
Earth was a task which only nature might accomplish,
and then only after eons of time had passed, no matter
how many impressed Corpsmen gave their lives for it.

When she had squandered her once-vast mineral
wealth, America next began to lay waste to the land
itself, in order to maintain the prodigious pace of her
consumption and to get the money she needed to continue importing minerals from places where they were
still plentiful.

Food had been conceived as the key to that—the
produce of those fertile plains that once had languished
unmolested for eons covered only by grasses. But as
more and more land was pressed into service, the sun
and wind leached its moisture, progressively exposing
layer after layer to erosion.

In some places there had never been enough water
to begin with, and what there was had not been
distributed to man's liking. So he tinkered, and wrought
works mighty considering his size, though puny by
nature's standards.

They were enough, however, to upset her balance.
Soils thinned, and nutrients escaped to choke once
free-running streams to death with algae and silt. What
remained was not enough, and so it was augmented
with chemicals with never a thought to what natural
forces would do to them after they had served man's
immediate purpose. The ever-dwindling harvests could
not feed the hordes of pests; they must be preserved to
feed the hordes of people. In the war that followed, friend
could not be and was not distinguished from foe. All
were ruthlessly exterminated without regard to whether
it was enemy or ally, and striking down his friends, as
he had, man doubled the might of his antagonists.

In an earlier day the tragedy could never have reached

the proportions that it did. From time immemorial nature herself had winnowed the ranks of the husbandmen and individually punished those who bruised her precious soil. But here again the meddling of men had thrown the system out of kilter. The stewardship of the land had long since passed from the hands of occupants to those of the moneylenders who never touched the land itself, but whose fingers continually groped for the pulse of human greed—and all too often found it.

Now, all this was finished—the continental middle was in some cases scoured down to the bedrock, the once-fertile mountain valleys had become salt deserts, each doomed to remain barren until centuries of meager rainfall had soaked through them and carried the salts back to the depths. And perhaps in a thousand, or ten thousand, or a hundred thousand years the great aquifers which had carried it up to the surface would themselves be cleansed of the pollutants man had put in them.

Mere man had destroyed it all, but mere man could not undo the destruction—not with all his sober resolve, not with all the good intentions that had been born of terror.

Nevertheless, he was making a pretense at self-discipline, though in the view of many, self-flagellation would have been the more appropriate term, provided only that it be extended to the entire species.

Of course it wasn't. It affected only a part of it—the weakest, most helpless part of it, those innocents and their progeny who, though they had not benefited from the rape of the planet, were nevertheless selected by those in command to pay the price for it—to become the slave caste of the 21st century. The Corpse.

It was Wyckoff's timely recognition of the futility, the uselessness, the wastefulness of such projects that had saved his own skin. *Glory alone rises to the pinnacle,* he had concluded; *blame retreats into the depths of the largest available mass.* So, unconsciously—but fortunately—having concluded that his presence and his efforts would change nothing, he had deserted the Corps and come back here, to New York City, and lost himself in its immensity to live the life of an outcast.

Wyckoff shook his head unconsciously, as if to break off an unappealing train of thought, and turned his attention back to the news sheet. On impulse, he turned to the shipping news. Wyckoff felt an urge to learn a little more about Knowles, now that he was gone.

He found the *Corona* listed in port at Matagorda, scheduled to depart on the twenty-third for a colony called Zahn. Zahn? The name sounded odd to Wyckoff. He knew of other worlds: those closest, like Herschel and Wolfingham, which had had time to build up substantial populations and with whom there was some trade; those frequently in the news, like Wells, and Verne, and Palmer and Chandler and Mitchell. But these were but a handful out of the hundreds that had been seeded.

He put the printout down, swallowed the rest of his coffee, paid his bill, and left with a pocketful of small-denomination notes. He could now wander where he would.

He went downtown and mingled in the crowds, strolling through stores filled with things he could never have afforded to buy and which, before he had acquired his new suit, he would never have dared to enter. Later he had lunch in a swank grill in the theater section, and flirted with a girl at the table in the corner. He had not ever had the nerve to do a thing like that before.

He had almost reached the point of walking over to try an introduction when she was joined by a burly man who looked like he would be jealously protective, so Wyckoff turned his mind back to his dinner.

So far, he had not done anything constructive with his new situation. He had concentrated instead on fulfilling his heretofore unfulfillable desires. But he knew the money would not last forever at this rate, and he had to find a way to make his newfound capital work for him.

He considered many possibilities, not a few of them illegal. In the part of the city most familiar to Wyckoff, the line between the two was often blurred, with the illegality of an act dependent not so much on the character of the act as the identity and politics of the actor. Wyckoff had always had difficulty distinguishing the flourishing policy games from the legal lottery, the illegal bookies from the licensed bookmakers, the loan sharks from the legitimate bankers, and so on, ad nauseam. He had no idea yet what the enterprise would be, but Wyckoff was certain that in this new society he now envisioned for himself there was a niche he could fill, and that he would find the roots of it within his contacts, down in his old haunts. One of them would surely find him a buyer for Knowle's medallion.

He decided the sooner that happened the better, with the bulk of the day already gone. The area around the scene of Knowles' murder would surely have cooled off, assuming there had ever been a genuine search for his killer.

Wyckoff hopped a bus and headed south, crossing under the river through the tunnel. At the other end there was an area of relative safety, where normal people worked during the day, and where his attire, though it would be somewhat unusual, would not be entirely out of place. He got off the bus there and started walking south, toward the docks, where he had acquaintances.

But once he got beyond the immediate area of the shops he realized it was a mistake. There was a car creeping suspiciously down the street behind him.

This one, like Knowles', was a red Mallory Electric. It might even have been the same car. But whether or not it was, the significance to him of the two men in it was the same to Wyckoff as Knowles' killers had been to Knowles: they were enemies; they wanted what he had. They would take it if they could, as they had almost certainly stolen the car they drove.

Wyckoff looked around him to assess the possibilities

for defense or flight. He had already abandoned hope of deterrence—there was almost nobody on the street. The raw cold wind to which he was now so oblivious still plagued the less fortunate, and there were few of them who cared to brave a stroll.

Panic welled. Wyckoff knew what these men wanted, and what they would do to get it. People who killed for no reason, such as those who had killed Knowles, would hardly treat a victim gently, and he looked affluent. Where Wyckoff the bum would have been safe, Wyckoff the dude was in mortal danger.

He looked ahead. There was no help there; just a long line of warehouses behind the docks. Wyckoff was still too far away to make a run for the docks.

So instead he began a retreat, back the way he had come, which told the men in the car that he knew what they planned.

The car stopped and went into reverse, first pacing him and then speeding up, to get between him and the relative safety of the crowds farther down the street. It then stopped again, and the passenger door opened. A rough-looking man leapt out and started after him. In the meantime the car sped forward again so that the driver could cut him off from the other direction.

Wyckoff was no stranger to street violence, though he avoided fighting whenever he could. He was unarmed, though, and he knew the others almost certainly wouldn't be. And outnumbered, he knew before the beginning what the end must be. He could not retreat to a place where neither car nor assailant could follow, because such a place did not exist. There was, therefore, only one thing he could do: he must attack, immediately, while he could still limit the confrontation to one opponent at a time.

He looked around for something he might use for a weapon. There was nothing in sight that could fill the bill, but there was a nearby instrument which might help some—the battered lid of a galvanized steel gar-

bage can. Wyckoff bent down and picked it up by its
twisted handle.

Turning, he faced the first adversary.

The man stopped as soon as Wyckoff picked up the
lid. He had a sneer on his face and a knife in his right
hand.

Wyckoff waited, standing perfectly still, for the other
to close in.

The man did, throwing the knife from hand to hand
as he took small, cautious steps toward his victim. His
behavior was intended to intimidate Wyckoff, to demonstrate he was an experienced knife fighter.

Wyckoff had no doubt of this. He had faced such
people before, and he knew there would be that instant
when the knife entered the favored hand—usually the
right one—and the weight was thrown on the left foot.
Then his attacker would spring. He cast a quick glance
behind him, knowing that he still had a second or two.
The other man was getting out of the car, but he was
still too far away to be an immediate menace.

Wyckoff glanced at the man's feet, noted that two
more steps would put him in attack position, and estimated the time. He waited for the man to take the first
step, and while his foot was in the air, quickly ducked,
reaching down with the lid and scooping it full of snow.
He brought it up just as the man was about to start his
second and final step.

He threw the blinding, frigid snow into the man's
face. As it hit him, Wyckoff plunged forward, his weight
also on his left foot. He brought the lid around and
smashed its edge into his opponent's lower jaw, then
down against his knife hand. The man fell backward,
striking the ground and sprawling. The knife fell from
his hand and Wyckoff scooped it up.

Behind him, the snow crunched heavily. Rising from
his stooped position, he raised the lid overhead, and
caught the blow from the jackhandle squarely in its
middle. Then he lunged, bringing the knife up in an
underhand thrust below the attacker's ribs.

The man dropped the jackhandle. A look of disbelief washed over his face, and he crumpled into the snow.

The other man, now risen, ran past him, headed for the car. Wyckoff leaped up to follow, though he knew by now that he was safe, having demonstrated convincingly that he was no easy victim. Somehow, though, perhaps because deep down inside he felt a need to strike a blow against such parasites—or to vicariously avenge the murdered Knowles—he continued his pursuit.

Whatever his reason, he remained committed. In the snowbank, comparatively unencumbered by the light suit, he had an easier time than the other, and reached him just as his quarry was grabbing for the door handle.

Wyckoff was not the squeamish sort. Having killed one of them, he knew he should do no less for the other. He raised the knife, prepared to cut the man's throat.

As he did so the man went suddenly limp and turned his head fearfully, glaring at Wyckoff through eyes filled with terror.

Wyckoff could feel no sympathy for the man. He was obviously a crazy—he had that wild, abandoned look that some of them acquired, particularly if they were users of recreational drugs. He was momentarily helpless.

Wyckoff knew then that though this man justly deserved to die, he could not play the part of executioner. He could kill in self-defense, as he just had, but not in cold blood.

Yet at the same time, he could not allow this man to go unpunished, or permit him his freedom in a condition to immediately go out and attack some other helpless victim, and he had to have time to think about what the punishment and the prevention might be.

To gain time without moving the knife, he launched a punch at the man's chops with his free hand, putting into it rather more energy than he intended. The man saw it coming and flinched, and made his situation worse. He caught it on the nose, which broke.

Wyckoff released him and watched him fall to the

ground, blood spurting into the snow, steaming briefly before it froze. Breathing heavily from the exertion, he took the time to glance around to see if there had been any witnesses to the engagement. He didn't see anybody close, but far down the street behind him there was a car, and it looked like it might be a police car.

Further observation confirmed his suspicion—it was the police, and they were headed his way. He had to leave, and in a hurry, before they got near enough to see what had happened. If they did, he knew he had no chance. No court would ever buy his story. He would never see daylight again.

He might have tried to make it on foot, had there been cover in the areas of the neighborhood with which he was intimate, but there wasn't any. The only practical means of escape appeared to be the car.

Wyckoff was committed to that course as soon as a glance told him the key was in it. He dropped the bloody knife on the ground, jumped into the car, threw the switch, and sped off, hoping the coils had enough charge left to get him far away from here. As he rounded the turn that would cut off his view completely, Wyckoff looked into the mirror. The cops had seen the bodies. They were stopping, but either they had not noticed that his car had pulled away from that exact spot or they were in contact with another car and depending on it to intercept Wyckoff. If they were they might not give chase, and perhaps he could get lost in traffic. He was fairly certain that from the distance they would not have been able to see the car's license number.

Assuming they would not follow, and that he could not be intercepted, Wyckoff headed north again, and sped through the tunnel which would take him back downtown. He could ditch the car there and get away free.

He did not know how to program the car's computer so it could use the automated highways, and in any event he had no particular destination in mind, so he kept it on manual. He drove at a slow, steady speed, leaving the tunnel as planned, but then took the wrong turn. As a result, he wound up on the freeway which led to the airport, and where six lanes of dense traffic prevented him from getting off again quickly enough to go back downtown.

Oh well, it did not greatly matter. When he got to the airport he could turn around. He had nothing else to do anyhow, and he might even take a look inside the place. Better yet, it suddenly dawned on him, the airport parking lot would be the ideal place to leave the Mallory. If he put it there it wouldn't be discovered for days. Yes, that was it. And while he was at it, he could wipe it down and get his prints off it, too. He found himself suddenly sweating in spite of the suit.

He pulled into the long-term lot, stopped at the gate, where an attendant handed him a time-stamped card, and then drove off toward a spot near the center. He parked the car between two others whose snow-covered windshields indicated they had already been here several days, and switched off the key.

Opening the glove box to look for a rag, he came up with a handful of tissues. They would do, he thought. He began wiping vigorously at every surface he might possibly have touched, being careful to touch nothing anew. He finished and sat there for a while with the soiled tissues grasped in his hand, looking around to see if anything else in the car needed attention.

At last he permitted himself to relax. He needed a rest. In all his life he had never had so much adventure and excitement in any one day. He wondered how much more of it there would be.

Almost absentmindedly he stuck his hand into his hip pocket to feel the medallion, which he had been on his way to sell. He found it inside the folds of the rental papers for Knowles' car—they came out with it. He had forgotten he had this, and it suddenly occurred to him that he could, once and for all, satisfy his curiosity as to whether this was the same car, and whether the man he had killed had been one of Knowles' murderers—he could compare the license numbers.

But he never got around to it. He was distracted by the fact that the papers listed Knowles' local address as room 1892, the Carlton Arms Motel, here at the airport. Wyckoff could see it from where he now sat, and a plush establishment it was, too. Knowles had indeed been doing all right.

Greed struck him instantly. What might there be inside the room? Luggage, certainly. More money? Probably. Maybe jewelry, and who knew what else. It would be a haul, one that could keep Wyckoff going for months if he was careful—one that could easily provide all the capital he would need. And certainly, if he didn't take it someone else would, and it would go to waste. He had no choice. Without thinking about it any more, he picked up the papers, stuffed them into a pocket, got out of the car, and slammed the door.

Chapter Three

The Carlton Arms was decidedly plush. Inside the spacious lobby the floors were marble, covered at intervals by real Persian carpets. Crystal chandeliers hung from the ceiling in the best of 18th-century tradition, framing a glittering fountain, and at each end of the lobby a polished marble staircase led to a mezzanine. It was, Wyckoff quickly realized, an oasis for the wealthy—but who else, he asked himself, could afford to travel anyhow?

The motel desk was on the second level. Wyckoff ascended the stairs, striving to appear dignified as he did so. Around him beautiful but aloof people did what beautiful people do.

Cautiously, he approached the desk, hoping his strained nerves didn't show. He stood there a moment, until an attendant came up.

"May I help you, sir?" The voice had an unctuous tone. Wyckoff found himself wondering how often it was necessary for the man to oil his tongue.

"I'd like my key, please; room 1892."

"Certainly, sir."

The attendant turned and walked to a rack. He took out not only a computerized keycard but an envelope, and returned to where Wyckoff stood. "Here you are, Mr. Knowles."

"Thank you." Wyckoff took the items, and glanced at the envelope with Knowles' name written across the front. This looked bad. If there was somebody else here at the hotel who knew Knowles, and was writing him notes—but, no, Wyckoff had torn open the envelope. It was an airline ticket for the 23rd—New York to Matagorda. He slipped it back into the envelope. It was one more asset to add to his growing collection. Cashed in, it would keep him for a month.

He buzzed the elevator, stepped aboard when it arrived, and got off at the 18th floor. Wyckoff fiddled with the keycard as he walked down the corridor. This would be the touchiest part. He had no way of knowing if Knowles had a companion in the room or not, or if other spacemen were staying at the hotel.

This last was unlikely, since it was a long, long way from Matagorda, but you never knew.

He listened at the door for a while, and since he heard no sounds inside, decided it was safe to enter. He put the key into the lock, slowly turned the knob, then pushed the door open cautiously. He was in luck— there was no one inside.

The room was opulent, from the round satin-draped bed to the steaming hot tub in the corner. It was the sort of thing Wyckoff had often seen portrayed on the TV screen down at the mission, but never dreamed really existed. Everything was first class.

He spent long minutes just staring, then began looking in drawers and closets. There was a great deal of jewelry, and a substantial amount of cash. The closets and dresser drawers were filled with clothing, all of it luxurious. It looked as though Knowles had planned to stay for months. He appeared to have brought everything he owned.

Wyckoff wondered, at first, why he would do that, but then remembered the transfer. Knowles was leav-

ing his old ship and getting aboard a new one. He had
to transfer his belongings, too.

Wyckoff smiled. He had finally gotten a break. He
would be set for life. While he was here, he could
systematically loot this room, turn its contents into
cash, and then disappear into the stream of humanity
within the city. He got started immediately, loading a
case with jewelry. He was glad he still had the car. It
would provide the transportation he needed to get to
town, where his acquaintances would turn these baubles into money.

Wyckoff worked all day, smuggling load after load of
loot out of the room under the very noses of the hotel
employees. They would notice the next day, of course.
He knew maids always reported a disappearance of
luggage, which represented the motel's security for its
unpaid bill, but by that time Wyckoff would be finished.

He spent long hours making his rounds, seeking the
best deals. Toward evening, his pockets bulging with
money, he arrived back at the airport, where he again
parked the car and carefully wiped the prints from its
interior. He knew what he was about to do next was
foolish, but to Wyckoff, it was a final flourish to extract
the maximum possible benefit from his good fortune.
He returned to the room, ordered an elaborate meal
sent up, including the most expensive wine on the list,
then took a leisurely soak in the hot tub as he watched a
classic movie called *The Caine Mutiny* on TV.

The dinner arrived just as he was getting dressed
again, and for a while he sat there eating, savoring good
food cooked in a manner he could easily get used to.
Then he was startled by a knock at the door.

Momentary fright quickly waned. It could only be
someone from the hotel, perhaps a maid with some
last-minute duties in his room. With labor so cheap,
they were all over the place, like mice. He put on the
robe he'd found in the closet and opened the door.

It was not a maid, though it was a young woman. She
was dressed to party and she looked distraught. "You're

not Emory," she said, startled by his appearance in the doorway.

"Uh, no, he's out. Who are you?" Wyckoff's question, under these circumstances, was strictly utilitarian. Had conditions been different, his motivation might have differed, too. He would certainly have had no objection to making friends with someone as attractive as she.

"Arlene. Where is he? I have to talk to him."

Her brusque answer startled him, ripped his attention rudely away from the exquisite figure so subtly enhanced by the satiny gown she wore; from the strings of what looked like genuine natural pearls that disappeared down the top of it; from the long, slinky blond hair that trailed down her back, and bounced with a life of its own whenever she tossed her head. *No*, he resolved. *Not for me—not now.* Instead, he answered as matter-of-factly as he could manage. "Uh—like I said, he's out. I don't know where. He didn't tell me where he was going. He's been gone all day."

Wyckoff was talking gas. So far, he'd managed to keep the fact concealed, but he didn't want any prolonged contact with any of Knowles' acquaintances who might decide to ask embarrassing questions. He'd have to get rid of her.

"Can I give him a message?"

"No. I'll just wait for him, if that's all right." Before Wyckoff could stop her she brushed past him, leaving a trail of subtle feminine scents.

Wyckoff decided she smelled like an expensive woman. She was decidedly headstrong, too; he sensed he'd better handle her carefully. He knew what he must do next: get out, leaving the woman to wait for Knowles, cash in the airline ticket, and beat it back to the city.

He offered her some wine, which she took, and some food, which she declined. He had not bothered to introduce himself, and she did not look as though she was in the mood for conversation anyway.

Wyckoff went into the other room, donned the polyinsulated suit, retrieved the airline ticket, and went back to where the woman waited. "I have to go out, too," he explained. "Got some business to take care of. You can wait, if you like. I'm sure Emory wouldn't mind."

She met that suggestion with a snarl. Obviously the wine wasn't all she'd had to drink in the recent past.

"You can't cash it? Why not?"

"Because it was issued against a ship's voucher. We can't give the cash to you, Mr. Knowles. It belongs to the ship."

"Well, I, uh—what I really wanted was to change my schedule. I figured I could make different connections, go early." Wyckoff was decidedly uncomfortable with the suspicious tone that had appeared in the attendant's voice. He hoped this would change it.

It did. Suspicion drained away completely. Cordiality returned. "Why didn't you say so? I can take care of that for you, Mr. Knowles. How soon would you like to go?"

Wyckoff hadn't been ready for that one. He did have a scheme in mind, though. If he could get a new ticket issued for today, he might be able to sell it right here at the airport. He could still get a credit or two out of the situation, and it wouldn't matter where the money came from, so, he replied, "When's the next flight?"

"This evening at 10:09, Mr. Knowles. I can book you on that if you like."

"Yeah, do that."

The man did. After punching a few buttons he came up with a new ticket and boarding pass. "Is your luggage at the Carlton, Mr. Knowles?"

"No. I won't be taking any this time."

The man handed him the ticket.

For a while, Wyckoff hung around the lounge, watching for a possible buyer. He looked for people in western dress, or who spoke with a drawl and who might, therefore, be heading in that direction.

He couldn't get anyone interested—except the airport police. One of them came over to talk to him, and though he eyed him suspiciously, was obviously intimidated by Wyckoff's expensive apparel. "You don't look poor, Mister. How come you're bothering these folks trying to sell a ticket? Why don't you just cash it in?"

Think fast, Wyckoff said to himself. And he did. "You mean, I can do that?" he asked, trying to sound incredulous.

"Sure. Provided it's your ticket. Is it?"

"Certainly, it's my ticket."

"Why don't we just double-check that. Come with me, please." He pointed to the ticket counter.

Wyckoff shrugged his shoulders and stepped in front of the cop, who marched him up to the front of what was now a fairly long line. He motioned to the attendant, who bent over while he whispered.

Wyckoff watched, terrified. He thought of running, but that, he knew, would do no good. It was better to tough it out.

Finally, the cop pulled him aside. "Ship's voucher—that's what the man told me. You tried to steal the money. I could lock you up for that. Maybe I should." He smiled.

"Uh—look," said Wyckoff, "we can settle this like gentlemen, can't we?" He knew the routine from here on in. He accompanied the cop to the washroom and left a couple of minutes later, fifty credits lighter.

Burned by one of the oldest shakedowns he knew of, Wyckoff simmered. He didn't know what else to do to dispose of the ticket. As he stood there he could see other cops talking to the one who'd stopped him. He knew what that meant—he'd have to pay off every one of them unless he could get away.

He had to get out of the airport, but that looked difficult, considering how many horny-handed cops there were, and how far he'd have to travel to do it.

Even as he thought about it, he started moving, going first to an escalator. That took him down one floor, to where the powered walkways were. These would be busy, and perhaps the two who'd gotten onto the escalator behind him would lose track.

He stepped on one marked gates H-1 to H-14. It moved along at a brisk pace, which he augmented by taking giant steps. People beside him held boarding passes in their hands and stared blankly ahead, intent on reaching their own destinations. Wyckoff became conscious of time, looked around for a clock. He found one; 9:51. Too bad, he thought. In a few minutes this ticket will be worthless anyhow.

He took a glance behind him. His two shadows were still on him. They must be calling his bluff—following him to see if he really did get on the plane, or if he was planning to turn around and leave the airport—good evidence to them that he was up to something unlawful.

Wyckoff made a decision. He'd get on the plane. Why shouldn't he? What else did he have to do? He could use a vacation anyhow, and now he could afford one. Besides, it would be warm down in south Texas. There would be no snow, the grass would be green, and there would be leaves on the trees. It would be uplifting. He made up his mind to do it.

Holding the boarding pass in front of him, he read off the flight and gate, and headed straight for it.

On the plane, he slept for the duration of the flight, though when he arrived at his destination he was anything but refreshed. Awakened by a flight attendant, he was astounded to see that the plane was empty. He was the only passenger who had not left it.

He rose, edged down the corridor, and started up the ramp to the lounge area, noting with satisfaction that despite the rapid change in climate he was still comfortable in the suit.

The lounge area was largely deserted, the hour being late, and Wyckoff had it mostly to himself. Other incoming passengers had already retrieved their luggage and moved on. They had taken all the cabs, too, Wyckoff noted with dismay. He put it down to bad luck, but all he could do was wait until one came back. He had no clear-cut idea where he wanted to go anyhow.

He sat down in a chair and closed his eyes, dozing for a few minutes before a voice woke him. He looked up.

"Hi!" the girl said, smiling. "Watcha doin' here?"

"I guess I fell off to sleep," he answered. "Uh—do I know you?"

"Ah'm Millie. Ya look kinda lonesome. Want some company?"

Ah. So that's it. He looked up at the girl. She was a freckle-faced blonde, with blue eyes made up in the characteristic manner of her profession—that of a party girl. Probably, he thought, she's one of the better ones. About thirty-five, she had enough age on her to make it interesting but not enough to turn his stomach. Physically, she wasn't all that bad, despite the drawl. Oh, well. In time, that would wear in, and conversation wasn't the object of these relationships.

Why not? he asked himself. It's been a long time. "Sure."

"You got a room?"

"No."

"We'll get one. You got a car?"

"No. I just got off a plane."

"That's okay. We can use mine. Uh—you know I'm a hooker, doncha?"

"Yeah, Millie. How much?"

"A hundred. That's if you don't want anything fancy, but I'm worth a lot more, if you know what I mean."

"Yeah, I know what you mean." He did. She'd be like the airplane ticket: start out looking good but wind up costing more than he bargained for. "I guess you'd be wanting that in advance?"

"It's only good business, honey. A girl's gotta be careful, and, after all, I am providin' the transportation."

Wyckoff reached into his pocket, gripped a couple of bills, and carefully separated them inside his pocket.

He didn't want to pull his whole wad out in front of her. He drew out a pair of fifties and handed them to her. She stuck them down her rather full-looking blouse, into that repository that nature had thoughtfully provided.

"Now, doncha go reachin' in there tryin' to get 'em back, y'hear? Come on, let's go party."

She led the way out of the building and into a parking lot to an ancient, beat-up, and nondescript car—an old-fashioned gasoline-powered job.

Wyckoff hadn't seen one in years. They were banned in cities, where there wasn't any such thing as a gas station anymore. But this was Texas, and no doubt they still had plenty of the stuff around.

She opened the door on the driver's side. "Get in 'n' slide over, honey. I'll drive."

Wyckoff did, noting that the interior wasn't in very good shape, either. The seat was torn, and on the passenger's side there was a spring sticking up. He scrunched over closer to Millie to avoid sitting on it.

"S'all right; you cuddle right on up, 'cause Millie's gonna show you a real good time."

Maybe she will, thought Wyckoff. She certainly seems friendly enough. He never gave a thought to the possibility that whoring might not be her only business.

The car left the airport, and for a while, Millie drove down the main road. Wyckoff, of course, didn't have any idea what their destination was. He simply assumed she had her own favorite motel nearby; that probably she was getting a cut of the rent from the operator.

She turned off the main road after about a half mile, onto a gravel road that seemed awfully lonely. It had no other traffic and no lights. "Shortcut," she explained. "I'm gettin' a little impatient. How 'bout you?"

"Yeah," answered Wyckoff.

"Why don't we stop right here, then—have us a quickie, just t'get warmed up, huh?"

Wyckoff still hadn't figured it out. He should have. This wasn't the way hookers operated. They were in the business of selling time—they didn't waste it. But before he had that theory worked out, she had the car stopped on the side of the road and the ignition switched off.

"There," she said, "ain't this nice? C'mere." She grabbed him and threw her arms around his neck, pulling him toward pursed lips.

It was then that the feeling of the situation's basic wrongness hit Wyckoff. Unfortunately, it was also when the blackjack hit him. The lights went out before he even got a taste of his hundred credits' worth.

Chapter Four

"Lordy, yew are alive, after all. I was afraid yew was day-ud."

Wyckoff didn't quite know how to answer; what was more, he didn't know if it was physically possible to answer. His mouth felt like it was upholstered with fuzz. He tried to move, and pain throbbed.

Despite the pain, he ordered his hands to feel the seams of his pockets. Open, all of them; and flat, all flat! God, she'd got it all; every credit. Wyckoff groaned, both from the agony of his wounds and from the greater agony of his loss. He'd had over eight thousand credits when he'd met Millie. Now he was wiped out. He looked up, into the face of his new benefactor. He wore a uniform—a cop!

"Where am I?" he asked, bracing himself for yet another variety of drawl. He could only hope that with exposure this would get easier. It seemed to work that way.

"T'the side a farm-market road 753, that's where. And you're lucky I spotted you. Coulda been there wouldn'a been nobody along for hours. You gonna be okay?"

"Yeah. I think so. I've been robbed. It was a hooker. Her name's Millie. Maybe you know her?"

"Sure. sure. I know all the hookers 'round these parts. They all got the same name—the same face. Mister, you can kiss your bankroll goodbye. Just thank your lucky stars they clouted you steada cuttin' your throat. That's the way we usually find you dudes."

Wyckoff struggled to rise, noted that he was on some kind of anthill and that the ants were biting him. He yelled, jumped to his feet, instantly regretted the act, and held his head in both hands.

"Take it easy," the man said. "No need t'get all stirred up. Here, lemme get 'em off you. Y'know, you're lucky. You coulda been dumped in a nest a fire ants. Then you'd have some real misery. What's your name, anyway?"

"Knowles; Emory Knowles. I'm from New York."

"Figures. They always pick on the dudes. You're lucky she left you your pants. Usually we find you guys plumb naked."

Wyckoff felt the rest of his pockets. He could tell by their flatness they were all empty—that is, all but two. Up on his lapels, the hidden pockets still bulged slightly. These had apparently been overlooked.

Somehow, that realization didn't comfort Wyckoff much. There was nothing of value in them, just the medallion, which was probably now worthless, and a piece of paper.

"Where was you headin', young feller?"

"Huh?" The twang was still throwing Wyckoff.

"I said, where was you goin' when you got took?"

"Uh—oh; I was to report to my ship." Wyckoff couldn't think of anything else to say. He couldn't tell this man he was running from the New York Police Department.

"Yeah. You're a spaceman, aintcha?"

"Yeah—chief storekeeper aboard the *Corona.* I have to report in by the twenty-third."

"This is the twenty-third, an' it's half over. You'd better get movin'."

"Uh—how? I'm broke, and I don't even know where the spaceport is."

"Relax, son. We ain't heartless 'round here. We'll gitcha there somehow. Believe me, this ain't the first time this little problem's come up. Trouble is, all you fellas ever think about is jumpin' into the sack with the first broad that comes along. You never stop to think some of 'em ain't as dumb as they look."

Wyckoff caught the innuendo—he had to be even dumber to fall for it. He tried to smile. "You got that right, Sheriff."

"Constable." The man smiled, toothlessly. " 'Round here we still got that office. Guess we're a little behind the times. Tell you what. C'mon back to the station with me. I'll find ya transportation of some kind so you can get t'the spaceport."

Wyckoff followed him to his car and got in. The constable switched on his motor and rolled silently off the shoulder onto the gravel road. For a few minutes he talked on the radio, using a number code Wyckoff couldn't follow very well.

Then he turned to Wyckoff. "Change in plans. Gonna gitcha there fast—unless you wanta check into a hospital or somethin' instead."

"No. That's fine; spaceport'll do fine. I'm okay."

"Well, in that case, we'll go out on the expressway. Friend of mine on the DPS has got a radar trap set up. He'll stop you somebody headed for Matagorda an' gitcha a ride, okay?"

"Fine."

The constable dropped him off on the side of the road. Down in an underpass, invisible from the highway, lurked two state troopers with a timing device. Farther ahead, again out of sight, was a chase car. One of the troopers walked up to Wyckoff.

"You can just wait right here, Mr. Knowles. When we get somebody, we'll let you know. Shouldn't be too long. There's lotsa trucks headin' that way."

Wyckoff stood alongside the road and waited. Sure enough, in about five minutes, the trooper called to him.

"Go on up. We got one."

Moments later, Wyckoff was seated in the cab of an aged diesel rig, beside a driver who looked like he might have just rolled in off the range. He had red hair and a red beard, and all of it was curly. It ringed his face below the creased and crushed straw hat.

"Guess I was lucky you was there, stranger," he said to Wyckoff. "Trooper gimme my choice. Take you along or get a ticket. You must be somebody special."

"Just a guy with a bump on his head and poor taste in women."

"Hah! You run into one o' them too, huh? Probably the same one that got me last year—every once in a while they work the joints around the airport. Mine was a blonde, with freckles?"

"Yeah, so was mine. About thirty-five, blue eyes; called herself Millie."

"That just might be her, only she was callin' herself Lorraine when I met her. Didn't know she was back. We'll get her, now that she is, though; that is, we'll get both of 'em, 'specially the guy that's bashin' for her. Lotsa us truck drivers lost our bankrolls t'gals like her, and we ain't forgot it. You probably done us a favor."

Perhaps he had. Wyckoff wasn't particularly concerned over bygones. His big worry right now was what he was going to do at the spaceport once he got there.

Matagorda was big. It occupied all of the south end of the island of the same name, and a great deal of the shoreland around Copano Bay, which had once comprised the cities of Rockport and Fulton. With the coming of the port, these municipalities had been moved inland.

Matagorda Spaceport was the reason why the United States, despite all its other failings, still led the Earth in space commerce. Privately financed space travel had been born here late in the previous century, and the State of Texas had been wise enough to promote the site as an alternative to nationally funded efforts. It now flourished, controlled, appropriately enough, by the Railroad Commission, which explained why more people recognized the Texas Railroad Commissioner by sight than the President of the United States.

Thus, even after its oil and gas were depleted, foresight and an independent tradition had enabled Texas to remain the most affluent of all the states, and the only one which had to close and patrol its borders to prevent unauthorized entry. Had he not come by air, and thus proven he would not be a public charge, Wyckoff too, might have been turned away. Now that he was again financially embarrassed he knew he would be kicked out like a dead skunk as soon as somebody noticed.

But at least he could console himself with the fact that he had been somewhere and seen something that not very many ordinary people ever got a look at. Viewed in that light, things didn't seem quite so bad, and he relaxed to spend a little time gawking like a tourist. There would be plenty of time for regrets when disaster struck.

The scenery rolling by was quite interesting. The truck rumbled over the long bridge that connected the island and the mainland, and in the distance Wyckoff could see mile after mile of low buildings. He wondered where the ships were, but he guessed that the launch and recovery areas would be on the seaward side, as far away from habitation as possible.

The truck driver, who up until this time had seemed content to let Wyckoff have his thoughts as he must have had his own, broke the long silence. "I can take you as far as Operations, Mister. I got t'go there anyhow t'find out where t'drop m'load. But they'll be able t'give you directions t'your ship."

"Okay."

Up until this point, Wyckoff's plans had been woefully incomplete. He had no idea whatsoever what to do next. He'd gone along with the constable's plan only because to have objected might have looked suspicious, and he'd figured that once he'd gotten to the port he could just wander off and go back to someplace more interesting.

When they arrived at Matagorda, physical realities changed his plans. The truck went through half a dozen checkpoints, and had to show papers at every one of them. He had kept the medallion and orders in his hand since.

"They're so scared somebody's gonna sneak in here," said the driver. "I waste more time on this run than any other I make."

Wyckoff nodded agreement, but said nothing. He was thinking that it might be just as hard to get out.

The truck pulled up in front of the Operations building and stopped. "This is where I leave you, partner. Have a good trip, wherever you're goin'."

Wyckoff thanked him for the ride and jumped out. He glanced around to see what possibilities there might be to slip away. There were none. An armed, uniformed man with a clipboard strode up. "Yes, sir? Destination?"

"Uh—the *Corona*." He still had the paper and the medallion in his hand.

"*Corona*! You're late, man; she's in final countdown. Better hustle inside; they'll take care of you." He gestured.

Wyckoff, feeling that he was being carefully herded toward a place he had no business going, entered the Operations building. It was crowded with people, a situation that would have been ideal for ducking out, had the guard not interfered again.

He stuck his head in the doorway and yelled to a red-haired man at the counter. "Hey, Murphy! Here's *Corona*'s lost sheep." He pointed to Wyckoff.

Murphy motioned him forward. "Gotcha all set, Mr. Knowles. Just sign all these, and I'll stamp 'em. We'll get you out pronto."

"What are they?"

Wyckoff realized immediately it had been a mistake

to ask. Only the fact that they were so rushed prevented an inquiry which would have unmasked him then.

Murphy answered, "Just the usual: ship's articles, payroll assignment, insurance forms, tax waiver request, and so on. Routine stuff." He handed Wyckoff a ballpoint pen and gazed at him with watery blue eyes.

Wyckoff took the pen and painstakingly signed "Emory Knowles" to all of them, concentrating deeply lest he forget himself and sign his true name.

When he was finished, Murphy whacked each one in several places with rubber stamps, then scrawled his own initials.

"There you go, all set." He tore off the back copies of several sets of forms and handed them to Wyckoff. "Ship's waitin'."

"How do I get there?"

Murphy picked up a pager and yelled, "Greely!"

"Yeah?" a voice answered.

"Passenger for the *Corona*. Pick him up out front."

Turning to Wyckoff, he said, "Jeep'll be by directly." He pointed to the front door.

Wyckoff turned and walked out. Whatever had possessed him to get into this fix? Now he was going to space. There was no way out now, and surely he'd be recognized as an impostor as soon as he got aboard. He'd be arrested, and at least charged with the theft of Knowles' possessions—if not with his murder, and who knew what all else. Surely, he thought, there must be stiff penalties for impersonating a spaceman.

He did not have a whole lot of time to think about it on the way to the *Corona*. Greely drove like a fiend, pouring kilowatts into the jeep's motor, whipping around obstacles and taking pains not to miss any of the bumps on the tarmac. In a couple of minutes they were in the launch area and the *Corona* was looming large.

She rested in a cradle in the center of a huge dishlike affair, part of which was hinged to admit ships. Once inside, a gantry on each side positioned her at the focal

point of twenty banks of continuously firing lasers fed
by an orbital mirror, which beamed down megawatts of
power by microwave.

At the other end of the voyage, since she was headed
for a regularly designated colony planet, she would also
find a cradle with which to land. Always, Wyckoff knew,
this was the first thing done. Ships could land on their
Aschenbrenners, but this was enormously destructive
to the planetary surface, and somewhat dangerous to
the ships themselves.

Greely whipped the jeep up a ramp that led under the
cradle and stopped. Ahead was a gantry with a steel
mesh cage at the end of its boom.

"Here you are, Mr. Knowles. End of the line."

Wyckoff got out of the jeep and looked around. There
was a man near the cage, holding the door open and
motioning for him to hurry.

Wyckoff did. He fairly ran over and stepped in. The
man got in with him, and on the way demanded
Wyckoff's papers. Wyckoff began sweating, thinking perhaps this was a last-minute identity check. But no, the
man only wanted to know which deck to stop at. He
handed the papers back immediately.

Wyckoff began to wonder if he might not be safe after
all. No one had yet even remotely suspected he wasn't
Knowles. And, he thought, why should they? Why
would anybody anticipate the impersonation of a common spaceman? Well, maybe not a common spaceman;
a chief storekeeper, whatever that was. Anyhow, this
was a new ship, and Knowles was a part of her first
crew. It was unlikely that very many of the crew would
have met each other before, or that Knowles would
have any acquaintances on board. Wyckoff began to feel
a little easier about the whole thing. In their furious
effort to meet the ship's launch schedule, nobody had
even asked to see his medallion.

The cage reached the proper hatch, and the man
opened its door. Inside stood a steward, with his hand
extended. "Papers, sir."

Wyckoff handed him the sheaf.

The steward glanced at them quickly. "Bay H-38, to your right." He handed the papers back.

Wyckoff started off down the circular corridor, reading the door numbers as he passed by them. He realized, for the first time, how really huge the *Corona* was. The diameter of the circle he traversed must be at least 400 feet, and she was at least four times that long. He felt a shiver at the thought of anything that big flying, but reason immediately told him such fears were groundless.

As he walked, the P.A. system blasted out the same instructions, over and over again, warning all colonists and auxiliary crewmen to remain in quarters and strap in for blast-off. Bridge and engine-room personnel were advised that this would begin in twenty-five minutes.

He found Bay H-38, pushed the entry button, and walked through the sliding door. Inside, he found a spartan chamber containing a bunk, a cupboard with several sets of shipboard coveralls in it, a small table and lamp, a stool and washbasin, and little else. It looked clean and fairly comfortable, and since Wyckoff had no luggage, not even a toothbrush, it would be room enough.

A legend over the bunk advised it doubled as an acceleration couch. Wyckoff was about to get into it when the screen on the small computer terminal inset in the wall over the table lit up. "Chief Storekeeper Knowles—duty schedule," it read.

Wyckoff went over and examined it. The information pleased him. Here was the answer to at least some of the questions that had haunted him. This readout gave duty station, his working hours, and the name of his superior—First Mate Arlene Graham.

Wyckoff, bushed from his travels, decided to test the bunk. He stripped off the polyinsulated suit, hung it on a hook, climbed into the bunk, and hit the light switch. An instant later a persistent buzzing began over his head, and red letters started blinking across the terminal screen and on a panel of the bunk's headboard. He sat up to read them. "Activate Restraints—Hazardous Maneuver Imminent."

"Okay," Wyckoff said. "Don't get so bossy." He pressed the pressure-sensitive panel at the head of the bunk. The red disappeared, and in its place the screen lit green, displaying the words "Systems Operative."

From somewhere beneath the bunk, arms rose and clamped themselves loosely around him, then inflated and held him fast against the bunk.

He lay there, thinking for the first time about the immediate future. He decided his luck had not really been so bad. Probably, a chief storekeeper only supervised—smoothed out the bumps that rose in the operation. He hoped so, anyway. That sort of thing he could fake. He had managed survival on the street for all these years by being a competent observer and following his instincts. This could not be that much different, and certainly was a good deal less dangerous.

A final sounding blast of noise came over the P.A. "Blast-off in thirty seconds; secure all stations." The message was repeated at ten-second intervals until only ten were left. Then a countdown began.

Wyckoff waited for zero and braced himself. A roar erupted, and rose in intensity. The seconds ticked by, during which time the ship seemed to be gathering strength to leap, and then she did. Crushing weight bore down on Wyckoff's chest. His head, already aching, reacted to the acceleration with lancing pain. Even his eyeballs ached. His throat was dry and seemed to be trying to close up on him.

How long this lasted in terms of seconds or minutes, he did not know, but it seemed like hours before the klaxon sounded again: "Freefall in ten seconds—secure all loose objects. All colonists and auxiliary crew will remain in couches."

This time the countdown started with five, and when again it reached zero, the crushing weight vanished. In its place was a feeling of vertigo, and the air felt stuffy.

Wyckoff now appreciated the restraints. It was comforting to have something around him to help combat the feeling that he was falling endlessly toward some unknown target. Then the ship's ventilating system kicked in, ending the closed-in feeling, and adding a low throb to the darkness.

This was conducive to sleep, and Wyckoff dropped off. He slept soundly, and neither heard the P.A. announce that the main drive was being cut in, nor felt the restraints slip away. He slumbered comfortably while the ship plunged on, driven by her Aschenbrenners at a steady one-gee acceleration. For all his body knew, Wyckoff could have been on Earth, sacked out in his favorite flophouse.

Chapter Five

There was, however, one minor difference. He seemed to have received a relatively minor impression that the door had opened softly; that for an instant a beam of light had flashed across the bottom of the bunk. He had no recollection of a subtle scent that filled the air, or of the sound of rustling clothing being hung haphazardly and hurriedly. None of these things mattered to Wyckoff's subconscious.

Something else did—the sudden disturbance caused by someone else's weight on the bunk, a stronger scent, the touch of soft fingers on his shoulders, the sensation of warm breasts sliding across his shoulder blades.

Instantly, Wyckoff was popeyed awake—and scared to death about it. Knowles did know at least one other person aboard—intimately, it seemed, from the way she was nibbling on his earlobe.

He was overcome by both panic and curiosity. He resisted the impulse to bolt; confronting her might provoke an ugly incident that would end with his arrest and detention. No, he must have time to think.

Besides, he liked what she was doing, though he pretended still to be asleep. Her hands were busy, having wandered over his shoulders and down his chest, intent on provoking another sort of confrontation. And

Wyckoff confidently expected that he would find the will to rise and meet the challenge.

In those next few minutes instinct, not reason, ruled. The silence was broken by the sounds of explosive breathing, followed by furtive grunts and gasps. Then, in a crescendo of groaning and squealing, rationality fought its way back into the situation; silence again reigned as they lay there, clothed only in darkness and perspiration.

Wyckoff feared the next few moments. He knew she would speak to him and he would have to answer. What would she do? How would she handle an error so gross as this must be?

He got his chance to see in the next instant. "God, that was good. You're a real puzzler, Emory. How can you be so terrific in space and so lousy on the ground? I'll never understand that."

Wyckoff took that as rhetorical and didn't answer.

She rambled on. "It's probably not you at all. It's probably me. Space messes up a woman lots worse than it does a man. Our anatomies react differently up here. I need a size bigger in everything. Of course, on some of us it looks good, don't you think?"

"Um."

That answer didn't tell her a thing she didn't want to hear. In the meantime, she'd thought of another question. "Where were you all day yesterday, Emory? I waited and waited. Have you got some chick on the ground?"

Again, Wyckoff didn't answer. No point in rushing things.

"Never mind; I don't care, as long as you can satisfy me, too. Just think, Emory—two hundred and thirty-eight days we'll be gone. And if they all start out like this one, it'll be a great voyage. Can I move in here with you?"

"Um," Wyckoff grunted.

"Not very talkative today, are you? I guess you're tired after your shore leave. Want to go to sleep?"

"Um."

"Okay." She leaned over and kissed him, then flopped down beside him on the bunk.

Wyckoff knew he didn't dare allow himself to go back to sleep, so he lay there until her even breathing told him she had slipped off. He had figured out who she was. She was the Arlene he'd met in Knowles' hotel room. She was also Arlene Graham, first mate of the *Corona*. He had to get away from her. Where he would go, he didn't yet know, but he couldn't stay here. Sooner or later she'd turn the lights on.

He eased his way out of bed, tiptoeing over to the cupboard to get a pair of coveralls. He found a set, unzipped it, and crawled in. Luckily, they included foot coverings. He zipped up the front and started for the door, glancing first at the clock and then at the terminal. The clock read 4:00 A.M. The terminal said his shift started at 7:00 A.M. He had three hours to disappear.

He walked around the deck, to where a door breached the otherwise smooth wall. It had a pair of call buttons on it—an elevator. Beside it was a terminal, with a printed legend beside it.

Wyckoff read this, selected the key for the ship's directory, and punched it.

A display appeared, giving the number of the deck and a listing of what it was on it. Hastily, he punched up "Passengers," and the terminal told him they were on decks 23 through 35. He called the elevator, and when it came, selected deck 35. If there is any safe place for me aboard, he told himself, it's with the colonists. He wouldn't run into any old shipmates among them.

The car stopped, not at deck 35, but at deck Z, and the door opened. Wyckoff was not prepared for what he found there.

Immediately in front of the elevator door was a small desk. Seated on the chair in front of it was an armed crewman. Wyckoff looked on each side, where walls, one pierced by a hatch, converted the corridor into a cubicle.

At Wyckoff's arrival, the guard stood up. "Yes, sir?"

"Morning," Wyckoff replied, not altogether confidently. The line between "A.M." and "P.M." had become obscured.

"Uh, what can I do for you, sir?"

"Knowles; Chief Storekeeper," Wyckoff answered. He was determined to behave as brazenly as necessary to get where he wanted to go. "Open up."

"Sorry, Chief. Passenger quarters are off-limits to the crew."

"Not to the chief storekeeper they're not." Wyckoff intended to see just how much authority he really had.

"Sir, I'll need to see an authorization from the captain."

"Then call him." Wyckoff knew from checking the schedule that the captain would be off duty, probably asleep.

The guard hesitated.

"What's your name?" he demanded of the guard.

"R-Rosetti."

"Rosetti what?"

"Rosetti, sir."

"All right, Rosetti, call the captain, or hand me the phone and I will. Otherwise, you can stop this foolishness and open that hatch. The choice is yours."

The bluff worked.

"Yes, sir." The man's voice was surly, but he took a cardkey from a rack and unlocked a panel. Inside was the control switch. He flipped it and a door opened. It was built like an airlock, with a small chamber and another, inner door.

The first door closed behind him, leaving Wyckoff standing in the chamber trapped between the two. He glanced around. There were no controls inside at all, just a button marked "call." He wondered what reason there could be to keep the colonists under lock and key. Were they dangerous?

At length, the inner door also opened. Inside, he found the same long, circular corridor as in the crew quarters, except that there were far fewer doors and everything seemed to have been left unfinished. There was primer on the walls, for instance, but no finish coat. The companionways were bare steel—no rubber treads or carpet, as there was in the crew section.

And, apparently, the colonist section didn't have access to the axial elevator. Instead, it had one of its own. Wyckoff suspected it ran only between decks 23 and 35.

He found the directory and read it. Cargo was stowed between decks 15 and 22. Above that were colonists' quarters. Since his objective was to find a place to hide, he punched the button for the lowest deck when the elevator came. Inside, the car was just as bare and unfinished as everything else in passenger country.

The car stopped, and its door opened into the darkness of a cargo hold. For scant seconds after Wyckoff stepped out, light from its dim interior revealed only more bare deck. That, too, vanished as the door closed.

Wyckoff felt around the bulkhead for a switch. Logically, there should be one nearby. There was, and he flipped it, sending current through half a dozen bare bulbs ringing the central shaft. The hold was three times the height of a man, and divided into bays, all of which were full of crates held in place by heavy netting.

None of this interested him very much, so after taking a quick look around, and noting that the decks seemed to be connected by ladders and hatches adjoining the axial tube, he called the elevator and went up to deck 16.

Sixteen was deserted as well, so he repeated the procedure, intending to keep it up until he found somebody. He regretted not having worn the polyinsulated garment under his coverall, since it had occurred to him he might want to stay here now that he was in. Still, having the run of the ship, he could always return for it.

Deck seventeen was not empty. There was a man in it. He came at Wyckoff out of the darkness, bent, it seemed, on murder. Wyckoff barely had time to raise his arm and deflect the crowbar that the man swung at the top of his head.

There was a bone-jarring impact, though the weapon was sliding and hadn't spent its full force on Wyckoff's forearm.

Wyckoff grasped the man's arms, forcing them apart, and brought his knee up sharply into his groin. At a time like this, manners had no place in Wyckoff's strategy.

The man screamed in agony. His hands released their hold on the crowbar, and it fell clattering to the deck. Wyckoff kicked the man's feet out from under him and pushed, until his opponent also thudded to the bare deck.

Now, safely on top, and with his antagonist disarmed, he could take a look. Fear left him when he did. The guy was old, and much more lightly built than he. He would be no problem, even when he recovered from the disabling blow. He was obviously not a crewman, since he wore ordinary street clothing. The clothing, like the man, was old, tattered, and none too clean. Wyckoff decided he must be a passenger.

In a few moments the man's preoccupation with his misery ebbed. He opened his eyes, and stared at the name embroidered on Wyckoff's coverall.

"Knowles! My God, man, I'm sorry—b-but you were the last person I expected to see coming through that door. Are you all right?"

"Yeah, I'm fine," Wyckoff replied, hoping that the astonishment he felt didn't show on his face. *What was this? It wasn't that dark in here. He didn't know this guy, and the guy didn't know him. Had he blundered into another case of mistaken identity? The man's reaction at seeing his name tag suggested that, as though he knew the name but not the face.* Wyckoff decided to ride that theory a while.

"You can let me up now, Knowles."

"Can I? I don't know who you are."

"I'm Luddington."

"Yes," said Wyckoff, "of course you are."

"In the pocket; inside, on the left."

Wyckoff was still holding both the man's arms in a steel grip. He pinioned both with his right hand, and with his left, reached in and probed the pocket. His fingers found a slim leather-covered folder, which he extracted and held up to the light. Inside was an I.D. card with Luddington's picture on it. Beneath the picture there was a number, followed by the words, "U.S. Aeronautics and Space Administration—Criminal Investigation Division." On the opposite flap was a small gold badge. A cop!

Wyckoff's resolve wilted. While he tried to figure out what to do next he relaxed his grip, helped Luddington up, and handed the folder back to him. His mind was full of questions he dared not ask, yet there appeared to be no other way to clear the confusion he felt. Obviously, Luddington expected Knowles to be aboard, but didn't know him by sight. And just as obviously, he was engaged in some sort of covert activity. But what was it? How was Knowles involved? And what was such involvement going to do to his own situation? He decided to play along and find out as much as he could. Thankfully, Luddington hadn't demanded to see any credentials.

"What were you doing down here?" he asked, hoping he wasn't already supposed to know.

"Checking out the colonial supplies. It's just as we thought. Here—come take a look at what I've found." He reached down and picked up the crowbar, then motioned Wyckoff to follow. On the way he reached over to the wall and flipped the switch for the lights. The room was immediately flooded with brilliance.

Wyckoff looked around. He had not noticed before, but some of the netting had been dislodged, and some of the crates had been pried open. He raised the lid of the nearest one, which was marked "Milling Cutters," but as far as Wyckoff could tell, it contained only junk: dirty, rusty scrap metal, most of it looking as if it had simply been scooped up out of any handy industrial scrap heap.

He went on to another crate, this one marked "Lathe (1)-30 Cm.—w/mtr.—3 ph/60 cyc./220 v." This one was filled with what looked like old manhole covers. He looked over at Luddington, who shot back a glance of frustration.

"That was supposed to be the machinery and tools these poor people need to start the colony. How much will they be able to do with that junk?"

"Is it all like that?"

"Probably most of it is."

"Why?"

"Why? Didn't anybody brief you? For the money. The *Corona's* on government charter. The government paid for equipment, for tools, for supplies. Somebody intercepted that, if it was ever to be delivered to begin with, and diverted it somewhere else. Then they substituted scrap, thinking by the time it was uncrated we'd be lightyears away and in no position to complain."

"How could anybody get away with that? There are inspections, aren't there?"

"Are there? Look, it seems to me that you'd know more about that sort of thing than I would. Anyhow, the crew of the *Corona* is only a small part of the ring; we know that. There are people on the ground who are in this, too, and they've probably been stealing from every ship that goes out."

"There'll be another inspection when we get to Zahn."

"Of papers; sure. Whoever's doing this may own somebody there, too. Whoever it is will sneak aboard this ship and leave with it, figuring if there's anybody left alive in the colony when the next ship comes, it'll be the same thing all over again."

Wyckoff's mind was racing. He'd gone through all this effort, suffered all this misery, simply because he had allowed greed to drive him. The medallion, once so intriguing, had been equivalent to a ticket on the *Titanic*.

It had been bad enough to have been an impostor in

the crew, but before, he'd counted on being able to melt away and hide among the colonists. Now it didn't look to him like that was a healthy idea, either. The colonists, it seemed, might be doomed to starvation after they arrived, and certainly that fate interested Wyckoff about as much as a trip out the airlock would have.

Without being certain just how it had all come about, Wyckoff had, in a couple of days, gone from the status of opportunist to pawn in what looked like a really complicated intrigue. No doubt all the crews skimmed off the cream from any colony run they made, but this looked to him like it was designed to make it impossible for any of the passengers to survive, once they got on Zahn.

That took a particularly callous and unconscionable type of thief. If all his shipmates fit that mold, Wyckoff was in as deep trouble as a colonist as he would be if his impersonation were to be discovered.

For an instant he had a temptation he knew he must resist at all costs—to take Luddington into his confidence and admit the masquerade; to trust that Luddington would somehow be sympathetic and know what to do.

But wait a minute—Luddington was a cop, and all Wyckoff's experience argued against trusting one of them. He'd fit in better on the other side, even if it meant confessing to the impersonation. It might well be that the crewmen who were in this thing would be able to handle it if they knew Luddington was onto them. And how much help could Luddington have aboard? Not much—that was certain. Maybe a few agents scattered among the sixty or so spacehands of the Corona's company.

But that might not work out, either. The honest crewmen were bound to outnumber the conspirators. How many crewmen would it take to run a scam like this? Half a dozen influential officers among the crew could handle it easy. All they had to do was get the stuff unloaded at the end of the voyage. How much trouble would that be? What it added up to was that Luddington could always go public with his case and get all the help he needed—unless the conspirators had the information they needed to box these government people in. And that, Wyckoff thought, was something they might be willing to pay for.

He decided to take advantage of Luddington's confidence in him, find out how much the other man knew about his own adversaries. He must know a great deal, Wyckoff reasoned. His office was federal, and whatever else you might say about the federal government, it had the money to spend on investigations. The feds were thorough.

"So," he asked, trying to sound confident, "are they all in on it, Luddington?"

The older man raised his eyes from the crate he'd been inspecting and paused, then gave a hesitant answer. "We have to assume that most of the seniors are. We know the captain is. He's living too high not to be. Got a fortune in cash socked away somewhere, maybe right here on this ship. You're supposed to be in on all this, along with most of your section. But, you know that . . ."

"What about the mate?"

"Which one—first, second, or third?"

"Arlene Graham."

"She's questionable, which means we assume she is until we have proof to the contrary. What's your interest in her?"

Wyckoff didn't answer.

"Okay. I see. Well, watch the pillow talk, huh." Assuming he'd read Wyckoff's situation correctly, Luddington went on. "We have a very real problem, Knowles. We have to check out every single carton of colonial supplies, then make an inventory of what usable stuff is left and set up a rationing system, so that these people can survive until a rescue ship gets to the colony. That ship isn't even scheduled to leave until the

Corona is halfway to Zahn, and might not get there at all if anybody on it is involved in this, so it's probably going to be up to you to make the report."

Oh-oh! More complications. Again the wheels spun. A trailing ship meant the back door was covered, too. Never mind, the crew didn't have to know about that part, and meanwhile, what was to stop "Knowles" from jumping ship on Zahn? *Think hard about that.*

But in the meantime, better answer. "Me? Why me?"

"Because you're a crewman. You think they're going to let a passenger go back?"

"Why does anybody have to go back? We could just call."

Astute as he was most of the time, adept as he had been at reading Luddington, Wyckoff missed the sign of his most grievous error through simple carelessness. He had gotten overconfident. He had been gawking around, so he did not see the look of absolute incredulity that washed over Luddington's face, then quickly retreated as he regained his poise. In his ignorance he simply plodded on: "Why'd the government ever let this ship leave in the first place, if they knew this was going on? Why not stop these people on the ground?"

"Because we wanted to get them all in one fell swoop—wipe out the whole operation, get this bunch talking about what's going on on other ships. By the time we get to Zahn it's expected that you and I will be able to inform on all the crooked crewmen everywhere, and by the time the relief ship gets to Zahn, I'll have the goods on their planetbound accomplices."

"Yeah. I see what you mean. Look, Luddington. I go on duty at 0700. I'm gonna have to get going."

"I understand."

Wyckoff turned to leave, pressed the elevator button.

"Wait a minute, Knowles. I've got something for you."

"What?"

"A radio. I'll have to go to my quarters to get it. I wasn't expecting you to turn up quite so soon."

"What do I need a radio for?"

"So we can keep in touch. It's too dangerous for you to come down here looking for me, and we certainly can't use the ship's phones. Somebody would get suspicious. You know I can't get out of the passenger area. Wait here."

Wyckoff stood in the center of the bay, idly fumbling with a splinter broken from one of the crates. He couldn't wait to get out of here, into a spot where he could think clearly.

He found himself almost wishing he hadn't run from that cop, and that he was sitting in a jail cell now, instead of trying to hack his way out of this rap. At least in the city, when they eventually turned him loose, he'd come out in a place where he knew his way around, and where he had survival skills. As it was, he could very well end his life in a bean field with a hoe in his hand.

He was still lost in his thoughts when the elevator door opened again and Luddington stepped out. Wyckoff thought nothing of it when the older man stuck his hand in his jacket pocket. He expected it to come out with a radio in it. It didn't—it came out with a gun.

And it was not one of those ticklers—plazers, which fired a burst of charged plasma and merely knocked a man out. This was an old-fashioned slug thrower, the kind that brought the curtain down for keeps. Wyckoff wasted no time in raising his hands high above his head.

"Pretty close, Mister, but not close enough. I went back to my quarters to get you a radio, and I thought while I was there I might as well check your picture, too, to clear up a little suspicion I had. It's surprising how much you look like Knowles in dim light."

Luddington had been advancing steadily on Wyckoff, and Wyckoff had been backing up just as steadily, but he ran out of room and now was backed up against one of the stacks of net-covered crates.

"Now," Luddington growled, "I want the truth from you. In fact, I want your life history. Turn around."

Wyckoff hesitated just a bit too long. He had a natural reluctance to turn his back on any enemy, but doing it for somebody who had a good reason to shoot and a place to hide his body afterward made it even worse.

Luddington's impatience began to show. Before Wyckoff could make up his mind what to do next, Luddington had paid him back for that kick in the groin, and he was now turning slowly and painfully, while straining to keep from sinking to the floor. In desperation he grasped a handful of netting and hung on.

"That's better. Don't move a muscle, and keep your hands where I can see them."

Wyckoff could feel the cold muzzle of the gun on the back of his neck, boring in. He straightened up as best he could and hung onto the netting, deliberating whether to make one last desperate attempt to overpower Luddington.

He never got the opportunity. Something else joined the gun's muzzle on the back of his neck—a gas-powered syringe. Wyckoff's eyes involuntarily crossed and his vision went dark. An instant later he was flying blind, floating around in the dark in free fall, or so it seemed.

*   *   *

Like a rag wiping the fog from a window, something cleared both his thoughts and his vision. His next conscious thought was to ask himself why he was lying on the deck. The next one after that supplied the answer. Luddington had zapped him with some kind of drug.

The other man was squatting down beside him, the gas-powered syringe dangling limply from one hand. The gun butt was sticking out of a back pocket. His face wore a twisted frown.

"Okay, Mr. Wyckoff, you tell me—what should I do with you?"

Wyckoff gulped. So that was what Luddington meant

when he said he wanted a life story—babble drugs! No
doubt he'd sung like a birdie. "I didn't plan none of
this, Luddington."

"No, you didn't. But you sure gummed it up. Of all
the stupid, idiotic—Wyckoff, if I could get you to an
airlock, I'd dump you out."

Wyckoff gulped again—hard.

"How did you even expect to get away with impersonating a spaceman when you don't know radio's useless out here?"

"Huh?"

"That's what I mean—the only way to send a message
at faster-than-light speed is put it on a ship that's doing
better than "C" and going where you want the message
to go."

"I was doing all right until I met you. Look, Luddington, just let me hide out in here until we get to the
colony. I'll get off the ship then, and you'll never see
me again. I won't say anything, honest."

"And what do I do when they come looking for you?"

"Uh—then just let me go back where I was." Wyckoff
was flexible—he didn't mind humoring the man.

"So you can tell them who I am?"

"N-no, honest, Luddington. I wouldn't do that—no,
I wouldn't ever say anything."

Luddington stood up, and put his hands on his hips.
"Wyckoff, do you know how much time you can get for
what you've already done?"

"A b-bunch—I guess."

"A great big bunch—enough so that the government
would be more than happy to bring you back from
Zahn. You'd rot, Wyckoff—rot for the rest of your life
in the worst joint we could find for you. And there's no
way you could hide. There's no way off Zahn once you
get there. It wouldn't be so easy to stow away from a
colony. It's not like Matagorda; they're really careful."

Wyckoff felt well enough to sit up, but he was careful not to move quickly. He knew that Luddington,

now alerted, could step back, draw, and shoot him before he could attack.

"What I'm telling you, Wyckoff, is that you lucked out again. I'm going to let you go, but I want you to know that if you do talk, and anything happens to me, the word about you will still get back to my people, and my people will wipe you out—understand?"

Wyckoff gulped.

"So, you're going to get back into the elevator and work your con, if you can, and if you get caught you are going to say absolutely nothing about me, or what you've seen in here. Is that clear?"

"Uh—yeah, sure." Wyckoff felt a massive feeling of relief. Not all his luck, it seemed, was bad. Still, he tried to look scared. He was well aware of the fact that looking scared was an important and useful defense mechanism. The first thing a bum learned was that it almost always worked with cops.

Luddington pulled the gun out again, and motioned toward the elevator. Wyckoff rose to his feet and went to it. He pressed the button, and waited, gazing back at Luddington. "I won't forget this, Luddington. I mean it. I didn't do all this on purpose."

"You know, Wyckoff, I believe you—you're not that smart. Lucky, yes—smart, no. This is a new ship, and you might even have a chance of making it if you stay away from bad company. It might interest you to know we think your girlfriend's clean."

"My girlfriend? Oh, you mean Arlene."

"She might be the only senior who is."

The elevator door opened. Wyckoff stepped in, turned, and watched Luddington until the door closed again. On the way up he thought about what had just happened. He knew that Luddington had no choice but to do what he had—luck had nothing to do with it. He resolved always, until this ended, to keep an escape route clear.

Chapter Six

When the hatch opened, he found that Rosetti had been relieved early. In his place was a rough-looking woman who greeted him with a drawn plazer. The shock must have registered visibly on Wyckoff's face, because the woman had some comments.

"You went in there unarmed?"

"Sure. Nothing to worry about."

"Not yet, maybe. Rosetti told me you went below. That's the only reason I opened the hatch. By the way, Captain Hamil wants to see you in his quarters, right away."

"Okay, I'm on my way." He pushed the button for the other elevator.

"I'm Linda," the guard said. "I like to get acquainted on a new ship. My quarters are on "Q" deck. Look me up sometime, okay? I'm in cabin four."

"Sure," Wyckoff muttered. He was unused to all this attention from women. You didn't get that on the streets unless you went looking for it, and Wyckoff generally hadn't.

It was the last thing on his mind now, and he had plenty of other troubles to worry about, not the least of which was his scheduled meeting with the captain. He had no idea whether or not Knowles had ever met him, and no way of finding out, but if he didn't obey the order to report, it would all be over anyhow. The only thing he could do was walk in cold and hope the two had been strangers.

There was, he thought, a fair chance of that. To organize a theft of this magnitude, the thieves had to have had some organization. That meant that they had to know *about* each other, but not necessarily that any of them would have known Knowles personally. There was some reason for encouragement from what Luddington had said about the mate. If the only person he was sure knew Knowles by sight wasn't in on this, then he had some kind of chance.

The captain's quarters were on "C" deck, just two decks below the bridge. He had a whole bay to himself. Wyckoff pressed the buzzer labeled "H. Abdul Hamil," and waited.

A voice boomed out over the intercom. "Who's there?"

"Knowles," Wyckoff answered, his heart in his throat. "Reporting as ordered."

The powered door opened, and without hesitating an instant, Wyckoff walked through it. He turned the corner around the alcove and saw a man seated at a desk, looking at him over the tops of narrow, gold-rimmed glasses. He was in his fifties, with gray hair, cropped close. His movements reminded Wyckoff of the motions of a snake—nothing sudden, but very deliberate.

"Sit down, Knowles," the captain said, after an examination that seemed to consume an eternity.

Wyckoff did, taking a chair in front of the desk. He felt an urge to adjust it, but it was, like most shipboard furniture, secured to the deck. *So, the captain didn't know Knowles by sight.*

"What were you doing on the cargo decks, Knowles?"

"Making an inspection, sir."

"Why didn't you do that while we were on the ground?"

Thinking fast, Wyckoff decided an inspection wasn't objectionable in itself—only his timing had been bad.

He threw out his excuse. "I didn't have time, Captain. I was late coming aboard. Trouble at the airport."

The captain grunted, seeming to be satisfied with the answer. "Did everything check out?"

Now in the spirit of the con, and in his own element, Wyckoff felt confident of his answer. "One hundred percent, Captain. Every crate."

The captain chuckled. "We'll do all right this time," he said. "I was worried about trying it with so many crewmen I didn't know, but with the recommendation Bob Grey gave you, I knew I could count on you. How about a drink?"

"F-fine, Captain. I'd like that."

Hamil reached into a drawer and took out a bottle and a couple of glasses. "You know," he said, "when we get this crew shaped up, this'll get easier yet. It just takes time. That reminds me. I understand you and Arlene are acquainted. Is that so?"

"Y-yes. How did you know that?"

"She mentioned it. Said you sometimes partied when you were ashore."

"Uh-huh?"

"I had Kendall Bottari picked for her spot, but she had seniority, so she bumped him down to second. I'm kind of nervous about your relationship. You're going to have to be careful."

"Okay."

"Of course, if you can bring her around. . . ."

"I get you, Captain. Look, I don't know anybody aboard except her. Who can be trusted?"

"Me and you, Knowles—and I'm not so sure about you. Cheers!" He gulped down his drink in one swallow. "Seriously, Knowles, this is the biggest thing I ever put together. Maybe the biggest thing anybody ever did out here. We've done pretty good for a new ship. We have somebody covering just about every spot: Bottari and myself on the bridge, you in the cargo section, Bob Verity on the power deck. But we have to extend our influence. We need all the bridge officers, if we can get them. And if we can't, we have to get rid of them. I've already pretty well written Mason off."

Wyckoff tried to remember what he'd seen on the roster. "Mason's the . . ."

". . . third mate. I want the whole ship to be secure, Knowles—every one of them. So get your section lined up. Bring your storekeepers around. You've got the edge over the rest of us—they're all thieves to start with." Having delivered his little barb, Hamil stood, smiling weakly, to signal Wyckoff that the interview was over.

Wyckoff had apparently passed the captain's test, if that was what this had been.

"Keep in touch, Knowles."

"Yes, sir."

Once back in the corridor, he felt better about his situation. Evidently the captain had been able to select only part of his crew. It didn't sound like things were too far along. Probably, this was the way it worked with the colonial fleet. A new ship meant a new fief for its captain. The colonial fleet was divided up just as the gangs down on the ground divided cities into turf. Wyckoff could understand that.

At least, he thought, he had once again landed on his feet, in a position to pick his side. But wait a minute—was he really?

Wyckoff mulled it over. He didn't belong in either camp. He couldn't join the conspiracy because the police knew about it and were about to smash it. But on the other hand, even if the police were disposed to protect him, relief wouldn't be immediate. Luddington was their only force on board the *Corona*—if he was the only one. He'd hinted that he wasn't, and maybe that was true, but somehow Wyckoff was beginning to think that Knowles had been extremely important to the government's operation.

Wyckoff knew how that was supposed to work. The Feds were supposed to be smart and play all the angles, pitting everybody against everybody else, until they wound up unscathed upon a heap of bodies. It had always sounded like fable to him and probably was, but even so, Wyckoff couldn't quite picture himself enjoying the role of pawn. For one thing, it could be decidedly dangerous. All he had in the world was his life. He was already living that on a borrowed identity and, however this worked out, he was washed up as soon as the voyage was over. Getting involved with Luddington would mean appearing in court back on Earth, and Wyckoff knew he couldn't impersonate Knowles throughout a trial, even if the government went along.

His options, then, were few: melt into the colonial horde, if that were possible; try to help Luddington, and be accused of Knowles' murder when the voyage was over; help Hamil, and share in his guilt when the Feds finally busted the conspirators.

He wished there were a fourth alternative, but none was apparent; he'd have to choose one of the three.

But not necessarily right away. He might still buy himself some time to think it over, now that he knew Arlene wasn't a part of it—if he could shut her up. He thought he knew how that might be accomplished. He meant to take care of that now.

Chapter Seven

Wyckoff returned to his own quarters, hoping Arlene would still be there, and that she would still be asleep. He stepped through the door quickly, glancing down at the bunk, where tousled blond hair protruded from beneath a sheet.

Quickly, he closed the door again, and stood there in the darkness.

"E-Emory?"

Wyckoff flicked the wall switch, flooding the room with light. Arlene cringed beneath the cover, then peeked out at him and gasped, "You!"

She sat up. "Emory's not here."

"I know," Wyckoff answered. "Emory's not aboard."

"What?"

"I said, he's not aboard."

"But I slept with him last night."

Wyckoff grinned. "No, you didn't."

Arlene was on her feet instantly, pummeling him with tiny fists and screaming at him. "You creep! Taking advantage of me like that."

Wyckoff subdued her easily, clamping one hand over her mouth and pinning her to the mattress.

She struggled mightily but to no avail.

When at last she tired, Wyckoff started to explain.

"I've taken Knowles' place on this voyage. I didn't have any way of knowing you were going to hop in bed with me."

"Mhph!"

"Look, you had a good time. You said so."

"Mhph!"

"I'm going to uncover your mouth. Then I'm going to explain this. If you scream, I'll belt you. Understand?"

"Mhph!"

Wyckoff slid his hand away, keeping his eyes glued to her bare chest. When he saw it rise explosively he put his hand back, extinguishing her intended scream. He could see that more persuasion was necessary. "Look, Arlene, do you want to be arrested with the rest of them when we get back to Earth?"

He took his hand away again right after that, but poised to stop another outburst should one come.

"Arrested! Why? Who are you?"

"My name is Wyckoff. I'm a federal agent," he lied. He felt Arlene's body go limp under his grip, so he relaxed it, though he still kept hold of her.

"Where's Emory?"

"He's still in New York." Wyckoff didn't think it either wise or necessary to tell her he was also dead.

"I see. Just how do you expect to get away with impersonating him?"

"As far as I can tell, you're the only one aboard who knows what he looks like. That's why I would have had to contact you eventually, even if you hadn't barged in last night."

"Barged in! I didn't know it wasn't Emory—and you might have told me then. That was a dirty trick."

"I didn't want to spoil your mood. Besides, I've learned a lot since. I can do a better job of explaining now." That was certainly true enough.

"What is all this you're saying about being arrested?"

"Some of the crew have a conspiracy going, Arlene. They've stolen the colonists' supplies and sold them. The holds are full of junk. They're planning to dump the colonists on Zahn without any tools or equipment. They'll all starve—that is, they would have if the conspiracy hadn't been discovered."

She stared at him wide-eyed. "That's what the captain's been hinting at."

"What has he said to you?"

"He mentioned you—that is, he mentioned Emory. He said he was glad to see that Emory and I were friends; that Emory was a smart boy who knew how to take care of himself, and how to take care of me, too."

"The captain's one of them. He wants all his officers in it with him. He means to make a bundle out of this, but he needs a crew he can trust."

Arlene's expression became grave. "I see. How do you know I won't turn you in?"

"You're too bright a girl for that, Arlene. You'll stick with the winner. Besides, I might not be the only agent aboard the *Corona*."

"How many are there?"

"Never mind. Maybe there aren't any; or maybe there are a dozen. Even I wouldn't know that." And it was true; he didn't. The only one he knew about was Luddington.

Her expression changed. "I don't seem to have much of a choice. I'll have to relieve the caption of command and . . ."

Wyckoff hadn't expected this reaction. He didn't know for sure if it was possible, but it didn't sound very practical, considering the fact that they didn't know who all the conspirators were. He decided, in view of Luddington's remarks, that it wasn't a good suggestion. "No, Arlene," he said. "At least, not just yet. There are some people already on Zahn who are in on this. We have to get them, too." He hoped he was coming across sufficiently dedicated and grim.

"Then what are we going to do?"

"For the moment, nothing. Not until we know who's who. I can check things out. The captain trusts me. He told me most of my crew is dirty. Certainly, they'll introduce themselves. I'll tell him you're about to come over, too; that I'm working on you real hard."

Arlene relaxed a bit. She fluffed the pillow up and slid into a more upright position, pulling the sheet tightly under her chin. She was not, it appeared, an impulsive person, but then, to land the job she had, she couldn't very well have been a dummy. "I don't like this at all, Wyck—what did you say your name was?"

"Wyckoff—Stanislaus Wyckoff. But it might be better if you got in the habit of calling me Emory, since that's who I'm supposed to be."

"I still don't like it, and I don't understand how you got Emory to let you do it. Has Emory been arrested?"

"No. He's—there's nobody bothering him. Look, I don't like this either, but since we're in it, we have to make the best of it, and I need your help. I don't know any of these people. I don't know what it was Knowles was supposed to do on this ship, and. . . ."

"You what?!"

"I said, I don't know what Knowles' job was."

She jerked bolt upright and glared at him. "You're not a certified storekeeper?"

"No. And as a matter of fact, I've never been aboard a spaceship before. That's why I . . ."

"You expect to impersonate a trained spaceman and you've never been on a spaceship? I don't believe it. What kind of idiots is the government hiring these days? Look, Wyck—Emory. There are some things I can teach you and some things I can't, and it's the ones I can't teach you, the things you're expected to know instinctively, that are going to get you in trouble. I don't know as I want any part of this whole thing. Why can't we just forget that any of this ever happened?"

"Because we're both involved already. Don't forget, you're supposed to know me. Look, I'm no kid; I've been around. All you have to do is tell me what a chief storekeeper does, and I'll wing it from there."

She continued to stare at him in disbelief. "Well, I

suppose there's no other way. Okay, we'll make you a lazy one. You'll supervise—lightly. Let your underlings do the work, be wishywashy. They'll love it. Most spacehands are goldbricks anyhow, and thanks to union featherbedding and the fact that most everything is automated, there isn't a whole lot of work for anybody to do.

"Your work station is down on "R" deck. There's a small office with a computer terminal. You have two assistants. I don't know either of them, but we can check the roster and find out their names. You're responsible for all supplies on board that the crew uses, except for ordinance, which is the responsibility of the third mate, who also doubles as the artificer . . ."

"You said ordinance; does that mean guns? *Interesting*, thought Wyckoff. *That's why they're worried about this Mason guy.*

"Yes. Of course, we don't carry very many, or anything big—just some sidearms and a few rifles."

"That could be important. We'll make it a priority to check on the third mate, then. What else do I have to do?"

"Well, let's see. Oh, yes. Your responsibilities would also include the passengers' consumables during the voyage, and while we're in space, any freight consigned to the colony. But once we make planetfall that becomes the obligation of the colonial supercargo."

"What about moving around the ship. Can I do that?"

"Within limits. For instance, the bridge would normally be off-limits to you. So would the power deck. But I can get you into those areas, if necessary. The passenger decks are locked and guarded, and you're supposed to get authorization to go in there."

"I know. I was there a little while ago. I found that a little strange."

"It isn't. It's standard procedure—and for a very good reason. You see, we carry a pretty weird assortment of people, and not all of them are thrilled to be colonists."

"But I thought . . ."

"That everybody wanted to get off Earth? Get out to the wild, open spaces and be pioneers? That isn't the way it is. There have been attempts to take over ships and force the crews to return. Besides, there's disease to worry about. You'd be surprised how many dirty little bugs these people bring aboard, and what stray radiation can sometimes do to the disease organism. Crowded in like they are, anything that got started would spread pretty fast, and if it got into the business end of the ship, it'd be rough on everybody."

"I was down there!"

"So?"

"The guard didn't even ask me what I was doing. She . . ."

". . . Assumed that, as an officer, you took the necessary precautions. Did you?"

"No."

"Then assume she's one of them. If she is, she'd know about you—uh, Emory. She wouldn't question anything you did. Did you contact any of the passengers?"

"Well, yeah, one. But he's an agent, too."

"You'd better be a little more careful next time."

"I don't think I'll be going back. Are there any other places I can't go?"

"I can't think of any offhand—uh, the armory, naturally."

"All right. Look, maybe you could take me around, show me the ropes, okay?"

"Sure. In a little while."

"What's that supposed to mean?"

She smiled up at him. "Last night, I thought you were Emory. I need to make a value judgment."

Wyckoff gave a sigh. He reached over and turned off the light. Life was getting complicated.

Chapter Eight

The interlude left Wyckoff exhausted, and with the distinct impression that Arlene was basically insatiable. The real Knowles, he thought, must have been a person of uncommon stamina, to have been able to hunt excitement on the side. He wondered how long he'd be able to stand up under the strain.

He liked Arlene. She was a likable girl, though in common with many other women he had known, she displayed a possessive streak that worried him a little. But she seemed to be satisfied he was on the level with his story about being an undercover fed. *Undercover!* That was rich! He was that, literally, though the pun lost some of its appeal when he thought of the day of reckoning still to come.

It had been, he reflected, an incredible sequence of events, fast-paced and up until now exciting. He wasn't sure whether that was intrinsically good or bad, but it had certainly altered his lifestyle. And if it had not been for the inexorable manner in which the circumstances threatened to close in on him, he could perhaps even learn to enjoy it. Certainly Arlene's favors were a substantial start on that.

He wound up deciding that for the time being he would have to fall into the character, or characters, in which fate had cast him. It would be tricky to remember when to be whom, but he was streetwise, and if life on the streets did nothing else to the man it made him versatile. On the street, you were either a successful opportunist or a failure, and failures wound up either in prison or in graves.

So Wyckoff resolved not to fail. He would learn the rules and observe them; convert street wisdom to space wisdom; play his parts straight and reap whatever profits he could.

A slim arm crawled around his neck, raising his head up off the pillow. Another drifted toward his groin, and soft lips brushed his ear. Arlene, tired of being ignored, was into the afterplay, hoping, perhaps, that he might manage one more time.

Wyckoff meant to discourage that at all costs. He turned away to let her know his interest, if not his strength, had completely waned. Then he again broached the subject of the storekeeper's duties.

Arlene picked up the cue, ended her role as seductress, and became his tutor instead. As in everything else she did, she was thorough, competent, and professional.

She withdrew her arm, pulled the terminal keyboard from its rack, and laid it across her lap. With the punch of keys, the screen lit up. "Actually," she said, "you can learn almost everything you need to know from studying this."

"What is it?"

"The ship's library system. I've accessed it for you this time, but you should make a note of the password so you can do it yourself." She punched a couple more keys, as indicated by the help-menu. "It's all here— ship's articles, duty rosters, crew's roster, and most important, the tables of organization and equipment.

"Now, let's get into duties. All of these are standard, by the way—the space administration and the union sat down and worked it all out years ago. Every category of work falls into either supervisory or executory—in your particular case, supervisory, which makes it easy."

"How so?"

"Your help is all experienced. They know their duties by rote. They know what records have to be kept, what reports need to be filed, and so on. They'll do this routinely, and all you have to do is approve and sign. Never do this on the spot. Always stall, and either check with me or consult this file."

"Why?"

"Because this is a new ship, and you're a new officer. Your crew will want to find out how astute you are, test your limits of patience. They'll rate you according to their own standard."

"Oh?"

"There are as many types of officers as there are human personalities. What you have to do right away is establish your authority."

"I would have thought my rank would provide that."

"Only if you assert it. You can be either a firm, distant supervisor who maintains control by following the book and using the authority the articles give you, or one of the boys, who does it by persuasion. Both systems work, under normal circumstances, and both have advantages. But in your case, I think I'd recommend that you follow the book, even though you might learn more by getting chummy."

"Why is that?"

"Familiarity means sharing your past—talking about former shipmates and berths. You haven't got any to talk about; therefore, you have to be the remote, aloof type, friendly but correctly distant. It'd be a good idea to cultivate that impression with the rest of the officers, too. They aren't as inclined to be nosy as the deckhands are, because most of them have their own secrets to keep, but there will be some."

"Okay, Captain Bligh it is, then."

"Speaking of the captain, be careful with him, Emory. I mean it: watch him. They say he's a sly one. I've

heard a few stories. I think he could be really dangerous if he caught on to you."

She was doing it—calling him Emory. Wyckoff was
pleased with that development. It helped him maintain
the persona in his own mind, and he knew he'd have to
be able to do that automatically if he was to get out of
this.

Arlene went on. "You have to remember where we
are—in deep space, many light-years from port, out
where the master of a vessel has real authority. In some
cases that authority is life or death, and portside law
gives him protection if he exercises the power correctly. What that means is that while we're under way,
he's like a little king, and as long as an order's issued
under color of his office he has to be obeyed—subject,
of course, to being able to justify his actions when he
gets back.

"But besides the legal authority he has, he's got
control of the actions of some of the crew by virtue of
his conspiracy with them, and that means he can get
away with a lot more. He can count on them for support at any dirtside inquiry. That's where the danger
lies. If he ever doubts you're the genuine Emory
Knowles, or suspects that you have something to do
with the law, you'll have a fatal accident, and the odds
are that nobody'll ever be able to prove it was deliberate."

Sobered by this advice, Wyckoff studied as never
before. When it was time for them to go on duty, both
he and Arlene felt that he'd progressed far enough to be
a superficially plausible chief storekeeper. He would
not call the deck a floor, or the overhead a ceiling, or a
hatch a door, nor would he allow himself to express
perplexity over some bit of jargon he did not understand. Instead, he would pretend not to hear, or quickly
change the subject to conceal his ignorance.

Wyckoff settled into his small office on "R" deck, and
spent a great deal of time rummaging through his desk
and its accompanying cabinets. Most of what he found

was mundane—supplies and forms for use when it was not convenient for his people to log on to the ship's computer.

He had not bothered to assemble his crew and introduce himself to them. Instead, he met each of them separately, as duties demanded and as chance dictated. Arlene had advised that either method was proper, and he had chosen the latter because it demanded less vigilance and offered fewer possibilities for slip-ups. A mistake observed by one man might be noticed, but he would not necessarily mention it to anyone else, or be believed by anyone he told. This was therefore less costly to the impersonation.

He found that as chief storekeeper he theoretically had no off-duty hours. He was like the captain and the drive engineer—the only one of his kind on board and therefore on call all the time, dependent on the discretion of his subordinates on the three watches for any rest he did get. It soon appeared, however, that in the day-to-day routine, absent some crisis, there was little danger of disturbance, and he could therefore count on relative peace and quiet outside those office hours he set himself.

Customarily, a ship maintained the Earth standard time of its home port, even when on a planet whose diurnal period differed. This was the only way the order of the biorhythm could be preserved. The first watch was therefore the day watch, and was prestigious to be on. Like the captain, the drive engineer, the ship's surgeon, and the astrogator, the chief storekeeper was considered a senior, and theoretically stood the first watch, whether he was physically present or not. All other officers, including the bridge officers, rotated watches.

In practical terms, what this meant was that there would be times when Arlene was not available to coach him—when she would be too wrapped up in her own duties or too hemmed in by other people for consultation. As an added inconvenience, Wyckoff could not enter the control room without invitation by whoever was on watch, so he would in any such event have to resort to ship's intercom to talk to her. Considering her status, and the likely nature of any such emergency, that would be perilously dangerous.

There were compensations. As one of the conspirators, he found he could go almost anywhere else he wanted on the ship, just as he had visited the cargo holds on that first day. All he needed to do was recite some official purpose. Because he was responsible for seeing to it that every area had the requisite sanitary and housekeeping supplies, there was never a foray without an official purpose.

Chapter Nine

"Hello, Mister Knowles."

Wyckoff had been down to the engineering deck, where he had been taking inventory of some spare parts—work he'd dreamed up himself because he wanted to look around. Engineering was located on deck 14, which at first had appeared to him to be an odd place for it, until he realized that the *Corona*'s inertial guidance system had to be located amidships. He was also amazed to discover that, contrary to what he had believed, there was another way, besides the axial elevator, to get to deck 14. And deck 14 had become important to his recent thinking because that was where the pods containing the ship's three Aschenbrenner drive units were located.

Always on the lookout for good hidey-holes, Wyckoff had discovered that each pod had an access tunnel and a small room full of auxiliary instruments. These were used infrequently, generally only during the course of engine overhauls at one of the spaceyards, and if he had to disappear suddenly, Wyckoff intended to be ready. He made plans to stock all of these with food and water—just in case.

The engine room elevator was not as large as the axial, because it was for passengers only. It ran outside the inner hull, through a tube exposed to vacuum, protected only by the thin plastic streamlined hull.

He had been lost in the implication of this when the voice assaulted him. He did not recognize the sound of it, but when he looked up he saw that the speaker was the girl who had been on guard during his foray into the passenger area some eight days ago.

"Hello. Linda, isn't it?"

"You remembered. I'm flattered. It's been a long time."

"Yes, it has," Wyckoff replied. He pushed the button to take them to "R" deck, then glanced over at her.

Linda was a handsome hunk of woman, he decided, though a bit rough-looking compared to Arlene. She wore standard coveralls, though hers were tighter than they needed to be. When she moved it was evident that nothing restrained her ample bosom, which, even at one gee, rode high. She was perhaps twenty-five, brunette, with blue eyes, an uncommon combination. Wyckoff looked at her short-cropped hair, and decided it wasn't her natural color.

She noticed, dropped her eyes, and smiled coyly, giving her body a slight turn toward him. "I'm going off duty, Mr. Knowles. Would you punch 'Q' for me? That's where I live, you know." She smiled again.

Wyckoff caught the invitation in that remark, and reminded himself of an earlier resolution to fraternize. He disagreed with Arlene and thought it unlikely that Linda could be part of the team, especially when she was only a common spacehand, but she looked nosy, and she might just be a gossip as well. In his circumstances, Wyckoff appreciated the value of gossip.

Throwing caution to the winds, and ever mindful of how Arlene kept him drained, he nevertheless decided to respond with enthusiasm. "Oh," he said. "I was about to take a break, too. What a coincidence."

"Let's do it together. My roommate's on watch. We can go to my place, have a drink and relax. We deserve that, don't we?"

"Of course." After that, Wyckoff fell easily into the mood of her small talk. He was sure of her now. Strictly speaking, nobody on board a starship was supposed to possess alcohol. In practice, officers were commonly excepted, and were fairly open in admitting it. But no spacehand would unless he, or she, were confident of the discretion of the party to whom such an admission might be made. Linda couldn't be—yet. That meant she had plans to cultivate his friendship, which meant . . .

The elevator doors opened and they stepped out into a corridor which, while it didn't compare with officers' country, was still a long way above what the passengers had. Linda led him past a couple of grinning crewmen like he was a fish on a string, and in a few moments ushered him into a tiny cabin.

There were two bunks—one above the other—a table, a small closet, and a combination commode-shower stall. Linda invited him to sit on the bunk. He sat.

"Sorry there's no ice. I hope you like bourbon."

Wyckoff didn't—especially not straight. In his customary social circle, muscatel was the usual alcoholic drink, but he took the glass anyway and gave it an experimental sip. As he expected, the stuff burned unmercifully, and he recognized it as synthetic. Linda apparently wasn't affluent enough to have the real thing.

She sat down beside him, sipping her own drink and acting coy. Somehow the zipper of her garment had descended, revealing a most astonishing sight.

He was not particularly interested, but to keep in character, Wyckoff pretended to ogle. Then his vision began to blur strangely. He looked away, toward the door, where dainty things hanging on a hook began crawling around of their own accord. Glancing back at Linda's face, he noticed that it too became strangely animated. One side of it drooped, the other seemed frozen motionless. Her eyes stared back at him like ice-cold sapphires rimmed in black lace. That was the way his mind originally recorded the incident.

That memory did not linger long. When he left her

he had others—recollections of a furiously animalistic orgy beyond anything he had ever experienced with Arlene; of himself dressing with a sly look of sated pleasure rippling across his face; of Linda's hungry eyes staring still, craving more, and the promise in those eyes that there would be. With this impression he returned to "R" deck and went back to his work. *I was right*, he thought, in a vain effort to salve his conscience. *She will know everything that's going on board the* Corona, *but she's certainly no gossip. Getting it out of her is going to take some time.* Not so strangely, he found himself eager to continue with that phase of the investigation.

Chapter Ten

Captain Hamil's quarters were as close to plush as ships' space ever offered. Even accounting for the fact that he was master of the vessel, they were a trifle much. The bed on which Linda McElhaney lounged, nude, was covered with silk sheets, and the champagne she sipped from the Flemish crystal goblet was not only the real French stuff, but one of the best of recent years.

She was enjoying herself immensely. It wasn't often she had a chance to watch the captain squirm. Usually, it was the other way around. Hamil's nature was a perverse one. He sought, and normally was able to maintain, a smooth control all the time. He used whatever he had to and whatever was handy in order to do that—his rank, the weaknesses of the people around them, his own polished guile, flattery, and sometimes lightly veiled threats.

He did it all for power and money.

Linda was sure that none of his other apparent appetites were real. She believed them contrived, because Hamil knew he was supposed to have them and that it would look odd to others if he didn't.

She was supposed to be the captain's woman. Why? Because captains were supposed to have them, and

commonly did, so Hamil had her. It didn't bother her
that he carried the facade only as far as he had to or that
he was a mediocre lover. What did bother her was that
he hadn't extended her the customary privileges that
were a captain's woman's due. He didn't back her up
against his officers, he hadn't moved her into his quarters on a full-time basis, and he kept her on in the lowly
duty status consistent with her rank.

Linda knew other girls who'd made it much better
than she had, who'd risen rapidly through the ranks and
had something to show for their efforts—something to
keep them against the day when their looks failed.
Hamil hadn't given her that, and most likely never
would, so she didn't feel the least bit sorry for him now.

It might well be, she thought, that this is the end of
the line for Abdul, but if it is, it's his own fault.

She was glad she had coppered her own bets. That
had been the smartest move she'd ever made, hooking
up with Luddington. Not only would she have protection when Abdul got his, and the satisfaction of letting
him know she had helped, but there was a good chance
Hamil's bankroll would be there to comfort her in her
old age. He didn't know about any of it—yet. She was
in the process of educating him now.

She had the duration of this voyage to find his loot.
She knew it was somewhere aboard. Luddington seemed
to think so too, though Linda doubted it had any central place in his thinking, or in the government's case.
Shortly before Abdul had been given command of the
Corona, Luddington had cautiously approached her,
and tried very hard not only to play on her sense of
civic duty to bring her in against Hamil, but to hint that
she herself might have certain vulnerabilities, too.

Well, her sense of civic duty had not been very
strong, and growing up as she had, in what even in this
day and age was considered a rough part of Baltimore,
she was more than used to being threatened by the
authorities. So neither fear nor altruism had played
a part in her decision.

What had convinced her was mention, probably innocently, and certainly by accident, that Hamil had acquired a great deal of money that hadn't been traced and was thought to be hidden away somewhere in the form of cash.

She'd known Abdul only too well, even then. Now, as then, she was certain that his bankroll would be somewhere within easy reach, where he could keep an eye on it. The facts argued that he'd smuggled it aboard and hidden it somewhere on the ship, and if that was the case all she had to do was stay in favor and keep her eyes open. As the heat increased, he was bound to go for it.

She had just turned up the burner; now she sat back comfortably to watch him sweat, braced for the obvious question.

It came. "What is all this?" Abdul stared at the tape player in his hand—the one she had just pulled from her bag and handed to him. Knowing Abdul as she did, she knew his mind was seething and that his flustered manner, so atypical, was this time entirely real. Most likely, she was thinking, he suspects I'm springing some kind of extortion scheme on him. She decided to nip that in the bud. She didn't want to come off as an antagonist; her objective was to compel Abdul to cling to her as an ally.

"They're after you, Abdul. It's all on there—play it."

"W-what's on it?" His voice was actually plaintive.

"A conversation I had with a man you *think* is Emory Knowles. He isn't." She paused a moment to let the implication of that sink in, then added, "You're lucky I was suspicious, and that I could get to him as easily as I did." She didn't add the details of that—let jealousy rise.

"What do you mean, he isn't Knowles? Surely they checked his credentials before he came aboard—you can't fake those—" His voice trailed off on the inference that thought raised. Somebody *could* fake them, with all the government's resources. The captain blanched. "Not a cop?"

Now, Linda thought, *you pounce—and you set the hook.* "No, but you've got some of those aboard, including one in the passenger decks. His name's Luddington." She had some qualms about telling him that, but then, she couldn't protect everybody. Luddington could just take care of himself. She was pretty sure Luddington would never talk about her, even if Abdul got him— unless, of course, Abdul also caught on to her, and she wasn't about to let that happen. "Wyckoff—that's his real name—*appears* to be a nobody, and a stowaway at that. He came aboard at the last minute, flashing Knowles's medallion, but those fools at operations were in too much of a rush to get us launched—they didn't check it. I put him under and . . ."

"You what? Drugs! Linda, that's the most dangerous thing you could have done. What if he finds out?"

"He won't. I used scopolamine, not a hypo; just enough, in a glass of whiskey, to make him a willing subject for hypnosis. I loaded him up with phony memories later just to make sure. There's no way he can catch on. Go ahead, play the tape."

Hamil pressed a button on the device. There was a brief hiss, then voices:

Linda: "How's that? Are you comfortable?"

Knowles: "Uh-huh!"

Linda: "Feeling sleepy?"

Knowles: "Uh-huh!"

"Put it on fast forward—skip the preliminaries." The device whirred briefly, then a voice reemerged: ". . . are you, really?"

Knowles: "Stanislaus Wyckoff."

Linda: "What happened to Emory Knowles?"

Wyckoff: "Knowles is dead—murdered."

Linda: "Did you kill him?"

Wyckoff: "No."

Linda: "Who did?"

Wyckoff: "I don't know."

Linda: "Was it somebody from this ship?"

Wyckoff: "No."

Linda: "But you can't be sure?"

Wyckoff: "Yes, I'm sure."

Linda: "How did you get on board the *Corona*?"

Wyckoff: "I had Knowles's clothes and papers."

Linda: "How did you get these?"

Wyckoff: "I stole them."

Linda: "But you didn't kill him?"

Wyckoff: "He was drunk when I met him—unconscious when I took his stuff. He was alive then, in his car. Somebody else killed him after I left, and took the car."

Linda: "Why did you come aboard?"

Wyckoff: "It was an accident. I didn't want to."

Linda: "Somebody made you?"

Wyckoff: "Yes."

Linda: "Who?"

Wyckoff: "The police."

"The police?" Hamil was gaping, his mouth open wide. "I thought you said . . ."

"He isn't officially connected. Fast forward a little, Abdul. The next couple of minutes aren't important to us. Evidently Wyckoff came across Knowles's car after he'd had an accident, switched clothes with him, and left him somewhere where a couple of crazies finished him off and stole the car. Knowles's killers didn't know him either. Meanwhile, Wyckoff looted Knowles's hotel room. He met the first mate there, briefly, and then a chain of accidental events brought him aboard. He thought the airport police were after him. The man's quite an opportunist. That's enough. Here he starts talking about your operation. I questioned him about this after I found out he'd talked to Luddington."

Again, clear voices could be heard.

". . . neer, Horan."

"Back it up a hair."

There was a hum. ". . . est of them?"

"A little more."

Linda: "Now, who's in on this?"

Wyckoff: "I don't know all of them."

Linda: "Who are the ones you do know?"

Wyckoff: "The captain, for sure; the second mate, Verity; the drive engineer, Horan; one of my senior storekeepers, Fred Moroso . . ."

Linda: "What about Mason?"

Wyckoff: "Who?"

Linda: "Mason—the third mate."

Wyckoff: "I don't know."

Linda: "And Graham—what about her?"

Wyckoff: "She's with us."

Linda: "Us?"

Wyckoff: "Me—and I guess with Luddington, too. I mean, she isn't in on the stealing."

Linda: "How do you know?"

Wyckoff: "I know."

Linda: "Did you tell her about all this?"

Wyckoff: "No."

Linda: "What did you tell her?"

Wyckoff: "That I was working for the government."

Linda: "Did you tell her about the cargo?"

Wyckoff: "Yes."

Hamil stopped the tape. "This is bad, Linda. Graham will never come over, now that she knows there are cops on board. We'll have to get rid of all of them. It'll be awkward, but we can do it. Maybe this Wyckoff can even help us identify the rest of the cops. And after that, there's nothing on the record to implicate us. The cargo's certified by the supercargo at Matagorda, and it'll be certified on the other end."

Here, Linda had to make a judgment. It was a perilous one because it slammed the door on Hamil. But if she didn't tell him the rest, she knew he wouldn't be scared enough to bolt.

"There's one more thing, Abdul—the colonists."

"What about the colonists? They won't last long enough to hurt us."

"There's another ship right behind us."

"What!"

Now the captain searched through the disembodied words—Wyckoff's and hers—to find the part where Wyckoff had mentioned this.

Linda didn't know if it was true or not. Luddington had never told her about any other ship—that information had originated with Wyckoff—but it seemed reasonable to suppose that it was a fact. Conditions on Zahn were harsh, and ordinarily there wouldn't have been another contact for several years after the *Corona* touched there.

Linda didn't care, either. She would be fine in any case, because she knew how to keep out of trouble. She lay there, sipping champagne, and enjoying Abdul's misery.

Chapter Eleven

Wyckoff had never been a sedentary person. He had boundless energy, though for most of his life that had been misdirected, or directed solely toward the satisfaction of his own curiosity. That curiosity was also boundless, and so he fit easily into the shipboard style a chief storekeeper's berth permitted.

He wandered everywhere, a pager on his belt and portable terminal in his hand. The latter he seldom used with any official purpose, but it looked impressive to fling open a locker of supplies, punch into the ship's mainframe, and pretend to compare what was there against the inventory.

This not only got him into places where his presence might have otherwise looked suspicious, but it had a way of making crewmen disappear. On all ships the crew stole or misused supplies, and the *Corona* was no exception, and nobody wanted to be in proximity when the loss was discovered.

Normally Wyckoff had no specific objective in mind when he made his rounds beyond the satisfaction of his own curiosity, though he did derive a certain perverse pleasure at driving these idlers up the wall.

Tonight, however, it was different. Wyckoff had returned to the launch bays on the third watch to search for whatever it was that the captain had brought here on the first watch.

When he entered, the spaceman on watch at the lifeboat station had been quite relaxed—asleep, in fact, with his feet propped up and a magazine sprawled across his lap. Wyckoff would have preferred to let him doze; he didn't want any company. But he had not expected to find the man in that condition and had been excessively noisy when he had entered the hatch.

He made up for it by failure to comment, and the man, discovered in his dereliction, now sat bolt upright and wide awake, probably wondering why Wyckoff had not disciplined him. Wyckoff not only didn't care what the man did, but he suspected that inaction was insurance for the man's silence. He would be nervous about the incident for a while, and then gratefully forget it—and the fact that Wyckoff had been here. That was human nature.

Wyckoff wandered aimlessly around in the huge bay until he was satisfied that the man was not watching him. Then he went directly to boat No. 1 which, like Numbers 9 and 18, rested on *Corona's* big turntable, in front of launch tubes. This was the one he had seen the captain enter earlier that day. He had gone in with a small box, and he had emerged without it. Wyckoff had been lurking near one of the other boats, and the captain had not been aware of it.

He laid his pager and terminal aside and entered through the little lock, closing it behind him so that the lights would not be visible from the outside. In an hour he had carefully, and he hoped indetectably, turned the little craft inside out. The package he sought was concealed inside one of the medical kits.

It was a bundle of papers—papers Wyckoff suspected were quite valuable, though he lacked the sophistication to understand what they said. Consequently, he did not know quite what to do about the package, and since he feared the captain would check it periodically, decided to leave it where he'd found it until he could learn more about it.

Arlene was his only safe source of that information, and so, when she came off watch later that afternoon, Wyckoff was waiting in her quarters for her. He found her strangely disturbed, though she would not immediately tell him why.

He put it down to female moodiness, suggested that they have an early supper in the officers' mess, and put on his wittiest and most affable persona.

But even after they had eaten and exchanged endless small talk, her mood had persisted. Finally, Wyckoff gave up on her and decided to pop the question. "Arlene, what are bearer bonds?"

At first, her response was an annoyed stare, as though he had derailed a train of thought of great immediate moment to her. But then, abruptly, her entire attitude changed, and she was all ears. "What?" Though a whisper, the word carried a heavy load of astonishment.

"Bearer bonds."

The look then changed to one of consternation, as though she was thinking he ought already to know.

Wyckoff sat there, a minor panic rising. Had he said something that compromised his impersonation?

"Bearer bonds are bonds that don't have to be endorsed to be cashed," Arlene finally said. "All you need is possession. Why?"

"Because I saw the captain hide something in one of the lifeboats. I went back later and looked, and it was a big package of them."

Arlene's face immediately blanched, and her eyes grew large. Her silence and the look of fear that washed over her face endured long enough to cause him serious concern, and to look around to see who else might be watching.

But there was no one else in the room, and the nature of shipboard food being what it was, the lone crewman who tended the microwave and collected the used trays was lounging back in his cubicle.

As abruptly as the silence had stricken her, the words now appeared. "It must be true," she gasped. "I didn't believe him. It sounded too crazy."

"Who didn't you believe, Arlene? What's crazy?"

"M-Mason. He said he thought we were off course."

"Explain, Arlene."

"H-he mentioned when I came on today that he thought it looked like our heading might be a degree or two farther in-system than it should be."

"That doesn't sound very serious."

She turned to him and made an effort to maintain calm. "No, I guess not. I keep forgetting that you've never been out here before. Emory, a degree of arc, over ten or fifteen parsecs, can mean an enormous error in distance."

"Well, then, didn't you check it?"

"Of course I did. That's part of my job. But the astrogation computer confirms that we're right on the money."

"Then why's it such a big deal?"

"Emory, don't you see? Hamil's phonied up the course. He knows you're on to him. He doesn't intend to take the *Corona* to Zahn. He intends to scuttle her."

"Scuttle the ship? What about him? What good would that do him?"

"Emory, didn't you hear anything I said? There's a definite connection between the bonds and the lifeboat."

"Where could he go in a lifeboat? Even I know what a joke they are. They're not good for anything like that."

"That's true, Emory. Lifeboats are an anachronism—a carryover from when everything was interplanetary. Ships like the *Corona* still have them because the law requires it, which is silly, since they don't have interstellar capability. They're supposed to preserve a life until rescue, but if an accident doesn't occur within a planetary system or on a heavily traveled route, they're useless. Most captains I know regard them as expensive shuttles, and not very good ones at that.

"That's what frightens me, because you see, Emory, there *are* a couple of places Hamil could go, and the course Mason thinks we're on would be about right for one of them—Kang-Kao-Tze. He must be really desperate, though." Her look told Wyckoff she expected him to recognize that name.

Wyckoff didn't.

"It was a colony settled exclusively by Chinese, Emory. We're used to thinking that space exploration was always the worldwide effort it is now, but that's not so. Around the turn of the century there were a number of nations that tried it on their own. China was one of them. The Islamic Coalition was another. The old Russian Empire had half a dozen. They all took their ideologies with them, but except for Kang-Kao-Tze, they've all pretty much been reassimilated into the rest of the system—even Shia, though travel there is restricted. But Kang-Kao-Tze is closed—it hasn't had contact with off-worlders for half a century. The last time anybody went there and got out again, it was a communist dictatorship worse than anything Earth ever had."

"Then why would Hamil want to go there?"

"Maybe he's desperate. More likely it's a combination of that and that ego of his. Maybe he thinks he can buy his way back, perhaps by selling the ship, and arrange for quiet passage someplace else."

"How could he do that if nobody goes there?"

"I said it was a closed world—not that they didn't have trade. But they use their own ships, which call mostly at Shia. Shia's the Moslem colony, and it's closed to non-Moslems, even though it's part of the Solar Combine now. It shares a lot of the Kung mentality. They get along well enough when they trade."

"So you'd think he'd head there, wouldn't you?"

"It would seem reasonable, at first glance. Ethnically, Hamil's an Arab, but if he ever was a Moslem, he's since acquired all the vices the rest of us have. Also, in most ways, they're a pretty strait-laced bunch, and I doubt if that would fit his plans very well. They wouldn't buy a stolen ship and they wouldn't cover for him, but if he slipped in from Kung—well, a rich man can live quite comfortably, even on Shia, and when things cooled down, he could probably leave without any questions being asked."

"What are we going to do?"

"You're asking me? I should think you'd want to talk to Luddington. Right now, I don't have enough on Hamil to justify trying to relieve him—not unless the government will back me up. I'd be guilty of mutiny."

"Oh, come on, Arlene—against a crook like Hamil?"

"Absolutely. His thievery has nothing to do with his fitness for command and I have absolutely no hard evidence that he isn't fit."

"But he's getting ready to wreck the ship, Arlene."

"He stashed his loot in a lifeboat, Emory—that's *all* we can prove he did at this point and that's not enough. It'd be different if he was under arrest by the civil authority and they ordered me to confine him."

"All right. I'll tell Luddington."

"When?"

"As soon as I can get in there."

"Okay. Emory, don't you think we ought to let Mason in on this? He wouldn't have said what he said if he were working for Hamil."

"I'd want to ask Luddington about that, too. Okay?"

Chapter Twelve

The door to the passenger elevator had no sooner closed than Linda McElhaney whipped out the transceiver she carried on her belt and pushed the transmit button. "Abdul?"

"Here," the captain answered immediately.

"Luddington just called. He said Wyckoff just left, on his way forward, Luddington'll be right behind him and should pop in here any moment."

"Good. What did you tell Luddington?"

"Exactly what you said—that you've ordered the elevators sealed and are about to lock up everybody who isn't in on this, and that I'd help him get to a lifeboat so he could intercept the other ship."

"Lifeboat number nine!"

"Right, number nine. Okay. Here comes Luddington, Abdul."

"Call me back when he's launched."

"Right."

Wyckoff had intended to go straight back to his quarters and tell Arlene what Luddington had said, though he must properly embellish it first. In point of fact, Luddington had offered little in the way of encouragement, and had behaved as though he didn't trust

Wyckoff, which was probably the case. He had listened with interest, and apparently with great concern, and then advised Wyckoff that there was another agent among the crew with whom he could rapidly get in touch. He would consult and issue instructions, and something would happen before the watch was over. Wyckoff couldn't tell Arlene that—not if she was to go on believing his own story.

This was why, on the way up, he changed his mind and decided on a detour. When the elevator stopped at "H" deck he immediately punched the down button for the lifeboat bays. He had suddenly remembered who he was, what he was doing here, and how he had gotten here, and he decided it was time for Mother Wyckoff's little boy to start looking out for himself again.

The same crewman was on duty when he arrived— this time he was awake. He greeted Wyckoff nervously. As Wyckoff disappeared down the ladder leading off the catwalk, the man embarked on his busy-work routine and did not bother him. Wyckoff went directly to No. 1 and quickly slipped inside.

He emerged, only moments later, with Hamil's bankroll stuffed uncomfortably inside his shirt. He had already started up the ladder again when the flash came.

The flash was extraordinarily brilliant in this huge chamber, which was lit only dimly by naked bulbs scattered among the grillwork. At first, Wyckoff didn't know what it had been, but then, while the afterimage still lingered on his retinas, he quickly realized it had been a plazer bolt. He had once been shot with one himself. They hurt, and they knocked you out, but they didn't penetrate or kill, which made them an ideal shipboard weapon.

He glanced around to see who was there, and advanced a step or two up the ladder to the top. There, peeking over the surface of the catwalk, he saw not the shooter but the victim. The crewman on duty lay sprawled out across the grillwork.

Then he heard the voices . . .

". . . there's nobody else. Get going." The voice was Linda's.

Wyckoff crept higher, to where he could see over the panel that surrounded the crewman's work station. Linda stood with her back to him, plazer in hand, watching somebody below. In a moment the figure she watched descended the ladder on the other side of the catwalk and Wyckoff could see him, too—Luddington!

Luddington reached the bottom of the ladder and ran to the lifeboat on that side, No. 9, which he quickly entered.

It was then that Wyckoff really got scared. Once Luddington was in, Linda went to the control panel and things that frightened Wyckoff even more started happening. At the end of the launch tube, inner lock doors parted, and a section of the turntable with the boat on it began moving toward the opening.

In less than a minute the boat was inside the lock. When the doors closed the pumps started whining, and Wyckoff knew the air was being withdrawn from the launch chamber. Luddington had not gone inside to hide; Linda was going to launch him.

She did that as soon as the pumps stopped and the outer lock doors were out of the way. Throughout the launch bay there was a rumble, as the hydraulic catapult expelled the boat from the lock. Then there was nothing, until the whoosh of air that signaled the lock's repressurization. He took another careful step and turned his attention to Linda.

Wyckoff was baffled by it all. He could think of no reason why Luddington would do such a thing, and he hadn't known there was a connection between them, though now it was apparent she was the other agent he had alluded to, or one of them. Theories formed and raced through his mind—Linda forced Luddington to go? No, she had sounded encouraging. Luddington was going for help? That didn't seem reasonable, in view of what Arlene had told him.

While he pondered these imponderables the answer

came, not through shrewd deduction but by revelation
of treachery. All at once, Linda had a radio in her hand,
and was calling: "Abdul?"

Wyckoff's blood ran cold. She had called the captain
by his first name, and the captain had answered
immediately.

"Here, Linda."

"He's gone. He'll be waiting for the trailing ship,
expecting to send it to Kang-Kao-Tze. You can take
your new heading and start jugging the rest of them. I'll
be right up."

"Okay. Stop at "R" deck on the way and pick up
Wyckoff."

Wyckoff ducked, cringing at the top of the ladder just
below the level of the catwalk. Not only was Linda
working for both sides, they knew who he really was!
Worse, Luddington didn't know he'd been double-
crossed, and apparently had been told a course change
was only imminent—not that it had already occurred.
He hadn't believed Wyckoff, which meant that the
trailing ship wouldn't be intercepted and it would no
longer follow *Corona*.

His old plans wouldn't work anymore. He'd have to
fall back on his contingency plan, which his instincts,
fortunately, had forced on him.

He waited until Linda left. When he heard the elevator door close, he darted down the catwalk to the main
deck, where there was a door to the engineering elevator. He waited nervously until it came, hoping it wouldn't
also be in use.

When it did, he got in, and endured more anxious
moments before the door opened at the bottom. If
anybody saw him and reported his whereabouts, the
captain would be sure to search the engine pods, along
with every other possible hiding place on the ship.

He was lucky. The axial elevator was more convenient for power deck personnel to use, so he met no
one. He quickly made his way to his hidey-hole, flopped

down on the makeshift bunk he'd assembled through-out those last hectic days, and relaxed as best he could.

As the minutes passed, the urgency of the situation began to fade. He took stock of the facts. Though it wasn't at all flattering, he had to ask himself how important Wyckoff the bum was to Captain Hamil.

The answer he got was not very. The fact that Hamil knew his name meant that he also knew the rest—that Wyckoff was at the very most a simple small-time crook, not likely to be dangerous even if he was at large. Oh, they'd look for him, and when they got time they might even try to trace his route from "Z" deck, where Linda would remember seeing him only a few minutes before.

Or—Wyckoff smiled broadly when the thought struck him—maybe they would question the crew. If they did, Linda might find out he had been in the launch bay when she arrived. What if she decided he'd been in No. 9 when Luddington blasted off? Great!

No, he couldn't be that lucky. Really, considering who he was, he didn't need to be. If they didn't catch him after a while, they'd probably assume he'd found his way into the passenger decks and was hiding there.

Wyckoff began to wonder what would happen to the colonists. They would have no way of knowing what was going on, especially with Luddington gone, and in any case, they were already locked up and helpless. They couldn't do anything even if they did know.

He quit worrying about them and got back to his own situation, which was naturally of more interest to him. When he got to Kang, he would find a way to survive. Perhaps, he thought, pummeling the bundle still tucked beneath his shirt, he'd even prosper. In time, Wyckoff quit worrying even about himself. He let nature take its course, and went to sleep.

Chapter Thirteen

Time passed. Wyckoff's existence became drab routine—long periods of sleep, long periods of boring wakefulness. He had no way of knowing how long he had been in hiding. His only clues were the length of his whiskers and the dwindling of his food supplies, which were now entirely exhausted.

Most of the time he lived not only in silence but in darkness, since he feared lights might attract the attention of anyone who wandered near. Occasionally he turned them on to look at the banks of dials on the pod's console, though, ignorant as he was, they told him nothing. Each time he looked, their needles rested in the familiar positions. It never varied.

Wyckoff did not know how far away Kang-Kao-Tze was supposed to be when he had gone into hiding, but it seemed to him that if that was their destination, the ship was long overdue. He wondered if Arlene had been wrong. As the pangs of hunger began to gnaw harder and harder into his vitals, he tried to divine an explanation. He came up empty every time until his thoughts took him back to that day in the launch bay. What was it Linda had said? "You can take your new heading and . . ."

He realized for the first time that Kang was not their

111

destination anymore, if it ever had been, and this struck
him as both good news and bad news. Kang hadn't
sounded very attractive, but the Earth government might
have been able to do something to help them get away.

Now, where was he? Starving, that's where, Wyckoff
answered himself. He knew he'd have to end his her-
mitage before very long, and he decided the ideal time
was now.

He could not bring himself to let go of the bundle of
bonds, even though it now stunk as badly as he did, so
he took it along as he cautiously crept through the
tunnel and back to the elevator. Along the way he was
tempted to peek into the drive room, but he decided
not to push his luck. Cleaned up, he might escape
notice, but as he was—hardly.

Instead, he summoned the elevator and headed for
"Z" deck, which was the first one after engineering that
connected with the axial elevator. There shouldn't be
anybody in the corridor on that side, as he knew for
sure there always was on the passenger side.

Arriving silently, holding his breath, and with his
heart in his mouth, Wyckoff strained his ears to listen
as he waited alongside the elevator tube.

The elevator was not in motion anywhere along its
long path. Wyckoff pushed the call button, then waited,
poised to run back to the engineering car. The moment
of crisis would come when the axial car arrived, because
both doors—the one on the engineering corridor and
the one on the passenger corridor—would open at the
same time, and anybody in the passenger corridor would
be able to look through and see him.

There was always somebody there. Wyckoff hoped it
wouldn't be Linda.

When the elevator arrived, Wyckoff jumped in as fast
as he could and huddled as near the circular wall as he
could to minimize exposure. The curve couldn't completely hide him, but any concealment would help.

Incredibly, nothing happened, and the doors began
to close. Wyckoff decided to risk a peek, and at the last

instant looked out on the passenger side. He was relieved. Unaccountably, there was at that moment no guard in evidence.

He hadn't counted on everything going as smoothly as it had. No doubt trouble would come, sometime before he'd made his way to the storage lockers, located between decks "J" through "N," and replenished his larder. That would be the tricky part, because not only did these lockers coexist with crew quarters, but he could only risk one trip, so he'd have to be extremely picky about what he took. It would not be like last time.

He got off the elevator at "N" deck, which was the lowest possible, and made his way to the hullside ring, where most of the lockers were located. He didn't know what watch it was, or even if the mutineers stood watches anymore, but the lack of traffic seemed to indicate it was the third. He hadn't had to hide once on the entire journey.

And that, Wyckoff told himself, when he'd finally arrived, is not only uncanny, but impossible. He had been in these sections often before his masquerade failed. He knew them well, and knew that however drastic the changes might have been, there should have been more happening here than this. Something was definitely wrong. It was as though he was alone on board.

Wyckoff selected a quantity of foods, mostly dried, since they were precooked, lightweight, and needed only water to be edible. He collected them in a net sack and stashed them in a convenient location. He had decided to do a little exploring before making his way below.

He circled around the ring until he came to a ladder tube. These ran between decks in the crew section, though they were rarely used. He hoped to find an empty cabin where he could clean up, and he thought he might know of one that would be unoccupied—Linda's.

Something *was* wrong! There hadn't been a sound

throughout the whole trip; not a shadow he hadn't cast himself. The only explanation possible was also unthinkable: the entire crew was gone!

Linda's quarters were not simply empty; they hadn't been occupied in a long time. Dishes with desiccated remnants of food clinging to them revealed that. And a plant he remembered seeing when he'd been in here had died from lack of attention. Nor did it appear that her departure had been planned, or that she had taken anything with her. Clothing—Linda's and her roommate's—still hung in their small lockers or lay folded in drawers. Cosmetics displayed the same dehydrated look the plant had.

Wyckoff sat down on the unmade lower bunk, noting that as he did so, dust rose in a small cloud. Then, he remembered the bottle of synthetic bourbon and reached for it. He uncorked the bottle, raised it, and took a long pull. Immediately, he wished he hadn't, and spit the bulk of it out onto the deck. Then he sat for long moments, holding the bottle by its neck. The implications of the situation were starting to sink in.

Wyckoff knew, from what Arlene had told him, that the *Corona* had been vastly overmanned. The ship was highly automated—it could be navigated with fewer than half a dozen crewmen. That would account for his lack of encounters. Those few would rattle around in her like dried-out peas in a pod. But the counterfoil of that was that something had to have happened to the rest of them, and to Wyckoff the only logical answer was that they had been herded into one of the launch bay airlocks and flushed out into space. No doubt that same solution would have been applied to the passengers, and if so, with the additional consumables available, the mutineers could stay in space for a very long time and go as far as their fuel would take them.

Now, he appreciated the remarkable brilliance Hamil had displayed in releasing Luddington, and the stupidity of the government's tactics. The *Corona* could surface years later in another part of the human sphere of space, insulated by vast amounts of objective time, and probably move to ground quite freely. Wyckoff didn't entirely understand the difference between subjective and objective time, but he knew there were such differences despite the tricks the drivefields played on conventional physical laws. Arlene told him they didn't amount to much, but she hadn't been talking about really long distances at the time.

He set the bottle down on the deck without bothering to recork it. It was time to retrieve his supplies and make his way back to the drivepod.

He did, in fact, go back. He even picked up the bag and carried it to the elevator. But the lack of evidence of human presence nagged him. All the while he'd been in Linda's quarters he had listened for sounds that the elevator was being used, and there had been none. There should have been, he knew, even if there were only a few people on board. Even for an automated ship there were essential activities, and even mutineers who had thrown off conventional shipboard habits would still perform these.

For over an hour he stood next to the elevator tube, sometimes with his ear glued to the tube's skin. Not a sound did he hear—not even the air rushing through the relief tubes that ran along the car's inner tracks. It was not being used.

Wyckoff then made a hasty change in plans. He found the ladder tube on this deck and used it to get to his old quarters on "H" deck. The climb was a laborious one; about halfway up he began to feel foolish about taking this route. Still, if he were alert for the sound of the elevator, so might someone else be, and the last thing Wyckoff wanted to do was run into the wrong person and wind up breathing vacuum himself.

"H" deck was as deserted as "Q" deck had been, and showed the same signs of neglect. He found his cabin door wide open and everything pretty much as it had been when he had left it. His clothes, including the polyinsulated suit, were hanging in the locker, as were

Arlene's. It was as though she had simply walked out and left it all.

The thoughts of Arlene saddened him. He liked her, and his relationship with her had been one of the closest and the longest of his life, despite the fact that it had rested on the lie of his impersonation. Now she was almost certainly dead, her remains floating out among the stars.

Wyckoff showered and shaved, oblivious to the possibility of discovery. Then he once again put on the polyinsulated suit that had gotten him into this mess. Turning down the collar, he felt the lapels. The medallion and the orders were still there in the secret pockets.

He got on the elevator and used it to check each deck below him, standing in the open doorway and looking out whenever the car stopped. All were the same. He reached deck "X," and tarried there a moment. Looking down, he noticed that only boat No. 18 still stood before a launch tube. One and nine were empty, and probably their launch tubes had been used to dispose of the colonists.

It hit him suddenly. No 1 gone? Why? Who would have used it? Not Hamil—he had no reason anymore. He and the mutineers had *Corona* all to themselves, and all the opposition either locked up or shot out the airlocks. He dared to hope: perhaps it had been Arlene. Maybe she had had the time to get there before they came for her. Then, as rapidly and as abruptly as his spirits had lifted on that thought, they plunged again. Slower death would have been such an effort's only yield.

Still, if this had happened, it would have been quite a kick in the head for the captain to see his bundle—all he'd worked so hard for, schemed so ingeniously to get—receding into interstellar space. That, Wyckoff thought, would be a fitting coup for whoever had left in the boat. And Hamil would never know that his loot had never left at all. Wyckoff, too, was one up on the captain.

He decided then that he mustn't get caught with the bonds, so he ditched them under the dustcover of one of the control consoles. Then he left again, dragging the bag of supplies down the ladder to the elevator on deck "Z." At the other end his curiosity was again aroused. He listened at the bulkheads, changing his station often, working his way all around the power deck. Not once did he hear voices or footsteps, or the clank of a dropped tool echo from the steel deck. Not once did machinery alter in pitch. In short, the sounds on the power deck were as inanimate as all the others on the *Corona*.

Wyckoff opened a hatch and looked inside. Not one light showed, except the diodes on the instruments. The power deck was unmanned.

And that, even Wyckoff knew, was absolutely unimaginable, regardless of how sloppy the mutineers might otherwise be. Trained spacemen simply wouldn't do this.

He switched on the lights and dropped the bag of supplies in the middle of the deck, deciding to find out once and for all what was taking place. He seized the telephone receiver from its cradle on the wall above Verity's desk, and stabbed his index finger down to the call button for the bridge. The phone rang—he recognized the familiar signal that buzzed in his ear—but nobody answered. He broke the connection and started punching other numbers from the handwritten list taped on the wall. He started with the captain's quarters. Nothing. He repeated the operation half a dozen times more. Not once did anyone answer.

Wyckoff now knew real panic. It was one thing to be a fugitive aboard a ship in mutiny, in danger of being caught and killed. That, at least, presented an opportunity to put up resistance. But to be on a derelict plunging through space at who knew what velocity until collision occurred or he died of old age—that was something else again. Wyckoff was momentarily unprepared to handle that.

He raced for the axial elevator and rode it to the

bridge, where its door opened onto another cavern of darkness.

He found the lights, switched them on—and gasped. On the deck was a thick steel bar, surrounded by shards of fractured plastic, pieces of glass, and ragged-edged electronic components, some trailing long wisps of copper wire. The astrogation computer had been smashed to ruin.

For the first time in his adult life, Wyckoff bawled openly. He was through, even though all the other controls appeared to be unharmed. He sat down in the center of the deck and let it all out. I can't fall off the floor, he thought bitterly.

There was absolutely no doubt about it now—he was the only living soul on board. Boat No. 1 had not carried Arlene, or some other astute crewman, off to temporary safety. It had carried Hamil and part of his crew away from the scene of this great crime. They had probably launched while passing within some colonial system, close enough so that the boat could reach it. If it were a new enough colony, Hamil could have come down in some uninhabited part, where he might disappear for years.

And no one would ever know what happened to the *Corona*. Even had he possessed the skill to maneuver the ship, Wyckoff could never find human space again with the astrogation computer smashed. Perhaps Hamil had left the ship intact because he knew that Wyckoff was still aboard, unaware that Hamil had scored the winning blow.

Wyckoff descended to "C" deck and entered the captain's lush quarters for a look around. He found the signs he expected to find, and something else he didn't— Linda's body, shrunken and partially mummified by the dry shipboard air, just as her plant had been. Maybe Hamil hadn't suspected the right thief after all, he thought.

Chilled at the coldbloodedness of the captain's acts, Wyckoff left the cabin, closing the door tightly behind him. Then he went forward, back to the bridge. He was master of this vessel now, by default. He stepped into the control room and thought about that.

Wyckoff decided to open the shutters across the nose ports and take a look out at space. He'd never seen raw emptiness before. He fiddled around with the buttons on the console until he got the directory to screen, then punched out the control command to roll the shutters.

The view outside disappointed him. It was not exactly ugly, but it was formless. There appeared to be a dark hole in front of the ship, surrounded by a halo of brilliant lights so compressed that it was hard to tell if they represented suns or not. The outer edges of the halo extended across the periphery, as though the ship's nose was buried in it, so he couldn't see to the sides.

He closed the shutters, feeling deep disappointment. This was not a fit diversion for a captain—but what was? What could he do to tease his mind into accepting this inevitable and awful fate? All throughout the *Corona*, there was only one tiny globule of sentience—his own brain. Amusement would derive from it, or not at all.

Absent-mindedly, he picked up the microphone on one arm of the chair, and tried to remember what the pilot had said into his during the flight from New York to Matagorda. Beyond "This is your captain speaking," he couldn't recall. He raised the microphone to his lips and said solemnly, "This is the captain speaking. We are now . . ."

He stopped. He hadn't switched it on. What good would it do to talk into a dead mike? He paused, found the switch, and threw it, then raised the mike again. He hadn't asked himself what good it would do to speak into a live one—he was afraid to. Now, what was the name of that old movie he'd seen back at the Carlton Arms? He tried to think—Mutiny? Mutiny on the Cai— the Caine Mutiny—that was it. He remembered part of it. "This is the captain speaking—no; this is Captain Wyckoff speaking. All hands hear this—there will be no liberty for this crew until the person who stole the strawberries from the Officers' Mess surrenders himself for punishment. I will not tolerate thievery aboard my ship—" No, that didn't sound right; Bogart had been so much more convincing, so bitter. Besides, those hadn't exactly been the right words. Wyckoff strained to recollect them. He tapped the microphone against his chin, and the amplified thumps echoed forth from speakers all over the ship.

Without warning the phone rang. Wyckoff leapt from the chair as though he'd been shot. He'd been wrong— Hamil hadn't really left. He was still here.

Wyckoff's mind raced, his thoughts tumbling over each other. Once or twice one of them was rational. One was the thought that Hamil wouldn't call, he'd pounce, armed and ready to kill without warning.

So sweaty palms gripped the receiver and raised it from its cradle toward a face now blanched pure white with terror. "Hello?"

"Emory?"

"Arlene? Arlene, you're not dead! Where are you?"

"Locked in the passengers' quarters with everybody else. We haven't been able to break out, and we were afraid to try with that maniac, Hamil, out there. Where are you? Where have you been?"

"Up on the bridge now, but I've been hiding." Wyckoff was finally, after the lapse of some six or seven eternal seconds, realizing that not only was he not alone, but he was talking to someone who could astrogate this ship. "What do you mean, locked in? There's nobody else on board but me—that is, I thought so, anyhow. Linda's dead. I think Hamil left in a lifeboat. There's one missing."

"I hope you're right, Emory. If they're still aboard, they would have heard you on the P.A. You'd better get out of the control room, just in case. Maybe you could get us out of here?"

"I'll be right down to try, Arlene."

"Don't hang up, Emory. I mean it—watch yourself; get a weapon of some kind if you can."

"I can see one from here, Arlene. Don't worry about me. I'll get you out." He hung up the phone, picked up the iron bar, and raced for the elevator.

Chapter Fourteen

Wyckoff, now feeling like a full-fledged member of the *Corona's* new crew, although he wasn't captain any more, had free entry to the bridge. He stood there now, flanked by Arlene and former Third Mate Mason, who'd just jumped two grades in rank.

"Is it bad as it looks, Arlene?"

"It's as bad as it can get, Emory. I seem to have forgotten—you told me your real name, but . . ."

"Call me Wyckoff. Can you get us home?"

He knew it was a dumb question as soon as the words were out of his mouth, and instantly felt like a fool.

Arlene and Mason looked at him with pity in their eyes.

Arlene broke a long silence. "There's no hope of that, Em—Wyckoff. Not that I can see, anyway. Maybe later, when things have had time to jell, we'll think of something, but without the computer, there's no way to tell what direction we're traveling or how far we've gone."

"Can't we just back up or turn around, Arlene?"

"It's not that simple. Hamil knew what he was doing. He changed headings at least once, perhaps more than once. We could have gone through dozens of entrance and emergence points while the drive was on, and it

123

was probably on for a long time after he left. The computer could keep track of this, but nothing else can."

"But we can see out now, with the drive off."

"It's no help, Wyckoff," Mason said. "We can't equate what we see from here with what was where we've been. We can't even tell how far we've traveled. To a man's eyes, a star's a star. You can't tell one from most others. Stars that look bright from Earth are pinpoints from here, if you can see them at all—even to the so-called beacon stars."

Arlene looked at Wyckoff and tried again to be kind. "He's right, Wyckoff. Finding anything at all familiar would be sheer chance, even if we cruised until our fuel ran out."

"Then, what are we going to do?"

Again, there was a long silence. Finally, Arlene took Wyckoff aside and gazed at him for longer moments still. "This isn't going to be easy for any of us, Wyckoff. We'll do what the *Corona* started out to do—populate a colony we don't even have a planet for yet."

Wyckoff's eyes got suddenly big.

"That's assuming we can find one. We might not. All we can do is take a good look around, pick out the best possibility, and go for it. We can't go home again—ever."

Wyckoff thought for a moment, and his face became very grim. "Arlene, remember what I told you. This ship's full of junk—scrap metal. How are we going to do anything with that?"

"I've thought about that, Wyckoff. There is one difference. The colony on Zahn existed in relative isolation. Ours will have the *Corona*, and its shipboard workshops and library. It won't be easy, but at least we have a ready source of raw materials, and we can make some of the machinery we'll need."

Wyckoff could think of nothing else to say. He had no experience outside hustling in the jungle of the big city streets, and no skills that he could see any use for on a virgin planet. For the first time ever, he found himself trying to think in long-range terms, but try as he might, he couldn't see himself fitting into any future he could then perceive.

Wyckoff had left his old quarters on "H" deck and moved into Arlene's cabin on "C" deck, where she exercised her prerogative to keep him as her Captain's "Man."

Under other circumstances, Wyckoff might have felt his manhood compromised by this situation, but things were rapidly changing aboard the *Corona*, and he found he liked the new ship better. Part of the reason was that he now felt himself part of it. Arlene had exercised another prerogative—one in which the rest of the officers joined her unanimously. As a result, Wyckoff was no longer a stowaway—he had rank and status. He was now, in fact and officially, the chief storekeeper aboard the *Corona*, and expected to discharge the duties of that office.

After the initial shock of liberation, what remained of the crew had began putting things back together, and because their own hides depended on it, they worked a good deal more harmoniously.

In the interval, the story of Hamil's final days had been pieced together in a way that seemed a rational narrative, and which had begun to be accepted as fact by everyone, including Wyckoff.

It went like this: Having dispatched Luddington as a red herring, Hamil changed course, probably heading for Shia. On the way, with the help of Bottari, Linda, Drive Engineer Verity, and a handful of the ordinary spacehands, he began quietly to collect and imprison the others on the lower decks, which already had high-security systems. This went on until he had them all.

Somewhere along the way he discovered the loss of his bonds. He probably suspected Linda, whom he thereafter killed. Verity discovered this and became frightened, suspecting he might be next, so he disappeared among the colonials.

Hamil was thought to have left the ship in boat No. 1

within the Shia system, after smashing the astrogation computer—probably with Bottari, and perhaps with *Corona*'s astrogator and surgeon, who were also missing. No one knew what happened after that. Probably also, they never suspected Wyckoff was still at large outside the passengers' quarters, which they quite naturally wouldn't have entered and searched, but which they would have regarded as a natural haven for a bum like him.

Assuming that the uncontrolled *Corona* would plunge onward forever after those left aboard her starved to death, Hamil made good his escape, and the only consolation the rest of them had was that he had escaped as a pauper.

For those on the *Corona*, Wyckoff's reappearance had changed the odds for survival, but did nothing to increase Hamil's chances of getting caught. They could only hope that the authorities would keep looking for him, and that he would be caught, but they would never know.

Wyckoff took his job seriously, and worked hard. He found that once he understood the duties, he could perform them quite well. His understanding had been aided by the knowledge that the commodities he dealt with were not only necessary to his own survival, but were all there were available.

The colonists were not told of the change in destination. They believed that a mutiny had occurred and then been put down, and that this was why for a time part of the crew had lived among them, so on the colonial decks, the changes were not radical ones.

That was a situation that bothered Wyckoff a whole lot. He knew human nature as he knew little else, and his instincts screamed that any lies told now would come back later and bite them.

He brought the question up at the first staff meeting Arlene held, after she had officially assumed command, but failed to get any support from the others. Not that this would have done much good, anyhow. Ships are monarchies, and can never be anything else if ever they expect to reach the next port.

So Arlene exercised her authority as captain and said no to Wyckoff's suggestion that they organize the colonists politically. "Time enough for that if we ever find a world to go down on. Once we're on the ground, they might still wreck *Corona*, but at least the survivors will be able to breathe."

Wyckoff found that Arlene's resolution extended to their private relationship. Although he had figured Arlene for a leaner, and himself as the most logical and influential leanee, he found that, in this case at least, he was in error. He decided, however, that it had to be done, and resolved to do it his way.

"This is outrageous, Mr. Wyckoff. Those records are confidential. You could go to jail for what you just did."

Wyckoff gazed calmly back at the man who glared at him from the other side of their improvised table in one of the cargo holds. It was an empty crate—one that he and Luddington had opened, and from which Wyckoff had carefully removed the assortment of junk. "So sue me, Mr. Fu. After all, you are a lawyer—the only one aboard, far as I could tell. You ought to be able to do that with your eyes closed. Of course, there are a couple of things you'll need first—like a court, maybe? I must say, it sure didn't look like you wanted anybody to know that."

Yasha Fu knew that he had violated a popular myth by getting as upset as he had. His ancestry was Manchu, and such people were supposed not to have volatile temperaments. But in this case and at this instant, nothing could have been farther from the truth. He was incensed, and, he insisted, righteously. Having duly served his sentence, he was entitled to anonymity, and a new start in life.

But his training was also beginning to show, and the combination of both these forces enabled him to get control again. Cool, calm control—the dangerous kind. "Why, Wyckoff? It must have taken you days to dig me out."

"I got problems, Fu. I need advice."

"I see." Fu shifted his stance. He could play games as well as anybody. "Aside from the fact that there are no courts until we get to Zahn, I'm not licensed anymore—anywhere. I've been disbarred, as you very well know."

"You think I care about that?"

"I think that's all you care about. Look, Wyckoff, shaking me down is a waste of time. I'm an ex-con—and they made me give it all back. All I've got left is the gold in my teeth."

"I better not be wasting time, Fu. You're an educated man, and educated men are too valuable to hoe beans."

"What are you talking about, Wyckoff?"

"I searched you out because we're all in big trouble—trouble only educated men can handle—and if you disappoint me, I'll probably get mad and do something awful to you."

Wyckoff had meant that as a sort of comic threat, to signal Fu that he was serious but not really mean. "Look, Fu. What if I told you that this ship was lost and never would make it to Zahn?"

He paused, staring intensely at Fu, whose mouth hung open. Tiring of waiting for a reply that never came, he added, "There wasn't any mutiny, Fu. *Corona* had a crooked captain and some crooked crewmen. They were stealing from stores, and when they got caught, they smashed the navigation system and jumped ship in a lifeboat. Worse, before they did it, they changed our course, and now we don't even know where Zahn is."

Fu gazed back soberly, and paused long moments before he replied. "You're serious, aren't you?"

Wyckoff nodded. "Yes, I'm serious." He could see that Fu finally understood and believed him. "You can see why we have to work up to this, and why we can't just announce it over the P.A."

"What a ghastly thought," Fu replied, a worried look washing across his formerly placid face. "The colonists would riot. They'd tear the ship apart with their bare hands—after they'd taken care of you, and anybody else in the crew they could reach."

Wyckoff leaned back, folded his arms, and shot Fu a grim glance. "I figure it the same way, Fu. That's why it might be better if you told them."

"ME!"

"Sure. I mean, who's gonna get sore at you? And don't tell me you can't handle it; I know better. That's what you guys are trained for."

Fu grunted a professional grunt. He hadn't forgotten how to do that, and thereby gained a moment or two to think. "Something about you bothers me, Wyckoff."

"What?"

"Why it's you, for one thing. And why are we meeting down here in a cargo hold like a couple of crooks?"

"Because maybe that's what we are, Fu."

"I don't follow you."

"The rest of them don't know I'm down here talking to you. They're counting on the croaker."

"Who?"

"The croaker—the doctor. What's his name—?"

A grin washed over Fu's face. "Dr. Mallarkey. An amusing name, would you not agree?"

Wyckoff ignored the question. Archaic slang was a diversion for the literate. "Whatever. He took care of the people who got hurt during the mutiny, so they leveled with him. Arlene says . . ."

"Who?"

"The captain. She said the colonists had confidence in him, and he'd find a way to break the news easy. He didn't like the idea. His advice was to keep on lying about what happened, and so far, that's all he's done. To me, that means he can't cut it, and big trouble for us later on. I'd feel a whole lot better with a real expert

running things. I think you ought to try to get control
down here."

"Is that so? You people *lose* control and I'm supposed
to stick *my* neck out? You're part of the crew of a
colonial ship. You people are supposed to be pros, too."
He rose to his feet, ready to leave.

"I'm down here on my own, Fu, with a long, sad
story of my own to tell. The rest of them don't know I
came. Since you haven't got anything better to do anyhow, how about you sit back down and listen?" He
grabbed Fu's sleeve and pulled him back down to his
seat.

"Incredible. I can't believe anybody would do a thing
like that."

"Check these crates, like I did. You'll believe it."

"But even if we find a planet, we'd be starting from
scratch, with almost nothing. I don't know, Wyckoff."

"Sure you do. That's why I picked you. Besides, it's
either that or give up, and I'm sure you wouldn't be
suggesting that. After all, people have been in worse
spots and wiggled out."

"Hm. I suppose you could say that, Wyckoff, though
it's difficult to imagine anything worse than this. But
you're right—there are precedents. The same thing
happened to the *Mayflower*."

"The what?"

"The ship the Plymouth colony came on to America.
They got lost, too, and never did get where they originally intended to go. The colonists aboard her were just
as upset as ours are going to be, but they made do, and
so will we."

"You see what I mean? You've got a way with words.
They'll listen to you, where all they'd do is lynch us. I
think I made the right choice in you, Fu."

"I hope you're right. Look, Wyckoff, I agree this has
to be done—we have to get some kind of political
organization going, we won't be just moving into an
established one, as we had thought. But—and I'm not

just considering my own feelings here—I think it'd be a mistake to tell them . . ."

"Tell them what?" Wyckoff asked, gazing bug-eyed at his companion.

"About my sordid past. I think it would hurt my credibility."

"Suit yourself," Wyckoff replied. "I can't see where it's got anything to do with your ability. Seems to me we should be worried about the future, not the past."

Fu nodded, and took another glance around the hold before he rose to his feet to follow Wyckoff out the hatch. "Thanks for saying that, Wyckoff. There are times when I need reassurances, and this is one of them. Aren't you going to ask me what I did?"

Wyckoff turned and stuck out his hand to shake. His gaze was firm. "Nope," he said, grinning. "I figure you'll tell me someday when you're in a braggin' mood. Besides, I always heard there were too many lawyers back on Earth anyhow." He strode to the elevator, entered the waiting car, and pushed the button for "Z" deck.

On the bridge, the mood was apprehensive. Days of observation had resulted in the selection of several likely target suns within relatively short distances of one another, and the *Corona* was now running full speed toward the nearest of them.

Short two bridge officers, Arlene put herself and Mason on double watches, with the result that Wyckoff saw less and less of her when she was awake. Not only did he have his own duties to see to, but he knew she did not especially like for him to visit her on the bridge.

Whenever Wyckoff wanted both company and information, he haunted the control room on Mason's watch. Mason was busy, too, but he seemed more tolerant of interruption than Arlene was.

They became friends, and Mason taught Wyckoff a great deal. He was the one who finally explained to

Wyckoff, in clear terms, why they couldn't find their way back.

"We can't believe our eyes," he explained, "or our instruments. We don't know where the *Corona* goes when the drive kicks in full power. The drivefields do something strange to the space around us."

"What?" It had been both a natural and a naive question.

Mason answered truthfully, "We don't know the exact mechanism, but the best theory has it that the drivefield creates a sudden local distortion of the space it occupies, in the direction of its travel—sort of a tube, or wormhole. Because space itself is what's moving relative to the rest of the universe—and for us, it's like riding a wave—we don't have the light barrier to worry about, but there are other problems. Orientation is one of them—it's hard to tell where you're going."

"Then, how can we go anywhere?"

"We drop the power below the point where the changes take place, and we come out of it to take a look around."

"But you just said you can't trust your eyes, or the instruments."

"What I meant was that we can't equate apparent distance with those the ship actually traverses. Does that make any sense?"

"Not a bit."

"All right. Let me explain something else. There's a theory that we can't tell by looking what the shape of the universe really is, but that it probably isn't spherical, or any other regular shape. What happens when the drivefields operate seems to support the conclusion that it's highly convoluted—something like a human brain, or a prune or raisin. Gravitational forces pucker it up."

"Uh-huh. Well, how come it doesn't look puckered?"

"The light follows the contours of the gravitational stress. To our instruments, which work on electromagnetic or optical principles, it appears to travel in straight lines. It would be like tying a granny knot in an optical fiber, and then trying to look at it from the inside. You wouldn't see the knot because it wouldn't affect the course of the light traveling on the inside. We can't observe things any other way, but we do know there are many differences between the time it should take for us to get to where we want to go and the time it actually does. Reason tells us that somehow, the action of the drivefields enables us to penetrate the folds and take a shortcut through them."

"Did anybody ever think of taking a look while a ship's outside?"

"Sure. We would if we could. In fact, I believe you said you tried."

"I opened the shutters."

"What did you see?"

"Gobs and gobs of light."

"Then you understand the problem. You can't observe under those conditions, and if you drop down, then you're back inside. For all we know, the Earth and the farthest star may be only a dozen folds away."

"And that's why we can't go back."

"We could go back, Wyckoff, if we knew where to go. But that's not the only problem. There's another obstacle—time."

"Arlene said that was nothing."

"She's right in one respect—the action of the drivefields enables us to escape some of the consequences of time dilation, provided we don't journey too far. Some ships apparently have, we think; those that never came back—or, more properly, haven't come back *yet*."

"I don't know what that means."

"It means not enough objective time has elapsed. They might pop up a thousand years from now."

"Oh."

"If we ever did make it, we'd have to face the possibility that the Earth would be thousands of years ahead of us."

The conversation was starting to give Wyckoff a headache. He didn't understand what Mason was talking about, and what was worse, didn't think Mason understood either. He decided to change the subject. "That system we're headed for now—what's it like?"

"We hope it'll be like Sol. The spectrum's right, and what we can tell about its motion from this distance suggests it has planets. Of course, it might not have any we could live on."

"What do we do then?"

"Go on to the next one and check it out. By and by we'll find something."

"Unless we run out of food first."

"The odds are good we won't; however, the sooner we can do it, the larger our reserves will be when we go down. That might be very important, because we might not be able to make use of what grows there."

Wyckoff got a little upset when he heard that. "How come?"

"Because not all life is organized the same way. Sometimes it's poisonous to us, but mostly it's just unusable by terrestrial forms. Most of Earth's plant life has a molecular twist to the right in its basic cellular organization, but we've encountered lots of left-handed systems. On the other hand, with proteins, it's the opposite."

"That doesn't sound like much of a difference."

"No, but what it means is if you made bread out of left-handed flour your body could eat it but it would all pass right through. None of it would be absorbed, so you'd starve."

"Well, what are we going to do if planets like that are all we find?"

"Change the ecology. We brought seed for terrestrial crops. If we have enough time, we'll be all right. In fact, it could be an advantage, because it would help eliminate troubles with pests eating our crops up."

"That's if we have time. What if we don't?"

"Then Hamil wins, after all."

* * *

They did not have time. The first system they explored had nothing they could use. Its life zone was wide but empty. The second was in decline, its inner planets losing water vapor so rapidly that the one possibility would be only marginally habitable, and even that not for long. The third had only gas giants. The fourth was a binary with planets in a trading cycle, and no life on any of them.

They were disheartened, but they could only go on, and they did, toward another local cluster of stars.

By the time they broke out of the last jump, they were very close to the bottom margin of reserves. If the ecology was wrong on any planets they found, they would be in very deep trouble.

Chapter Fifteen

The nose ports were open, and all who were allowed in the control room visited often to peer out. Visually, the view was spectacular, but only that. When it came to interpretation, only the ship's instruments told the real story. The story was good—a stable sun, a broad life zone, and a very young and watery Earth-sized world within it. It had two fair-sized satellites, each almost 500 miles in diameter, and a diurnal period of slightly more than 17 hours. It would perhaps be a little on the warm side there, but it had already given birth to life and was fully oxygenated.

Certainly it would not have any natives, because its life had been far too brief for anything so complex to evolve. There might not even be land animal forms, perhaps no flowering plants, if Earth's own evolutionary past was any guide.

"So, there you have it, Yasha. How does it sound?" Wyckoff had taken Arlene partially into his confidence, and through persuasion, convinced her that they must have a workable liaison with the colonists. She hadn't at first been exactly thrilled that he had taken it upon himself to organize this, but as time wore on, her confidence in Wyckoff's instincts grew and her own duties became more demanding. She was then content to let him have his head, and to hold these sessions with the emerging colonial leadership.

"Like money from home, Wyckoff. Just the sort of encouragement we needed."

Wyckoff glanced around the makeshift table at the faces of the handful of men and women who were in Fu's confidence. At this point he made no pretense at remembering everybody's name—that could come later.

"Up until now," Fu continued, "we've kept this among ourselves, but now that we have a definite destination, we can broaden the organizational base a little. There are a few people who already suspect something is going on—those who mix a little more than usual, and, of course, the doctor."

"Then let's get them in on it," Wyckoff answered.

"Yes. As a matter of fact, that's probably the most workable strategy. Those who have figured it out will be too smug with themselves to do any complaining, but I think I'd rather pass on Mallarkey," Fu added.

Around the table other heads nodded agreement.

"He'll soon be too busy to bother us much anyhow."

"Busy?" Wyckoff was puzzled. "Is somebody sick?"

"Not yet," Fu replied, with a broad grin. "But he will be when he finds out he has to fill in for the vet. We don't have one aboard, because Zahn was supposed to be crawling with them already." Subdued chuckles rose from several participants, and it was evident that the man was not especially well liked.

"By the way, that's illustrative of our basic problem. All the theorists, the real experts, are waiting for us on Zahn. They went in first to get things ready for us. What *Corona* was bringing were the craftsmen, with the hands-on skills and experience. I expect most of them are going to be extraordinarily competent, but now they'll have to do as scientists and engineers as well."

Wyckoff wanted a political organization, not politics, and he said so. He reverted to the previous point. "I don't like it. A guy like Mallarkey is important, whatever his personality, and he might be easier to control on the inside. Sooner or later he'll find out what we're up to. What if he talks to the wrong people?"

"What do you suggest, Wyckoff?"

"Clue him in—give him some kind of title to keep him happy. Like you said, pretty soon he'll be busy enough in his own job, considering his own skin depends on it. And while we're up here it doesn't matter anyway—the ship's captain is in charge."

Fu emitted a sigh. "Okay." Fu was still clearly the colonial leader, and he got away with making that decision on his own.

Out of the corner of his eye, Wyckoff saw evidence that that might not last, as a crusty old geezer opened his mouth and came within a hair of speaking out.

Wyckoff didn't care whether they always agreed—he cared only that they were organized and capable of taking and keeping authority. He had an instinctive feeling that none of this would work unless there was broad support. "Tell me what happens next," he said. "The captain's gonna want to know."

"Well," Fu replied, "we thought maybe we'd approach things from the colonist's committee angle—you know, hold a meeting of as many of them as we can get in one place and suggest a committee be elected to deal with the captain."

"But you've got me for that, Fu."

"Sure, we know that—but they don't. Besides, it wouldn't change anything as far as you're concerned. It'd be a sham. What really counts is that when the news finally does hit, there's an organization they're used to dealing with that they can look to for answers. To get that, we have to hold an election—oh, and we'll need a goat."

"Huh?"

"A goat—somebody to blame for the bum food we're getting, and for all the scarcities and stuff."

"This is the first I've heard of any such thing."

"Right, now you're catching on, Wyckoff. You're doing

a great job—too good, in fact. Throttle back and let this committee get itself elected. We need to work a few miracles."

"I guess I could arrange that okay."

"Good. We'll have to work pretty fast if we want to get established by the time the captain finds us a planet. In the meantime, there's something else we ought to be doing."

"What's that? And by the way, we may already have found a planet."

"Hm." Fu paused and considered. "Then, the colonists can't be told about it just yet—not until we're ready. But getting back to my point, it'd help if you give me access to the Colonial Bureau's records. We need to identify anybody with talents we'll be depending on when we get down. More important, we could use that kind of help now, with the planning."

"I thought you said that was illegal," Wyckoff retorted, grinning. He watched for a reaction on Yasha's face, and strangely enough, saw one. *Habits do die hard*, he thought.

"I'll get you what you need," he agreed, though with some reluctance. He was sticking his neck out farther and farther. Arlene didn't know about any of this. She thought this was a simple liaison. She didn't know he was organizing the colonists politically or that he had personally dipped into those records. It occurred to him that she might not like it—that she might regard it as a usurpation of her own authority. But Fu was right. Such people were going to be crucial, and they were needed right away.

Wyckoff was pleased. He was pleased because he noted everybody else was pleased, and that was good enough for him. His fears, once substantial, began to ebb. A few cautious probes at Arlene convinced Wyckoff that she would not have objected to anything he had so far done. Consequently, he felt safe in then stating that it was his intention to embark on just such a course, but stopped just short of presenting her with a fait accompli.

He began to make hasty plans for the landing, and furtive expeditions into the colony section to seek out and confer the artisans and craftsmen Fu had briefed. Though the bulk of the passengers would be farmers, and simple ones at that, they would need what these people would have to make for them. The craftsmen would, as a consequence, become very important, and Wyckoff was appalled to find that already, before anything had been accomplished, some of their heads were swelling. He could envision an aristocracy arising on their destination planet and resolved to frustrate such a development if he could, though Fu, when warned of his suspicions, did not agree.

"You have to remember, Wyckoff, that people are political animals, and that they have a tendency to choose the kind of system that works best for them, whether they really like it or not. It might be that what we'll need on our new home planet is some system of feudal tenures like they had on Earth in the Middle Ages. After all, the cultural collapse is going to be comparable."

"There won't be a cultural collapse, Yasha—not if I can help it," Wyckoff had replied. Thereafter he had endless speculative arguments with Fu about how the colony's government might end up.

Because he was below, engaged in one of these arguments, Wykoff was nowhere near the bridge when an astounding discovery was made, and did not hear of it until the end of the second watch, when he arrived at the "C" deck quarters to have dinner with Arlene. As it turned out, he did not need to deceive the colonists into thinking they had yet no haven planet. It now appeared that might be true.

As captain, Arlene routinely avoided the officers' mess, preferring to utilize the quarters' own cooking facilities. Wyckoff liked this domestic touch. He had grown quite used to it, and he was particularly satisfied to find that at last he fit the mold of a working-class man—something he had always regarded as unreachable in his Earth-bound social setting.

But Arlene was not in the quarters, though she was off watch, and she had not removed anything to eat from the freezer.

Wyckoff cleaned up and changed clothes, expecting she would pop in at any moment. When she didn't, he forgot he was hungry and went up to the bridge to see if she was there.

She was. So was Mason, and Verity, the reformed conspirator and drive engineer, which was quite unusual. He was still not out of the doghouse, even though he had taken amnesty and been restored to duty on a probationary basis.

Wyckoff approached the little knot of people completely unnoticed, and stood on tiptoes to look over Arlene's head. They were thumbing through a stack of computer-enhanced photographs of the planet they were approaching.

"What's happening?" he asked, tapping Arlene on the shoulder to get her attention.

She looked around, an expression of slight annoyance on her face, which rapidly changed when she realized who it was. "We think there's a ship in orbit around our planet."

Wyckoff pushed his way ahead to where he could see a little better. There was a blotchy-looking photograph of the planet lying on the desktop that showed a tiny dot alongside its equator. "It doesn't look like much from here. How do you know it's a ship?"

Arlene replied, a note of grave concern in her voice. "It's at the very outer limits of resolution, but we can tell by the way it behaves. Its motion suggests a certain size and density, and we can estimate its mass. A natural satellite couldn't have the same mass and stay in the orbit this is in. It's a ship, Wyckoff."

"Then who's in it?"

"You mean, what's in it. It can't be human, Wyckoff.

That's the scary part. This is a colonization effort by some other species, and they aren't likely to take it kindly if we try to horn in."

"You mean, we're gonna have to fight them?"

"That's out of the question, Wyckoff. No, I mean, we'd have to move on—find another world."

"But we're close to the bottom of the barrel on supplies, Arlene. We can't do that—we can't just give up." He looked up and caught Mason's glance. He could tell immediately that the first mate agreed with him.

"I didn't say we were giving up, Wyckoff. But now we'll have to be careful. Maybe we'll get lucky and find out we just made a mistake, or it'll leave again, or something equally miraculous."

"What're you going to do now?"

"I'm going to put the *Corona* in a solar orbit and send a lifeboat in for a closer look. I want the planetary surface, both those moons, and all near-planet orbital space checked out before we show ourselves." She turned to Mason. "I guess you're the crew for that one, Rick."

Mason nodded, noted the pleading look on Wyckoff's face, and said, "Half the crew, Captain. I could use an observer to help me spot." He was looking at Wyckoff when he said that.

Wyckoff, his tongue fairly hanging out in anticipation of Arlene's answer, was not the least bit bashful about calling in a marker. Lately, he'd learned a lot about such things from Yasha Fu. He understood the process, and agreed: the others owed him—owed him everything they now possessed. When he followed Mason into the lifeboat and settled in its second couch, Wyckoff marked the account "paid."

Chapter Sixteen

Between the time the photographs had been taken and the *Corona* was maneuvered, by microjumps, into a solar orbit on the other side of the primary and hidden among the detritus of the system's asteroid belt, the enigma grew. The object had inexplicably disappeared from sight. Arlene insisted it must have gone down to the surface, unwilling to believe that the miracle to which she'd alluded in jest had actually come to pass. She waited tensely for boat 18 to return and report.

The expedition took six days, observing radio silence all the way. When it returned, Mason insisted that was the correct explanation. He believed a ship had been there in orbit, that it had been no mirage.

And that was what he said in his report to Arlene: "We think they tried to land when we approached, and that they're wrecked on the surface, Captain. Our instruments picked up surface radioactivity in concentrations too large to be natural. It has to be the debris from a power plant. But we couldn't get a visual sighting even in low orbit, and I hesitated to land because there might still be survivors, or even a settlement."

"Did you see any signs of that?"

"No. If there is a colony, it can't be a very large one.

There aren't any of the usual earmarks of civilization—no radio noise or traffic, no atmospheric pollutants, no dams on streams, no lights visible on the nightside, and no indication of agricultural activity."

"There wouldn't be any of that on a brand new colony, either—not until a substantial population arrived."

"Maybe this was the first ship."

"Maybe. Then again, it might have been nothing more than an exploration party. Rick, I'm going to park the *Corona* in a high orbit around the planet, and then I want you to go back down, in force, and check the surface out thoroughly. Start with the wreck—and make that an armed party."

Mason nodded, then turned and left.

Wyckoff followed him. This time he didn't ask Arlene's permission to tag along. He knew she would have forbidden him to do that if it really bothered her, and he would have yielded to her authority. Wyckoff was in thorough agreement with the course she was choosing. If they had to fight for this world they would. They didn't have any choice.

But it turned out not to be necessary. All they found were ghosts. Rick was able to give Arlene a fairly detailed report this time. "It was a real mess, Captain. Whatever it was, it hit hard. It plowed the ground up right down to bedrock, as though the engines failed just when it was about to settle. But something bothers me; the wreckage looks recent, but it isn't new enough to be the vehicle we saw in orbit."

"*Thought* we saw in orbit, Rick."

Mason blinked, but continued. "We found parts of skeletons inside. The ship had burned, but lots of the bones had been broken before they were charred. We brought some of them back for study, but in the shape they're in, I doubt if we'll learn anything useful about what the creatures were like. Beyond that, there wasn't much to bring back except photographs. Would you like to see them?"

"Yes, I would."

Mason spread them out, and the captain spent a few minutes studying them before handing the pile back to him. "Odd configuration for a space vehicle, wasn't it?"

"What? Oh, yes, I noticed the nose, too. It does look sort of incomplete. Maybe they were already breaking up on the way down. With the damage the crash caused, it's hard to tell."

Arlene put the photographs down and looked up at him. She had made her decision. "I guess that does it then, Rick. We'll find a good spot and set the *Corona* down.

The spot selected would have been ideal had there been a landing web. It was on the southern shore of the northernmost continent, where a broad river trailed down through a range of coastal mountains, and across flat prairie to the sea.

They chose it because the river would provide transportation from the site of the landing to the settlement they contemplated building some fifty kilometers downstream. It had to be that far away to get outside the destructive perimeter of the ship's drivefields, should she ever go into space again.

Arlene expressed a hope they all shared—that *Corona* would someday rise again. She did not like the idea of this great ship rotting on the planetary surface, where the elements could pound its fragile systems into ruin in a few short years, but at present, there was no alternative but to leave it here. Its shops and power plant were needed by the colony to turn out such implements and tools as they could to replace those Hamil's gang had stolen.

Wyckoff found the situation tailor-made for self-fulfillment. He worked like a demon at his first real job, and despite his lack of formal education, he did it very well. He literally blossomed, using his natural drive and leadership ability in a productive way for the first time in his life.

He was one of the people. The story of his arrival on the *Corona* and the pivotal role he had played in averting disaster circulated freely. He was respected, not simply as a hero, but as one of their own who had beaten the system; who had been where they were and had risen above it. They couldn't fool him, and they knew better than to try. Nor would he listen to excuses. Laments that something was impossible fell on deaf ears. He didn't want to hear that, and he didn't, so they wound up doing it anyway.

He and Fu made an effective team, though often Wyckoff cringed at some of the things Yasha suggested. For instance, Fu insisted that they set up a national government, though the entire colony, crew included, numbered less than 1,500 people. Somehow, he got the rest of the committee to go along, held an impromptu election, and in one day, had their ratification by voice vote.

Small as the colony was, the parliament amounted to no more than a council. All its voting members were colonists, and Fu was not only one of these, but chairman. The nonvoting members consisted of the *Corona*'s officers, and the captain retained veto power over any act of the civilian authority that in any way affected the ship.

If Wyckoff didn't understand, then it was his own fault. Certainly, Fu made valiant efforts to explain.

"We need to plant the seeds now, Wyckoff, while somebody still has visible legitimate power, and we have to contrive a system that'll work in this environment a dozen generations from now, after we're dead and gone. If we do this wrong there won't be just one nation, there'll be dozens, perhaps hundreds, like it was in Europe."

"Okay. Only, the way it looks to me, someday this planet's gonna wind up with a king."

"It could happen, I guess. Something wrong with that?"

"Yeah, plenty. Seems to me, instead of getting better, we'd be going backward. What's the matter with the way we did it back home?"

"Nothing—for back there, and in another time, Wyckoff. But tell me, would you want to be back there now, the way it was, if you could go?"

It took Wyckoff far less time to answer than he might have imagined it would only a short time ago. "No, I guess not. What did you mean by another time?"

"I mean, certain political systems are best for certain cultural levels, and cultural levels rise and fall, Wyckoff. That was what was wrong with the one you had at home. It had stagnated—it was out of sync with reality. You called it a democracy and held elections, and you told yourselves the people were in control of the government, but it wasn't that way at all."

"It wasn't?"

"The United States ceased to be a democracy in 1932. After that you had a bureaucracy. The country was ruled by a collective mind with only one objective—to maintain its own existence. And it did, easily, because not only didn't you elect them, most of the time the electorate didn't know they existed, much less who they were. The Russian bureaucracy was even worse. We British had a better system by far."

"We British? I thought you lived in Singapore."

"Part of the Empire, old boy; still a member of the Commonwealth. When it became independent, the new regime realized it always would be. That's why they didn't tinker with its organization. But, getting back to business, Wyckoff, the bureaucracy was awfully efficient in that one thing. The trouble was, what the people wanted done when they voted for their representatives never did get done."

Yasha's normally steely gaze became even more intense, almost a stare, and his voice strengthened, as though approaching a subject on which he was rabid. "Nothing could change the bureaucracy that grew up after that—not even Congress. The monster could always outlast any opposition. It was so big that by the time any given Congress could even figure out how it worked it was out of office. Lots of individual congressmen tried to get reform movements started, but all the bureaucrats had to do was stall them. Sooner or later an elected official loses an election, or retires, or dies. None of those things happen to bureaucracies." He paused briefly and smiled at his pupil. It was as though, having cast this venom out, he was feeling physical relief.

"So what's that got to do with us? Was that going to be your next question, Wyckoff?"

"I guess so. What *does* it have to do with us?"

"Try to compare the way that system works to what we just did, and with our speed and the way everybody got a shot at the question. You'll find you can't, and that's my point—we have to pick the right system for this colony, and do it now, while we still have both the power to do it and the knowledge. We lucked out, Wyckoff. The inedible native plant life this planet has furnished us is a means of controlling its development, and that's important with a population so small and no further contact with the homeworld."

"You mean it's good for people to starve?" Wyckoff's fingers began to drum on his chin, occasionally pulling at the beard he didn't have.

"Nobody's starving, Wyckoff, thanks to people like you. We've managed to set up a tight little community down here and make a good beginning toward self-sufficiency despite the fact that we started out by getting shortchanged. People are working hard to make it go—people who are basically individualistic misfits, like you and me, to whom such behavior is unnatural. Why?"

"Why? Because it beats starving. How's that for a reason?"

"You can do better. Think—what's the rest of it?"

"There's no place else to go."

Yasha rose, stretched, hitched his pants and stuffed in the errant shirttail his lean waist found so difficult to manage. It pulled right out again, but he seemed not to notice. "Exactly. For all practical purposes we're still aboard ship: we still depend on the resources it provides, which makes every one of us vulnerable to sovereign authority. That's what we have to preserve, Wyckoff, whether we call our leader a president or a prime minister or a king, or make up a brand-new title. The power and the authority have to repose somewhere the people can see it. The idea of having it there has to be indelibly imprinted—it has to become a part of the political animal that lives on this world.

"We have to do that immediately, because none of this is going to last, Wyckoff. If we don't make sure the people want to stay here and keep this civilization flourishing, they'll run off to the frontier, just like they ran from the English colonies when North America was being settled."

"But there's nothing to eat. You just got done saying—"

"That'll change. Before the next human generation grows up, our food plants will've gone through dozens, perhaps hundreds, of generations. Without native pests they'll have a natural ecological advantage over native plants. Crop yields should be fantastic. Before you know it this world will support human life anywhere on its surface, unless we do something to stop it."

This sounded insane to Wyckoff. "Why would we want to do that?" He reached for the bowl of native "peanuts," scooped up a handful, and began munching nervously.

"To keep our descendants from slaughtering each other with stone axes and bronze swords—how's that for an answer?"

"Sounds kind of dumb to me," Wyckoff answered, his panic gone now that he understood this was merely the lead-in for another of Yasha's political lessons. He liked Yasha well enough, but sometimes talking to him could be absolutely maddening. To Wyckoff, the prime purpose of conversation was entertainment. Yasha, on the other hand, perceived words as tools.

Fu waited patiently for Wyckoff's customary look of

resignation to appear. "Sure, until you stop to think it out—and I'd recommend you do that. I'd recommend we all do it, because the first generation has to be really dedicated to heading off calamity or it won't get stopped. The point is that as people spread out, differences are going to arise, and that could mean separate nations. Unless there's some really powerful force to hold them together under a planetary government, we might wind up with Earth all over again. Certainly they'll find plenty of things to fight about."

Wyckoff, so often intimidated by Fu's fervor, raised his arms in gesture, hands palm outward—as though, like Moses, he could staunch the torrent. "Yasha, you're getting all worked up. Calm down. There's enough for everybody. They don't have to fight. There's no reason to."

"Since when has that been a consideration, Wyckoff?" The question sounded almost angry, though true anger had no place in Fu's orderly lifestyle. "Besides," he went on, "I'm talking about the future—centuries from now. Just like with the plants, there'll be a human population explosion, too. It works the same way for us as it does for anything else; whatever there is the race will expand toward the capability of consuming it.

"It's a political fact, Wyckoff. The quickest way to barbarism would be to go too fast for our control system. As long as it's a matter of survival, we could probably get by with the ship and its crew as a symbol of power. But sooner or later, maybe a generation or two down the line, the best and most efficient system would probably be a constitutional monarchy organized along the same lines as the English. What's the matter?" Wyckoff had jumped to his feet, and Fu now found himself staring up at his companion, who towered over him. Could it be that he had touched a genuinely sensitive chord?

But no; Wyckoff's intention was merely to pace, as he often did at such times. *A true man of action*, Yasha mused. He admired those who could think on their feet.

"I don't like it. If it was that good, why did we fight a war to get out of it?"

"We? You mean, the U.S.? That's a good question, Wyckoff. It shows you're thinking, and that's good too. And I'm afraid I don't have any really convincing argument to make against it, except to say that all this happened at a time in history when the whole world was out of kilter. But how's that different from now? The same thing could easily happen here; some of the same basic social pressures are present. In fact, that's exactly what I meant before, when I said that as we spread out, differences will arise and we'll find things to fight about—that is precisely the reason why we had the American revolution. You don't have revolutions if your system has flexible design, if it provides a way to correct for stress.

"In the case of the Crown vs. the Colonies, outside forces were at work that slowed the process down: you had protracted foreign wars, a slightly unbalanced sovereign, and a chicken-hearted but stubborn parliamentary leadership. Also, when you stop to think about it, the revolution left far more unchanged than it changed. The form of the legislature was different; you had a president instead of a king—but your legal system and local government, which are the fundamental shapers of any society, stayed close enough that even today the decisions of English courts are cited as authority in U.S. cases. That same legal system, the common law, followed the British flag around the world. It was adopted in some pretty strange places, like India and Israel and most of the former British colonies in Africa.

"This is because it was a good system, and the reason it was a good system is that it developed out of a good system and met specific needs as they arose, yet maintained its stability. England has been going strong for over a thousand years, Wyckoff; longer, without substantial change, than almost any other you can think of, and the system matched the culture, minor change for minor change. We know their system works, and we know how it worked at every stage of its development. We could do worse."

"I don't know," Wyckoff moaned. "I just don't know."

"Got questions, huh?"

"Lots of them. For instance, where'd a Chinese guy get a name like Yasha? That's Russian."

"Plain dumb luck, Wyckoff. My mother liked it."

Wyckoff left the session with his head spinning. For a long time he thought about what Fu had said, with little real understanding of what it really meant. Gradually, though, he began to understand that cooperation among this small population was crucial, and that what little culture they had must not be allowed to fragment itself by running away from its problems, but instead must be turned inward and attack them. He had to admit that there was a lot to be said for knowing exactly where you stood in the system, and being able to move up in it if you possessed ability.

In that respect, Wyckoff held up his end. He established himself as a resourceful innovator and an effective remover of seemingly insurmountable obstacles.

For instance, there were no plows, so Wyckoff rooted out an old Japanese swordsmith and told him to make them out of the scrap in *Corona*'s holds. Never mind that he was an artisan and not a mere mechanic—he knew how to work steel. His efforts were rewarded by a patent of land signed by the captain of the *Corona*, as local representative of the United States, on whose behalf she had laid claim, by right of discovery, to the entire planet.

There were no tractors or animals to pull the plows, so Wyckoff selected teams of sulking teenagers and set them to competing with one another for acreage tilled.

There was no lumber for buildings, so he set a crew to work on the river bank making bricks. Because transportation from the ship to the settlement was difficult, he set a small crew to work digging a canal from the river to the dimpled crater in which the *Corona* rested.

Wyckoff did not know how to do any of these things himself, but he knew they could be done, since the ship's library described the techniques. Nor did he bother to learn how—his time was too valuable to waste on that. Instead, he formed a little cadre of his brightest colonials and set them to work extracting the information and supervising these individual projects.

He had become an executive and firmly believed in the executive method—that a true leader does no work, except to see that others are working. Always, suitable rewards for exceptional performance were bestowed by the representative of the absent sovereign.

Wyckoff had little time with Arlene, who kept as busy as he did. They met infrequently at their quarters aboard ship to eat or to sleep, and it was on these occasions that they exchanged news—as they did when the first crops were finally in, and when Wyckoff returned to the ship from the settlement down the river. "It'll be squeaky for a while, Arlene, but most everybody I talked to seems to think we can make it. The farmers say it looks like rich land, and they think now that they've got a crop in the ground it'll grow okay. Too bad about those left-handed watchamacallits," he chuckled.

Arlene took the news without much enthusiasm. Wyckoff could tell she was not very happy to be where she was, and she had lately been looking a little wan. She was holding up, that was true, but she was not without her own laments about her situation.

"What would I do without you to buoy up my morale?" she told him. "You're good for me. Without you I'm just another bossy broad on the downslope of forty. Nobody would pay any attention to me, but they like you, so they follow you. You're earthy, and they identify with you; even Mason does."

Wyckoff was naturally flattered. At the same time, he was slightly alarmed. Arlene was a high-strung person and she was stuck in what for her was a decidedly unnatural situation. He knew the civil responsibility which had been thrust upon her was onerous, and that she wanted free of it. She was a ship's captain, and a ship's captain should be running a ship, not a colony.

"One of these days," she continued, "maybe in a year or two, when they don't need her quite so much, I'll take *Corona* back up where she belongs."

"What good will she do us in orbit?"

"Not just into orbit, Wyckoff. Out there exploring, to see what's nearby, or maybe to try to find a way for us to get home."

"We are home," Wyckoff replied.

"What?"

Wyckoff looked up at her face, found it blanched and white, and knew that the words had struck her bitterly, though he hadn't meant them to. But the damage was done; he had to explain. "It's official. The Colonial Council voted almost unanimously for it. From now on, we call this planet 'Home.' "

She recovered quickly from the shock, though Wyckoff could tell much of her response was forced.

"Not very imaginative," she said, "but nice—catchy." She struggled to say the name and couldn't. It stuck in her throat like a gorget. Striving mightily, as if to drive homesickness from her mind, she changed the subject and asked a banal question. "How are the crops doing?"

In total sympathy to her gloomy mood, Wyckoff answered as matter-of-factly as he could manage. "The farmers still aren't sure about them. Some of the seeds take, some of them don't. They're hoping enough do so there'll be food for everybody, but they don't know yet, and they don't know about the weather, either. Most of them are a little bit pessimistic about our chances. They say maybe if they had better equipment, the right fertilizers and stuff, they could do lots better."

"Maybe somewhere on this pla—Home—there's something Earthmen can eat."

"People are looking, Arlene. It'd help a whole lot if

they had some horses to pull those plows and things, but they can't make any animals until there's something for *them* to eat." Wyckoff's voice trailed off, and he stopped talking in order to dive into the dinner Arlene had just removed from the microwave and placed in front of him. He ate like it was his last meal.

"Good!" he said, when he was finished. "A steak would have been better, though."

"Getting to be a gourmet, huh?"

"It's easy to get hooked. Anyway, we'll have some sooner than you think. I wonder how long those frozen embryos keep?"

"Years, Wyckoff." Suddenly, she burst into tears.

"Now, what's the matter with you? What did I do?"

"It's not you, Wyckoff; it's me. I keep thinking about what happened to us, and how far away from our *real* home we are, and that we're lost . . ." Her voice trailed off into sobs.

He tried his best to comfort her, and couldn't. There was only one thing he could do, and he did it—held her and let her cry it out.

It took a while, and it was obvious there was much turbulent emotion she had to get rid of. Wyckoff hoped that when it was over it would be the last time she thought of Earth for a while. That was hard on her, particularly as she had finally realized the most important ambition of her existence and become captain, and now had to sit here, on what to her was just another dirtball, and waste it. Too bad she wasn't more like himself—a wish she had often expressed. It would have been easier.

Yet he'd complained as often and as loudly as anybody, and maybe with as much justification.

Suddenly, as though vocalizing this would divert her, Wyckoff too, was letting go. Most of his life he'd been stuck in New York. That was all he'd seen—all he'd thought there was. And then he'd gotten on the ship, where it was a little better, but now he was stuck down here with a bunch of farmers. "And even they talk over my head, Arlene. Oh, they don't mean to, but they do. It's the same here on the ship. Let's face it, Arlene. I'm ignorant. I've never been anyplace and never done anything, and there's not one thing I can do that nine out of ten people around me can't do better. There's not one thing I know that nobody else knows."

"I'd trade places with you anytime," she blurted.

"What?"

"Nothing—just thinking out loud."

But he had in fact heard her words. Unashamedly, he realized what she said was true. She would have. So would many of the others. Wyckoff had the one talent that made him invaluable to the faltering colony—the adaptability most others had lacked. Without him, without his instincts, which had impelled him to hide from Hamil, they wouldn't be on Home now, but locked up in *Corona* starving to death. Wyckoff did not understand why he went on no matter what, but he did, and that made him the most important person in the colony— more important even than the captain. That kind of thinking took a little time to get used to.

He looked over at Arlene, wondering what he might possibly say to bring an end to this black mood, and found that she was now asleep.

Chapter Seventeen

The site of *Corona*'s planetfall had been chosen partly because it bordered on the subtropical, and therefore would have mild winters and a long growing season. Not all the plants the humans brought liked summer; some preferred cooler seasons. Corn, for instance, liked the warmth of high summer, while oats and barley could best flourish in Home's cooler and rainier winter.

The time of the corn came and went, and after it was harvested the farmers immediately put the fall crops in. They toiled ever harder to prepare new fields farther up the river toward the ship, and to establish orchards.

They were fortunate that there had been no great profit in the seed, else Hamil and the conspirators might have stolen that, too. Surely, then, the colony would have failed, but as things turned out, it didn't seem to be doing at all badly.

That was Wyckoff's impression as he pedaled toward the river, down the narrow and still bumpy path that followed the proposed canal route from the ship to the river. Bicycles weren't his favorite form of transportation, but they had high mechanical efficiency, were within the manufacturing capability of the colony's shops, and used no precious fuel, so they were de rigueur for travelers of high civil station.

159

Normally, Wyckoff might have expected company for most of the way from workers excavating the canal bed, but that too was a seasonal thing, and during planting and harvesting times, work on the canal was secondary. So today Wyckoff rode alone, and in silence.

At length, he reached the bank of the river, where the diggers had constructed a little shack to store tools and equipment. Here, Wyckoff would abandon the bicycle and transfer to a canoe. These were made of galvanized sheet-steel, with the ribs and keels corrugated in, so they were light and durable. Paddling them downstream was easy because the current was a fairly brisk one. Going back depended on the season of the year, but for most of the warmer times a steady wind blew inland from the ocean and made it possible to use sail power to go upstream.

Wyckoff chose a canoe and tipped it upright, then strained to push its farther end into the water. Then he noticed there were no paddles or sail in it and walked to the shack to look for some inside. That was when he saw the tracks.

Ordinarily, Wyckoff paid little attention to such things, but something as obvious as this great muddy footprint, right in the middle of the shack's doorsill where he was about to plant his own foot, was impossible to ignore.

He stopped, squinted into the morning sun, and tried to tell himself that what he was seeing was the distorted footprint of a barefoot human child, the same as many others he could see in the dirt around the entrance. This attempt at self-deceit failed miserably, and as he scanned the area he found many more—all unequivocally nonhuman, and some very clearly overprinting real human tracks, where comparison was easy.

Wyckoff had made a profound discovery, and it scared him to death. He did not know what to do next. He was not sophisticated enough to determine how large a creature made the tracks, or if it was dangerous to humans.

But even Wyckoff was astute enough to draw the one inescapable conclusion—you cannot have a predator without prey, and Home had no land-dwelling animals. She had, in fact, only very primitive sea life—marine worms, mollusk-like creatures, something that resembled jellyfish, and some creatures enough like primitive crustaceans that the experts predicted an insectlike land form would someday evolve from them. Wyckoff should not, therefore, have worried.

Unfortunately, he did. He knew the vessel of another race had crashed here on this planet, and he didn't know what sort of creatures they were or what they might have brought along with them. The only possible explanation for what he had just seen was that the aliens had had their own animal forms aboard, some of which survived the crash of the ship and now wandered free across the length and breadth of Home.

And that scared him. He was almost a thousand kilometers from the crash site of the alien ship, which meant either that the creatures spread out widely, or that they enjoyed eating meat and were stalking humans as a source of it. As soon as that occurred to him, he began looking around for something that might be useful as a weapon.

No one went armed on Home. There had been no reason to, until now. But men were resourceful creatures; they could contrive killing devices from many things. Wyckoff reached down and ripped a plank from the platform in front of the doorway, noting that from the far end a long, rusty spike still protruded. Thus armed, he cautiously opened the door a crack and peered in.

The morning sun was on his right, and the shack's doorway faced the river, which was south, so Wyckoff did not have the benefit of direct light to see by. What he had—a bright beam of sunlight streaming through a knothole in the planking—was more than adequate to make out the creature which had left the tracks. There it lay on a pile of burlap sacks in one corner of the shack—apparently asleep. Wyckoff reflected on his terror of only moments ago, when he had had visions of slashing claws and bared fangs, snarling in anticipation of combat. He put the plank down on the floor and watched as the creature opened its eyes and stretched languorously.

Wyckoff's fears now seemed foolish. He felt a strange sensation, an impression his memory searched out and retrieved from his own childhood—a satisfyingly safe, stable impression. He squatted down and picked the furry little creature up. He felt as though his very heart were melting.

"Wyckoff, what is that thing?"

"I don't know. I found him sacked out in the boat-house down by the river. Ain't he cute?"

"Y-yes, he is," Arlene muttered. The creature Wyckoff held in one arm stared out at her blankly and content-edly. It looked a little like a baby koala bear. "Wyckoff, he's also inexplicable. Where could he possibly have come from? He certainly didn't evolve on Home."

"Then he must have come off that wrecked ship. He could have been a pet or something—maybe the only thing that got off it alive. You want to hold him?"

"No, not just yet. He might . . ."

"Bite? Naw, he won't. He's real friendly. He let me walk right up to him. Didn't even blink. Go on, take him."

Reluctantly, Arlene extended her arms. The creature did not seem to mind the transfer, and settled in for a ride.

"There, you see. It's okay."

"How do you know he won't get mean when he gets bigger, Wyckoff? It might be just a baby, and all babies are gentle."

"I don't know, Arlene. But I figure we can take care of that when the time comes, if it ever comes. I never had a pet before, unless you count rats. I did have one of those once."

"What does he eat?"

"I don't know that, either—for sure. But I guess he

eats the stuff that grows here. It stands to reason he'd have to, or he would have starved before now."

"That might be okay, then, Wyckoff. But I don't see how we could justify keeping him around if he ate terrestrial food—not with everything in the colony rationed for people."

"What if he did, Arlene? We're not that short anymore, since the crops have started coming in. Why, the farmers are already hatching some of those frozen chicken eggs—and they've got to feed them."

"They'll *eat* the chickens later, Wyckoff. Are you going to eat him?"

"Of course not. I wouldn't eat little—uh . . ."

"Got a problem already, haven't you?"

"I'll find a name for him."

"Maybe he's not a him."

"Yeah. You're right. It'd have to be a name that'd fit a—a whatever it is."

Wyckoff reached out to take the creature back, and he seemed to want to go, so Arlene let it. Something had changed, though its expression remained as unreadable as before. It was as though it suddenly didn't like her.

That possibility did not seem to bother her. She did not forbid Wyckoff to keep the creature, perhaps because such an order might not have stuck anyhow, even if she had given it. Wyckoff had become far too important a person on this world for even the captain to seek out confrontation.

So Wyckoff kept his beast and named it Jerry, which would fit either sex, if Jerry's sex was ever determined. As it turned out, Jerry ate terrestrial food, and seemed to thrive on it. This reinforced the theory that Jerry was an escaped pet. "See, Arlene. He would'a died if he hadn't found me."

Confrontation did come, and the result was as might have been predicted. Arlene forbade Wyckoff to bring Jerry into the ship, but Wyckoff did it anyway, and Jerry followed him around, waddling on his short legs, wherever he went. Jerry acquired another enemy—Dr. Mallarkey—and he proved that, cute as he was, he had both a temper and some weaponry.

Mallarkey was naturally curious about extraterrestrial life forms. After all, he had never before examined one, since they were absolutely barred from Earth. Jerry bit him savagely on his bulbous nose, thereby preserving both his dignity and the body substances Mallarkey had been about to collect. Wyckoff had naturally taken Jerry's part, and he resolved that however curious science was, its prurience would not be satisfied at the cost of any holes in Jerry's hide.

Friction increased between Wyckoff and Arlene, too. She insisted that Jerry not spend the nights aboard the ship, particularly not in her boudoir. Wyckoff attempted to obey, and built a little doghouse for Jerry outside the aft airlock.

But the first night alone, Jerry found his way back into their quarters, having apparently untied the knot on his tether, and Arlene found him at the foot of the bed when she woke up the next morning.

"He's lonesome, Arlene, that's all. And he's not hurting anything up here. There's no mess or anything."

And there wasn't. Arlene made sure of that. She checked the cabin thoroughly, inspecting every corner. But of course she couldn't rule out transgressions in other parts of the ship.

So, despite her opposition, Jerry moved in with them, and was Wyckoff's constant companion. Wyckoff pompously insisted that Jerry had proven he was housebroken, and that he had no other bad habits, so he ought to be allowed to stay.

They held a little ceremony when the canal opened. Since it was Wyckoff's idea, he officiated, but he insisted that Arlene have the honor of blowing the last two earthen barriers that would let the water in.

The explosions tore a hole in the embankment and the force of the water did the rest. It boiled in, muddy and violent, leaving the ship on its island in the middle, an island created when the drivefields had torn away a ring of overburden around the hull's perimeter.

"See," Wyckoff grinned, "just like King Arthur's joint, until we fill part of it in to make docks. Now that we have this canal, we can float stuff in instead of lugging it on our backs."

"I am impressed, Wyckoff. What do you do about the current out in the river? It's pretty strong, isn't it?"

"That's the next surprise. Watch." He picked up a handset and called somebody named Dailey.

Pretty soon there came a screeching sound, high-pitched and still far way. The whistle provided the focus needed to locate its source, which was a small boat now halfway down the canal. Following it was a plume of smoke, which rose to the top of the canal bank and was immediately carried away by the brisk wind blowing from the port beam.

"How do you like it, Arlene?"

"What is it?"

"It's a steamboat."

"That's a couple of centuries out of date, Wyckoff. Why not something a little more modern, like a gas turbine? *Corona*'s shops could make the parts."

"Yeah, they could, all right. But that wouldn't teach these people anything. This stuff will, and they can make it all themselves, just like they made the boat. All they took from the ship was scrap iron, and pretty soon they won't even need that. They'll be making their own iron pretty soon, but the kind of alloys they'd need for turbine blades will be beyond our capability for a long time yet. Besides, it takes fuel to run it, and this works just fine on the same local coal the smith uses."

Arlene seemed suitably impressed. Instinctively, Wyckoff had realized that a culture had to grow at its own pace, and do things for itself. If it didn't, it would die as soon as it lost the technological help it had been getting.

The boat huffed and puffed its way down the canal

and entered the moat, where eager hands grasped out for lines thrown to them. It docked in front of the stairway that had been constructed from the ship's central elevator to the water's edge.

"It'll unload its cargo—in this case, food for us—pick up another load of iron, and go back, Arlene. How'd you like to take a ride on it?"

"Well, it looks safe enough," she answered, "but I really shouldn't be taking the time. I've got work to do."

"You're not doing anything that can't wait. And you haven't seen the town in a long time. It's built up a lot since you were there. They're really doing great things. Come on—give Yasha and the guys a chance to brag a little. They deserve it."

She was weakening; Wyckoff could tell. He waited patiently for the inevitable to happen, and it did.

"Well, I suppose I could go for a little while. How long will we be gone?"

"Downstream's pretty fast. Upstream is slower, because of the current. Then, they'll have to unload and reload—probably until early tomorrow morning." He waited apprehensively.

"Why not?" she said at last. "It's been a long time between vacations."

"Fine. Let's get a few things and get going."

They went aboard, collected what they needed, and were about to depart when Wyckoff's face took on a worried look.

"What's wrong, Wyckoff?"

"I can't find Jerry. He must have gone off someplace with somebody else."

"You were planning to take him along?"

"Sure. He's no trouble."

"No!"

"Aw, Arlene, cut it out. What do you have against the little guy? He's never done anything to you."

"I can't help it, Wyckoff. We just don't get along for some reason. I can't explain it, but sometimes I get uncomfortable when he's around. It's like he has a bunch of different moods, and like I can feel them. I wish you'd find some other place to keep him besides our cabin."

Wyckoff eventually yielded. He didn't want this to spoil the trip for her, and he understood. Arlene wasn't the only one Jerry affected that way. There were others. It seemed you either liked him or you didn't—there wasn't any halfway point. Wyckoff did like him, very much, but then, he liked almost everybody. And in the end he left without Jerry, confident someone else would look after him while he was gone.

Besides, it would have taken too long to search for him. He'd never learned to come when he was called, and the *Corona*'s huge bulk was now comparatively empty with all the colonists gone, and with more than half her regular crew spending at least part of their time in town. Only the officers stayed aboard full time these days.

Next morning, on their way back, Wyckoff had reason to feel satisfied. He knew that Arlene had greatly enjoyed the trip, and their overnight stay in what to her were primitive conditions added a certain something to their relationship. She was her old self again—calm, contented, and uninhibited. Where aboard ship she fretted over their predicament, here she was without troubles, or else she had managed to shove them out of her conscious mind. Either way, Wyckoff didn't care. It was enough that she seemed to be happy again.

She sat now alongside him, in the boat's fantail, the only place not cluttered with bags of grain and baskets of vegetables, and watched the paddlewheel churn the muddy water white. For a long time she didn't speak, and when she did she reinforced Wyckoff's assumption that she was now a happier person. "You've done some amazing things, Wyckoff. I'm proud of you."

"These people did it all, Arlene, not me. Most of them never had a chance to show what they could do before. Now they have, and they can see where it all comes from, and that it's theirs. That's a big thing to people like us."

"Like us?"

"Well, me, I mean. On Earth, what could I have been except a bum? The Earth didn't need me, or want me. It didn't want these people, either. I guess we were too slow or something, and everybody else passed us by. Here, on Home, it's different. Everybody's got a job. Everybody does what he does best, the best he knows how, and nobody worries that somebody else will come along and take it because they can look around and see there's going to be enough for everybody someday."

"You say that like you mean it, Wyckoff."

"Yeah, I mean it," he replied, somewhat shocked.

"That's why that old fear haunts me—has haunted me since the day we landed," she said tearfully. "That someday, sooner or later, another alien ship might come to this planet you're calling Home, and that they might, in fact, try to take it."

Wyckoff responded to that with some boastful, macho utterances. He blustered and threatened horrible vengeance on anybody who might try that. In that way he made it clear that he, too, had considered the possibility of such an encounter. Thereafter, he was uncharacteristically silent and morose.

They steamed into the *Corona*'s moat and docked, and crewmen began unloading the cargo, which they placed in the elevator car. Arlene and Wyckoff waited until the car had a full load, so the boat could leave and get back to town before dark. Then they went up with it, but took the liberty of diverting it to their quarters before sending it back down to the cargo deck.

"I wonder where he is."

"You haven't found Jerry yet?" Arlene had gone directly to the shower and was soaping up, but Wyckoff was still searching.

"I guess he's in somebody else's cabin, or he'd have been here."

"Find him later. Come on in—the water's great."

After a few moments of futile searching, Wyckoff joined her in the shower, and for a few moments his pet was forgotten. But when the splashing ceased, and the cabin was dripping with condensation, he climbed out of the shower capsule wrapped in a towel and mopping water from his eyes to see a side of Jerry that was new to all of them.

Chapter Eighteen

The animal look was gone. So was Wyckoff's conception of Jerry as a pet. The creature, now standing uncharacteristically erect and wearing a sort of coverall, held a gun in its hairy little hand—pointed directly at him.

Wyckoff stopped short, and held the towel around him. The shock had been so great he didn't know what else to do. What he'd thought of as his pet had been something else all along. There were some drastic adjustments to make in his thinking.

Behind Wyckoff, Arlene was still clowning around, unaware that there was anything wrong. There was a whacking sound, as the end of her towel snapped against his rump, stinging him badly enough to cause him to jump.

When Jerry's gun hand tensed in response, Wyckoff yelled out, "Arlene, stop—look."

She did, catching the urgency of his tone, and gasped at the sight. "God, Wyckoff, what is all this? What's he doing wearing clothes—and what's he doing with a gun?"

Jerry hadn't moved, but had kept the gun trained on both of them. Now he did. His other hand pointed to their respective piles of clothing.

171

"H-he wants us to get dressed, Arlene."

"Wyckoff, you realize this is no animal? This is intelligence—intelligence of a very high order. This is a *crewman* from that alien ship."

"I know."

"It tricked you. It tricked us all. But what does it want?"

Wyckoff had finished drying himself and was reaching for his pants. Arlene was still huddling in her towel. She was still in shock, and in no hurry to get dressed. It was obvious the creature wanted to take them somewhere, and that she might not like what would happen if it did.

And then Jerry waved the gun at her, his gesture unmistakable in meaning.

Arlene hastily dropped the towel and began dressing, finishing at about the same time Wyckoff did.

Then they waited and watched Jerry, still motionless and still resolutely covering them.

"Now what, Jerry?" Wyckoff demanded, not really expecting an answer. He had yet to hear Jerry make a sound. As far as Wyckoff knew, he was mute.

"Up," the creature said, in a strangely high, though guttural voice. It was the first sound either one of them had ever heard it make. It waved the gun toward the door.

Wyckoff's jaw hung open. He was beginning to think of Jerry as an "it" instead of a "he," as Arlene always had.

"It wants us to go to the bridge, Wyckoff. But why?"

"UP!"

That was enough. Impatience was not restricted to the human race, obviously. The ugly menace buried in that last growling utterance surfaced. They turned and marched to the elevator, where Wyckoff fumbled to push the "up" button.

When the car came, they all got in, Jerry with his back to the door and carefully watching both of them while the car moved upward.

At the top, when the door opened, the humans got another shock. There was more than one Jerry; in fact, there were seven of them. And they were all here in the control room, all armed, and all dressed in the same sacklike garments.

"That's what it was, Wyckoff," Arlene whispered. "It wasn't that Jerry acted different at different times—it was because it wasn't the same one all the time."

But the aliens were not alone in the control room. Mason was a prisoner there, and Verity, together with five of the spacehands—all, Wyckoff was willing to bet, who had been aboard this morning. They were all penned into one corner, and the 'Jerry' who had escorted them to the bridge gestured that this was where he wanted the two of them.

Mason was the first to speak to Arlene. "Captain, they got you, too!"

"Where did all these creatures come from, Mason? And what do they want?"

"I think they want our ship, Captain. They must be survivors from the crashed shuttle. They must have traveled here from the crash site, ditched their clothing and weapons, and waited for their chance. As for how they got aboard, your guess is as good as mine. I woke up with a gunbarrel up my nose. We didn't have any reason to guard the ship. But I always thought there was only one Jerry."

"So did I," Wyckoff groaned. "He really sucked me in. They must have been counting on that. We couldn't tell one from another, so they slipped aboard one by one and hid. If anybody saw one, they wouldn't pay any attention—they'd think it was Jerry. I shouldn't have let him run loose like I did."

"At least," Arlene replied, "I know now what it was I didn't like about him."

One of the creatures went to the control room door and closed it. Another headed for Verity, whom it herded into another corner of the room. A third seemed intent on separating Wyckoff from the bridge officers and motioned him into yet a third corner with several of the spacehands. None was far enough away from the others so that conversational tones could not be heard and understood, so when one of the creatures stood in the center of the deck and screamed, "UP," all the humans heard him.

"You want us to raise ship?" Arlene asked.

"UP!" The creature waved its gun even more menacingly at her.

She tried to explain. "We cannot go to space. We cannot astrogate. Our astrogation computer has been destroyed. Do you understand?"

There was some reason to think that he would, since he knew a human word. It would seem reasonable that the creatures had made a study of the human language before embarking on such a venture. But if it did understand, it evidently did not care.

The creature pointed upward with what would have been the index finger if he had been human, but which was merely one of four opposable digits on his hand. "Up—our ship up."

" 'Our ship,' huh? Do you suppose he'll shoot somebody if we don't take *Corona* up, Rick?"

"I'd hate to risk it, Captain. It didn't sound to me like that's what he meant, though."

"Then, what did he mean?"

"Let's turn on the console, and pretend we're getting ready to do what he wants. Things are getting too tense to suit me."

"Good idea. We'll start with the video monitors and see if there's anybody else still loose." She moved to the command chair and used its remote unit to fire the big board up. All throughout the ship, and from speakers outside it, klaxons sounded. That would leave little doubt in anyone within earshot that something was wrong aboard. One by one she switched around the cameras, but there was nobody visible in any of the areas they panned. Next, she started the main scanner, which immediately produced a blip. At first she thought it was one of the synchronous satellites they'd launched to map the planet and monitor the weather, but it wasn't. It was too low. "Rick," she whispered gravely, "there's a ship in orbit. That's what it meant."

"I see it, Captain. But why does it want the *Corona* to go up? It doesn't make sense. Out there we could run; down here we're a sitting duck."

"They'd shoot us all if we tried to run."

"UP!" the little creature screamed again. To punctuate his demand he fired a shot, which just missed Arlene's foot.

"We'd better do it, Rick. That's a slugthrower. He'll ruin something vital or kill somebody next. Start the prelaunch sequence. That'll take a while, and make them think we're busy while we figure something out."

"What do we do about the power deck? Verity should be down there."

"He'll have to handle it from the bridge. Let me see if I can get him over here." She pointed a finger at him and motioned, making certain that the creature who was guarding her noticed.

He did, and he seemed to understand that Verity was needed now that the ship's systems were being activated.

"Verity, get the drive warmed up."

"What? Captain, you can't be serious."

"We have to. They want us to, and right now I don't see any way we can argue."

Verity looked at her as if to say, 'I hope you know what you're doing,' but he went over to the auxiliary engineering board and booted the drive start-up program.

"There's one chance," she said, in a voice unnecessarily loud, hoping the aliens would not catch on. "We know what's coming and they don't. When we blast, I'll do it wide open. It'll pin them all to the deck, and the rest of you disarm them before they can get back up. Okay?"

A series of grunts rose in answer, and she started a short ten-to-zero countdown as soon as the board showed the *Corona* was buttoned up and airtight. But on the count of one, every single alien flopped down prone on the deck and kept his weapon trained on the humans. They might not have understood the words, but they knew what high-gee forces did. There wasn't time for Arlene to do anything else. She lifted the ship.

Chapter Nineteen

They drifted in freefall, only intermittently grasping for handholds whenever it was necessary to fire the ship's main drive and rise to a higher orbit. It was a stern chase, and thus took time.

Arlene was strapped into her command chair, as was Verity, but the others now stood in a clump in one corner, mostly up near the overhead where an elastic cord ran all the way around the bridge complex. The nose port shutters had been withdrawn. The *Corona*'s crew and the aliens alike watched through it as the alien vessel hove into view.

"Captain," Mason whispered, "time is running out."

"I know it, Rick. But so far they haven't made any obvious mistakes. I wish now we'd been more careful. At least we should have kept the armory locked."

"It was locked, Captain. They must have found a way to break in. Or," he added sheepishly, "Jerry memorized the combination while he watched me open it. How could we have been so blind?"

"It's done, Rick. Quit worrying about it and try to think of an answer to this."

The 'this' to which she referred was a module about a tenth the size of the *Corona* that now loomed directly ahead of them. It was a dull-metallic glob, featuring

many unsightly warts, bulges, protrusions and antennae
for decoration. It didn't look like it was meant to enter
an atmosphere.

"Where are the engines on that thing, Captain? I
don't see any."

"I don't either. Maybe they retract inboard."

"Could be. But why would they bother? They didn't
streamline anything else."

"Maybe they use a different kind of drive than we
do."

"The wrecked ship had pods like our Aschenbrenners
do."

"Then maybe—hey, look!"

Mason turned his attention back to the port. Through
it, and ahead, a tender could be seen emerging from
the other vessel. It was small, perhaps large enough to
contain four or five of the little aliens, but it was towing
a cable.

They watched it grow in size as it approached. Soon
it reached the end of its tether and stopped. Its cockpit
cowling opened and out came a suited figure who began
detaching the cable, which appeared to terminate in a
large plate. Then the tender backed off.

As soon as *Corona* was near enough, the creature
placed the plate on the hull and pushed off in the
direction of the tender, which he reached without the
use of any artificial propulsion. He reentered it, and it
drifted back to the other vessel.

Then the distance between the two craft started to
close.

"It's an electromagnet, Rick. We're being reeled in
toward the alien ship."

"I see," Mason answered. "I wonder why."

"They brought *Corona* up here for a reason, Rick.
Maybe something's wrong with their ship, and they
need ours in order to get home."

"That thought has crossed my mind, Captain. It also
occurs to me that the module we're approaching really
might not have any propulsion capable of planetfall.

Our vessel might have been the aliens' only way up from the planet."

"Then we'd better stop them real quick, Rick. And there's a way—if we quietly power down. They can't restart the drive sequence without the passwords. See if you can get that idea across to Verity without stirring up the Jerrys. Maybe later they'll let one of us near the console again."

Mason nodded, then slowly edged his way over to the engineer's station, and began mumbling something incomprehensible, even to Arlene, who was closer than the nearest alien. He rejoined the captain a moment later, with a big smile on his face. "I use my pig Latin so seldom these days I'm losing fluency," he said.

They settled down to silent watching, but it wasn't long before Mason had some even more puzzling questions. As soon as the two vessels were drawn close, other suited aliens appeared. Some herded metal girders out through a cargo lock and guided them toward the *Corona*. Others carried strangely shaped equipment, which they attached to the large cable.

Then, at last, the alien purpose became clear. The girders were to bridge the distance between the two, and the equipment they carried was to be used to weld them in place. The humans watched this activity, aghast.

The suited aliens worked rapidly, and for several hours, blinding flashes from their arcs flared in through the ship's ports. When they were finished, the two vessels were firmly joined by a webbing of stoutly braced girders and the magnet was withdrawn.

All the while the human beings on the *Corona*'s bridge had silently waited and watched for some opportunity to take action against the aliens. The aliens, however, had been shrewd enough to keep their distance, and always held their weapons ready. The opportunity had never appeared, and as time passed, the possibility of escape became slimmer and slimmer.

As soon as the task outside was completed, two of the aliens left the room, and went, apparently, to the captain's suite. In any event they returned, about five minutes later, each towing a spacesuit and its backpack. They had one for Arlene and one for Wyckoff. These were placed in front of the humans and the appropriate gesture-command given.

"Where do you think they're taking us, Arlene?"

"To their ship, obviously," she replied, somewhat irritated. "Why else would they bring us these?"

"Sorry. I guess it was a dumb question, huh?"

Her tone softened, became apologetic. "I'm the one who should be sorry, Wyckoff. And no, it wasn't a dumb question. There are lots of reasons they could have done it. Maybe they have to do something else outside the hull, and don't know how."

"That might explain you, but how about me? What could they possibly want me for?"

"All I can say is, ask Jerry, if you can figure out which one he is."

They were herded into the axial elevator under guard and taken to the planetside lock, which rested between the ship's three huge landing jacks. Arlene was a little surprised at this, and remarked that the aliens didn't seem to know about the others on the lifeboat decks, which were much nearer.

They reached the lock, cycled through, and were then turned over to suited figures outside, who had brought the tender. They rode this into a large lock on the other vessel, which led then into a broad corridor.

Amazingly, with the first step out of this lock there was increasing weight, and by the time they had taken ten they felt almost a full gee.

Chapter Twenty

The Jerrys now breathed the bumpy vessel's air, standing cautiously by with helmets removed, gesturing to the humans to follow suit. The humans did, and their helmets were immediately confiscated. "It smells like we're in a big bag of armpits," Wyckoff groaned, and moved to grab his helmet back. He quickly retreated when a gun, tightly grasped in a tiny, hairy paw, thrust toward his chops. Each motion he made thereafter the weapons followed. He could almost hear the eyeballs click. Now, he thought, we really *are* trapped.

Small as it had appeared from the outside, the ship they were on seemed fairly roomy within. Moreover, they did not have to stoop, as both Arlene and Wyckoff had assumed they would, because of their captors' three-foot stature. They could stand upright, with plenty of overhead room.

But it was not until they arrived in what they took to be the vessel's control room that they understood why. Not all the aliens were of the teddy bear species.

The two others they saw were fully as tall and as bulky as humans. One was thinner than the other, and like it, hairless. Its skin was milky white and shiny, almost like scales, though if it had such they were too tiny to make out. This one wore a heavy hooded garment of some type of brocade material, decorated, of all things, with a gaudy flowered pattern.

"That turns my stomach," Arlene whispered. She had immediately categorized it as female—one with abominable taste, though there was no way to tell if it was, or if in fact these alien races even had separate sexes.

The other alien was much more imposing, and it was clear it was in charge. Its skin at least had pigment, but evidently the natural color did not entirely please it, as it wore paint as well—blazing oranges and crimson, arranged in seemingly random jagged-line designs.

Its clothing consisted of a kimonolike garment of a silky smooth substance with curious iridescent qualities. Its upper limbs, uncovered, were thickly muscled, almost to the point where it had no neck below its bulbous head. The jaws opened sideways like an insects, though it was clearly endoskeletal. Two oddly lidded eyes, set in the human arrangement under a bulging brow, completed its facial ensemble, but there were no indications of either nostrils or ears.

Nevertheless, it rapidly proved it did communicate by sound. It jabbered in great breathless burps at the little aliens and the other big one for several minutes after the humans had entered, gesturing, and from time to time, pointing at the humans. It seemed to be the source of the odor, and the air became increasingly foul.

The humans were petrified. Nothing so disconcerting can happen to a person than to be ushered into strange surroundings, for an unknown reason, and then to be simply ignored. They were like cattle in the auction ring.

Wyckoff had experienced the feeling many times before, on those occasions when he had been detained by the police. He didn't like it, and he said so in a loud voice that boomed through the chamber and very effectively stopped all other conversation. "What do you guys want with us?"

The larger alien roared out a word, which the humans heard as "silence!" The creature reached a knobby multi-digited hand beneath its robe, and drew forth a device which it pointed at the deck where the two of them stood. Immediately, Wyckoff's weight doubled. It was an agony even to try to move. He could do nothing except to strain to hold himself erect so he could observe the aliens.

The big alien's voice had come with strange echoes. Wyckoff could distinguish two distinct patterns—one gibberish, the other perfectly understandable, though flat and toneless English. The English, he discovered to his amazement, came out of a sort of cabinet behind him. He jerked his head painfully around to look at it.

His description was slightly flawed. It was not a cabinet—not in the usual sense. It had rollers and it moved. It seemed to be some sort of robot.

He turned again to look at Arlene, found she was shaking perceptibly and about to lose control of herself. He knew he couldn't let that happen to his girl. He had to reassure her, and Wyckoff's way to do that was to make small talk. "Well, at least we've got somebody we can talk to, Arlene. Wonder how that thing does it."

She didn't answer him. She just looked miserable.

He decided it wasn't going to work and that it was, in fact, time to shut up. But that was when the big alien decided it was ready to talk to them.

"Which of you," it asked through the translation device, "is Captain Graham?"

"She is," Wyckoff answered, recoiling. To his everlasting disgust, the painted alien seemed to have developed an even worse case of halitosis.

"Then you would be Mr. Wyckoff. Let her answer, Mr. Wyckoff." It turned to Arlene, who was still shaking, but who looked determined not to let her fear show. "Captain, I wish to move this assemblage into a higher orbit."

"What?"

"I repeat, we are too close to the planet. You must

order your crew to move us farther out—at least two more planetary diameters."

"Are you mad? We're unstable with this 'thing' attached. We'll tumble."

"Do not attempt deceit, Captain Graham. Your technology is generally inferior, but I know your capabilities exactly. I am aware that your ship is highly maneuverable and has adequate stabilizing systems. I watched you take it to the surface when you arrived. Your crew will manage."

"You what?"

"I watched you." The creature handed Arlene a handset that must have come from the *Corona* with one of the little aliens and said, "Call Mr. Mason and give the necessary orders."

"I will not." She set her jaw and assumed a determined pose, folding her arms across her chest. As an afterthought, she added a question. "How do you know so much about us?"

The painted alien ignored her question. "Then I will instruct my crew to do it." He muttered into a device of his own, in a language the machine did not translate, then stared blankly at her.

"Wait a minute," Arlene broke out at last, after a long period of hesitation. She knew she couldn't risk letting them wreck the ship, as well they might if they tried to maneuver it. She took the radio. "Mason?"

"Yes, Captain? Are you all right?"

"So far. Have they monkeyed with the controls?"

"Not yet. Are they about to?"

"Not if I can help it. Has the situation changed any?"

"No. Status quo, but we aren't stable in this orbit. We're going down slowly but surely."

Arlene paused. She had been entertaining some hope that Mason would find a way to overpower his captors, since at the moment humans outnumbered them, but the hope then died. "Take us out to 25,000 miles, Rick."

"Twenty-five thousand? Captain, may I ask why so far?"

"Because that's where Double-Ugly here wants to go, and he says he'll try to move the ship if we don't. I assume that mean's he'll try to tow it with his own, and I don't think we want to risk that."

Rick didn't ask who Double-Ugly was. He assumed she meant an alien. "I am sitting here at the console awaiting maneuvering orders, Captain."

"No," Arlene answered hastily. The implication of Mason's words was hardly lost on her. He had just told her he was in a position to cut the power, but she didn't want anybody hurt. Losing *Corona* would certainly doom the colony below. "Stabilize the orbit and *then* make any *necessary adjustments*, Mr. Mason." Arlene was by now pretty sure the robot only translated words. The flat, monotonous, synthesized voice probably couldn't pick up any but the grossest of inflections, and those she had employed were subtle in the extreme.

The human ear, by contrast, easily caught it all. "Understood. I'm starting a firing sequence, Captain—countdown of ten, if that'll be of any help."

She must have known what Mason was thinking—that she and Wyckoff, forewarned and ready for the really crushing acceleration he could deliver, might have the opportunity to try to seize a weapon, but looking around, she also had to be pessimistic. It hadn't worked before and wouldn't work now. Not only were they too closely guarded, but excessive thrust might endanger *Corona*, in her current delicate condition. "No, Rick," she said forcefully. "I don't think that will do it."

The orbit was thus attained, while the aliens watched on another screen and seemed pleased. The big one, in order to spare Wyckoff from being crushed, had released him from the gravity trap. He invited the two humans to sit on the cushions strewn about the deck by the departing Jerrys, who then left the chamber. Only the alien in the atrociously flowered robe remained.

"Very good, Captain Graham," the painted alien said, "you are very sensible for a female."

"For a female! What has that got to do with it?"

"The races that have females seldom allow them the responsibility you hold. That is all I meant. What does 'double-ugly' mean? I noted that the machine did not translate this term, but I assume you used it in reference to me and that it is uncomplimentary." He paused. "I can hardly take offense at the antics of barbarians, of course, but I am curious."

"It means . . ."

". . . Boss." Wyckoff chimed in and interrupted the captain. His wink told her he thought his was the cooler head and he wanted her to calm down.

"Let her answer, Mr. Wyckoff. I rather admire her spirit. In fact, all you creatures seem to have a certain something. It is a shame you are such uncivilized savages."

"Now, wait a minute—who attacked who? Who are you people? What do you want, anyway?" Despite Wyckoff's best efforts, Arlene was on her feet and fuming, the anger that had been building suddenly too much for her.

"I am Lylard, Lord Temporal," the alien said coolly and matter-of-factly, as though anyone should have already known. "I want to go home. That is all I want, and all of my purpose that I will explain to you. To get there I required your ship. Since it occurred to me you would not give it to me willingly, I took it."

"But you had a ship."

"Half a ship, Captain. The other half is wrecked down there on the planet, as I'm sure you already know. There was an unfortunate accident. More unfortunate yet, the module destroyed in the accident contained my spatial drive."

"We found the wreck. But in the condition it was in we hardly expected any survivors. How did those creatures manage that?"

"My servants, the Dorians? Simple. They were already on the surface, waiting to be picked up. They were not in the module that crashed. I must say, you *are* dense. What a disappointment!"

Lylard apparently did not expect lesser life to take offense at his insults. He calmly continued. "Had I anticipated the accident, of course, I would have left them there and thus avoided the problem, but since it did happen, I must improvise. You will, of course, lend me all possible assistance."

Arlene gulped. Despite the impersonal effect of the translation device, or perhaps because of it, that remark had emerged as particularly cold-blooded.

But the moment of truth had come. Rick's idea had been a good one, and by now he'd have cycled the systems through. Shut down, the *Corona* would be useless to the aliens. She couldn't be moved so much as an inch without the right passwords. Arlene knew these, and so did Mason and Verity, and they were the only ones who knew them. And though the Dorians had watched the control program initiate, it was, in her opinion, most unlikely that they had followed closely enough to be able to duplicate the operation. "No," she told the alien resolutely. "This is as far as you go. Here we are; here we sit until we rot."

Lylard's expressions were, of course, unreadable to her, though she watched him closely anyhow, as she spoke.

His next remark was obviously intended to sound even more bloodthirsty than his last, but it lacked the same punch. "Captain, I am quite sure that you believe I am now helpless, and perhaps I would be if you did not have a substantial colony on the surface. They are a disadvantage to you. They serve me as hostages, as do those crew members not directly involved in your ship's operation. I am prepared to sacrifice all of these if that is necessary to gain your cooperation. Do you understand that?"

That was tough talking, yet not a realistic threat in

human eyes. They hadn't seen anything on the approach to this vessel that even looked like a weapon.

Arlene glanced at Wyckoff to read his expression and thus his thoughts. His jaw was set, and it was obvious he also thought the alien was running a bluff.

Thus fortified, she then replied, "You *are* helpless. You welded your ship to mine. Now, even if you were armed, you couldn't maneuver unless I let you—and I won't let you."

"I see," the alien added, after a suitable interval. "You want a demonstration? Is that it, *barbarian*?"

Wyckoff watched Arlene's expression change from confidence to grave concern. Now it was his turn to read thoughts, as she weighed odds. He saw them all, as clearly as though they coursed through his own mind: would this creature now begin to torture her crew, herself included? Could she take that—hold firm, watch, and keep her silence whatever Lylard did, even as the last crewman died? He knew that this might ultimately be what she would have to do—that if she didn't she would, most assuredly, be placing the colony in jeopardy.

He turned his attention back to the alien, half expecting to see him drooling over an array of hot coals and pincers. But the alien shared neither Wyckoff's arcane ideas nor Arlene's indecision. While Wyckoff conjectured and Arlene dithered, Lylard busied himself at a keyboard.

When continued silence became onerous, Arlene broke it with bravado. "Is this supposed to make me think you're launching missiles?"

"Nothing so childishly crude," the flat machine voice boomed emotionlessly.

Artificial or not, the tone was chilling. Arlene grew tense. The inside of her suit was now noticeably wet with perspiration, but she was doing her best not to allow her concern to show.

She looked over at Wyckoff, and searched for some supportive expression, but Wyckoff had suddenly retreated into silence. He was inclined to do that in times

of stress, and more than once Arlene had expressed
envy over this ability. She, like most people, was largely
devoted to hysterical reaction—do something, even if
it's wrong—which was almost always the worst response
possible. Wyckoff didn't suffer this failing and it made
him a cool hand—a survivor.

Abruptly, Lylard turned and faced the humans, obviously finished with his nefarious preparations. "Call
your ship," he ordered, handing Arlene the same
handset.

Arlene took it and pressed the talk key. "Rick," she
screamed, as though expecting Lylard to interrupt, "keep
them trapped in orbit—whatever they do, don't give
in."

But Lylard did not interrupt, and there was a faint
hint of annoyance in Mason's voice when he replied.
"Captain, I've been trying to reach you . . ."

"Is everybody all right?"

"We're fine. But I can't raise the colony."

Can't raise the colony! The implication of that remark
was devastating. Lifting ship on Aschenbrenners was a
planet-shaking event—literally. Nobody could ignore it.
Every colonist on Home should be staring up into
space looking for *Corona.* Anybody with a radio should
be listening for an explanation. The colony should be
calling frantically, trying to find out why *Corona*
had lifted—if the colony still existed! Was it possible
that Lylard's race really did have weapons that powerful?

She had to know, but she could only function through
Mason's eyes. "Rick, can you see *anything*?"

"We're scanning." His voice trailed off. "Captain, it's
no use—the colony's gone! There's not a trace of it—it's
like it was never there."

"Gone?"

"My screen's on maximum magnification, and I'm
looking right at it—where it was, that is! The ground's
bare—no buildings, no canal, no crops. Everything's
just gone—even the crater our drive made. Captain, it
looks just like it did before we landed there."

Arlene glared at the alien. No force known to human science could have created the effects that Mason described! She had called Lylard's bluff and he had covered it by somehow obliterating the entire colony. She had blundered. She gathered herself up into a scream.

The scream never came. Wyckoff had crept near, and the grip of his hand on her shoulder had somehow lent her the strength of will to stop it, and the resolve then to have her own vengeance against the alien. It would die—maybe after the last surviving human being did, but surely, nonetheless. She knew the human will, and if there was no other way, then the surviving humans would demolish *Corona*.

While these thoughts had been whirling through Arlene's head the alien had nonchalantly turned his attention back to his console, and had just finished punching in another long sequence of commands.

"Captain!" The voice was not Lylard's. It came from the handset the captain still held. It was the first mate.

The urgency in his voice stirred another instinct in Arlene, and she answered promptly, though with detachment.

"Go ahead, Mason. I'm still here."

"So's the colony! I don't know how, Captain, but all of a sudden it's all back where it was! We've got Yasha Fu standing by on the ship-to-surface channel. He can't understand why I'm upset—he says nothing's happened since *Corona* lifted."

There was a long moment of silence, during which the alien gestured for Arlene to return the handset.

She gave it to him without explaining to the first mate.

Lylard turned it off. "Now, Captain, shall we discuss this some more?"

But it was Wyckoff's turn to talk again. Having gone into a sort of huddle with himself, he had emerged with an opinion—that what Mason described smacked of magic. As an ignorant man himself, Wyckoff constantly confronted illusion, and he knew its value to clever schemers. This lord, it seemed, could put on an impressive show, but then, so could most other educated men of Wyckoff's acquaintance. He was less convinced than Arlene was—she was genuinely shaken.

He became her voice. "Something new from the trick bag—like the weight?" he said, turning to the alien.

"What does it matter to you, you oaf, so long as I could do it." He turned to address Arlene. "I assure you, Captain, the colony really was gone. Perhaps you would like to see this done again? Perhaps you would like me to do it while you send one of your lifeboats to the surface to look for your colony? Yes, Captain, I know about those. Also, I control their use, so long as I have your ship. I could live on that planet if I had to, just as your kind can. I would not like to, but I could. I would not remain here to rot as you suggested.

"But perhaps you would now like to reassess your position?"

Arlene was already doing that. Lylard had mentioned something she had not previously considered important— the lifeboats. Now she did consider them, and their importance. If and when *Corona* went, those sixteen lifeboats still aboard her had to go up with her, else Lylard would still hold an insurmountable advantage over the more numerous humans on Home. Arlene needed more time to think, and since conversation seemed to have the effect of stopping the action, she decided to keep talking. "And if I do cooperate?"

"There will be no reason to molest your people," Lylard replied. "They may continue to enjoy the planet as best they can. I assure you, I do not want it. My only interest is to get home, and I am not an unreasonable being. I will not require an immediate decision of you. I will allow you time to deliberate upon it."

"I want to talk to Yasha Fu."

"Who?"

"Yasha Fu—the leader of the colony. I want his personal assurance that everything is all right."

"You do not trust your first mate?"

"I trust him. It's you I don't trust."

"Very well, Captain. Take this and call down." He handed the set back to her.

Yasha Fu did confirm that the colony was safe, though his voice was grave. He had been in communication with *Corona* long enough for Mason to explain in detail the circumstances of its departure.

Lylard made no effort to interfere in the discourse, and accepted the handset without comment when Arlene was finished with it. He had himself been engaged in conversation with his companion in the flowered robe, though on this occasion the interpreting device did not translate their words into English. After an exchange of some length that creature left, and in a few moments a pair of the Dorians arrived to escort the humans from Lylard's chamber.

They were taken to another, fairly bare room containing nothing but a sort of couch with extremely stiff cushions, where the two of them sat after the Dorians locked the door. For a long time neither spoke.

Wyckoff was first to break the silence. He grinned toothily, and tried to break the ice as well. "Well, at least the air's a little fresher." He paused, as though waiting for applause. It didn't come, so he moved on to a serious subject. "How do you think he did that trick, Arlene?"

Contrasted to her former silence, Arlene's response was strange. It was almost explosive, as though her words had been pent up until Wyckoff appeared with the key. "God, I wish I knew! I wish I knew for sure it *was* a trick."

"Maybe Yasha's right—nothing did happen. Maybe Lylard has a way to make everybody *think* he did something. I knew a dude once who could do stuff like that—hypnotize people. He made one guy think he was a duck, and . . ."

"Not possible, Wyckoff."

"How do you know what's possible for them?"

There was a brief pause, then hesitant words followed in a voice that at first sounded close to cracking. "You're right. I guess that's the part that really bothers me, Wyckoff," she snapped back, steadily regaining control, and striving to restore strength to her voice. "I don't know."

"What are we going to do?"

"At the moment, nothing. We have to have time to think this out. There was something strange about that whole episode. I wish I knew specifically what—it all happened so fast, though."

Wyckoff rose to his feet and started to pace. "You know what I've been thinking, Arlene?"

"What?"

"There are probably as many of us up here on the ship as there are aliens." He slammed a fist savagely into an open palm. "They got the jump on us before because they hit us when we weren't looking, but . . ."

"Exactly what I've been thinking, Wyckoff, and this is why we need to take our time and study the situation. We have to be ready for opportunity when it comes. Meanwhile . . ."

"Meanwhile, what?" He stopped to examine the tiny seam between the hatch and its sill.

Arlene rose to her feet and started to strip off the clumsy spacesuit, useless now anyhow without a helmet. "Even with the passwords there'd be problems for them, if you know what I mean, and they'd obviously rather have our help than not."

"I don't know about that, Arlene." The implication of what she was doing was not lost on him. It told him she was resigned to being captive in this capsule for a long time. Was she giving up?

"He wants us for something—either to fly the *Corona*, or to show him how to do it. If he was sure his people could handle it by themselves he'd have pushed us overboard a long time ago." She paused, and cast an annoyed look at Wyckoff, whose fiddling was suddenly getting to her. It might improve his situation, but it wasn't helping hers. Sympathetically, she twirled a lock of hair around thumb and forefinger and gritted her teeth.

"You don't think they could?"

"Maybe they could, but they evidently don't want to. It stands to reason that it's safer with us doing it. They've had one accident, so maybe they're not overly anxious to risk another." Then she blurted, as an afterthought, "I wonder what he meant by 'half a ship'— must you fidget like that?"

Wyckoff stopped short, paused an instant, then turned a red face toward her. "Sorry," he mumbled, then added, "beats me. Maybe his talking machine didn't get that part right." He settled down next to her and pulled the lock of hair from her fingers. His own were creeping up the nape of her neck.

She shivered and pulled away, as though for some reason she found the caress irritating. "No. No, I don't think so. But since you raised the subject, what do *you* think of that translator?"

Wyckoff acknowledged her mood with a flinch, then rose to his feet to resume pacing. "Pretty handy gadget to have around, I'd say."

"Uh-huh. I'd say so, too. But have you considered what else it means?"

Wyckoff responded with the obligatory pause. Why didn't people just say what they meant, like he did, and get it over with?

"The translator's a computer, Wyckoff. We have such computers, though none that can match the performance of that one. Ours will only do written translations, and then only within very narrow limits. Lylard's can handle the spoken languages, idioms and all, including some fairly modern ones. It must be drawing from an absolutely fabulous memory."

"So?"

"So, where did the data in that memory come from?"

The question threw him for an instant, then her meaning became clear. "I get it. The computer learned from somebody! It had to get its English from other men!"

"Exactly. There had to be an interspecies contact. The fact that we don't know anything about it means it wasn't one of their ships visiting Earth but one of ours, perhaps one of the missing ones, visiting them. But wherever it happened, there's an outside chance that the data base this thing draws from also contains the astrogational information we need to find our way home again."

She paused, behaving as though she expected the same exuberance from Wyckoff. When he didn't respond, she found her second wind. "Don't you understand, Wyckoff? I'm talking about our REAL home— Earth!" Her voice was suddenly creaky and her eyes had become misty.

She paused once again, sniffled and straightened, and redirected her gaze at Wyckoff. Her expression changed, to reflect a growing self-consciousness, as though she suddenly realized how melodramatic she must have sounded.

Wyckoff's reaction to all of this had been disappointing. It consisted chiefly of a look of alarm more likely engendered by her ebullience, rather than her words. But then, what else could she have expected? He'd made it clear long ago that Earth had not been so kind to him as it had been to her.

Arlene let this pass and continued, somewhat more subdued. "I can't help thinking that if we could take them—well, it'd be a whole lot better than blowing up the ship." She was smiling then, trying to look cheerful. It took all the will power she had just to keep that face on.

Neither implication was lost on Wyckoff. "Yeah, I think I see what you're getting at. If they need us, maybe we need them, too. But aren't you forgetting something? They've already got us."

"For the time being, yes," she answered resolutely. "But as you said, there are nine of us. This vessel is too small, even considering the physical size of the Dorians, to hold very many of them, and that means rough numerical equality even now. We might be able to juggle the odds even more."

"How?" Wyckoff grunted. He had thrown his weight against the couch in an effort to move it, and see what lay beneath. He could not—it appeared to be securely fixed to the deck.

"Hey! Easy," she protested. "Save that energy for when we really need it."

"Sorry. What were you going to say?" By then, Wyckoff was flat on the floor, trying to look underneath.

"What I meant was that when Lylard took *Corona*, he also took potluck. He got the crewmen who were aboard at the time, but most of our specialists are missing. Granted, he's got the bridge officers and Verity, so he could manage if he had to, with just these and the automated systems. But thanks to union feather-bedding, and the *Corona*'s size, he won't know who's really essential on long voyages and who isn't. She's a big ship and there are only five spacehands aboard out of almost fifty." She paused and smiled, as if to suggest that Wyckoff ought to read an implication into that. "I intend to convince him that all the crew is needed to handle the ship in deep space, and try to persuade him to bring more up."

"Neat—if you can pull it off. But how? He's not going to let us land again." Wyckoff doggedly continued his examination of the room. He had already been around it minutely at least four times. This time he seemed to be concentrating on knee level and below.

"Suppose I agreed to cooperate and told him there are specialists down on Home that I need, and without whom the ship could not be safely astrogated. What else could he do but let me have them?"

"And then we just wait for a chance to take them, right? Yeah, I can see how he might go for that," Wyckoff grunted. It had suddenly occurred to him that the couch might lift up from sockets set into the deck. He tried it and discovered it did.

He had also nearly dumped Arlene off. She squealed her annoyance and pummeled his shoulder.

"I'll fix it, all right?"

She did not respond to the specific question, but stepped aside to allow him to reseat the couch's legs. It was back to business for her. "A chance will eventually come if we can stall long enough. But even if it doesn't, it gives us a way to protect the people in the colony, if we refuse to leave without assurances that they're all right. That weapon—if that's what it is—has to have a finite range. And if we can get beyond that, maybe we can start thinking about saving ourselves."

"They've got the guns, Arlene. A lot of people will get killed."

"A lot of people would get killed anyway, Wyckoff. Maybe none would survive. Could you picture Lylard keeping any of us around after he got what he wanted— especially if he got *everything* he said he wanted? I can't. And remember what he said about the Jerrys? He would have left them down there to starve. He's a cold-blooded monster."

Wyckoff grunted a detached acknowledgement. His explorations had finally convinced him that there was no way out of the room, and no weapons-grade material within it. He now saw the couch simply as a couch— with a girl on it. He settled in and threw a lanky arm across Arlene's shoulder. This time she didn't pull away. Wyckoff held her close and in contemplative silence for long moments before adding, "Yeah, isn't he? I wonder what a Lord Temporal is, anyhow?"

She snuggled closer and literally purred her response. "Who knows? It sounds like a title of nobility, doesn't it? Maybe the machine couldn't translate it right and it came out that way. It doesn't matter. What do you think of my plan?"

Wyckoff shrugged, hesitated, and then answered by hedging. "It'll take some more thinking, Arlene, but anything beats nothing. I say what have we got to lose by trying it?" He paused, straightened, and picked at the couch's fabric, pulling a tiny object from one of its folds. It was about the size of a match head. He held it between thumb and forefinger, out where she could see it.

"What is that?" Arlene screeched, recoiling as though the thing he held might sting or bite.

"Beats me," Wyckoff replied nonchalantly. "It was just sticking in the cushion. It looks like some kind of pin with a fancy head."

Arlene seized it from him and examined it carefully, holding it up to the light. Her face contorted into a grimace of rage. "God! Wyckoff, it's a bug—a microphone. That devil's been listening to us!"

Wyckoff stared back at her, open-mouthed.

"I should have expected it. It's an old trick—the police and military do it. Segregate prisoners in pairs so they'll babble to each other . . ." She stopped short and paused, as though thinking deeply.

"Then we're okay, Arlene. You didn't mention . . . ?"

"I didn't, and you couldn't. But what about the others—there's no way to warn them. Unless they get lucky, like you did, they'll never notice the bugs."

"*Lucky*?" Wyckoff decided he was not only offended, but angry. Why did people always do that to him? And Arlene, of all people. She certainly ought to know better after the things she'd seen him do. "Luck had nothing to do with it," he snorted. "I knew . . ."

"You didn't even know what you had when you found it—you had to ask me. If I hadn't told you, you still wouldn't know. It was luck, Wyckoff—just plain dumb luck."

Wyckoff glared back at her, but said nothing more. He quietly moved away from her, seeking out the farthest corner of the chamber. He found that even there he could not sit still for very long. It was as if the deck beneath him bit into his flesh if he rested on it too long.

He looked over at Arlene, who also seemed both

retiring and agitated, whose face was sullen and whose gaze was glaring. He was suddenly aware of a growing urge to lash out, to strike at something. It did not matter what, so long as he possessed the power to crush it. He felt his muscles tensing, the blood pulsing in his temples and the hollow, empty feeling that comes to a man when the body dumps its adrenals. He made ready to spring.

"Flann! Stop!" The Dorian, Zheh-rhe', the lone male among them, only slightly bigger himself but far stronger than any of his surviving wives, easily moved Flann physically. Moving her mind was another matter, and for long, agonized instants after making the attempt, he was not even certain he had reached her.

But at length she did respond, and answered him, seemingly annoyed at the interruption.

Zheh-rhe' breathed a sigh of relief. He had not been a fixed part of the link, as Flann had been, but he had been able to feel it, and from the instant her control had started slipping, he had known it must be broken.

Abruptly, Flann realized what had happened, too. Integrated deeply into the linkage, she had not been aware of any problems. It had been like looking at a large object from too close a range, where there are distortions of vision that can only be corrected by seeing from a distance. Failure had not been apparent to her in her linked state. "Will they be safe?" she asked, with genuine concern.

"For a short time, perhaps. But we must move them, and soon. Wyckoff must have more room. He must be able to keep away from her."

"Back to their own ship? Will Lylard permit this?"

"He would no doubt refuse if asked; therefore, we shall not ask. We will move them on our own initiative and take the risk. The temporal is enormously busy—too busy to notice."

"A pity we failed," the female remarked. "We need a victory so. If only I could have gained control of him—

established a permanent link—it would have given us an insight into everything the humans did."

"It was against all odds for it to work. They are, after all, an alien species totally unrelated to us. Still, it was worth trying, and I am glad we did; unless, of course, he kills her."

"I had higher hopes," Flann admitted. "Wyckoff is so—so impressionable. His head was a comfortable place for me."

"For me as well," Zheh-rhe' replied. _Too bad we never found another like it._

This last was unspoken, though Flann heard it, and that, in and of itself, was remarkable. Only occasionally could lengthy or complex thoughts make the leap from mind to mind. Emotions, simple ideas, solitary words—these were relatively easy within the Dorian species, and almost as easy with Wyckoff. Zheh-rhe's name, for instance, had passed from Dorian to English in just that manner.

This was why the Dorians had risked the experiment just completed, which had failed so miserably. They had hoped that upon discovery of the first hidden microphone, the human captain would be concentrating on the passwords. At that instant Flann had pounced, forging the link as firmly as she could, doing her best to reinforce whatever emotions Captain Graham experienced.

And she had. Across the line between the species, unfortunately, there was little certainty. The strongest signal prevailed, to be seized upon by the most sensitive mind, and while Flann understood enough of the human language to pick out the information she sought, she had not been given the opportunity. The human captain screened her thoughts—not intentionally, of course, but with emotion so powerful it threatened her own safety—with rage so enormous it overwhelmed all else.

Worse, in her efforts to pierce this barrier, Flann had added her own strength of will, and reinforced this, enveloping the far more sensitive Wyckoff. It made a veritable emotional bomb of him.

The Dorians had known of the risk, of course. Dorians had lived with their empathic faculty for a long time. While they were alone as a species it had been a survival mechanism—an evolutionary crutch. Dorians did not wage war against themselves as other species of sapients did. No Dorian could stand that kind of pain.

And perhaps it could be said to still promote survival, though in the view of modern Dorr, the trait was a curse and not a boon. The coming of the temporals had made it so, and Dorr, so safe from itself, had learned to fear and obey outsiders.

On the other hand, discovery of the humans, down on the planet they called Home, had been enigmatic for another reason—isolated sensitivity to Dorian minds, though not in any great degree to each others'.

This was part of the reason the situation between Wyckoff and the captain was potentially so dangerous— were misfortune to befall Wyckoff, the Dorians would feel it almost as though it had befallen one of them. They could therefore not permit any such thing, and must protect him.

Flann had used the interval to regain her composure and strength. This done, she addressed the obvious subject: "What next?"

"We must try other ways, Flann, and keep on trying until we find a method that works. We must regain access to Dorr. We must deliver our people, and the humans' desire to find their own home again will be the key to that. We have been given the opportunity. It is up to us to find the courage to seize it."

Zheh-rhe' took Flann's arm and led her to a rack containing two Dorian-sized space suits. "We must move them one at a time, Flann, and we must be very careful. A chance like this may never come again."

Chapter Twenty-One

"Now what? Look at the fix we're in." Wyckoff was adamant. He had been pacing as best he could in freefall, pushing himself off first one bulkhead and then another, and every now and then he let loose with an outburst like this one. "If you'd kept your mouth shut about blowing up the ship, we wouldn't be locked up in here." He pushed his way to a position from which he could look straight at her.

This wasn't simply a lovers' quarrel anymore. Their relationship was in a bad way, and Arlene refused to believe this was her fault, or that she had been the one to change. The most persuasive evidence argued for her side. Wyckoff *had* changed since coming aboard *Corona*— changed drastically.

The difference now was that Arlene was having trouble perceiving the metamorphosis as beneficial, and Wyckoff as friendly. In the beginning he had been docile and controllable. At the moment he was neither of these things—he was a loose cannon. Arlene had never imagined he could be this way.

She was scared of him, so she cowered in a corner and tried to ignore him. She hoped if she did he'd stop screaming at her. He had before, on the first two occasions.

But he seemed more persistent this time. He hung there, glaring. She could finally stand it no longer, so she hurled a recrimination. "Why didn't *you* think to check for bugs?"

"Because I'm supposed to be the dumb one and you're supposed to be the smart one. Besides, I did look. I'm the one who found it—remember?"

He was right, of course. She should have. But she wasn't about to tell him that. They were in a fix, but maybe the aliens were, too. Maybe that was why nothing was happening. There was a certain consolation in such thoughts.

They had seen neither hide nor hair of Lylard after the initial conversation. Since the bug had been destroyed he'd evidently assumed they wouldn't say anything useful to him. They had been taken to separate chambers and held in isolation for what they judged was about four days.

They had no idea why. The teddies had come, bringing their helmets, and hustled them into their suits. They were taken separately to *Corona* on the tender and once aboard brought here. On the way, Arlene had seen something that made her gasp in disbelief, but which also convinced her the aliens could never make use of the *Corona*.

On the way to the stern locks she had seen teddies in suits working on the hull. A section of the skin had been removed, and trailed the ship on a long line. They had been cutting through the inner hull during the minute or so she had been able to watch.

The rear locks had gaped wide open, and it had been clear that there was no air in most of the stern half of the ship. This was confirmed by an observation that the axial elevator shaft was plugged between deck "22" and deck "Z"—that part of *Corona* which had been the passengers' section.

Why the aliens had done this was still a complete mystery, but it was readily apparent that if they continued, and unless they braced the ship exceedingly well, it would probably not be able to stand the acceleration the Aschenbrenners were capable of delivering, and *Corona* would never again be capable of landing on anything larger than one of Home's small moons.

Wyckoff must have seen everything Arlene had, of course, but she had avoided discussing it with him because, in addition to the present strained condition of their relationship, they could not be sure their quarters, where they were now confined, were not also bugged. Reason suggested it would be far better for the colony to let the aliens discover their mistakes the hard way.

Of course, it might not work out like that even if she kept quiet. Verity and Mason would certainly be aware of the danger, and might discuss it among themselves. And Lylard would certainly be listening when they did.

Even so, there was still the human hole card—sabotage—whether Lylard swallowed her story about needing all those crewmen or not. He wouldn't if he had listened attentively. If he worked very hard he and the Dorians could probably prevent insurrection, but sabotage was another matter entirely. It would be next to impossible to prevent knowledgeable crewmen, dedicated to *Corona*'s destruction, from accomplishing that with relative ease. Somebody, sometime, would get the chance.

As captain, Arlene must be resigned to that end. She must assume that death for everybody aboard lay at the end of the trail, whether by asphyxiation, starvation, or a bullet from the aliens' guns. The best the humans could hope for was that Lylard would not molest the colony before he left.

It was not Lylard's mystery weapon that worried the captain anymore. As time passed, evidence mounted that this secret weapon might indeed have been a bluff— that maybe Lylard wouldn't harm the colony with it because he couldn't. Certainly, visibly flattening the colony would have been far more convincing than what he really had done—or appeared to have done. But bluff or not, by using it, Lylard had gained more credible weapons—*Corona*'s lifeboats. A couple of them, sent crashing into the settlement, would be enough to bring human civilization on Home to an early and abrupt end—if that occurred to him.

Even with so much idle time on her hands, and no matter how carefully Mason's words were analyzed, a theory that would explain how the aliens had managed still eluded the captain. It was not simply that she lacked first-hand information—the first mate was neither stupid nor inexperienced. He would have reported exactly what he saw. He had used tamperproof instruments—or so they might have appeared but for Fu's disclaimer.

All things considered, Wyckoff's mass hypnosis hypothesis, outlandish as it had sounded, could still demand first place among the possible explanations. Nothing else came remotely close to fitting Mason's observation. Certainly, even a race capable of generating artificial shipboard gravity couldn't destroy something completely and then recreate it.

All speculation abruptly ended with a resounding thud. Wyckoff let out a blood-curdling scream, and Arlene felt herself tugged rudely from the corner where she had been huddling.

Dazed, jolted so abruptly out of the darkness of her concentration that she thought at first the drive was on and the ship was being moved, she strained to listen for sounds that *Corona* was breaking up. For a moment she held her breath, convinced the hull would be breached at any moment and the air would rush out.

Arlene waited, terrorized, holding her breath as though this would do any good against hard vacuum, but nothing else happened.

She pushed against the bulkhead and rose to her feet, and found that weight, though not her normal weight, was back. There had been none of the pre-launch sequence warnings that the drive was being activated—unless their circuits had been damaged or disconnected. She waited pensive moments more, then promptly forgot all her fears when she glanced down at Wyckoff.

He had landed hard, having been floating high to begin with. Like Humpty Dumpty, he had assumed a lofty perch where he could gaze down at everything. Like Humpty Dumpty, his fall had been a great one.

She rushed over to him and pulled him out of the corner. He was bleeding from a cut on the back of his head, which evidently had struck a wall cabinet as he descended. The blood was running down the back of his neck.

She rushed into the adjoining head for a wet towel and mopped it away, then pushed back one of his closed eyelids. His eyeball had rolled back, which usually indicated a concussion. She knew she had to get him to his feet, and struggled to drag him away from the wall.

She could not have managed at Earth-normal, but like she, he was lighter, so at length she managed to get him to the corner of the bunk and prop him upright. He started coming out of it, so she left him there while she rummaged through the head's tiny medicine cabinet for bandages.

By the time she returned he was conscious again, but still dazed and glassy-eyed.

She took the wet towel and blotted away more blood, this time provoking a wince of pain. He grabbed the towel away from her.

"All right, do it yourself," she said, rising to her feet. "I guess you're going to be okay after all. You're still your stubborn self." Her tone was sarcastic rather than angry. Their anger had fled in the face of the crisis.

"What happened? Are we moving?"

"I can't tell. If we are I don't think it'll be for long, the shape the ship's in. I suppose they could have circumvented the controls, though that'd give them only manual capability. It might explain why there wasn't any warning before it happened. If that's the case, you might be wise to stay where you are. You can't fall off the deck."

But just as she said that, they both did. Suddenly, they were both plunging toward the ceiling, which fortunately, being overhead, did not contain any furniture, as the regular deck did. And the attraction, when it hit, was far weaker than the first assault had been. They collapsed together in a pile, screaming.

"Grab yourself a strap, Wyckoff. We're not under way. That's a gravitational field, and it may reverse again."

They crawled to the bulkhead and grasped the handholds that now lay limp on the ceiling. These were designed to be used in freefall, and couldn't be relied upon to take the strain if the field reversed again, but they were better than nothing. And certainly the field had to reverse again—the aliens could hardly leave it as it was.

"Now what?" Wyckoff was hanging on tightly to his strap with one hand and feeling the back of his head with the other.

"You might thank me for pulling you out of the corner. You'd have hit that cabinet again if I hadn't."

"I've been picking on you pretty bad, haven't I?"

"Yes, you have."

"I'm sorry, Arlene. I guess I just had to blame somebody. But none of this is your fault. It's mine. I'm the one who brought Jerry into the ship."

That was it. He didn't say any more, and Arlene appeared to be thankful. At any rate, she did not respond with recriminations of her own.

The field did reverse again, but this time the increase was slow and gradual. First, it went off entirely, then built up in the opposite direction, so even if they hadn't been holding tightly to the straps they would have been all right.

Again on the deck, they took no further chances, but got into the bunk and strapped in tightly. For a while Arlene poked and prodded Wyckoff, trying to keep him awake because she knew sleep could be dangerous to him with the concussion he had.

He dropped off anyway, and she eventually gave up on her effort and fell asleep herself.

When she awoke, there was a difference. Her weight was now a full gee. A glance at the monitor screen in the overhead told her that a full watch had elapsed since the field had gone on. While they had slept, the aliens must have managed to stabilize it. It remained to be seen what other progress Lylard might have made.

Wyckoff continued to snore. His breathing appeared to be normal but Arlene decided to wake him anyhow and make certain he was all right. "Wyckoff, wake up. It's morning."

When he failed to stir she gave him a frantic poke, after which he snorted ambiguously. She gave him another, harder, and he rose stiffly against the restraints, moaned and winced, then felt the top of his head.

"Got a headache, huh?" Arlene's question was followed by a sigh of relief.

"And how!"

"I'll get you something for it. Wait here."

"Lylard got our drive going after all, I guess," he said, gulping the medication and chasing it with water.

"No. But he's obviously trying to modify the ship. I wish I knew why, and I wish I could be sure lack of passwords really will stop him from taking it out. Lylard has obviously got the technical reach on us. Generating gravitational fields is a long way past our science."

"Maybe he'll fool around and wreck it, and we won't have to."

"That's the part that really worries me. He's acting so confident, and experiment on the scale he seems to be using would be foolish unless he really didn't need our help."

For the sake of Arlene's composure, Wyckoff had kept his own similar opinion to himself. He saw Lylard as a practical being, even if he wasn't human. He believed Lylard knew how to get to people, and through people, to get what he wanted. He wasn't 100 percent certain Lylard hadn't already made the grade. *I trust Rick*, he thought, *but I'll never be sure about Verity again—not after the way he helped Hamil. But how do I keep her from thinking about that?*

Change the subject, came the answer. Wyckoff released his restraints and climbed gingerly out of bed, still feeling rocky. "I wonder if they'll ever let us out of here?" He walked over to the door and tried the "open" button. The door wouldn't budge.

"Don't waste your time. It's still locked as tight as ever." Arlene was rummaging around in the freezer. "Want something to eat?"

"Yeah, sure. I guess so."

Arlene popped a couple of dinners into the microwave and waited ten seconds or so while they heated. She took one out and placed it on the counter in front of Wyckoff. "Eat. Enjoy life while you can. The future doesn't look too bright for us."

Wyckoff slid into one of the high stools that were bolted to the deck next to the counter, picked up a fork, and dug in. He had raised a bite to his lips and was poised to gobble when something clicked in the door. On *Corona*, doors made such noises only when cardkeys were stuck in them. He got no further with breakfast.

Arlene had heard it, too. She was still over at the microwave, lifting out her own food. She put it down, picked up the knife she had used to cut the tough plastic seals off the packages, and slid it down the counter to Wyckoff.

He quickly tucked it into his waistband and covered it up with his shirttail, then assumed that peculiarly wide-eyed and disarming gaze he affected so well.

The door had receded completely by then, though the opening was hardly filled. Two Dorians stood within it, flanking a wheeled translating robot and pointing stun weapons at the humans. One of them obviously understood human nature pretty well. With a nod, and a wave of his weapon, he motioned the humans away from the door.

As they backed away and the Dorians entered, Wyckoff was almost certain the slightly larger one was Jerry. Except for the hectic episode in the control room, he had not seen Dorians close enough together to permit comparison, but now he could see that they did differ slightly in physical detail, the same as human beings did.

Wyckoff's retreat had taken him all the way to the bunk. So far, he had been following Arlene's lead. She had already reached the bunk and was sitting on the edge. He didn't want to do that—he wanted to retain his mobility. He had already decided to try to take these two, though he intended to do it without using the knife.

The Dorians obviously were not going to make it easy for him to try anything. They always kept the robot between them. "Sit, Wyckoff. Beside the captain." The larger Dorian jabbed savagely with his weapon.

Wyckoff decided to wait a while to make his move so he did as the Dorian ordered. He promised himself he would remain cool, and pick his time with care. He could not totally suppress his animosity, however. "Is that you, Jerry?" he asked through a snarl.

"Yes, Wyckoff."

Arlene suddenly found her tongue. She had had composure but now suddenly lost it. It was like a spring inside her had suddenly unwound. "What do you want, Jerry? What's happening to my ship? What have you done to the rest of my crew?"

Wyckoff was startled by her actions, and for a moment was afraid she might try to jump the Dorian. She had never liked him very well to begin with.

But Jerry stepped even farther away and remained on his guard. "Your crew is fine, Captain. For the moment. So is the colony. As for your ship, the modifications we are making will be beneficial and may even lead you back to your own world again. That is one of the things I came here to discuss."

Arlene's face lit up. She was silent, contemplating what that meant, so Wyckoff gained the floor.

"Just like nothing ever happened, huh, Jerry?" Wyckoff's hackles rose steadily. "Like you didn't ever double-cross us?"

"I understand how you feel, Wyckoff. I . . ."

"You do, huh . . ."

". . . Know how it must have looked to you, but . . ."

"How'd you like to have your tail pulled out by the roots, huh? Put the plazer down and see what happens."

"Here!" Jerry's hand dropped as the volume of his voice rose. He took three rapid steps forward, and before Wyckoff could rise, he found a plazer dangling under his nose in Jerry's limp hand.

Wyckoff shook his head. "Uh-uh. No, you don't. I'm onto you, Jerry. I reach for that and your buddy pops me—uh-uh."

Jerry dropped the weapon on Wyckoff's foot and, turning to his companion, said, "Give him your weapon, also. We must not waste time."

Wyckoff's mouth was hanging wide open by then. Popeyed, he turned to Arlene, who sat rigidly still as the other Dorian dropped its plazer at her feet, and then back to the Dorians, eyes searching them for signs of the presence of more subtle armament.

"We are now totally unarmed, Wyckoff. You have our weapons, plus the knife. We have proven our good faith. Now it is your turn. I beg you to listen."

"How'd you know about the knife?"

"I knew, Wyckoff. Does it matter how?"

Wycoff stared down at his waist. The hilt of the knife bulged out in a lump, but not enough to suggest that was what it was. He accepted this as the explanation, but even though things were apparently as Jerry said they were, he was still wary. In his experience an adversary simply did not do a thing like this unless he had some other advantage. He continued, cautiously, to look for the gimmick he was sure was buried somewhere in this peculiar situation.

Arlene was somewhat less affected, perhaps because she had never been as wrapped up in Jerry as Wyckoff had been. She also recognized a possible deception. There was, after all, no way they could tell what lay outside the door. For all they knew there might be half a dozen guns on the other side. However, practicality ruled her even more sternly than it did Wyckoff when her vessel was concerned. She wanted to know the details. "If you want us to believe any of this, Jerry," she said grimly, "then you'd better have a good explanation for what you did."

"As I said," Jerry replied, "that was part of our purpose in coming." Turning to Wyckoff, he added, "I really do understand how you must feel about that, and I am sorry."

"Yeah, sure."

Apparently, the Dorian decided that Arlene's sympathies were greater. He addressed his remarks to her from then on. "Circumstances make all of us what we are, Captain. It is not a thing of the will. We Dorians are prisoners as much as you are."

"Prisoners! With the run of the ship?"

"Surely, Captain, you will concede that the threat of immediate force is not the only way a people may be coerced. Our entire race is hostage to Lylard and the other temporals. So is Lady Bane's and so, I now think, is your own. Wherever temporals go, they dominate. My own words should be sufficient proof to you that they must have reached Earth." He paused to watch the growing horror on Arlene's face.

But the captain did not reveal her emotions in words, and Jerry did not belabor the point. He might nurture the seed of fear he found in the captain, and watch it grow, but this growth maintained its own pace. "As for having the run of the ship," he continued, "it is possible for us to move this freely only because Lylard is now all alone, and enormously busy, so he cannot keep close track of us."

"But you're helping him. He was trapped up here until you got us into this. Now, you're tearing up my ship . . ."

"We are modifying it, Captain; making it better. In that respect Lylard's aims coincide with ours. In fact, none of it could be done without Lylard, because only Lylard knows what must be done and how to do it. Do not confuse intemperate habits with incompetence. Lylard is a temporal, and there are no incompetent temporals."

Wyckoff had thus far been content to let Arlene do their talking. He still could not bring himself to address Jerry in a civil manner. His words were intentionally surly. "So far, Jerry, all you've done is whine about how great he is and how helpless you are. What are you trying to tell us?"

"I am trying to tell you exactly that, Wyckoff . . ."

"All I see is one critter with stinky breath and paint all over his ugly face—one of him, and a lot of you, doing whatever he wants. Men won't take that, Jerry. Maybe Dorians will, but men won't."

Jerry's tone remained flat, thanks to the transmitter, but his mannerisms betrayed a great agitation. He was squirming like a worm contemplating the hook. "Wyckoff, will you listen! You are as impulsive as Lady Bane. She . . ."

"That's the second time you've mentioned Lady Bane. Who's Lady Bane? Is she the other big one?"

"Yes, Wyckoff; the Kruj'jan."

"What about her?"

"It is unimportant at this moment, Wyckoff. Lady Bane is another of Lylard's hostages. She is a barbarian—her people are backward savages who are preoccupied with weapons, and with making war."

"Sounds like she's the one we should be doing business with," Wyckoff said, turning to Arlene.

Jerry's exasperation began to show even more. "I said

I had no time to waste, Captain, and I don't. I came
here to explain how things are. I thought you would at
least be interested in protecting yourselves and your
people. If that is not so, tell me now. We Dorians will
try to find another way."

"Is he listening?"

"Who, Captain?"

"Lylard."

"Of course not. Why should you think so?"

"Never mind. What is it you want to tell us?"

Jerry settled back, bracing himself on his tail, which
he held stiffly. "I said I would explain how things are,
and within the limits of time left to us I will. The facts
are, Captain, that the temporals dominate whatever
they touch. They can do this because they are not
confined, as we are, to a single progressive interval of
time. They can move outside it at will. But that has
been demonstrated to you already." He paused.

"What?" Arlene's word had been uttered as a long,
drawn-out hiss, but it was apparently comprehensible
to the machine, and Jerry understood.

"What happened to your colony—what your first mate
saw—was real, Captain. The colony was really gone.
Think about it for a moment and it will be obvious. The
planet below appeared as it had before you landed,
because Lylard's module had moved along the timeline
to a point beyond your view."

Arlene was staring at the Dorian with her mouth
hanging open. Wyckoff, whose ignorance permitted him
less appreciation for the significance of the statement,
was not impressed. "I knew all along it was a trick," he
said smugly.

"Wait a minute, Wyckoff." Arlene had reached out
and grasped him physically, clinging to his arm as though
it represented reality to her. "Lylard said he watched
us land. We had been searching for him—we had seen
him before we got close . . ."

"The same, Captain. A fraction of a second out of

phase with real time—into what temporals call 'stasis'—and Lylard's module was effectively invisible."

"He was waiting—he knew we were coming!"

"Are you beginning to understand what I meant when I said he was formidable?"

"I'm not sure I even believe you. Wait a minute. Why should somebody who could see the future have an accident?"

"Because he could not see the future, Captain. That is to say, he could not see his own future."

"I don't know what you mean."

"It is very complicated, Captain. We cannot take the time to discuss it now. There are other, more important matters we must cover. The capability I just described has permitted the temporal to dominate vast regions of space and countless races within it. They . . ."

"Is it some kind of empire?"

"Oh, no, Captain, it is only a step above anarchy. When you know more you will see why that not only can be, but must be. But please control your curiosity and allow me to concentrate on explanations that are really important."

"I'm sorry. I didn't mean to do that."

"You are lost, Captain."

"Huh? Yes, we are. How . . ."

"We were among you humans aboard your ship for a long time, Captain. Even if we had not picked up smatterings of your language, and, of course, we did, we would have understood that simply from your behavior. And then there is that faint area on *Corona*'s bridge where the deck bears scars. We see a little differently than humans do, Captain. Our eyes polarize the light that enters them."

"Oh. Go on, Jerry." She was becoming an avid listener.

"Lylard's astrogation computer is aboard this module, Captain. It is fully functional, and even now my companions are laboring to tie it into your control system."

"But he said his spatial module crashed. We found the wreckage, and there aren't any engines on this part . . .

"And you assumed his ship was like the *Corona*? Ah, but Captain Graham, it isn't. That's the fortunate part."

"I know designs would differ, but . . ."

"I cannot explain Lylard's preference, Captain. It is enough for me to understand that for some reason the designers did not follow the human custom of using small shuttles. Certainly, that seems a safer method, and eliminates the possibility of misfortune such as befell Lylard, but perhaps it was more advantageous to be able to lift large cargos. Whatever the reason, all the instrumentation was fortuitously aboard the orbiting module, which, by the way, is the reason your ship is being, as you put it, torn up. It is more efficient, since there is room, to bring the entire module aboard instead of tearing systems out. This way a few cables connect the two systems without risk of damage to the components. It was practical."

"Perhaps," Arlene grunted, "provided she'll hold together under thrust."

"There is no danger, Captain. Lylard will make certain it is safe. Not only that, as you surely have noticed, his module now supplies *Corona* with an artificial gravitational field. This can be adjusted very finely. It can be synchronized with the engines' thrust and used to cancel out any stresses that appear. *Corona* should even be safer than she was before."

"All right!" Wyckoff was now interested again, and seemed friendlier. "Then all we have to do is wait until he's finished and take over again, right?"

"That is our intention, Wyckoff," Jerry replied.

"We hope we will be successful, but it will certainly not be that simple. He must not know that it is happening, though he will assume we are plotting the attempt. Among the temporals, suspicion is a cardinal virtue."

"Like you said, he's all alone, Jerry. Unless you guys are planning to help him some more, that is."

The Dorian either did not recognize the sarcasm or did not care about it. In any event, his response ignored it. "We will have to maintain that appearance,

Wyckoff. So will you humans. Lylard has his counterpart to your passwords. Lylard alone will possess the routing keys we need to use his astrogation computer.

"So you see," he said, turning to face the humans, "we may, for a time, have a balanced situation—Lylard's computer and your vessel, your passwords and Lylard's keys, or none of us go anywhere. And for the time that that situation persists, all of us will also stay alive."

"I don't see how that can possibly work, Jerry. Lylard's been content to keep us prisoner—he hasn't approached us with any kind of proposition yet."

"He will, Captain. As I said, Lylard has been very busy. Also, he thinks he already has complete control of your ship, and that your present value to him is as simple hostages. When he discovers he cannot activate your space drive, you will have another encounter."

"When do you think that will be, Jerry?"

"When I tell him, and when I suggest that your cooperation may be gained by promising to return you to your homeworld. To make it ever more persuasive, perhaps I could also suggest this as a reason you have not yet destroyed your vessel. You could do that, I presume?"

Arlene allowed him to presume, and did not respond vocally.

Wyckoff took up pursuit of the original thought. "And then, when we find out where these keys are, we take over?"

"Essentially, that will be the plan, Wyckoff. But, as usual, you oversimplify. You see, we already know where the keys are—Lylard carries them on his person. The real difficulty lies in determining which keys are safe to use. Some are not, but only Lylard knows which ones these are."

"What's wrong with them?"

"They are only partly functional, Wyckoff, and if used, they will fail. Temporals employ these as traps for the unwary, who may attempt to do what we now contemplate."

"Then we'll just have to persuade Lylard to tell us which are which," Wyckoff retorted, grinning wolfishly. In his mind he once again envisioned a brazier full of glowing coals, and an array of pincers, but this time the victim was Lylard, not a human being.

"Are you suggesting torture? Would that work on a human being, Wyckoff?"

"Maybe—on some of them."

"I do not think it would work on Lylard. I think I know what he would do, and I do not think he would suffer for a moment."

"No? Why not?"

"He would offer us a key, and we would have no way of knowing it was the wrong one until it failed, and we were marooned. Once we were, he would have restored his bargaining position."

"That's when I'd really whomp him."

"In order to persuade him to repeat the procedure? Sooner or later *Corona*'s fuel would be exhausted. The nearer that time you came, the stronger he would get. Lylard is stubborn, and he would gamble on himself. I know him." He paused, as though to let this sink in.

"I have already suggested a far less risky way," Jerry continued, "one that preserves all options: cooperation, while we patiently observe Lylard and attempt to identify the keys he uses."

"He's going to let us sit there and watch him?" Wyckoff chuckled.

"No, of course he isn't. Not you, or I, or any human or Dorian, Wyckoff. No, that task will fall to Lady Bane. I sincerely hope she is equal to it."

"Why wouldn't he be just as careful with her around?"

"Because he takes her even less seriously than we do, Wyckoff. We humor her and defer to her, principally because compared to us, she is large and dangerous and more easily controlled with wit than might. But Lady Bane is only an ignorant barbarian, whom Lylard, not entirely with justification, believes lacks the capacity to comprehend the technology that surrounds her. He allows her freedom of movement."

"It doesn't sound as though you like her very much," Arlene replied.

"She can be very tiresome at times, Captain. No doubt you will someday discover this for yourself if you live very long."

"Yet you seem to think she will help?"

"I think so, Captain. Lady Bane appears to be fascinated with you humans—in particular, with yourself—though it is my opinion she regards you as a rival."

"A rival—why?"

"You are another imperious female. You have high station, just as she does, and you command males."

"I see."

"Perhaps you do, perhaps you don't, Captain. In any event, Lady Bane is in a position to help and I think she could be persuaded to join in the mutiny. After all, she wants your job."

"*My job!*"

"Well, actually it's your station she covets, Captain, as though ability depended on position. Kruj'jan logic is exceedingly strange. She'll probably try to assassinate you someday, when she's finished studying you, but you should be reasonably safe for the time being. I think she'd probably like to be a temporal, too."

Arlene gazed at the little Dorian for a long moment. "I don't think I like that idea, Jerry. I'm not sure I like any of your ideas."

"There's something we haven't talked about Captain, and that's this: What might the temporals be doing to Earth right now? As things are, your people would be helpless against them, because they're time-bound.

"But suppose together we managed to overthrow Lylard? You then will command a temporal vessel, and Earth will become a temporal power. Do you understand what that would mean?"

She stared at him as she pondered this remark.

Wyckoff interrupted this, with a remark that decided

her at last. "He makes sense, Arlene. Right now, we're sitting here on our hands, doing nothing while Lylard's rebuilding the ship. You and Jerry both said he was smart. What if he finds a way to get it working by himself? What happens to us when he doesn't need us anymore?" He answered his own question with a gesture, drawing an index finger briskly across his throat.

Jerry seemed to understand that. In any event, it was his cue to chime in. "He'll try that, too, Captain. Remember, now that he has the resources of your colony, time literally means nothing to him."

"You'd let him? You wouldn't stop him?" Arlene was livid.

"I have a world of my own to save, Captain. I wouldn't stop him. We Dorians and Lady Bane would carry on alone, and do what we have to do, as best we can. We are not as strong as a combination that included you humans would be, and we have a greater problem. You see, for us, simply to kill Lylard is not a solution. Both our cultures have long been embedded in temporal fiefs, as yours may soon be, and there is no way to separate them from temporal influence again. For us, the best that can be expected would be a substitution of overlords. We cannot permit the rest of the temporals to select one of their own. We must take the power for ourselves."

"I see." She looked at Wyckoff, trying to find for herself the same rationality he seemed to have acquired about the situation.

His returning gaze was calm, firm, and reassuring. He wanted a commitment from her to match his own. He trusted the Dorian again.

She seemed not quite ready to give him a commitment; not as ready to trust her people and her ship to creatures whose conniving had already deprived her of her rightful control of it without a great deal more reassurance. "I want to think this out, Jerry. While I'm thinking, I want my crew freed."

"Captain! Be reasonable! I cannot do what you are

asking—Lylard would never permit it. We Dorians are free only because he needs our labor." He turned to Wyckoff. "You must dissuade her, Wyckoff."

But Wyckoff was not so disposed, and said nothing. He and Arlene had just finished a long interval of bad relations. It had been unpleasant for both of them, and while it had endured, they had both made their most grievous errors yet. They did much better, he thought, as a team, and if this was what she wanted, that would be his way, too.

Arlene was still waiting for her answer. "I can't take everything you say on faith, Jerry. I need some proof of it."

"I have given you arms, Captain."

"Plazers, Jerry? Mere ticklers? And only two of these against all of you, and who knows what else Lylard has?"

"Very well, Captain. I think you take foolish risks, but I will arrange for you to talk to the other humans."

"Both of us will go."

"You double the risk, Captain," the Dorian protested. "There is no logical reason . . ."

"I am the captain," Arlene replied, her jaw jutting out like a granite boulder. "I command this ship—not you, not the temporal, not anybody else—and logic has nothing to do with it."

The gesture provoked a long pause in the alien before he answered, and what might have been his race's equivalent of a sigh of resignation; the humans couldn't tell. "Agreed, then."

"And I also want to talk to Lady Bane."

"Captain, your demands become impossible, and you keep adding more of them with every concession I make. I have explained about the Kruj'jan—she is best left to we Dorians, who know her. Lady Bane is fully capable of clawing your throat out in a fit of anger."

"I have claws of my own, Jerry. Besides, your male ego is showing—you presume we won't get along. Maybe she'd appreciate a chance to talk to another woman. I know I would." She continued to press her point by gazing at the Dorian, and by watching, out of the corner of her eye, the crack of a smile that was beginning to wash across Wyckoff's face.

Jerry took it longer than a human being would have, but eventually the silence got to him. "Very well, Captain. Your position is irrational, dangerous, and foolishly places our entire conspiracy in jeopardy. Nevertheless, as you say, you are the captain."

"Fine. Let's get started."

"Not so fast, Captain. Preparations must be made."

"Now, Jerry, don't give me any excuses. The only preparation you have to make is to ensure that Lylard doesn't see us. That ought to be easy if he's as busy as you say."

Jerry protested no further. He turned to his companion, and the robot translated his words to her for the humans: "Go, Flann. Locate the Lord Lylard and inform the others of what we are about to do. Also, we shall require a Kruj'jan-English link from the central computer to be routed into Bane's terminal. Attend to it."

"That will be dangerous," Flann replied. "It will be necessary to mislabel it, so Lylard does not become curious and intercept."

"Yes, it will, but if we must take this clumsy human to Bane's quarters, she will be less conspicuous without a robot following her."

The humans did not read sarcasm in the remark, of course, but they presumed it was there, just as they presumed that Jerry's face contained a frown, although they could not recognize it.

The three of them waited in silence until Flann returned.

Chapter Twenty-Two

"They could surely have found some better quarters for you." Arlene gazed around the sparsely furnished chamber down in what had been the passengers' section on the outward voyage. Almost everything removable had, of course, been stripped from *Corona* and taken to the town that was growing on Home.

"I guess they figured all we needed was a place to eat and sleep," Mason replied, "and I must admit we've been comfortable enough, even before we had weight. Verity's been driving himself nutty trying to figure that one out. He claims he could if he could get into the computer."

Verity took the opportunity to assert his position: "We've had this in theory for more than half a century, Captain. It's the hardware that was missing. When am I going to get a look at theirs, Captain?"

"I don't know, Verity. Maybe never. For all I know we humans may be sticking our noses in a rat trap. The Dorians claim they're our friends, and that they want to work with us, but they obviously don't trust us, and I certainly don't trust them." She turned to the first mate, her silent gaze a cue for him to express his opinion.

"They brought you here, Captain. And from what you've told us so far, I can see logic in what they've done. After all, they were down there with us and our ship, and meanwhile, their only way home was in a decaying orbit. Given the same set of circumstances in reverse, would we have risked having them say no?"

"They could have just waited for Lylard to starve," Verity volunteered. "My calculations show that almost certainly would have happened before the orbit became critical."

"The Dorians aren't like that," Wyckoff boomed. "Besides, Lylard might not be the kind that would have waited to check out that way. He might have decided to blast his module, instead. And anyway," he turned to Arlene, "he said they didn't know which of those keys were booby trapped."

"Well, that's a point for Jerry, guys," the captain sighed. "He claims that Lylard has to get back—that if he doesn't, another temporal will take his place. Of course, he could be making all of it up—he's already made some of it up."

"What? What'd he make up, Arlene?"

"My, but you really *have* forgiven him, haven't you, Wyckoff? He's got you jumping down people's throats for him."

"All I said was, what did he make up?"

"I wish I knew, specifically. But all I'm really sure of is that Jerry was either listening to what came through the microphone we found, or he's still working for Lylard and Lylard listened and told him what we said."

Wyckoff's mouth was hanging open. He did not speak.

Mason did. "What's the difference, Captain?"

"The difference? The difference is—and this is crucial— that if Jerry was the one who listened, the Dorians could really be working for themselves and against Lylard, just as he claims. —But not necessarily working with us," she added, as an afterthought.

"I see." Mason's face was covered with a grim look.

Arlene must have doubted he really did, since she went on explaining. "He knew things he shouldn't have known, Rick. He harped on the fact that we were lost, and he kept hinting that the temporals might be on Earth. He not only had information he couldn't have gotten any other way, but he knew where we were touchy. He concentrated on the things we mentioned that were bothering us the most."

Wyckoff, still standing on the sidelines, came to Jerry's defense again. "I believe him, Arlene," he said. "I know he's on the level. I can feel it."

"He's up to something, Wyckoff. And he's holding out on us."

"He couldn't tell us everything. He doesn't have time."

"Your loyalty is admirable, Wyckoff, but it's irrational." Arlene turned to the others. "Anybody look for bugs in here?"

Verity nodded. "We suspected there might be, Captain, and we had lots of time."

"You didn't find any?"

"Nothing."

"Nobody talked to the aliens?"

"They left us alone, Captain."

"Did you talk among yourselves—about the passwords, I mean? Did you mention that there *even were* any passwords?"

Heads nodded in the negative. She had expected that, of course. They had been suspicious enough to look for listening devices; they would have been careful. She paused an extra moment, then looked straight at Wyckoff. "Well," she began, "we did mention that passwords were necessary to start the drive. And so," she said, extra loudly, so that Wyckoff couldn't ignore her, "did Jerry."

Wyckoff looked sheepishly around at the others. "Maybe he made a lucky guess."

"And maybe he didn't. That's why I wanted to talk to Lady Bane. I suspect Lady Bane will have some things to say about the Dorians, just as the Dorians did about her. I can't believe she's as bubble-brained as Jerry claims she is. I know there's some other reason he doesn't want me to talk to her."

"It sounds like her relationship with the temporal is a fairly cordial one, Captain," Mason observed. "Perhaps the Dorians hesitate to trust her."

"Uh-uh, Rick—couldn't be. At least, not according to Jerry. He told us that we'll be depending on her to supply a reliable course. They'd have to trust her— we'd have to trust her."

"Are you sure you could get along with her, Captain? Jerry could have genuine fear of a clash. After all, they have the advantage of experience."

"I can get along with anybody I have to, Rick—for a while, anyway. Well, enough of this. Conjecture is entertaining, but it won't answer questions like that, will it?"

Again, heads nodded in agreement. "All right; I'm going to risk my throat in spite of Jerry. After that I'll make him bring me back and we'll confer again. This is one decision I can't make for the race. I'll want a consensus—input from all of you on what we should do, and then a vote. Agreed?"

The heads nodded in the affirmative.

Chapter Twenty-Three

Arlene was nervous, but determined not to let it show, and thankful therefore that this scaled alien had no acquaintance with human characteristics.

They each sat on a low but heavily padded chair obviously designed to fit the shorter Kruj'jan legs, with a translating robot between them, and took each other's measure.

In the doorway Jerry waited, leaning against the jamb, partly propped on his tail, until Lady Bane noticed he was still there. She flicked a switch on the red cube in her delicately scaled hand and said something in her own language.

The machine translated it into Dorian, which of course was gibberish to Arlene, but the effect was that Jerry immediately disappeared and the door hissed shut.

"Where did he go, Lady Bane?" the startled Arlene asked. She was by no means certain that Jerry had not, in fact, been genuinely concerned with her safety, or that he had not been hanging around specifically to protect her. She could see simply by looking at Lady Bane's long, bony, three-fingered hands, and the retracted claws each bore, that the Kruj'jan, technically unarmed, was still deadly.

"He did as commanded, Captain. He closed the door

from the outside. Who knows where he went; who cares."

Arlene was astonished at those remarks, but thought better of asking for an explanation. What was important was the working of their plan, not whether relations between the races were cordial.

"These Dorians are timid as offal worms, Captain— this male as much as the others. It remains to be seen whether you humans are any better."

"We shall strive to be, Lady Bane," Arlene replied cautiously, having already decided that Kruj'jan must be very direct beings. This was confirmed by Lady Bane's next words.

"I hate Lylard, Captain. I will enjoy killing him."

"Lady Bane, may I ask how much of the plan the Dorians have explained to you?"

"As you are the human leader, you may ask, Captain, but I cannot tell you."

"Why not?" Arlene was now enormously disturbed. She was starting to shake, and she earnestly hoped the Kruj'jan did not notice.

"Why not? Because the plan is not a Dorian plan—it is my plan. And," she added, "I ordered you brought here so that it might be explained to you."

"I see, Lady Bane. I promise I shall listen closely." Her shivering was now almost uncontrollable. She had concluded that Lady Bane was either quite mad or her entire race was flaky.

"To begin with, Captain, I want it clearly understood that I am the leader. I am the most qualified, and I do, after all, possess the keys."

"You do? The Dorians told me that Lylard had these."

Lady Bane turned to face Arlene, and for the first time Arlene thought she detected a faint hint of irritation. She could not be certain, but she resolved to take no more chances. She had been wrong, the Dorians right. From now on she would listen, not speak. "Please expound, Lady Bane."

"They amuse themselves with falsehoods, Captain,

though this demeans them. Lylard does the same, though he is a being of immense power, whom I respect and revere. Lylard is not an offal worm, Captain. Offal worms possess no power, therefore none can be taken from them. Hence there is no triumph in overcoming one like the Dorian. Lylard is another matter."

"Of course he is, Lady Bane. I will attest to that." Arlene's confusion mounted. Perhaps Jerry was right. Certainly, it was difficult to understand how the Kruj'jan could both hate and revere the temporal.

"There will be glory to be gained in overcoming Lylard, Captain. It must be mine. My consort and I will then rule securely."

"I did not know you had a consort, Lady Bane," Arlene replied, trying desperately to strengthen her own resolution.

"I do not, as yet. That is why I hate Lylard so. He has interfered. Had I remained on Kruj I would by now have had suitors—many, many suitors. I should have ultimately chosen the greatest among them. I can still do that when we return, however, and I shall."

"Why did you go with Lylard if you hate him so much, Lady Bane?"

"That is a foolish question, Captain. Why are you here?"

"Why, because at the moment, I can't help it."

For an instant Lady Bane's claws twitched, and a tiny ruff of featherlike projections rose around her neck. Her eyes closed to vertical slits, the equivalent of a squint. "For the moment, Captain, neither can I, but when I kill Lylard and take his place, it is Kruj which will dominate the temporal culture, and the others will be hostage to me."

"You are one of Lylard's hostages?"

"I am. I hate him so." It sounded almost like an afterthought. She added, "Against Lylard, my people are weak, because the warriors worship me."

"You are their god?"

"No, they merely lust for me, as they shall until I

have selected my consort. But it is not my fault—this is my good time." She paused, as though waiting for Arlene to say something, but continued, sounding somewhat defensive, when the human didn't. "Surely I am entitled to that. Why should I have to give it up?"

"Why is that your good time?"

"You pry, Captain."

"I wish to understand your circumstances."

"You are a female. Surely, you know them well enough. Would you be happy with your belly full of eggs, ignored and lonely while the males were free to make merry?"

"I don't know, I've nev—" She stopped, perhaps just in time. She had been about to make an admission that could place her in great danger. She resolved to proceed with more care. "I understand you now, Lady Bane. For me this is also *my* good time. I feel constrained to point out, however, that we appear to be very different biologically."

"I have already observed that, Captain. It appears that you are feebly armed. I note with interest that your claws are small and weak. Your race must have immense inner strengths, otherwise it should not have survived. But perhaps," she added, "you have thus far faced only other weaklings."

"We do have such inner strengths, Lady Bane," Arlene assured her. She was beginning get the rhythm of the conversation. Better, she was gaining an insight into Kruj'jan culture, though this, of course, would be enormously superficial.

Jerry had called her race barbaric, and obviously it was, but the attitudes Lady Bane displayed—her forthrightness, her utter lack of appreciation for social deception—pointed out plainly that it had parallels among primitive human cultures.

Arlene began to sort these out mentally. Such cultures did not conceal their emotions to minimize encounters—they wanted them, to determine social standing. The elite, the aristocratic, the nobility—they were the individuals, or perhaps clans, tribes, or families, that could lick the rest of the population in combat.

So, knowing that, Arlene immediately knew some other things about Bane. First of all, Kruj would necessarily have a planetary government of sorts. Second, Bane was probably the lone surviving child of an ambitious Kruj'jan family, or maybe the only child of whoever it was that ruled the planet. Third, Lylard had selected her as hostage for that very reason. These were the obvious conclusions to be drawn; there were others much more subtle and, she believed, more important.

She knew, for instance, that Bane's people would be practical enough to plot and plan their strategy, rather than dash head-on into disaster and extermination. They admired power, and they quite obviously preferred to take it over rather than destroy it.

She did not know how long Kruj had been subject to Lylard, but she suspected it had not been very long, and that meant that Lady Bane would follow the game plan so long as it appeared to her that she might take the temporal's power. She hoped the Dorians had understood things the same way she did. She could be fairly confident they had, since they appeared to fully appreciate deception and Lady Bane did not. Arlene at once resolved that she would become this creature's friend.

Lady Bane endured the intervening silence without objection and without apparent notice. She did not appear to be a being who wasted words—she used them sparingly and economically. Now, having at last concluded that the conversation demanded her efforts to keep it alive, she spoke. "It will be a long time before we fight, Captain, but I shall certainly enjoy it."

"Yes, as shall I, Lady Bane. In the interval, Lylard is our foe."

"Lylard is our foe, Captain, and after him the rest of the temporals, and while we battle these your throat shall be safe from my claws."

"And yours from mine, Lady Bane." She suddenly re-

alized then that everything that had been said up to this
point had been preliminary—this was the apex of the
conversation, which had led the two of them to truce.
"Tell me, Lady Bane, what your plan is, and what
assistance you will require from me."

The Kruj'jan turned to the human, her feather ruff
now flattened and lying smoothly across milk-white shoulders of iridescent scales. Even through the translator
her voice seemed calm and serene. "I require only your
obedience, Captain, and that of your crew. Listen carefully. I shall expound."

Arlene braced herself, resolving to remain alert for
any sign of trouble. Truce or not, she knew that one
careless word from her could destroy the rapport which
had been established.

Chapter Twenty-Four

"It's every bit as bad as he said it was, Wyckoff. Lady Bane told me in so many words that she intended to fight me when the temporals had been taken care of. She evidently doesn't see any need to lie. I hope she isn't as candid with Lylard."

"He's probably used to it, Arlene, so he doesn't take her seriously."

"I can't count on that. It's a mistake to assume that others think as you do, especially other sapients."

"Other what? Oh, you mean aliens. Yeah, I know."

"I meant Jerry."

"I know that, too. What have you decided to do?"

"Bane and I talked about the Dorians, Wyckoff. She doesn't have much use for them and I'm sure she wouldn't lie for Jerry—or even for herself, for that matter. I'm still convinced the Dorians are holding things back from us, but the fact that Lady Bane is in is a good sign. By the way, I think she'll do just fine with her part. She may not have a talent for lying, but she's an expert at concealing the truth. I couldn't get a thing out of her that she didn't want to tell me."

"Yeah," Wyckoff agreed. "Sometimes, that's the worst kind of lie there is."

"So, anyway," Arlene continued, without acknowl-

235

edging that concession, "I'm still convinced that Jerry is holding back on us, too, but I don't think we'll have to worry about any of the aliens until Lylard's down. Lady Bane wasn't bashful when it came to talking about the Dorians. She laughed when I suggested Jerry could astrogate the ship."

"The Dorians have practically rebuilt it."

"Lady Bane says that's what makes them contemptible to her: their slavishness. She calls them offal worms. She says Dorians can follow directions just like a computer can, but Lylard has to supervise everything they do. Lylard always told her that *both* Kruj and Dorr were barbaric planets. Isn't that interesting?"

"Yeah."

"It should especially interest you. You're Jerry's buddy. I just hope you can see now that it wouldn't be smart for us to let the Dorians learn to operate *Corona*."

"They can't learn anything from me, Arlene."

"I will be eternally grateful for that, Wyckoff."

Chapter Twenty-Five

"Ready, Barbarian?"

"Ready, Lord." Lady Bane *was* ready, in more ways than one. She sat slightly behind Lylard and to his right, holding a radio transceiver in one hand and the switching controls for a pair of translating robots in the other.

"Human mode," the nearer robot blared in Kruj'jan.

She threw the appropriate switch, all the while wondering how this was going to work—the arrangement seemed so clumsy. Still, it was fortunate that Lylard needed somebody, and that the task was simple enough for her to handle, and that he regarded her as too slow-witted to constitute a threat.

Fortunate it was also that Lylard had never bothered to learn the language of a subject race, not even that of the Dorians, and thus was totally dependent upon machine translation. And the machines, of course, though they were entirely adequate to do the job, had no discretion when it came to which language they translated into. Lady Bane was thus enlisted, because she could do that much, do it as fast as demanded, and because Lylard could not trust a Dorian to do it.

She understood neither the words the temporal then uttered into the handset's microphone, nor the equally incomprehensible gibberish that came back in reply, but she was next aware of a subtle change in the direction of down. She shifted her body on her chair in order to compensate.

There had been a lengthy briefing on this part of the operation, both by the human captain and the Dorians, and Lady Bane knew that the next few minutes, while *Corona*'s engines pushed her slowly and safely away from the planet, would be relatively uneventful. Her real task would begin when that was over, when Lylard inserted a routing key into his console's slot and began to feed a spatial course into the astrogation computer. Then, she would be busy.

There was a difference in the Lord Temporal's behavior in moments of stress. Busy, he was more tolerable. He needed leisure to be boorish.

Most of the time his behavior was suitably nasty. Facing brutal facts, Lady Bane could only conclude that it was his nature to be nasty and that his personality truly stank worse than his breath did. After all, he couldn't help that he didn't speak with inspired air, as the other beings aboard did, but with swallowed air; or that of all Kruj'jan senses the olfactory was most acute. He could have done something about his attitudes, and certainly, not all the cruelties he practiced on others were absolutely necessary to maintain control over them.

She took the time to glance back at Lylard, who watched a screen set beneath a hood and out of her immediate view. On it, she knew, would be a logarithmic display of all the nearby star systems, and from these Lylard would select a target star. That was the instant for which she waited.

She had seen a lot of Lylard's control room since they had become trapped here, and this was not the first time he had called upon her to help him. There had been another time when he had needed her assistance even more desperately than he did now, because there had been no one else alive aboard this module.

That had been a turning point for Lady Bane. Before

that she had simply been a captive, a minion of a vanquished people, a token of Lylard's might which the other temporals could envy. Temporals did such things. They cherished their living trophies, and judged each other's worth in terms of races held subject. Lady Bane's race, being fierce, seemed to her to be of especial import to him, all of it psychological, since so far as she knew Kruj had no commercial value to Temporal society.

That had always particularly rankled Lady Bane—the fact that Lylard was essentially a common trader, gathering goods and hawking them to his cronies, but all the while lording it over nontemporals. It rankled her because her own race, culturally and evolutionarily so much more deserving of imperial station, had thus far been denied it.

She had tempered her bitterness somewhat of late, as she began to realize that destinies are difficult things to perceive, and even more difficult to unravel from one another. And in this voyage, fateful as it seemed to be to so many other unfortunate peoples, the true destiny of Kruj now lay inchoate, awaiting only the touch of the imperial hand. That hand, Lady Bane believed, with an assurance born of faultless logic, was her own.

So she had prepared herself, and served her demon lord, and learned from him. She had waited, and endured the final insult of tutelage by the Dorians, and their insinuation that they, not she, would take the succession. *So they think*, she snickered silently, *so they think. I have my humans now, my magnificent humans, and I have my keys.*

On Corona's bridge the arrangements for translation were much the same as in what humans had come to know as temporal control, though this was sheer coincidence, as none of them had ever seen the inside. The principle differences were that there was only one robot and that the human species alone was represented. That had been a major point in the uneasy agreement between Arlene and Lylard, and the subject of the most intense negotiation.

This interlude had proven quite enlightening, though this was unintentional on Lylard's part. The temporal turned out to be far more practical when he knew his opponent had bargaining power than when he had believed the humans were helpless. The difference was like day and night, and he was, consequently, far more disposed to answer Arlene's questions than he might otherwise have been. Sometimes, she asked questions of no possible relevance to the maneuvering of the ship, but most of the time she tried to justify asking, and this was the method which yielded the greatest amount of useful information.

Lylard had, of course, hedged as much as possible. He would not, for instance, discuss the location of Earth. That part of the voyage, he insisted, would be conditional on human performance in getting him back to his own base, from which any further expeditions would be mounted. He would insist on compensation, in an amount arbitrated, if necessary, by the Temporal Guild.

"That is intended to throw you off guard," Jerry had warned the humans, after the incident was related to him. "He never intends to let you try to go there. He means to overcome you somehow and take back this ship. I assume he did not elaborate on the function of the guild."

"No, he didn't," Arlene had answered. "Why should that be a secret?"

"Because, Captain, the temporals are organized out of necessity. They would not otherwise be able to avoid self-destructive conflict. Temporal society is unwieldy, its members quarrelsome, the subject races many, and the number of great temporals, as opposed to lesser lords, is small. The great lords are inclined to discourage the proliferation of temporal knowledge, so Lylard would be fearful of punishment should he be unable to control you humans. You are technically advanced, so control would be difficult—so difficult Lylard would not risk failure. He will not keep his bargain."

Arlene had answered that she had never believed he would, and the conversation had ended with the remaining questions unanswered.

The humans simply added them to a long list of things they didn't know and followed the Dorian's advice to be wary.

And that was the reason the reconstituted *Corona* was now being operated from two control stations, despite the fact that both Lylard and Verity agreed consolidation of the controls would not be inordinately difficult. It was also why only humans occupied the bridge and only Lylard and Bane were in the temporal module—neither side wanted the Dorians involved in the test that was about to take place. The Dorians did not appear to take offense.

Testing the system was Lylard's idea, and not a bad one from the humans' standpoint. It would be far better to detect any structural weaknesses or control problems while in the vicinity of Home than somewhere out in the wilds of deep space. In the event of disaster, at least they knew that Home could feed them, and with the Home system in the middle of a rectangle of space ten parsecs on a side they were within the extreme theoretical range of *Corona*'s lifeboats. To extend that a bit more, one lifeboat, under robotic control, remained in orbit around Home's sun, where it was supposed to respond to distress signals from boats heading in-system.

At the end of this test the agreement called for the *Corona* to be resupplied, and for the rest of the human crew to come aboard, at which time Lylard would again be allowed to have his Dorians. The test was about to commence.

"Captain Graham?" The flat machine voice rang out loud and relatively clear from the translator robot immediately behind the console where she sat.

"Ready," she answered.

"I am also ready. My astrogation program has booted. You may move to solar orbit."

Arlene assumed that was all the temporal had to say, and switched to her intercom. "Minimal thrust, Verity. Take it very easy until we know what kind of job the Dorians did."

Wyckoff, sitting in a couch in the corner, his regular station since the mutiny whenever *Corona* was under-way, could detect no difference, though he knew the ship had begun to move because the gravitational field was automatically corrected to compensate. He did not mind this at all. It was much more pleasant than the old way, where his body had to take care of these things.

They reached the prescribed orbit in less than two standard hours. In the interim Arlene and Mason spent most of their time talking either to Lylard or Verity, and checking one or another of the ship's many systems. In normal times the computer handled almost all of this routine work, but as it was, there had been too many subsystems cut off from the master control for that to be practical, and in addition, there were a number of new systems for which no data were available. Given time, a chance to study these, and the opportunity to cross-connect them, *Corona* could eventually be completely reautomated, but as things were, the entire human crew would be needed to operate her safely on a long voyage.

This time it was Arlene who called down to the temporal, to inform him that *Corona* had reached the departure point for her first jump. He answered that he was ready with a plot and began reading off figures for her to relay to Verity. She did this without comment, and when Verity had confirmed receipt by reading them back to her she ordered the jump to begin.

The rest was anticlimactic. A ten-parsec jump would consume fifty-one and a fraction standard hours. The wait until the next one, which would come as close as celestial mechanics would allow to a right angle, would be filled first with furious but boring systems checks and then with tedium.

Wyckoff, of course, had no essential duties to perform while this was going on. He did not possess the technical competence to help. He tried to make that up by preparing snacks for the others, who quickly pronounced him an utter failure as a gourmet cook and ended that short career.

As a result, he was reduced to killing time by napping, and thus it happened that by the time the systems checks had been completed and everybody else was exhausted, he was still fresh as a daisy. Then he got a job—the others gave him a watch to stand while they retired to nearby couches and dropped off to sleep.

Half a dozen times, Wyckoff performed this lonely but important duty flawlessly. Two more jumps were smoothly accomplished and entirely without mishap and Corona was now on the downhill leg of the test.

But by the time he embarked on his seventh successive watch, Wyckoff had reached the epitome of boredom himself. With nothing to do and nobody to talk to, Wyckoff first passed the time by daydreaming. He was, of course, exceedingly good at this. Time was, daydreams had been all he had for diversion—it seemed like a million years ago. Who would ever have thought that a guy like him would wind up in a place like this, doing what he was doing now?

He had drifted with the tide; gone wherever the currents in this fickle stream that constituted life decided to take him. Well, he mused, it had certainly been interesting. It was also a little dangerous, true, but circumstances had chased out all the mediocrity with which his existence had once been filled.

The pace had been so fast and so furious it had been a very long time since Wyckoff had stopped to ask himself where he was really going and how it was all finally going to wind up. Before Lylard had come he had believed he had really found his personal niche in life, but the instant he had started to feel comfortable in it himself, he began to drift away from Arlene, who definitely wasn't comfortable in hers. And since Lylard had come, with all the turmoil he brought with him, Wyckoff had sorely missed the certainty of that old existence and found resumption of shipboard lifestyle wearisome. Again, friction had developed between the two of them, partly because, he reasoned, he was so ill fitted to help her with _Corona_'s operation.

He gave a sigh and looked up at the console, where the terminal screen was counting down the time until the next jump. There were still four hours, sixteen minutes, and forty-nine seconds to go before he would rise up from his seat and give Arlene's shoulder a nudge.

Forty-eight seconds, forty-seven seconds, forty-six seconds, forty-five, forty-four—Wyckoff's eyelids clicked shut with every change of the red numerals. It was a new game to him—an idle, mindless experiment without any purpose except to determine if he could ever perfectly match, with the human time-sense, the electronic precision of an idiotic clock. He found he could come rather close most of the time, providing he fell into the correct cadence. At first that took great effort, since he had a distinct tendency toward prematurity. Anticipation was a handicap from which the clock did not suffer, and Wyckoff labored to conquer his.

Eventually, he did, and he was proud. He could now almost perfectly match the performance of the clock. He could do it with every beat, or every second beat, or even every third. That became his next challenge—to see just how long he could keep his newly contrived biological clock in sync with the real one.

The intervals began to stretch out, longer and longer. Up to ten he was almost always able to do it. Beyond that, it became much more difficult. Eventually, though with enormous effort, he reached a benchmark—fifteen seconds. But he could not seem to cross this barrier no matter how hard he tried, no matter how deeply he concentrated.

And his concentration was deep—as deep as ever it had been, almost as deep as the mind approached at the boundary of sleep. Having reached this apparently insurmountable barrier, Wyckoff's entire will was dedicated to overcoming it. He had no doubt he would, if only he had the time, and he knew he almost certainly had it—over four hours before the gong would sound the preliminary ten-minute warning that the jump was ending. That was time enough.

Wyckoff concerned himself only with the gong. The test had settled down to such routine, and its execution had been reduced to such perfection, that he had no reason to expect any other emergencies, and in any event, it would make no real difference because the system was not dependent on human alertness to detect malfunctions. To handle these, it had automated alarms which were more sensitive and therefore much more reliable.

These systems were not designed to detect biological malfunctions, and while Wyckoff pursued his trivial dalliance, one of these occurred. It was a mere gurgle of sound passing through the radio's open circuit, not a pattern exact enough to require or even permit a translation. To the robot it was only noise.

To a sapient being, had one been listening, it would have been immediately recognized as the rattle of death.

Wyckoff did not hear it. He was thereafter wakened by the gong, as was Mason, who had the next watch. Both stirred at the same instant, Mason with a residual weariness which of late had never seemed to leave him, Wyckoff with a slightly guilty conscience for sleeping on watch and a sigh of relief that the first mate appeared not to have noticed.

Mason went to the console and made ready for the next maneuver while the captain obliviously slept on. It was the custom on the bridge for one to rise with the first gong and the other with the second.

When the second sounded, Arlene arose and joined him at the controls while Wyckoff remained where he had been snoozing. He never had managed to get past fifteen seconds.

While the others were busy relaying the next batch of data to Verity, he continued with the experiment. When they were finished, he joined Arlene, who turned the watch over to Rick and retired to the galley to prepare some palatable food.

"This is a little beneath my dignity, you know," she told Wyckoff. "The master of a spacegoing vessel should not have to double as mess officer."

"I tried, Arlene. I tried."

"I know. You made one dish that wasn't *too* bad, but everything else gave me heartburn."

"Glopnik," Wyckoff said proudly. "Russian stew. I learned that one from Grandpa. He ate it during their civil war. Of course, he always made his with rat meat . . ."

"Enough of that kind of talk. I've decided I don't need your help. Go away, before you ruin my appetite."

He didn't, of course. He stayed and helped, and returned with her to the bridge, bearing the tray of lunch for the three of them. She did, in fact, eat very little.

"He sounded kind of funny this time, Captain."

"Who sounded funny, Rick?"

"Lylard."

"How could you possibly tell—everything sounds the same. A robotic voice is a robotic voice."

"There was a difference. I can't explain it, and I can't even tell you what the difference was—timing, maybe. You know how it is—every voice you hear is different from every other."

"He hasn't got anybody to relieve him like we do. He stands every watch by himself. I doubt Lady Bane is much company."

"He also hasn't got any duties while he's on watch, the way we have. All he's responsible for is crunching the numbers and passing them on. By the way, Verity noticed it, too."

"Why would he be talking to Lylard?"

"He wasn't. He said the numbers didn't sound right to him. But we checked them out, read them back twice—once with each other, and I did it once with Lylard."

Arlene had a grim look on her face by then. She was a seasoned shipmaster, and a really experienced space-hand gave a hunch the respect it deserved. Too often, a hunch was nothing more than a collation of data gleaned from the subconscious—important data the conscious mind should have noticed but hadn't. Captains who thus paid attention to them were rewarded by extended lifespans. "Do you suppose he could be ill or something? I mean, after all, we don't know a thing about him."

"If he is, and if it got really serious, I think he could be expected to say something. He hasn't been bashful about demanding help yet. Still, maybe I should call and talk to him myself."

"He's awfully grouchy, Captain. Be prepared to have your head bitten off if you do that."

Arlene did not call. Instead, she stayed awake during Mason's watch, stood her own, and attempted to do the same on Wyckoff's. It was too much for her endurance, however, and she finally fell asleep in Wyckoff's arms.

Because he was still bored, and because Arlene's presence on the same couch limited his locomotion even more severely, Wyckoff again committed the unpardonable offense of falling asleep on his watch.

He awoke to find that the others were nowhere near as concerned with his dereliction as they were with the fact that suddenly *Corona* had broken out of the jump and Home was nowhere to be found.

Mason was on the horn to Verity and the two of them were frantically checking systems to try to find out why the jump had terminated prematurely. Arlene was holding a finger in one ear while she leaned on the translator robot and tried to talk to Lylard. From his vantage point on the couch where he had been sleeping, Wyckoff could not make up his mind which of the two appeared more frustrated.

He rose and walked over to where Arlene was standing, waiting for Mason to get a break so that she could talk to him. "What's the matter?"

"We aren't where we're supposed to be, Wyckoff, and Lylard insists that we are."

Mason finished on the power deck phone and joined them, his face a mask of gloom. "Nothing, Captain. The maneuver checks out perfectly against every figure Lylard gave us . . ." his voice trailed off.

"Every one except time," Arlene continued for him.

"Twelve hours, nine minutes, and 54.6 seconds early, to be exact, and not a clue as to why. Did he have any explanation?"

"He says the figures he gave us came out of his astrogation computer and he read them right off the screen. He doesn't understand why we couldn't handle the last jump after three successful prior jumps."

"Does he know how to compensate, or where we are?"

"I asked him that. He claims to be working on it and says he'll have some more figures for us in a little while."

Mason emitted a grunt in reply.

"Also, though I didn't come right out and ask him if he was sick, I commented that he sounded different."

"And?"

"He said it was my imagination."

"Maybe we ought to take a chance on going in there."

"Only as a last resort, Rick. Let's wait and see whether there's some other explanation for all this. It could very well be a translation error of some kind, despite what happened on the other three jumps."

"I don't see how, Captain; we worked all that out before we ever started. Lylard taught Verity and me his numeral system and we taught him ours. We each have conversion tables."

Wyckoff had been more or less left out of things. Suddenly, Arlene noticed him. "I don't want to put this on the intercom, Wyckoff, because you never know who might be listening, but I want you to go down to the power deck and borrow any crewmen Verity can spare."

"Okay, for what?"

"To break into Lylard's module if we have to. You might want to talk to Jerry about the best way to do that. It's all right to tell him what happened. He may even be able to offer some explanation."

Wyckoff nodded, then trotted off to the elevator. Twenty minutes later he was back, followed by two human crewmen and the Dorian, to report that Jerry was as mystified as they were.

"Settle everybody down wherever you can, then, Wyckoff. While you were gone Lylard called in some correction figures. We've checked them out. They look all right and we're about to try them."

"Won't Verity need these guys?"

"He says not."

"All right. I'll take them down to our place. We'll have a party—play cards or something. Uh, you'll let me know what's happening, won't you?"

He received a nod in reply, and then departed.

Aboard *Corona* the intercom signal was a loud gong, which usually sounded once, unless the caller was impatient and hit the talk bar more than once. Then resonance helped it along, and the result of successive punching was deafening.

It was quite effective at waking people, and when Arlene called down from the bridge, the three humans and the Dorian were all sleeping soundly in one big pile on two mattresses pulled from the bunks.

Wyckoff managed to reach the microphone before anybody else did, though the race was a close one.

"Bring everybody up here, Wyckoff," Arlene said grimly.

"Is something else wrong, Arlene?"

"I'll explain when you get here."

"We're on our way."

A couple of minutes later he arrived, breathless, in the control room, followed by his little force.

Arlene directed the others to seats and then retired into a corner with Wyckoff to break the news to him. "We're still lost, Wyckoff, but we're pretty sure now that we know why."

"Yeah? Why?"

"We think Lady Bane did something to Lylard, and that we've been talking to her for the last couple of days, not him."

Wyckoff's face reflected astonishment. "How could she get away with a thing like that?"

"Easier than you might think. The translator would provide her with a way to disguise her voice—enough, let's say, to fool somebody who wasn't familiar with his mannerisms, such as ourselves. And Bane herself should know Lylard's habits quite well."

"That's ridiculous. How could she expect to get away with a thing like that—trying to run this ship all by herself? Jerry said . . ."

"Yes, he did. And that's the part that worries us—for a couple of different reasons. We knew that Jerry was holding out on us. I mean, even you are willing to concede that he didn't tell us any more than he had to, aren't you?"

"Yeah, so?"

"Maybe he wasn't telling the truth about those booby-trapped chips, either. Maybe, in spite of what each claims, the two of them are thicker than they let on, and ganged up against the rest of us."

Wyckoff's head began shaking vigorously. "Naw, I don't believe that, Arlene. I can't picture the two of them lasting five minutes in a room together without one of them getting killed, most likely Jerry."

"Well, we have to resolve that, and pretty soon, too. Let's get him over here."

Wyckoff motioned Jerry to join them, and Jerry, in turn, removed an object from his belt pouch and plugged it into the robot, which then followed him to where the humans were.

"I assume the problem still exists, Captain."

"Maybe worse than ever, Jerry." Arlene hesitated only an instant before she dropped the other shoe. "Tell me, Jerry. Physically, could Lady Bane overcome Lylard?"

It was clear that the question took Jerry by surprise. He paused a long time to consider his answer, and when he gave it, he still hedged. "If you mean, is she strong enough, yes. I am convinced that they would be a fairly even match physically. But Lady Bane would never attack Lylard."

"Why not?"

"For the same reason we Dorians wouldn't. I have already explained it all to you."

"How about if she believed she could get home without him?"

"But she couldn't. The keys . . ."

"If she decided to risk it, could she astrogate Lylard's module—and by that, I mean this ship, too?"

Jerry did not hesitate very long with his answer this time. "Yes, I suppose she could—until you caught on, or until she ran into one of his traps. So long as she had a translator handy—uh, no, wait a moment, Captain; I'll have to retract that statement. I don't think she could."

"Why did you change your mind?"

The Dorian remained silent.

"Jerry, I asked you a question. Answer me."

And suddenly he did, but very curiously. The sounds that came out of the robot were not exactly laughter— they were more like astonished grunts—but they came fairly close. "Captain, how many fingers have you got?"

Arlene was dumbfounded by the question; nevertheless, she stuttered her reply: "E-eight; ten if you count thumbs. Why?"

"And Lylard?"

"The same as humans—and Dorians, for that matter. What are you trying to tell me?"

"That Lady Bane has three per hand, Captain, and I think that was her downfall."

By this time all human eyes were on the Dorian. He began to behave nervously. "Well, don't you see, Captain? We all have different numeral systems. You humans use the base ten, as Lylard's culture did. Dorr uses the base twenty. In each case, the number of digits on the hands and feet suggested the numeral system adopted by our respective cultures, and in the case of Kruj, the count is to the base six. That, I think, is the reason your calculations do not agree with your observations."

Silence reigned among the humans, so the Dorian continued. "Lady Bane would have been familiar with Lylard's numeral system, of course, since she has to use it aboard his vessel. She could have read the numbers off the video screen easily enough. But I doubt if she would have had many occasions to convert them into her own system—yes, I think that's probably it."

"What's it?"

"Well, Captain, you or I doing it would have had the presence of mind to make the adjustment, because we appreciate how massive the error would be over such distances. Lady Bane is not that sophisticated. She undoubtedly took the easy way out and simply read off the decimal numbers for the robot to translate. When it did, she switched to human Kruj'jan mode and repeated them to you. You, in turn, gave them to Mr. Verity, who used them. And since the last jump was the only one where there was a visual checkpoint . . . Captain, this could be very, very bad business."

"No, Jerry, we know Lylard was still in control for the first three."

"You said you tried a course correction."

"Yes."

"And by then, Lady Bane knew something was wrong, I gather?"

"We told her. We were sure by then that Lylard was in some kind of trouble—we didn't know what."

"You still don't. Captain, there's another risk—the temporal drive."

"We don't know anything about that."

"I know. Neither, of course, does Lady Bane, but as you have just seen, she lacks inhibition, and might easily be tempted to tamper with that next if we get near a mass large enough for it to operate. We mustn't risk that."

"We're prepared to storm Lylard's module if we have to." She turned to Wyckoff. "I guess you'd better get ready to do that, Wyckoff."

Wyckoff had been leaning against the bulkhead, taking it all in without comment. He didn't have the slightest idea how to get inside, but he was ready to try. He started toward his men, who waited in the corner.

Jerry called him back, then turned to Arlene. "I suspect that may be unnecessary, Captain, if I know Kruj'jan nature, and I think I do. You see, having made the attempt at revolution, and having failed, Lady Bane will now see herself as unworthy."

"Unworthy?"

"Yes, Captain. As a result, she may yield to a more authoritarian figure such as yourself, if you are firm, and more important, if you convince her that you, and only you, can do what she could not."

"I don't understand."

"It is the way her people are, Captain. Their thinking is very rigid, very simplistic. They are concerned with ends, not means, and consequently, if you show clear evidence that you can overcome her, she will obey you."

A wave of fear washed over Arlene's face. "She said one day, when Lylard was vanquished, she and I would fight. If Lylard's dead . . ."

"It will not come to a physical contest, Captain. Don't you see? If you exhibit your superior power and ability, and demand she yield, and if you promise to correct these errors and take her home, Lady Bane will believe, because that is what she wants to believe. She wants to feel that Kruj will be saved from further torment at the hands of the temporals. Of course, she may only postpone her ambition of combat with you until a later time, but postpone it she will—if you demonstrate to her that she has a reason."

"I should order her to open the module?"

"Yes, Captain, that would be a first step."

"If she refuses?"

"She will not."

"What if Lylard is really still alive?"

"I don't think there's even a remote chance that he is, but if he is, so much the better. Things should be easier."

"Gratitude? From him?"

"Hardly, Captain. What I meant was he would then surely have to substitute one of us for Lady Bane if he wanted any help. He would certainly hesitate to give an assassin a second chance."

"I see. Well, then, there is no reason to wait any longer, is there? Why don't you go with Wyckoff, Jerry?"

"I will."

"Wyckoff?"

"Yeah?"

"Call me when you're in position, okay?"

"Right, Arlene."

"And don't get hurt."

"I won't." He winked at her.

Ten tense minutes passed before Arlene got her call. When Wyckoff's voice blasted out of the handset she held, she jumped almost off her seat. She hastily twisted the volume knob down. "Go ahead, Wyckoff."

"We're down here at Lylard's module. The hatch is closed and locked. It looks pretty tough, but Jerry says he thinks he could cut through in about an hour if he had a laser torch. I'm thinking of sending for one."

"You don't sound very optimistic, Wyckoff."

"I'm not. According to Jerry, Bane'd be a rough customer, and he isn't even sure these plazers'd stop her."

"I hope he's wrong about that and right about the rest of it, Wyckoff."

"I guess we're ready whenever you are, Arlene."

"I'll leave the key open so you can hear. That may provide you with some margin of safety."

"Okay."

Wyckoff turned up the volume of the handset. He and the rest of the humans huddled near and listened, as did Jerry, although without his robot translator he could not follow very well.

"Lady Bane?" Even through the small and relatively tinny speaker the words came through loud and clear. "Lady Bane, we know you've done something to Lylard, that you've taken control of that module. We've gotten lost because of you, Lady Bane. Your numbers didn't work. Your attempt to correct the error only made things worse. Do you understand that, Lady Bane?"

There was no answer.

Arlene paused only a moment before she continued. Wyckoff thought he knew why—to give Lylard, in the event they were mistaken over his fate, a chance to intervene and deny what she said.

No such disclaimer was forthcoming, which in his opinion just about clinched it. He drew the plazer from its holster and pointed it at the hatch.

Arlene's voice blasted out again, with a strengthened volume and new vigor.

"You are all alone, Lady Bane. By yourself you can never hope to reach your home, but we can find it and take you there, and we will if you come out now."

There was a long silence. Then the handset echoed with the translator's synthesized voice. "This is my ship now, human."

"Not for very long, Lady Bane. We can take it, and we will; you know we will."

Again there was silence.

"Which will you choose, Lady Bane? Death here, alone in space, or a chance to free Kruj from temporal rule?"

"I am Lord Temporal now, human. The right is mine by conquest."

"Because you killed Lylard? How did you do it, Lady Bane—strike from behind?"

"I did it. How I did it does not matter. I now claim what was his."

"This ship was never his, Lady Bane, because he could not make use of it. And neither can you, but I can."

Again, there was no answer.

"Lady Bane, I will wait no longer. If you do not come out immediately, I will order my people to begin cutting through the module with fire and to burn you down as soon as they reach you. Is that what you want Lady Bane?"

"No."

"Then, do as I say. We humans will treat you fairly."

"You *will* take me home."

"We will try, Lady Bane."

"You will free my world?"

"We will help as much as we can," Arlene answered.

Slow down, Arlene, Wyckoff urged silently. *Don't give it all away.*

She didn't have to. Lady Bane must already have been convinced of the hopelessness of her situation. Probably, as Jerry had predicted, it was only a question of getting her into a receptive frame of mind, permitting her a graceful way to save face. He and Yasha had discussed that subject on a couple of occasions, though at the time he had not been aware how central it was to most oriental cultures. "Always leave your opponent an escape hatch," Yasha admonished. "Leave him with something yet to lose and his cowardice will be your ally."

Arlene had just successfully practiced that strategy on the Kruj'jan, and it seemed to be working. In any event, the lock on the temporal module began, in that instant, to cycle.

Wyckoff had ordered Lady Bane bound before bringing her to the bridge. He remembered what Arlene had told him of her first interview with the Kruj'jan, and he didn't want to take a chance on anything happening to her. Somehow, this had all seemed too easy—a creature as rough as this one just giving up.

The best evidence that something was wrong lay below, in the temporal module—proof of what the alien woman could do: the dead and now decomposing body of the lord temporal. Bane had, as Arlene had suggested, taken him from behind, crushing his oddly shaped skull with a blow from a metal bar. He had, no doubt, died instantly, and probably with no idea of what had hit him.

On the way up to the bridge Lady Bane had expressed her own laments—the ease with which the temporal had passed. She regarded it as necessary, though highly regrettable, that Lylard had not suffered in the proportions that his captive subjects had.

Wyckoff couldn't help feeling a little sorry for both Bane and her victim. He did wonder why she had picked that particular time to cave the temporal's roof in. It didn't make any sense unless she believed that they could get along without him. Jerry expressed a similar opinion.

He took her into the control room and parked her in the middle of the deck. Arlene and Mason were there, of course, and Jerry had followed him in the door.

"All right, Lady Bane," Arlene began. "I want you to tell me what this was all about."

"The robot's not translating, Captain," Jerry explained. "You need a Kruj'jan element. I have one in my pouch." He hurried to plug it into the translator.

"Remove the Dorian, Captain," the robot's voice immediately bellowed. "I will say nothing while he is present."

Arlene looked over at Jerry, but he had already started for the door, and saved her the trouble of asking him to leave.

When he was gone Lady Bane became more talkative. She made it apparent she did not like the Dorians. "You think they are your friends, Captain. They are not. They plotted against Lylard, and they will do the same against you."

Wyckoff knew Arlene shared this sentiment, so he was surprised at her next words, which were defensive of the Dorians.

"We all plotted against Lylard, Lady Bane, and certainly, you plotted against me. But I see no evidence that the Dorians did it."

"For myself, I will admit to what you charge, Captain. We of Kruj are a warrior people. And though we do on occasion use guile to defeat our enemies, we prefer the more honorable way.

"But it is not the same with the Dorians. For them, treachery is the method of choice."

"When I see proof of treachery, Lady Bane, I'll act against them. Until then, they're friends, as you would have been had you behaved yourself. Now, I asked you a question; I want it answered. Why did you take it upon yourself to assassinate Lylard?"

"It was time for him to die, Captain. I did not need him anymore, and he was dangerous while he was alive."

"*You* didn't need him anymore! Lady Bane, he was your way home."

"Ah, so, the Dorians did not tell you. I was right. There, Captain, is your proof."

Arlene was squinting at the Kruj'jan, as though it hurt her eyes to look at the alien woman's garments. "I have seen nothing of the sort, Lady Bane."

"Wyckoff has the evidence."

"Now, wait a minute," he protested. "All I took off

her was this stuff, while I was shaking her down for weapons." He held up a slim case of some plastic material and handed it to Arlene.

She fiddled for the catch, found it finally, and snapped up the lid. The inside was padded with a sort of velvet, and a dozen or so thin cylinders studded with gold spikes were set in individual sockets. "What are these, Lady Bane?" Arlene demanded, shaking the box under the alien woman's nose.

"They are routing keys, Captain—guild bonded routing keys."

"You took them away from Lylard?"

"Indirectly, Captain."

"What does that mean?"

"That I took them, but that Lylard didn't know they still existed."

"There was only supposed to be one set of keys, according to Jerry, and Lylard was supposed to have them. What's a guild bonded key?"

"A duplicate of the keys to be used on a particular voyage, Captain, copied and certified by the major house of the temporal guild to be genuine. I'm quite certain the Dorian didn't mention them."

"No, he didn't. Why would Lylard have these extra keys?"

"There is a price for the answer. Release my bonds."

"Not just yet, Lady Bane. Perhaps after a few more questions."

"Very well, Captain. These were not Lylard's keys, and he thought they had been destroyed. They belonged to one of his partners."

"Yes," Arlene retorted, drawing the word out into a sort of hiss. "I had forgotten all about his partners, but he did say that they were all killed in the crash of the other module."

"That isn't quite correct, Captain. Release me or I speak no more."

Arlene took a moment to consider that. She decided

to do it. "Put her on the corner couch and cut her loose, Wyckoff," she ordered, "but keep her covered."

Wyckoff complied. He could tell that having him do it was very impressive to the alien. She seemed to him to be in awe of Arlene, for no other reason than that males obeyed her orders.

"Now then, Lady Bane, suppose you explain your situation from the beginning."

"Since I was taken hostage?"

"No, since this voyage began, or from the time of the accident. Whatever is a good starting point for you—but keep it relevant."

"Then I will start with the beginning of the voyage, Captain.

"Lylard organized the venture, but it was an ambitious undertaking, too large for his own resources. As is sometimes done among the temporals, he sought out partners, to whom he promised a share. As it happened, he found five of them, though one was a young bharph pair."

"I don't know what that is, Lady Bane. Explain." Arlene was craning her neck toward the translating robot.

"That race forms pair bonds, such as you and Wyckoff have, though in the bharph they are of exceptional intensity, to the extent that they eventually become physically ill when separated. The pair begins to merge into a single personality, although there remain two bodies. It is the pair, rather than either sex, which becomes the individual. For this reason, bharph are an exception to the guild's rule against female temporals."

"What difference would that have made?"

"I was preparing to explain that when you interrupted, Captain."

"Sorry. Go on, then."

"Temporals are not trusting of one another, Captain. The partners necessarily went along on the voyage in order to protect their investment. Had they not gone, Lylard would surely have stolen from them. However, they were also in danger from one another and so they sought guild auspices. Guild agents searched the vessel and its occupants for weapons—there are none aboard except what you humans brought. They also supplied each temporal with a set of the keys I mentioned.

"The temporals then embarked and touched at a number of worlds, trading and looting. When they reached your world they sent the Dorians down alone."

"Why?"

"To do the work, Captain. Certainly, you do not think the temporals would labor?"

"Labor at what, Lady Bane? There wasn't anybody here for them to trade with or steal from."

"The Dorians were sent there to gather biologicals, Captain, and to flesh out the cargo. They were on the way back at the time and there was still room in the spatial module which they didn't want to waste. There are an endless variety of life forms, Captain, and among these the expedition contemplated finding purchasers for drugs which can be made from certain plants. Plants are therefore a big part of temporal commerce."

"Go on."

"Lylard's living quarters, and that of the bharph pair, were aboard the temporal module, while those of the other two were on the spatial module. That is why, after the Dorians were taken down, that module returned to orbit.

"For some reason I never discovered, the bharph male decided to descend to the surface when the spatial module returned for the Dorians. Perhaps he was in need of some substance they were expected to be bringing back. In any case, the female was in her bad time, and was gravid, so remained aboard the temporal module with Lylard, myself, and Lylard's remaining partner.

"When the accident occurred, Lylard found himself in a position of advantage—he was awake but the rest of us were sleeping. He used the same iron bar I killed him with to assassinate his remaining partners. Lylard knew that he would be delayed for a long time and that the others would be competing with him for life supporting resources and for control of the module . . ."

"Wait a minute, Lady Bane. You said he might be delayed for a long time. Don't you mean, trapped permanently?"

"No, Captain. Lylard wasn't really trapped here. And again, I see the Dorians didn't tell you. He had a means of escape, even before you came. That is why he was concerned about the surviving temporals."

"How?"

"Down the time line. He still had temporal capability. It would have been extremely hazardous, but he might still have been able to reach a region where there was a chance of rescue. If he succeeded, not only would he have the profits of the voyage, but first chance of taking over the fiefs of his dead companions. To do that, though, he had to survive."

"Why didn't he kill you?"

"There were many reasons, Captain. For one thing, he had not had time. For another, he was greedy, and he regarded me as a valuable property. For a third, I would not have been an easy victim. He knew that, and chose to bide his time rather than to confront me. My own strategy was essentially the same. It was the arrival of you humans that temporarily saved Lylard from me."

"We saved him from you?"

"Not from death itself—that would have been postponed a while—but from much, much pain. I already had the routing keys by then, but I did not know how to use them. I hoped to overpower Lylard and persuade him to teach me."

"I think I understand what you meant by that, but how did you get these keys? Why didn't Lylard collect them?"

"He did. That is, he tried to get them all, though not quite hard enough. He found two sets immediately, and then stopped looking because he thought this set was down on the surface."

She paused, as though to give the humans the opportunity to catch up with her reasoning. When none offered comment, she continued. "It occurred to me that the bharph male had no reason to mistrust the female and would not necessarily have taken his keys to the surface with him. If he hadn't, I wanted them. After Lylard and I had pushed the bodies out the airlock, I decided to search the bharph quarters more thoroughly than he had. Your arrival distracted him, and provided me the opportunity to do that, since Lylard was too busy to worry about what I was doing. I found them and hid them."

Lady Bane paused. Evidently she had said her say and was now ready to receive the captain's praise.

Arlene was not about to give her anything but a scolding. "Killing Lylard was senseless, Lady Bane. All our chances of getting home probably died with him. We still don't know which keys have traps."

"Is it not just as useful to know which one does not?"

Arlene stared at the alien woman with her mouth wide open. "Of course," she replied when she finally found voice. She reached for the case. "Show me which one it is."

"It is none of those, Captain. It is down in the module, still in the computer. Lylard called it his test key. I do not know what else it can do, but I watched him use it to turn things on in there. After I killed him I compared the markings on it to those in that case. None of the symbols match."

Arlene gave out a sigh. It was clear to anyone who heard it, except perhaps Lady Bane, that it was an expression of frustration. She could not convey that to the alien woman, either with gestures or the robot's sterile words. Finally, though, she reached a decision.

She turned to the alien and said, "Lady Bane, we humans are going to have to work a few things out among ourselves. While we do that, I must confine you to your quarters, as I have already done with the Dorians. We simply cannot take the chance that anything else will go wrong. Do you understand me?"

"I understand, Captain. I disagree that in the case of myself any such measures are necessary. With the Dorians, yes—they have lied to you; they are seven. I have not lied to you, and am but one being."

"I must insist, Lady Bane. You love your people and I love mine. In my place, could you do less?"

Lady Bane did not respond. Arlene had adroitly imprisoned her within a cage of logic, a finer and sturdier cell than any forged in iron. She tempered the sentence by promising to reconsider when they reached Home again.

"If we ever do reach Home again," she commented sadly to Wyckoff after he had returned from the alien woman's quarters. "It doesn't sound promising."

Chapter Twenty-Six

The humans had gathered in the control room, working in shifts, making small experimental maneuvers through which they hoped to repeat at least a part of the course out.

Those who had been asleep, as Wyckoff had been, had been awakened by a squeal, to find Mason bent over the console. They had ended the last jump prematurely, and had emerged within a gas cloud. The first mate was examining this with the instruments. Arlene asked him how far into it they'd gone.

"Not very," he answered. "We can back out with no trouble, as soon as the drive program's been reset, but I have no idea where we are."

"I didn't expect you would. I just wish Bane had asked for help as soon as she killed Lylard." She gave a sigh. "Oh, well, what's done is done. Keep at it, Rick. Find us a way out of it. Keep an eye open for likely systems, too. We might just be starting another small colony."

Mason didn't like the sound of that. He knew what she meant. Food would run out one of these days. There would be no way to tell when until Wyckoff finished his inventory. He had a fair idea what they'd come to orbit with, but the aliens had gobbled indis-

creetly, thinking that resupply would be easy. Now it
wasn't.

The chief storekeeper took the opportunity to report
to the captain. Perhaps he hoped to reassure the others, who certainly needed reassurance then. "We're not
too bad off food-wise, Arlene. There's enough of us and
eight of them, and the Dorians probably don't eat as
much as we do. Of course, we'll have to do something
pretty soon. How are we doing otherwise?"

"Not very well, Wyckoff. Verity's been studying the
computers in Lylard's module. He says that in some
ways they're way past anything we could have built,
and so far he hasn't been able to make much sense of
the big one."

"Yeah, I've seen it, Arlene. Takes up a whole deck all
by itself. But maybe, if we can get it working right, it'll
know where we are."

"There's a problem with that. The test key seems to
turn the whole system on and plot spatial maneuvers,
which is fine, as far as it goes. But according to both
Lady Bane and Jerry, the regular temporal routing keys
coordinate the two systems, and they run in sync. We
still have to figure out how that's done, assuming the
test key has that capability.

"But that's not the only catch. Knowing where we are
in relation to where Lylard came from might get us
back to Home, but there's a very slim chance we could
locate Earth. Apparently, the translator units don't store
location data, just the information about the language,
so that if the robot hears a language it can translate.
There's speculation that the temporals have a main data
base that does do this, but I don't see how we could get
to it."

"Yeah, well, I still haven't got that bunch figured
out."

"You were there when Jerry explained it. They travel
time, Wyckoff. That's what happened to Lylard's module when you and Rick went looking for it, and how he
managed that trick with the colony. As soon as his

instruments picked us up he ducked into what the temporals call stasis. Don't ask me to explain that, but the result was that we had no way to tell he was there.

"Then, after we were captured, he did it again, but this time I know he moved us backward because the crater and the canal were gone."

"Yeah, that part I understand, Arlene. But if he could do all that, why did he let that accident happen? Why didn't he just go back and fix it so it wouldn't happen? And while we're at it, how come he didn't know Bane was going to kill him?"

"Remember what Jerry said when I asked him that? He said that Lylard couldn't see into his own future. As for going back, he couldn't. He'd have created what the philosophers call a paradox, and it's pretty generally agreed you can't have a temporal paradox."

"What's a paradox?" Wyckoff demanded, suspicious that once again the talk was rising over his head.

"It's a contradiction," Arlene hastily explained, aware that he was in difficulty, and anxious to avoid confrontation.

"The classic example involves the man with the time machine who uses it to go back and murder an ancestor, usually his grandfather, before that ancestor reaches puberty. Logically, this is impossible."

"Provided Grandma's not playing around."

"You have to assume it's a biologically necessary ancestor, Wyckoff."

"Well, that closes that loophole."

"It wasn't a loophole, Wyckoff. You tried to cheat. You can't cheat Mother Nature. But the logic goes further than that. It's also reasonable to assume that the same individual can't appear more than once in the same instant of time—in other words, he couldn't meet himself."

"But if he moved back and forth like you just said he did, wouldn't he have to do that? Wouldn't that get him mixed up in one of those paradoxes?"

"Maybe not, Wyckoff. I suspect that either the temporal system permits some kind of observation while the traveler's moving through it, so that it wouldn't bother the observer if he didn't stop, or that the mechanism prevents paradoxes by blocking him from entering time periods he's been in before. We'll have to be very careful about using it ourselves until we know how that part works."

"I don't know as I want to try that, Arlene."

"We'll figure it out eventually, Wyckoff. Time travel might be new to science, but it's old to philosophy and mathematics. Besides, we have to use it."

"Why?"

"Because it's the only astrogational system to which this vessel is presently capable of orienting. The only common point of reference has to be buried someplace in that big computer's memory or in another computer someplace in temporal territory. If it's in the module's data base, then we've been fortunate. If it isn't, then we'll have to go out and find it."

"I don't understand what you mean."

"The temporal transport system relies on the ability to move back and forth along the timestream and to break out at will. Since all material things move in both media, spatial distances are interchangeable with temporal distances. If you've moved through one, you've necessarily also moved through another, but—and this is the difference—there is no temporal equivalent to the physical light barrier. Now do you understand?"

"No."

"Then think of it this way. You're in one part of New York. You want to go to some other part. What do you do?"

"Hop a bus."

"Okay. Suppose the bus doesn't go where you want to go?"

"Then I get one that goes someplace where I can catch another bus that does."

"What if the bus isn't there when you get there?"

"I have to wait for it."

"All right. But suppose you had a time machine, and you knew exactly when the bus would get there. You move in time in the appropriate direction until just before the buses meet, and then you get off one and on the other. You don't have to wait."

"Okay."

"So Lylard's ship was in orbit around Home. Home's moving, along with its sun, in a long orbit of galactic center. Naturally, since he's within its gravitational field, he moves along with it. At different points along the time line it crosses an infinite number of spatial points, some of which are reasonably proximate to points through which other bodies move in different, and perhaps more favorable, directions.

"So if he wants to go someplace, he calculates the best spatio-temporal route, assuming he hasn't got a preprogrammed routing key already, and uses his equipment to take it. Unlike the rest of us, the temporals can totally disregard time dilation. To them, it's meaningless. That, according to the Dorians, is because there seem to be a number of temporal bands, each possessing a different degree of temporal energy. Stasis is merely the lowest of these and has almost no energy. It's like the powered walkways in airports."

"Yeah, I see it now. That's why Lylard needed us. He didn't want to just take a chance on making a temporal jump and being lucky enough to run into somebody who'd help him. He wanted to be sure he'd be able to get to the next bus stop."

"Local travel to him, Wyckoff, but very important. He owed both his dilemma and his survival to the fact that his ship was in two parts. The part we took aboard had the temporal generator and main computer in it. The other half had the spatial drive system. When the temporals wanted to descend, they uncoupled it and used it for a shuttle. When it crashed, Lylard was stuck in orbit around Home, able to move in time but not in space, so he waited for us to arrive and then took our ship."

"So now we've got a whole ship, and we can do what he did—if we ever figure out how." His voice trailed off, and a look of gloom washed over his face. "And the rest of them—they can't help . . ."

"They're barbarians, like us, Wyckoff. Oh, they have a general idea of how things are supposed to work but none of them really understand the mechanism. The Dorians, for instance, did a magnificent job of installing the module. Verity says the ship is almost as sound as it was before, but they were only following Lylard's instructions. The Dorians are very good at that, according to the princess."

"Who?"

"The alien woman—Bane. Didn't you know she's got royal blood?"

"You're kidding?"

"Not at all. She's a real princess, and she's beautiful, too, to some. Of course, tastes do differ.

"But the plain facts are that on the whole, we humans are much more technically advanced than either her race or the Dorians, so it's up to us."

"Well, if she's a princess, what was she doing with Lylard?"

"Not a very good match, was it? I gather from Bane that the temporals came one day to trade, or more properly, to loot her planet. Lylard took her because she was precious among her own people, and therefore useful in helping him control them. To them, she was unique, and that's what the temporals do—they collect rare and precious things."

"I wonder what they took from Earth when they were there?"

"Who knows? But they must have found something that interested them or they wouldn't have an Earth language in their files."

A tone sounded. An instant later Verity's voice boomed through the intercom. "Captain, can you come to the module?"

"Something happened?"

"Something very interesting, Captain. We managed to boot the astrogation program on this big computer. I'm into a very interesting file."

"Marvelous, Verity. I'm amazed. I thought it would be months before we even got the screen to light."

"We got lucky, Captain. The Dorians were able to help some, and this thing is incredibly user-friendly. Of course, we have to work through the robots, and idioms throw it off, but . . ."

"I'll be right down, Verity." She turned to Wyckoff. "Maybe you'll get to meet some more of these temporals. You can ask them what they took."

Wyckoff had been inside the alien module before, with Verity and Mason right after the temporal had been killed. He had helped to remove the temporal's body and commit it to space. He had seen many wonders in the alien vessel, including some solid silver busbars as thick as his thigh, worth maybe twenty or thirty thousand credits apiece to his favorite fence in Brooklyn. Not that he thought much about money anymore. He was a reformed man, a respectable member of the *Corona*'s crew—so long as he didn't go back to Earth. There, he feared, he might still face a murder rap. The law had a long memory.

He liked it better where he was now, even though they were lost. He had a feeling they'd someday get out of this trouble, and that there were better days ahead. But in the meantime, there'd be adventure, and Wyckoff was hooked on that. Whatever else you might say about his lifestyle, it wasn't dull.

He was ignorant, certainly, but ignorance wasn't a permanent disease. It was curable. Meanwhile, as Arlene had once remarked, "ignorance is the mother of adventure." It seemed to Wyckoff that whenever anything important happened he was in the thick of it, and though this furnished excitement there were drawbacks too. He had to take responsibility for what he did, sometimes even when he couldn't talk to anybody else about it. It had been like this with Knowles' death and, more recently, with his napping on watch. Wyckoff's conscience hurt him, but not enough to tell anybody about either of those transgressions.

It was easier to take when he could look around him and see others in the same sad moral shape. Ignorance and evil weren't necessarily complementary characteristics. For instance, Verity had been just as evil, and he was anything but ignorant. But even at that he didn't really know any more about the mysterious machine in the center of the module than Wyckoff did. True, Wyckoff hadn't suspected that that big ball in the center was mercury. Who would? Mercury was something they put in thermometers, not in spheres six meters across.

Verity said this had to be part of the temporal generator, and that it was probably making the gravity too, but Verity was guessing. He might never figure out how the aliens did it.

He speculated, and Wyckoff listened, and nodded that the massive magnetic field that nearly tore the buckle from his belt was what held the thing spherical, but meanwhile he was wondering if the man-thick cables that surrounded it like a basket were made of silver as the busbars were.

It was the same with the deckful of crystals, all laced together with optical fibers. Verity was sure this was a part of the computer, but again, he didn't know any more about it than Wyckoff did. Certainly he couldn't have fixed it if it were to break. But he had—and Wyckoff was quite willing to concede him the credit for it—gotten it to do something.

As usual, whenever technical subjects were discussed, Wyckoff sat in the background where he could watch and listen, and indulge in his own speculation about them.

At that moment, Verity was huddled over a keyboard marked with alien symbols, fairly drooling at the display that had appeared on the holo tank the aliens used for a screen. Lady Bane, having been brought here by an armed spaceman, stood at his side.

"I'm sure I was right, Captain. That deck of crystals has to be linked to this. I'm sure that was the core of Lylard's computer. There's nothing else aboard that fits the bill."

He turned to the alien woman: "How about it, Princess?"

She replied through the nearby translating robot. "It is part of the astrogation equipment. I have seen it before. Lylard used to consult it to determine which key he would use next. It is part of the temporal drive, which is a powerful system, and with which I caution you not to meddle."

"You're not a whole lot of help, Princess. We already knew that, but we have to meddle if we're ever to make use of it."

Arlene interrupted what could have become a confrontation. "Does that mean the entire spatial astrogation system went up with the other module, Verity?"

"No, Captain. I don't think so. Otherwise, I shouldn't be getting what I'm getting. This computer is remarkable. Look at this. I think it's a logarithmic chart of the galaxy, and . . ."

"Don't you mean a simulation?"

"No, I don't think so. I think it's an actual master chart."

"How did you manage to get to it?"

A sheepish look covered Verity's face for an instant, then vanished as rapidly as it had appeared. "Through trial and error, mostly, Captain. We'd hit a key and see what happened. Enough punching, and, well, we worked up a list of routine instructions that every computer has—basic housekeeping commands, like calling the directory up to screen, or reading a file, and so forth. No big deal, really.

"Once we learned to call up files, we started doing that in the order in which they appeared in the directory. In most cases these were text files. We copied them optically so they could be routed through our library computer's readers and eventually translated by Lylard's robots.

"This one we're watching is completely different from anything else. I think it's a record of Lylard's course, or a map with that course superimposed on it, from where he started all the way to Home. The thing's been moving in little jumps, just like our own system would have displayed it, only it touched maybe a thousand different reference points, and every one moved."

"What is the significance of that?"

"It means that as the course ran, stellar motions were reflected in the display, and this thing was constantly updating them. It ran all the way from the other side of the galaxy."

"That's impossible. No computer could possibly be fast enough to do that."

"Ordinarily, I'd agree. If this was real time these aliens would have to be either incredibly old or that computer would have to be able to keep up. I think it would melt down first."

"So, another mystery."

"Yes, Captain. But this time I think I know the answer. There is a way it could have kept up. As a matter of fact, I think our own computer could probably do it if its components were reliable enough. I think the alien system would be, because it has no moving parts and nothing carries any current. It all seems to work on light. When it's working you can see the pulses moving around inside the crystals."

"You mean lasers?"

"Nothing like that, Captain; just ordinary light, but in the proper pulses and intensities. No doubt the photosensitivity of the individual crystals varies from location to location within them.

"So, since it would be absolutely reliable, why should the temporals, given their other capabilities, sit there and wait for an answer to grind out? I'll bet they wouldn't. I think they probably just fed in the problem and the program and then sent it the appropriate distance back in time, and when it was finally ready to crank out the answer it would reappear, perhaps a nanosecond after it left, to burp it out. It wouldn't make any difference what happened in real time. As far as the computer was concerned, the module wouldn't have moved while it was gone."

"An interesting theory, Verity. Where would it get its power?"

"I don't think it'd take that much. Not if it works like I think it does. Whatever it did need could go back with it, maybe using a really long-lived isotope for fuel. There are lots of them that could be used."

"You say you're running some kind of recording?"

"Yes."

"Then, we should be able to backtrack along it?"

"That's only a hypothesis right now, Captain, and only experiment will confirm it. We have to be sure, or we'll get lost again. I don't know if we'll have time. Like Wyckoff says, we'll be out of food in a month or so."

"It might take that long for us to work out the error Lady Bane's course correction introduced. No, there's only one logical choice for us to make when we do get ready to try it—the short course, back to Home."

"Captain, I don't know. We might be all right doing that, providing this thing was recording when the ship left orbit, but I don't know that it was."

"Well, then, Verity, you'll just have to find out, won't you?"

"Yes, ma'am. I guess so." He left, his head shaking slightly but noticeably, to return to his station.

"Weren't you a little rough on him, Arlene?"

"Sure I was. I meant to be. Otherwise, he might have just quit on us. Verity's not like you, Wyckoff. He's a *good* engineer. He *knows* an impossibility when he sees it."

"Oh, and I'm too dumb?"

"That's an advantage I'd hate to see you lose."

Chapter Twenty-Seven

"Ready, Verity?" The captain's voice was clear but weak, as though it might have had to battle its way past a lump.

The reply came back immediately, through the intercom station on her console: "Ready." Verity's voice was no less tense than Arlene's.

"Thrust."

An almost unnoticeable change in weight took place, more a directional than a quantitative one. *Corona* leapt ahead, into a milliparsec jump, headed for a star they thought was a little over half a light-year away.

Below, in the temporal module, Mason was standing by to observe whatever changes might take place on the galactic display. Not only was the experiment designed to detect such movement, but they hoped they might then be able to correlate distances, and convert data from that computer into terms understandable to human beings. As it was, since the display was logarithmic, there was no way they could use it to determine the distance to the star that was their immediate destination.

Mason watched for a while, until he was certain, then pressed the talk button on the intercom. That was a refinement of recent times, and now that the communications system was wired together, operation was very much easier.

"Movement, Captain," he reported. "Slight, but definitely there. I'm recording it on tape, just to make sure we don't lose track."

"Stay with it, Rick. We'll double the next jump. That ought to help."

Wyckoff ambled over and leaned against the bulkhead on Arlene's right. "Doing okay, huh?"

"Well, I don't think things are any worse than they were, if that's what you mean."

"Why are we going for that star? I heard Rick say it was first generation. I thought they weren't supposed to be any good."

"They don't have planets, Wyckoff, that's true, but we don't want it for that. We want its mass."

"Why?"

"Because time runs slower near a massive body than it does elsewhere. And according to the aliens, and the engineering manuals we've translated so far, we'll need that mass to enter stasis."

"We couldn't do it from where we are?"

"We couldn't get that much power out of our engines. The temporal drive has an optimum operational zone for any particular body. In the case of Home, it extended from planetary center to about 30,000 miles. If we had gone out a little farther, we would have ruined Lylard's demonstration. Too bad we didn't know that at the time."

"And when we get there, we try out the new drive?"

"We have to do it someday, Wyckoff. Actually, I'm looking forward to it."

"*You* are. Me, I'm not used to the regular system yet."

"It didn't hurt you any when Lylard did it. You didn't feel a thing."

"He knew what he was doing. We don't."

"We'll figure it out, Wyckoff. Pretty soon we'll be

back on Home, and as soon as we resupply we'll start looking for Earth."

"You really are anxious to get back, aren't you?"

"I guess I am. Shouldn't I be?"

"I don't know. Maybe so. Your situation's different from mine. There isn't anything for me to go back to."

"Me either, Wyckoff. My home is out in space, and I know I wouldn't be staying on Earth, even assuming we do get back. But I have to try to find it. It isn't that being away is so bad—it's that I didn't have a free choice in the matter. Hamil stole that from me. I guess what I'm really trying to say is that I want my option back." She looked at him and smiled weakly. "Can you understand that?"

"Yes. I got me a girl with a mind of her own. There's nothing wrong with that."

"I wonder if you really mean that, Wyckoff."

"Sure I do. Why wouldn't I?"

"Because deep down inside, Wyckoff, I think you're a whole lot more provincial than you let on. Go on, admit it. You're a traditionalist; you've got more peasant in you than you think you do. I remember that trip down the river. I saw the look on your face. You were as proud of those fields as I am of this ship—am I right?"

"Sure, but you've got to remember, I'm a city boy, and all that was new stuff. New stuff is exciting."

"I know what's bothering you, Wyckoff, and I know why you're afraid to go back. I know what happened to Emory. I found a tape the other day, and I played it. I know about your rendezvous with that girl—Linda."

She paused and waited for a reply, as though she knew her words would sting and that this would take a while to wear off. When Wyckoff persisted in silence, she reluctantly continued. "I have to admit I was upset at first."

"I don't know what you're talking about." Despite the disclaimer, it was obvious that he did. His face was red as a beet.

She tried to sound more conciliatory with her next remark. "I know. You weren't aware it was being made—you didn't even know it existed. Hamil's woman, Linda, recorded it after she drugged you. I think I was more upset about those circumstances than I was about Emory's murder."

All of a sudden things started adding up. Wyckoff could now see the causes for some of Arlene's peculiar behavior of late. Previously, he'd attributed it to that female mystique that has always baffled man. Now he knew it was rooted in simple jealousy. He asked himself whether or not this was rational, then answered his own question. Yes, in her place, he would have felt and behaved the same. "I guess I should have told you, Arlene, but somehow, the time just never seemed right. But you see why I can't ever go back, don't you?"

"Why can't you? You didn't kill him."

"No, but if it hadn't been for me, he wouldn't be dead now. I'm the one who fixed it so he could get killed."

"I disagree. I think he would have gotten killed anyway. Emory was basically an irresponsible slob whose only interest was in having a good time. I'm just glad you were handy when his luck finally ran out. And maybe if you hadn't been aboard, Hamil would have gotten away with what he was trying to pull. It's pretty obvious now that he only decided to run when he found out about you. You're a better man than Emory was, in every way."

Wyckoff was always embarrassed by compliments, even when they came from someone close. "Well," he said, intending to get her off the subject, "you see how it is between me and Earth."

"No, I don't, Wyckoff. I can understand how you might feel guilty, but I don't think you really are. And I'll bet a talk with Yasha would straighten you out. In any case, I wouldn't make you go back if you didn't want to."

"Captain?" the intercom squawked.

"Yes, Rick?" Arlene sounded as though she might have been grateful for the interruption.

"I can confirm it, this thing's tracking. There's a red blip showing on screen now. The blip is us—I'd book it."

"All right. That's good enough for me. Will we have the parallax to compute the remaining distance when we come out of this jump?"

"Yes, but just barely. There'd be a lot of guesswork in it."

"All right, then. I guess I'm coming down with buck fever—make it two jumps instead of one, then. Why be half safe?"

"Why indeed? We've had trouble enough on this voyage."

Arlene's prediction of the effects of the temporal field was slightly erroneous. They did feel it this time, perhaps because they were adjacent to an enormously more massive body.

The aliens had, of course, experienced this before, and it did not seem to bother them.

It bothered Wyckoff, who complained that his bodily processes had come to a standstill. Jerry's only advice was not to look at the digital clock the computer displayed, which appeared to be ticking off one second to every fifty or so of Wyckoff's heartbeats.

That was because the computer was processing data from its maintainer, a device that plunged independently even farther into the static field than *Corona* had, and whose job it was to alert the computer to obstacles and dangers that might lie ahead.

Its operating principles were still imperfectly understood. That was partially the fault of imprecise translation of the alien manuals. But what these seemed to suggest was happening was that the maintainer moved rapidly back and forth from the ship to points downwhen or upwhen, as the case might be, and on the occasions it was aboard, dumped its data into the memory. It could not depend on electromagnetic means to transmit its data.

Wyckoff followed the Dorian's advice and gradually felt better. This was fortunate, since the temporal route, though shorter by far in terms of travel time elapsed compared to their journey outward, was a complex and repetitious zigzag—a backward and forward routine involving many temporal touchpoints. Contrary to his expectations, the journey was anything but instantaneous.

Both Jerry and Lady Bane agreed that Lylard would have made it to Home much more quickly than the humans did, which was about the only thing they had agreed upon since Wyckoff had known them.

They were becoming more and more familiar to all the humans, involved as they necessarily were as consultants to the human crew. Consonant with Arlene's expressed intention, neither the Dorians nor Lady Bane had free run of *Corona*. No aliens ever traveled outside of quarters without an armed escort.

On the occasion of *Corona*'s return to the Home system, Arlene relaxed her rule a bit, and permitted both Jerry and Lady Bane to mount the bridge and watch their approach to the human colony through the unmasked nose portal. It was breathtaking.

To the humans, the true beauty of the occasion lay in the knowledge that the planet below was theirs; that it could nourish the race, even if it wasn't Earth.

Wyckoff stood in the center of a quartet composed of himself, Mason, Lady Bane, and the ubiquitous translating robot. "There it is," he murmured. "Good ol' Home! It doesn't look much different."

"Why should it?" Mason answered. But his voice had a tinge of nostalgia, just as Wyckoff's had. "We've returned approximately six weeks after the *Corona* left. I'll bet the people will be surprised to see us."

"They won't even know we're up here until we call them. How soon can we land?"

"*Corona* won't be going down, Wyckoff. We'll use the lifeboats for shuttles, and descend in them."

"I thought Verity said the ship was all right?"

"It is," the alien woman interjected. "It is because of the temporal generator. The temporals never land a module with a generator on it."

"Why not?"

"I do not know for certain, but I suspect that part of the reason is to prevent their victims from getting hold of one. In any case, this is wise, since we all will depend upon it to find our homes again. It would be foolish to risk damage to the vessel."

"Earth." Mason gasped the word, as though it burned his mouth. "What a story we can tell them when we do get back, eh, Wyckoff?" He gave his companion a friendly prod.

"I'm not sure I really want to go, Rick. But I'll tell you what I would like to do. I'd like to go back to the time where Hamil skipped out and pick him up. I'll bet that'd shock the pants off him."

"Yes, that might be fun. But you know, I think I feel like you do about this. I think I'd like to see the galaxy—after we find Earth again, that is—and maybe be a Lord Temporal myself. It sounds romantic."

The translator's speakers fairly sizzled with Lady Bane's retort. "The temporals I know are dishonorable, cowardly cutthroats, Mr. Mason. Some are bad enough, incredible as it may sound, to turn the stomachs of the Dorians, and Dorians are offal worms who live in fear of everything."

"What I meant was that they're like pirates, in the old Terran tradition, with a free lifestyle and all of space to roam and explore. Naturally, I hate them."

Lady Bane shot him a disdainful glance. It was clear that she wasn't deceived by the first mate's attempt at whitewashing the temporals.

Wyckoff noticed the way the Kruj'jan's ruff had raised, the way her muscles were bunching, and the way the retractable claws, normally folded back flat against the tops of her fingers, were twitching. He resolved to cool things down. He liked Lady Bane and always treated her with great civility. He thought she liked him, too, and counted on that fact to keep her under control. "You have to remember, princess, that thanks to you, Lylard didn't last long enough to push us around much. On the other hand, we had our own devil—Captain Hamil. We had enough time with him. It takes time for humans to learn to hate people, and it's hard work.

"Besides, according to Jerry, there are different kinds of temporals. He said every one aboard was different. Now, you couldn't have hated all of them like you did Lylard, Princess."

"I must admit, I did not find the bharph female as offensive as the others; however, like myself, she was unwilling, and she was oppressed."

"There, now do you see? Maybe there are some good pirates after all."

"I will reserve judgment until I have encountered all of them, Wyckoff. I might add that in the light of further data, the translator has refined its definition of your term. I am prepared to concede that the habits of the temporals coincide closely with this concept."

At last, Mason dared to speak again. "It fits a theory I've been working out," he said.

Wyckoff, still anxious to keep the conversation friendly, picked up on this opportunity to get it moving to another point, an effort in which, despite his intention, he largely failed. "What kind of theory?"

"One on temporal origins—where they came from, how they got to be what they are. I think you may very well be right about them being pirates. I get the impression there aren't a whole lot of them, by the usual standards."

"What's the theory?" Wyckoff turned slightly, to keep an eye on Lady Bane.

"Well, bear in mind that's all it is. I could be wrong, and I probably am. But this is what I think. Somewhere, or maybe somewhen—maybe millions or billions of years ago, or maybe in the far future—somebody stumbled on time travel. However it happened, it would be easy to see that conquering time is the only practical means of crossing long spatial distances. There's no other way to get from here to there without homogenizing your own reality. With this, your real time always stays the same, and you can compensate for what it does to those who don't travel with you.

"Whoever discovered the temporal drive didn't share it, at least not widely, and probably not willingly, in any case. If they had, there would be evidence of it, recognizable even by us nontemporals, and there isn't. Back in the days before space travel, one of the biggest unsolved questions was, where is everybody?

"So, instead, I think the knowledge spread very slowly, and very likely accidentally, like it did to us.

"Lady Bane, you spoke of an organization of temporals. The machine translates it out as guild, but 'mob' would probably be more appropriate, considering your description."

The princess did not speak, but she nodded her assent to that refinement.

"The fact that there are two separate ranks of temporals—high lords and ordinary ones—is especially informative, particularly since the distinction seems to be that the high temporals are those who can manufacture temporal vessels, and the inferior ones are those who, one way or another, gained possession of one. Would you not agree?"

"I would," the alien woman answered, then added an example. "Lylard and his ilk were of the lowlife."

This time it was Mason's turn to acknowledge with a nod.

Wyckoff was relieved at this, since he had begun to fear another emotional outburst. The princess seemed incensed at the very thought of Lylard or the mention of his name, however casually.

"Anyway," Mason droned on didactically, "between them, they've divided the universe all along the time line. They've got territories each more or less respects, their vassals among the lesser lords, and control of subject races of nontemporals such as we, whom they exploit."

"Chicken thieves," Lady Bane muttered, her tone somehow managing to ooze through the translator as vile contempt. "They trade among themselves with what they plunder from the barbarian civilizations. Any culture not temporal they call barbarian, even if it possesses technical ability exceeding their own, as sometimes happens. The temporals steal knowledge whenever they can, and technical information is a staple of their trade."

"What about all that junk we found squirreled away in the module's hold? What were they going to do with that?"

"Yeah, Princess, I've got to agree with Rick; some of that is worse than what the *Corona* was carrying."

"It all has value to somebody, Wyckoff," the alien woman replied. "Most of it, believe it or not, is primitive art, though it takes the right kind of perspective to see it that way. It was intended for what the temporals referred to as the luxury trade, which is another word for fools, in my judgment. Lylard and his partners had just finished collecting it and the expedition was returning to base when the accident happened.

"It is," Bane sighed, "a game the temporals play with one another. They pass their trinkets through as many hands as possible, and with each passage their fervor grows. Have you seen the gold and jewels they had?"

Wyckoff nodded. He could not help speculating how rich he would be if he had this back on Earth, but then Bane broke his bubble.

"This is what the temporals used when trading with the real primitives, who cannot get at whole asteroids of it as they can."

"Yeah," he added sourly, "more junk. After a while, everything turns to junk."

"Very profound, Wyckoff," Mason noted, "but erroneous. Some things don't: progress, learning, knowledge, good music, good literature, really good artwork;

these are the universe's real treasures. These are what I'd collect, if I were a temporal."

"Then, maybe we'd all better get busy, Rick—we *are* temporals now."

The last boatload of food and supplies had just cleared the lock, and Wyckoff was directing the crews who were stuffing it into storage lockers. As soon as they were finished, the *Corona* would be getting under way.

Below, on the planet, the colony looked a lot different. In the twenty years the ship and her crew had moved forward in time, its entire character had changed. Not only was the population larger, it was thoroughly at home with the idea of time travel. Those spacehands who'd left ship upon the initial return had taken care of that—and seen to it that when the *Corona* appeared in orbit again there was a warehouse full of artwork and spices to be traded on the next voyage.

Best of all, they had established a university of sorts. For a colony this small, the expense was proportionately enormous, but the benefits had been equal. In the interval, with the use of the translating robots and the backup system from *Corona*'s library computer, the scholars had succeeded in translating all the alien data into English. Sadly, but as expected, there were certain subjects that Lylard had completely omitted from his data base—among them, anything useful to astrogation, and data on the temporal system. They had anticipated the latter, since he had been a minor lord.

As the humans quickly discovered, the mere fact that they now possessed translations of manuals did not imbue them with automatic understanding of them. Untranslatable technical terms abounded, and when the robots encountered one of these, they thoughtfully left a blank for it, creating great frustration among the researchers.

There were, fortunately, also some illustrations. A group of these, dealing with the physical treatment of the temporal drive, became known as the doomsday list, because doing any of the things listed would unbalance the temporal field and destroy the ship.

The crew was required to memorize the doomsday list. Without it, the voyage they contemplated would have been suicidal. With it, and with the rest of the data they had salvaged and the experts who had been trained in the interim, they hoped the twenty years they'd sacrificed through their initial ignorance had been both expendable and worth it.

The "old" crewmen were now middle-aged, but others, like the officers, who were outside the local timeline, had replaced them. Some had families on Home and, if everything went well, would return to them a day, a week, or a month hence, looking slightly older, having turned the Einstein Effect around a full 180 degrees. They could do that, by means still very little understood, and within limits that were still very much undefined.

Unfortunately, they could not skip ahead and see whether or not that would happen. If they tried, all they would accomplish would be to squander yet more time, since the interval would then be closed to them.

Arlene was worried about the possibility *Corona* might not return, but not enough to call the mission off, especially now that they were sure the colony would flourish. She regarded rediscovery and return to Earth as obligatory. The information they now had was of immense value to the race—possibly even vital to its survival. Besides, they owed Bane a ride home, for what she had and was doing for them. They owed the Dorians, too, though they seemed to be much less attached to their home civilization than Lady Bane was, and as fired up as Mason was about learning their way around the universe.

Arlene believed renewed contact with Earth meant that all of humanity might someday enjoy the advantage the temporals now had—to travel where and when they wanted. The others paid that idea lip service. Only Wyckoff openly disagreed.

Somehow, he was certain, that wasn't in the cards. He believed Mason's theory was correct: the evidence would be there for them to find, unless things turned out otherwise.

On the last day before their scheduled embarkation, Wyckoff went into seclusion. He did not think of it as such, he knew only that he had his worst case of the shakes ever. He could not endure company; he must find counsel and comfort in his own thoughts or not at all. He returned to his sanctuary in the engine pod, where once before he had ridden out a storm. The pod was the same, only he was different, and it was that very difference which drove him there.

No one had disturbed him then; no one did now. He rested, sitting in the darkness on the same old pile of rags and junk that he had brought there so many years ago.

Years? Could he mean that? He decided he couldn't— for him it was only months, at most. He now existed outside the timeframe which most of the life on Home still shared with one another. He felt alien. He was losing his orientation. He was afraid that if he left again, the next time would be worse, and it was already all but unendurable for him to think that many of the friends he had a year ago were gone, and had been, in their own timeframe, gone for many years.

Once, not so long ago, he had labored under the delusion that temporal travel meant something else— that he could creep backward in time and visit what and who had been, and change what had been to something better. Causality was a bitter disappointment to Wyckoff. It struck him as unnecessarily brutal. Nevertheless, it was a fact that though a personal, real lifetime might be stretched out over a millennium or even more, the intervals between the temporal points it touched were lost. A temporal might emerge from stasis as far in the future as he wished, but he could never emerge in his own past.

A lump was growing in Wyckoff's throat. In the darkness, that which he could see in mind and memory was not only real again, but the only reality there was. He saw the light of Home's sun and felt its warmth. A brisk wind was blowing over freshly plowed fields, bringing their odor to him. They were the smells of living things, the growing plants that men of flesh and blood had cultivated.

And he knew in an instant that this is what had made the difference, made the planet home in fact as well as in name. The mark of man was upon it—and so was his mark. And that was good. He had at least that—an answer for the question that in even more uncertain times he had asked himself: *When I am gone, what will remain to show that I have ever been here?*

But was it enough? He did not know. Arlene's words echoed in his ears. She called him a peasant. He was, and he was not ashamed of that. Though he might call himself a lord, as many now did, yet if his hands touched the tools with which he built his world, and his feet followed the plow, he was what all successful men had always been: a part of the ecology, at peace with nature.

It was down there, on Home, that Wyckoff had first tasted such peace; enjoying the first really satisfying interlude of his entire existence, the first familiarity with his environment, the first interlocking of his destiny with that of other men. He did not know if he could bear the loss, though some of it, even now, was gone.

Yasha was gone. Yasha, that small, quick man, so cheerful that Wyckoff unconsciously compared him with a cricket. Yasha had been simple, straightforward, transparent, parochial, a peasant himself, yet certainly the most complex person Wyckoff had ever met, and possessed of the keenest intellect. Other men had built what culture there was on Home, Wyckoff among them, but Yasha Fu had given it its soul.

Good old Yasha. A smile washed over Wyckoff's face. He leaned back against the cool metal of the bulkhead and let recollection bloom.

He could see the two of them in his mind's eye, sitting in Yasha's tiny office, using his crude desk for a table. They had beer, which Wyckoff ordinarily didn't like very well, but which Yasha had himself brewed with rice, according to an old ancestral recipe, he boasted. It went down well but loosened Yasha's tongue and made him more talkative than Wyckoff could remember.

"I feel a little guilty, Yasha," he had said. "We could have raised a couple of chickens on the grain we're drinking up."

"Home can get along without so many chickens for a few more weeks. Never feel guilty about accepting a privilege you've earned, Wyckoff. It's unpatriotic."

Wyckoff had not replied. The alcoholic content of Yasha's brew was high and begat strange words, he thought. His own sobriety was in grave doubt, so he sat there dumbly.

"If it's your due—you take it. Refuse and you insult the public, who gave it to you. Worse, you risk destabilizing society. That's the part that really makes it unforgivable, Wyckoff. Don't ever forget that."

"I wouldn't even consider it," Wyckoff had replied sarcastically.

"Know what you are, Wyckoff? Huh?" Yasha was holding a cup in the same hand with which he was attempting to point. Tidal forces inside it were demanding release, sloshing over the rim, running down the tip, and dripping onto the rough-hewn boards of the tabletop in cadence with the shaking finger.

"What? What am I?"

"You're a legend, that's what."

Wyckoff remembered his answer to that. The answer had sounded inane: "I can't be. I'm not old enough."

"You will be, Wyckoff. To the rest of the people here on Home you'll be the next thing to immortal. You know what the captain's gonna do, don'cha?"

"I heard. I don't think I like it."

"It's the only way, Wyckoff. Home needs the time,

and those of you who go in search of Earth will need the peace of mind. It's got to be."

Wyckoff had put his cup down on the table and never picked it up again. He had finished the conversation stone-cold sober and with a slight headache. It was the last conversation he and Yasha ever had. He never saw him again.

But he remembered every word, even those he hadn't understood. By and by, he thought, maybe it'll start making sense.

Some of it did already—Yasha's prophecy that *Corona* and her crew would soon exist only in the memories of Home's oldest citizens, and that the stories they told to wide-eyed children would dim as the youngsters grew to maturity and repeated the tales. It would happen, Yasha insisted.

In some respects it already had. Wyckoff rubbed a shirtsleeve over eyes too moist for his pride to have endured, except in this darkness and solitude.

"You must always be there, Wyckoff—you and Arlene. The people of Home must always believe that someday you are coming back, because you are not merely founding a dynasty, which is easy. The two of you are the dynasty, which is unique in human history."

Wyckoff gave his face another dab with the sleeve. It felt soggy. He sniffled instead.

Pretty sneaky of Yasha. It wasn't that they hadn't thought about it themselves, he and Arlene, but Yasha took it upon himself to be the catalyst, and so they tied the knot. A royal couple at last, Yasha declared.

Whatever. Wyckoff had felt no different. The true impact hadn't hit him until now. Now he knew what it felt like to be a legend: lonely.

Chapter Twenty-Eight

Once again, *Corona* winked out of the Home system, attempting to retrace the course that had brought Lylard's party there. Being far from experienced in the use of the temporal system, they made mistakes, and many times at the beginning of the voyage they lost their way and had to backtrack, both in space and time. The reversal of course had a curious effect on the plotter display, and in the beginning gave them many anxious moments. Not only did the blip that served as its cursor and represented the ship change color from red to blue, but each display was a mirror image of the other.

The phenomenon had come as a complete surprise. There was absolutely nothing in any of the translated manuals that even hinted of the reason. They knew that in orthodox theory it should have been impossible to reverse the temporal course, but also that the human theorists responsible for this opinion were unacquainted with the static effect the temporal generator utilized. Of necessity then, assuming Earthly science erred through lack of data, they believed what they saw, and used it because it worked.

In this manner they did learn, more or less continually. Trial and error being the peerless teacher that it was, they also learned exceedingly well.

Still, there appeared to be only one point on the display they might possibly be able to identify with certainty—Lylard's point of origin. Neither the Dorians nor Bane knew how to find their own home systems, any more than the humans knew how to find theirs. Most of the Dorians had been picked up by Lylard long ago and had accompanied him on many of his travels. Jerry had been traded through several temporals before Lylard got him.

So the plan, born of necessity, was to barge into temporal territory and try to gain that knowledge. It was a bold plan, but the alternative was to search all time and space and hope that they would be lucky.

Corona thus proceeded much more slowly than she would have had the crew had real confidence in the course she ran, and life settled down aboard her, to become as routine as the run from Earth to Zahn was supposed to have been.

There was no real action on the bridge anymore. Once a few spatio-temporal hops had been made, that too became routine, and the nature of the journey being what it was, there was very good reason not to approach any planet closely—the major cost in energy was in passing in and out of temporal stasis or across the bands, not in moving along the time stream. So, for the most part, they stayed as far in-system as was possible.

Wyckoff, not being a spacehand except in the very broad sense, found himself with time on his hands and little to do. The main computer kept the inventory of supplies for the small complement they carried, and the trade goods, as he now called them, had long since lost their novelty. He was tired of looking at alien paintings and statuary which, as often as not, appeared disgustingly ugly to the human eye. Only alien music, some of which turned out to be hauntingly beautiful, managed to hold his attention, and he spent hours listening to recordings.

When he wasn't doing that and when his off-watch hours failed to coincide with Arlene's, he frequently found companionship in the Dorian, Jerry. The Dorians also had time on their hands, having been replaced in their duties on board the *Corona* by human crewmen who had rejoined the ship at Home. It was not that *Corona*'s officers were ungrateful for the Dorians' help, or that there was any animosity left over from the incident with Lylard; that had healed, and bygones were bygones. It was mostly that the Dorians lacked the training human spacemen had and were too small physically to perform many of the tasks as efficiently.

So since they had become the equivalent of passengers, most of them began to behave like passengers. Some haunted the terminals of *Corona*'s library system, soaking up such technical knowledge as their culture lacked and which the humans had not proscribed. The Dorians proved to be fantastically gifted linguists, and most, including Jerry, learned English in order to read without tying up the limited translating facilities the module had carried.

Of all the Dorians aboard, Jerry still seemed special. The others were friendly enough, but compared to him they seemed shy and retiring. He, on the contrary, professed not only to enjoy human company, but to enjoy studying Wyckoff. As a consequence, he became Wyckoff's more or less constant companion in tedium.

The two of them did occasionally triumph over this. They discovered that a certain root from among Lylard's spice cargo, when roasted, ground, and steeped, was remarkably like coffee. It was a little bitter for human taste, so Wyckoff drank his sweetened, but there was always a pot of it going at his station on "R" deck. The pot became the focus of many idle but philosophical conversations between the two of them.

Occasionally, though, Jerry abandoned his usually carefully neutral stance and gave unsolicited advice. It was thus following Arlene's announcement that the *Corona* would soon need fuel, and that she intended to look for a culture that could supply it. The fuel, tritium, took a fairly high technology to produce, and an even higher technology to need. It would be scarce, and the search for it a long one if conducted at random. More audacious surveys, and perhaps indiscriminate contacts, were contemplated.

"I advise caution, Wyckoff," Jerry said gravely. "Please tell the captain I said that."

Wyckoff noted the tone of Jerry's voice and asked him why.

"We must choose exactly the right culture with which to trade, and do it at precisely the correct time," Jerry answered. "Knowledge of temporal travel is the one commodity for which all sapient species will kill."

"I didn't know it was that dangerous to be smart, Jerry."

"I learned this from Lylard, Wyckoff. He was always very careful of such things. He never risked a contact with any culture that approached his own in technical competence. He always chose an era which would give him the advantage. I might add that when he could, Lylard always obtained his fuel from the bases of other temporals. They have such an arrangement with one another. He stopped at one such on the outward journey, though none but the temporals disembarked there."

"We might not find one, and even if we could, wouldn't it be pretty dangerous?"

"Why should it be dangerous, Wyckoff?"

"Well, here we are, bumbling around like we don't know what we're doing and all. Somebody's going to notice that . . ."

"And nobody will care. Temporals aren't normally very dangerous to one another, Wyckoff, except for the sort of intrigue Lylard got himself involved in. They'll take it for granted we're ordinary temporals."

"Well, I don't like it, Jerry. We won't know how to act."

"There's no prescribed temporal behavior, Wyckoff. I'd know if there was; I've been around enough of them. They're only different in the way they get around; otherwise, they have the same problems as anybody else. Those aboard Lylard's expedition were typical, and I observed them long and closely. Lylard was dominant among them, because he was the greediest. He used them, and told them lies—such as the one about the rich source of spices he knew of—in order to get their cooperation. He would not have been able to afford the expedition otherwise."

Wyckoff's tone changed—became a little more reassured. "I wouldn't think any temporal would have money problems, Jerry."

"Money? Oh, yes, I see. I am not used to a standard medium of exchange anymore. No, Wyckoff, that is not true. Fortunes rise and fall among the temporals just as they do among others. There is competition for resources even among those with all the universe to draw from. There will be local scarcities of some commodities. We are experiencing this in our quest for fuel."

"But Lylard just took what he wanted?"

"*Sometimes* he did. They all do that when they can get away with it. Everybody likes to get by as cheaply as he can. But it's dangerous. Sometimes temporals underestimate their victims and there's fighting, which is just another way of paying if you really stop to think about it, because valuable supplies are expended and irreplaceable equipment is destroyed.

"That is the principal reason the temporals seldom wage war among themselves, though they are ready enough to use force on barbarians. As a matter of fact, peace is the norm throughout the universe as I know it. The reason is that warlike peoples almost always use advanced technology, including interplanetary capability, to destroy themselves—as the Kruj'jans will doubtless do, if they ever get their paws on any ships. As a matter of fact, the human wars I have been reading about in your records may very well be unique among cultures which have achieved interstellar travel. It is miraculous that your people survived."

"What about *your* people, Jerry? What are they like? You never seem to talk about them." Wyckoff had not been alone in noting that peculiarity. Others had commented on it too. The Dorians were willing enough to talk about anything else, but they never seemed to pine for their homeworld as Lady Bane did. When pressed to discuss themselves, they answered evasively.

Jerry's reply was typical in that respect. "Now? What are they like now? I have no way to answer you. I do not know how to measure time in terms of my homeworld's units. I do not know how far the period during which I lived there is removed from that I presently occupy. For all I know, in this time my race may be extinct. But I can tell you we were not barbarians, as Lylard used to suggest. We did not have space travel, but we had aircraft, and many of the technical amenities your culture has. That steamboat the colonists built on Home would have been archaic in my culture."

Though he was astute enough to resist mentioning it, it occurred to Wyckoff that perhaps Jerry had just revealed a racial secret. *What if*, he asked himself, *the Dorian race is extinct, and Jerry and the other six guys are all there are? If it was us humans, would we like to talk about things like that?* He decided not to get any more personal than he already had, and asked a more innocent question. "So where does it all end, Jerry? I mean, here we are, and there you are, and we're both in trouble because of Lylard?"

"I assume you mean, how much has temporal meddling changed the course of galactic civilization? My answer, based on what I have personally seen, would have to be, not by very much. I do not know, of course, how many temporals there are, but I have some idea of how vast the galaxy is and I have some inkling of the true depth of time.

"Except for the temporals, time is an insurmountable barrier. Your people encountered it and felt the frustration long before you met Lylard. Unlike we who are here, most species will never progress beyond the slow, creeping posture yours had at that moment. Moreover, civilizations die, planets die, even suns die, so if life has any influence on the universe at all, it is not readily detectable.

"Nothing is static for long enough in galactic terms for any one species to comprehend it, much less dominate it, and that may be true even for the temporals. Mr. Mason is right about what he told you; were it to happen, signs of it would be strewn all along the time line of every inhabited world in the galaxy. It is not there, thus the temporals appear to be content merely to be temporals."

"What was Lylard's homeworld like, Jerry?"

The Dorian paused, as though to recollect and reflect upon his answer. "He had no home world in the sense that you mean, Wyckoff. It is my belief that none of the temporals do. I have been to what he had. So has Lady Bane. Except for those he brought there, the system he occupied was empty of life in the era he selected for his homewhen. He kept its location secret, since he was but a minor lord. He lived there like a criminal, in hiding."

"But what about this central computer Arlene talks about?"

"It may exist, but Lylard didn't have it. And there are, I understand, greater lords of sufficient power that they do not have to hide as Lylard hid himself from them, and who comprise the leadership of this guild of theirs. I have not personally seen any such, but I presume Lylard traded with them for the astrogational information he needed. He had to get it somewhere."

"And so will we?"

"So will we, Wyckoff."

Chapter Twenty-Nine

Arlene was starting to get antsy over their fuel situation. The humans were discovering that astrogation with these combined systems was both a long, tedious procedure and an expensive one in terms of energy.

The Aschenbrenner inertial drive was a fuel-efficient system, and many of the human vessels of the *Corona*'s class had simply not been in operation long enough to have required refueling. But the temporal generator proved to be such a heavy drain when under prolonged use that *Corona*'s reserves began to run low.

Thus there was a period of great anxiety as she passed through many and varied points of space and time reversing on Lylard's recorded course, when no noteworthy civilizations were found. Some relief was afforded by the fact that as experience with the systems grew, the "local" travel became shorter and shorter, much of the distance having been made up by fine-tuning their temporal travel. Still, the eventual exhaustion of the tritium in *Corona*'s tanks could now be calculated accurately, and it was only a matter of weeks.

The bridge crew kept the instruments on full time now, and examined each system they passed with a minuteness disdained only a short while ago, hoping to come across a culture with both the capability and need to refine the fuel they sought.

They found none. In all times they were able to explore during their passage, their current area of travel appeared to be singularly devoid of life-bearing systems. Either they were traversing great clouds of hydrogen, or they were passing huge first-generation suns which, though they burned fiercely, did not spawn rocky planets.

Had they not been searching for fuel, the lack of planets would not have mattered. At least passage through that region of space and time was not a positive, active peril, as the gas clouds were. The gas clouds contained enormous amounts of matter, but they were spread so thinly that the mass was useless. They had no foci, and it was the foci on which the temporal generator depended to augment the power it drew from *Corona*'s engines.

Time after time the captain had no alternative but to back the ship up to the next fork and follow another branch. The fuel load dwindled, but gradually the gas clouds gave way to wastelands of another kind, each in their own way as dangerous.

Corona reached a point where the plotter suggested the better course was upwhen, so they reversed and followed it as far as they could, then turned again. Traveling down the timeline led again to disappointment, into more of the same. The stellar character changed once more, though again not for the better, leading then into a broad patchwork thousands of light-years across, filled with nothing but white dwarfs and neutron stars. They abandoned that end of the temporal spectrum, concerned that the next phase of stellar evolution would lead them into a swarm of indetectable and deadly discontinuities.

Discontinuities were mentioned on the doomsday list. Though theoretically, the larger ones should have been ideal temporal transfer points since masses were at once so huge and so compact, they were warned against approaching them. No explanation was given.

The alternative passage *Corona* faced did not seem very attractive, either—it was through massive gobs of agitated hydrogen, interspersed with dust coalescing into lumps, constricting and falling into themselves. *Corona*'s crew was not, of course, compelled to stand by as this occurred in real time, but moved along the timeline in frictionless stasis.

Stasis was not an easy or a comfortable concept for the human mind, but it was undeniably a handy thing to have around. More than once the sudden grip of the temporal generator spared *Corona* a plunge into the flames, as she followed a shrinking volume across a smaller and smaller radius in order to reach the temporal boundary. More than once the maintainer sensed changes just in time to flick them safely into stasis the instant before thermonuclear reactions began, and before the radiation pressures hurled a star's outer envelope over *Corona*'s flimsy body.

Fortunately, in stasis they were safe, protected from any force that moved at less than an infinite velocity, simply because they could move leisurely out of its way as though it were frozen immobile.

The greatest peril *Corona* faced resulted not from what was present but from what was not present. There are always areas of any galaxy where matter is scarce, and where stars in any era are few and far between, because mechanical motions dictate their dispersal and movement, and thus create voids which require great care to cross. At any rate, *Corona* drifted into such a place, and it was here, in the most inhospitable part of this most inhospitable region, this spatial counterpart to Earth's own worst deserts, that signs of technically advanced life appeared most prominently. There was, it seemed, an oasis nearby.

The first evidence of it came from other vessels passing near enough for *Corona*'s instruments to detect them. Blips began to appear on the screen of the module's mass gauges, belying the presence of temporal fields that could not be originating from the far-off suns.

The humans were mystified at first, but the Dorians knew what it meant.

"Such heavy traffic indicates a trading base lies somewhere near," Jerry told the humans. "It is probably not as large as the one Lylard visited on the journey outward, but it should have the fuel we need."

"If we dare go in to get it," Arlene replied. "After all we went through to get this far, I'd hate to blow it now. How can you be sure that this is a temporal base?"

"Who but temporals could reach this place? Who will therefore suspect us of being anything else? If we can reach it, then we are also temporals. And why should anyone care who we are or where we come from, so long as we are peaceful and have goods to trade? I doubt the danger is great, Captain."

"Suppose we don't have anything anybody wants?"

"Lylard used to say that there is nothing everybody wants and nothing nobody wants. Lylard was but a minor Lord Temporal among those with whom he traveled, but he managed to survive them. He was not stupid, and we can learn from him."

Establishing vectors for the other ships was not difficult, nor did they have any difficulty matching course or keeping up. They suspected the other vessels were homing in on some kind of signal transmitted from the body they approached, and that instruments to detect this probably existed within the temporal module. The manuals contained no data on such a system, probably because it would have been useful to astrogation, and the humans had not found it because of their reluctance to tamper with equipment of unknown purpose and importance. Owing to the sheer volume of traffic around them, they were able to calculate where these would converge and determine the base's location, though the display plotter did not show the positions of vessels other than their own.

Arlene could not tell for certain how far away they were from it, and therefore hesitated to pull *Corona* from stasis. In their current state of near distress it was important that they complete any maneuver on as little fuel as possible.

When Mason announced that blips were becoming scarce on the mass gauges, though, she knew that their unseen companions were dropping in velocity, a clear indication that they were nearing the base. She hastily followed suit, and by fantastic coincidence, brought *Corona* out within visual range of it.

Visual was perhaps a misnomer. It was not visible to the naked eye, but it radiated brightly in the infrared, and so their instruments could see it. "It's huge," Arlene remarked. "It must be several thousand miles across."

"Thirty-seven hundred, Captain," Mason replied. "And undoubtedly artificial. Its surface seems to be nickel-iron. Its orbital motion suggests a much smaller mass than it would have if solid; therefore, it must be hollow."

"A dyson sphere?"

"No, I think not. There is no plume of radiation, as there would be if it was open to space. Entry must be controlled through locks, as on shipboard. I wonder why we have not been challenged?"

He continued to wonder until the radio began to blast away in a series of strange, high-pitched whistles. The translator device was tied in at once, and promptly recognized the speech, which it thereafter translated into English.

". . . tering the Bubawawa defense zone. Identify your vessel immediately or it will be destroyed." There was a momentary pause, and then the voice began again: "You are not broadcasting the proper recognition signal required for entering our defense zone. Identify your vessel immediately or it will be destroyed." Another pause: "You—"

"It's a tape or something, Arlene," Wyckoff shouted, "and it sounds like they mean business." He paused, then snickered, "Bubawawa, huh? What a dumb name!"

"Yeah," Mason replied sarcastically. "You'd think they'd pick something more sensible, like Honolulu or Walla Walla, wouldn't you?"

Arlene ignored them. She was not the kind who took refuge in humor when she was scared. To her, terror was a serious subject, and it deserved her full attention. She adjusted her headset and flipped a switch on her console to turn off her earphones and divert to the cabin speaker. Simultaneously, she located the channel on which the challenge was being broadcast, and keyed her microphone. "This is the Earth ship *Corona*—Captain Graham. Can anyone hear me?" She paused, knowing that there would be a substantial lag, then repeated her message twice more before she was interrupted.

The computerized voice was bland, of course, but even so it seemed gruff, simply from the context. "This is the traffic control supervisor, *Corona*. Why are you calling on a defense channel?"

"This is *Corona*—Captain Graham. We are answering your challenge; we are identifying our vessel."

"I repeat: Why are you calling on a defense channel?"

"And I repeat: We are responding to challenge."

"You are disrupting the entire station security system, *Corona*. Stop your vessel. Go to this frequency." The translator burped out a string of numbers.

Arlene punched them into her console keyboard, then tested: "This is *Corona*—Captain Graham."

"This is Station Security, *Corona*. You are in violation of station traffic rules. You have failed to request an approach vector; you have endangered other vessels with collision."

"Sorry," Arlene replied hastily, "but . . ."

"A corridor has been cleared. Leave our system immediately or you will be destroyed."

Arlene hesitated. She knew that they were defenseless if attacked. Not only did *Corona* lack armament of her own, she couldn't even retreat into the safety of stasis. The station was out here by itself, isolated both in space and in time, and at their distance from it, its attraction was below what their system required in order to operate. There seemed to be no alternative but to comply, or at least to pretend to comply while they continued talking. Without fuel they wouldn't last very much longer anyhow.

Meanwhile, Wyckoff popped up with a suggestion. "Tell him our equipment broke down, Arlene. Ask him to help us get in. Tell him we need extensive repairs, and fuel—lots of fuel. And tell him we have an extremely valuable cargo to sell."

She glanced back gratefully and nodded her head. "This is *Corona*—Captain Graham. We acknowledge. We are coming about."

"Tell him, Arlene!" Wyckoff nagged her. He knew he had to. Arlene just wasn't very good at deceit unless somebody really pushed her.

With this push, however, she did an adequate job, with the impersonal translator program concealing her frailties because it conveyed information only, not emotion.

As it turned out, she did not even need to begin the maneuver before greed took hold at the station. Another voice—a different one apparently, although they had only the speaker's word for it—burst out through the speaker. "*Corona*? Captain Graham? Acknowledge!"

"*Corona*! This is Captain Graham."

"This is the guild resident. I have been monitoring your transmissions. Is your vessel in acute distress?"

"Careful, Arlene," Wyckoff cautioned. "Don't let him get the idea you'd be a pushover."

She smiled an acknowledgement, then answered the alien. "Not exactly. Our propulsion systems are operative but communications are out, and most of our detection gear is giving us problems. This is why we didn't request an approach vector. We were trying to follow the other traffic in."

"I understand," the resident replied. "I don't seem to be able to find any record of your ship. I take it you've not been here before?"

"No," Arlene replied, and seemed relieved that she had a chance to tell the truth again, "we haven't."

"I'll have to have the security section check you out then. I'm sure you understand."

"Of course," Arlene answered, her voice trembling.

"I've spoken to their supervisor about the way his people behaved. It's so hard to get good help these days. Naturally, we have to choose aggressive types for these duties in order to have an effective defense, but they do have a tendency to overdo things."

"Of course," Arlene replied. "We understand."

"I was certain you would. I assure you, they'll behave themselves while they're aboard your vessel. And now, if you'll excuse me, I must get back to my other duties."

"Certainly," Arlene replied. She glanced over toward Wyckoff, her expression a strange mixture of bewilderment and relief.

He exuded confidence. "Now, you see? It worked. Arlene, you've got to learn to handle the con. Don't be afraid. These people don't know any better. They'll believe anything we tell them as long as it sounds reasonable."

After that, all conversation in the control room died quietly. It was as though everyone realized that nothing they could say would make any difference if the aliens didn't believe their story, and if they decided to just move in and take. Minutes ticked by and the tension built, as they sat waiting for clues of the aliens' intentions.

Then, out of the darkness a tug appeared, brightly lighted and blasting out intermittent bursts of microwave radiation to warn other traffic out of its way. When it had approached near enough, its crew advised that it would be docking and that a pilot and a valuer would be coming aboard the Earthship. The pilot would then guide *Corona* into a repair lock, provided the valuer found, on inspection of their cargo, that they had sufficient means to pay. The humans had no reason to speculate on what would happen if it was decided they couldn't pay—they knew. The answer was implicit in the arrangement.

Chapter Thirty

This is getting complicated, Wyckoff said to himself, as he directed the gaunt figure of the valuer to the storage holds.

The alien had been given a portable modem when he entered the cramped cargo bays. Wyckoff carried its mate, and both were patched into a translator robot standing outside. Thus the two of them could wander through constricted corridors, past cupboards and bins stuffed with merchandise, and still communicate without difficulty. Without physical difficulty, that is.

This alien, however, appeared unusually taciturn. He had little to say as he wandered through the storage area examining the artifacts the humans had taken from Lylard. He seemed never to get the idea that he should replace the netting after he had loosened it, and Wyckoff was getting irritated because the job fell to him.

Nevertheless, he followed the valuer through his excursion on three decks, stoically replacing netting and trying to read the alien's expression. That, he knew, was a hopeless task. The alien's face was covered with a sort of beard that bristled several inches past his skin, and through which his eyes were almost invisible. His head resembled a hairy bowling ball, though missing a fingerhole because his mouth was all but indetectable unless he spoke.

That had been exasperatingly seldom while he rummaged through Lylard's collection, until they reached the area where the homemade crafts of the colonists were stored, and what had been an unemotional episode suddenly changed character.

Except for the hand-forged weapons and cutlery—the products of the old smith and the apprentices he had trained—most of the stuff was both amateurish and unattractive to Wyckoff. The pottery, for instance, was rough and crudely formed. Its decoration was even worse. The carved wooden statuary was stylized, and to him appeared formless.

But the valuer spent an inordinate amount of time examining it, far longer than he had devoted to the things Lylard had collected.

It was not until he had moved on to sample the spices that he made any direct comment, and then he was noncommittal about details. "I think," he said at last, "that I can pass your ship for entry. As for these spices and biologicals I cannot yet say, since the opinion of experts from individual consumer races is necessary to determine their suitability. But you appear to have done well with the alien artforms, particularly the last batches I examined. I have seldom seen anything so crudely primitive, yet so remarkably beautiful. They will find a market."

Wyckoff privately considered that remark a gross insult, but he kept his opinion to himself and escorted the valuer back to the tug. "They like our stuff real well," he later told Arlene.

There was much for everyone to do after that. The ship was moved inside a huge pressurized blister on the asteroid's surface, and they were assured she would be refueled as soon as the cargo was traded and credit was available.

By then, Mason and Verity had evolved a theory to explain the station's construction. The temporals had apparently tugged a nickel-iron body into the desired position and blown it up like a balloon.

"It'd be easy with enough power," Verity explained, "and they'd have that. First you bore through the body with a particle beam. You fill it with ice, plug the holes, roast the surface with the same beam until it's molten, and let the steam do the rest. It'd blow up just like a balloon. I'll bet we'll find the temporals use a lot of these."

Wyckoff didn't understand this explanation, but he was thrilled to be where he was. And for once he felt important because he knew, as did the rest of the crew, that the sale of the cargo was something he could handle better than anybody else. "None of the rest of you have any experience dealing with hot goods," he told them, "but I've been doing it most of my life. It's like any other specialty—you've got to know the ropes and you've got to know the territory."

To learn the territory he and Jerry made a number of quick, exploratory forays inside the station, which turned out to be far more complex than the human dreamed it could be. Aside from the natural gravitational field on the outside surface, the temporals had a central generator within the cavity, which exactly reversed the natural field. Getting in, therefore, was somewhat awkward, requiring entry through a cagelike affair with its own internally generated field.

But once inside, the entire immensity of the base was more or less open, though it was not empty. On the contrary, radiating out from the central module, like three-dimensional spokework, were thousands of hollow girders that not only supported what was attached to them but formed the nucleus of the transportation system. Travel on the base was largely done through elevators, and because of the way the spokes were arranged, you could get from one place to another in a surprisingly short time simply by shuttling through the central sphere.

Looking at all this, the former bum from New York

was properly awed. Certainly, he thought, it's bigger than I'm used to, but it can't be any wilder, and it has to work pretty much the same way as any other city. In that thought, he took comfort. Here, he was in his element.

And he had guessed right. This huge city had everything the familiar ones did, including its affluent sections and its slums, its industrial and mercantile neighborhoods and its playgrounds, its police force and its underworld. Every city, anywhere, had to have these things because they were either inherent in the urban system or essential to function, and Wyckoff was not surprised to find them here.

The only major differences he could see were in the form and faces of the base's inhabitants, and these were physical and superficial, not fundamental—bizarre flesh on the old familiar urban skeleton. The melting pot was orders of magnitude larger. Instead of just white and black and brown you had all these differences and more . . . weird form, weird decoration—natural and unnatural—wide variation in such things as body hair, skin tone, size, and method of locomotion.

All were, of necessity, oxygen breathers, and plants to supply this gas grew everywhere, but it was clear to anyone passing throughout the neighborhoods that there were subtle local preferences in such things as gravity, temperature, and humidity. Sometimes the elevators the two visitors rode traveled through such areas, and they wondered how the structure could stand the stresses.

"I have been in such places before, Wyckoff," Jerry confided. "Somehow they compensate for things like that. As a whole, the entire base gravitational system does balance, and that, apparently, is all that really matters."

Wyckoff drank in the experiences he was having, as though they were savory wines. As soon as he had seen the immense variety of life forms that occupied the sphere he lost all fear that somehow the humans would be singled out and somehow excluded. They would not be—humans were not unusual enough. Wyckoff found he went as unnoticed among the common people as any individual of any other race represented here. Perhaps it would be different in the inner sphere, from which the temporals controlled it all, and perhaps not. He did not really think it would be. As far as Wyckoff could determine from what he'd observed, the only thing that mattered here was whether or not you could pay for what you wanted. If you could, no one seemed to care what that might be.

He knew, for instance, from talking to creatures he encountered, that every conceivable form of vice existed within the sphere. Slaves could be purchased here, or sold, and in fact, many in the city were, or had once been, members of that category. Vicious drugs were traded, and used, by exponents of such races as affected them. Stolen property made its rounds, as did various types of personal weapons. These weapons seemed to be the only things that greatly interested the base constabulary; otherwise, they seemed content to let the people do more or less as they pleased.

Chapter Thirty-One

Wyckoff reported to the rest, assuring them that they could move in perfect safety throughout the base. Many of them thereafter did, including Lady Bane, who set out to explore the shops and salons of the elite sections. She returned, heavily laden with some of the gaudiest garments ever seen aboard *Corona*, and with a tab to match. Arlene promptly forbade her ever again to pledge the ship's credit, under pain of restriction to quarters. Lady Bane didn't appreciate that at all.

The inner sphere was the Wall Street of the temporal base. It was operated by the Guild, of course, in theory if not in fact. The humans suspected that in this case, at least, the term "Guild" really meant a particular Major Lord Temporal who was privileged to skim off revenues.

In any event, here one could trade commodities in blocks through commission brokers, and sell to professional dealers, instead of taking display space down on the lower levels and selling to individuals. Both arrangements were offered and both had advantages and disadvantages. Under either method the Guild got its cut, of course—commissions under the former, and a sort of sales tax under the latter arrangement.

The humans decided that, at least for now, they had best stick to the block system, since it was faster and since they had no idea what other commodities they should be trading for.

They were relieved to discover that while the temporals did not have money, they did have a system of credit that seemed to be acceptable throughout all of temporal territory, which, of course, really meant all space and time. If they employed the Guild brokers, they got the conversion service as a part of the package, whereas if they sold below then each separate transaction that was recorded for them entitled the Guild to a fee.

They also discovered that they had really possessed some temporal exchange all along, and hadn't realized it. Guild credit accounts were recorded electronically, and in Lylard's module there were specially coded chips which evidenced his own supply of credit with the temporal guild. Had they known what they were and that it was safe to use them . . .

The brokers did a competent job, and seemed well worth what they cost. Of course, they had an advantage in the human artifacts, which indeed sold well. Other temporals snapped them up greedily. Many remarked gleefully, as the valuer had, that the articles exuded the beastliness of their makers. Word of them got around, spreading quickly among those who found such things exciting. They congregated near, eager to touch anything personal to these exotic dawn-creatures. It was all Wyckoff could do to hold a straight face.

Being the commercial spokesman for the humans, Wyckoff dealt with many of these beings at arm's length. In time, he got to know them and their habits so well that he could perceive no essential difference between himself and they. Once the sapience of an alien was conceded, it seemed to him, and something of his temperament was learned, his face and form ceased to matter.

Of course, he recognized that technology also played a part in this. Thanks to that there was no language barrier of any great consequence, and everybody sounded essentially like everyone else. The translators were themselves levelers and equalizers.

Only the major temporals seemed to rate any special treatment, but it was rare to encounter them. Since the entire facility seemed oriented toward one thing—trade—and as the trade benefited them the most, they stayed out of the way and let their system work naturally.

The more Wyckoff learned of the guild operation the slicker it sounded and the more he envied those in control. It seemed that absolutely nothing occurred on this facility that did not ultimately yield the guild a profit. Its fingers were into everything, however small, however insignificant it seemed to be. Wyckoff was astonished at the figure he got when he tried to calculate their daily take on translating services alone.

One of his first observations upon arrival was that no two people seemed to speak the same language. Because of the variety of races in the base, this in itself did not surprise him, but what was astonishing was that there was nothing like a commercial language—no lingua franca, such as other trading centers had.

Then he realized that this would have been bad for business—the Guild's business in translator services. Translator robots—modern ones, not clumsy antiques like those they had gotten from Lylard—were everywhere. Any needful being with a Guild Masterchip could plug it in and one of these would follow him and translate every nearby utterance for him as long as his credit lasted.

Very soon after arriving here Wyckoff had concluded that his prior conception of temporal lifestyle was completely unrealistic. He had pictured this base as a fort, with an armed and armored temporal huddled inside it waiting to be besieged.

It wasn't like that at all. To be sure, the base was a very unusual place, but it was not organized for fighting. It existed to make a profit—and did so very handily. The guild was even clever enough to stake its customers for a while, if they had no ready credit but were acceptable risks. They operated like the gambling houses down at Atlantic City, and treated their high rollers with care.

He had run up quite a bill on his own translator before he realized some of the more astute denizens, like certain humans he had known, talked for the sheer enjoyment of it. In the course of selling *Corona*'s cargo, he had entertained a good many of these.

Wyckoff regarded information as an excellent investment. He knew that anything learned had its survival value, and sooner or later revealed this to the person who learned it. The streets of New York had taught him that his first day on them.

True, he wasn't in New York anymore, but he didn't see why that should make any real difference. Certainly, the objective was the same as it always had been—survival in a social system over which he didn't have control.

Wyckoff hadn't been here very long before he realized that despite outward appearances, the alien city, like any large human city, was essentially just a vast ocean of life whose denizens might swim along at different speeds and in different directions but who all really were merely struggling to get from one end of life to the other.

Having adopted that philosophy, it wasn't a radical step for him to presume that somewhere in that vast throng was the alien equivalent of himself, as he had once been. He set about to find him, believing that once having found him, he would also understand him.

He was wrong. He was never certain that he had found "him" or even "her." Eventually, he contented himself with contemplating the ravings of 'it,' and never in any part of the rambling conversation the two of them had did it ever mention a name. From a strictly personal standpoint, therefore, Wyckoff regarded the venture as a failure. Academically, which was the only way he could rationally look at it, he was compelled to conclude that the creature was surviving only marginally, since it was addicted badly to one of the alien drugs, unkempt, uncouth, and at times incoherent.

Yet it was also a veritable cornucopia of information about both the city and the temporals who ruled it. In some outlandish way that Wyckoff never succeeded in fully comprehending, it claimed it had been and still was, itself, a temporal.

"I am lost," it told him, in a voice that slurred and wailed beside the bland tones of the machine's translation. "All of us are lost. The universe has thrown us up."

With that, Wyckoff had discreetly scooted himself across the bench on which the two of them sat, fearful that perhaps the being might be speaking literally, as its earthly counterparts did on occasion. It was drinking an intoxicating beverage from a plastic flask, dipping its siphonlike tongue in and out of the wide mouth. It had purchased this from an itinerant vendor and on Wyckoff's tab—its price to pick its soggy brains. Soon, Wyckoff knew, it might become ill, but he also knew that nothing he could do would prevent it from consuming all the drug the bottle contained.

He was resolved to learn as much as he could from it before this happened. He knew from other conversations that there were in fact a great many such stories, and that certainly not all of them could be true, if any, in fact, were.

Back on Earth these had their counterparts. More than once he had sat and listened, for lack of anything better to do, while some Bowery bard raved out a chronicle of his fall from wealth and grace. Then, as now, the objective seemed a common one—to gain the means of obtaining the next dose of whatever it was that took away the pain.

Normally, when he heard such a story, Wyckoff settled back and treated it as entertainment if he had time. He had time now, since it would be hours before it was necessary for him to return to the core and check the day's sales.

"I knew the first temporal," the being raved. "I killed him."

Wyckoff glanced over at his inebriated companion and smiled. The creature looked so puny, with his stick arms and legs, and with his comically banded blue and yellow fur.

"Yeah?" Wyckoff decided to humor the creature anyway.

"Indeed," the being affirmed. "It was a kindness."

"Funny," Wyckoff chided. "You don't look old enough."

"Age has no meaning to such as we, Earther. That is the curse of the temporal. Once you have left your rightful time you can never find it again, even if you manage to find your world."

"We're going to find ours," Wyckoff assured it, wondering as he said this if somewhere down the line, after he got through kidding himself, he would wind up like this. He hoped not, and he didn't think so.

"Oh, certainly you will, Earther. Anyway, you'll try. They all try—some for as long as the credit lasts. They pour it into the guild's open palm and sit there drooling at any hope. But it's all a scam to get the last dregs of treasure away from poor, helpless people. They all wind up at the Chartmaster sooner or later. They come with hope and leave with despair, knowing they can't go home again."

"Where is he? How do I find him?"

"Who?"

"This Chartmaster." Wyckoff would have been shaking the little creature if he could have stood to touch his matted, grimy fur.

"Not 'he,' Earther, 'it.' The Chartmaster's a machine."

"A computer?"

"That, and more."

"Some kind of robot?"

"More even than that—almost alive."

"Where?"

"Everywhere—here, the next base, the next one after that, scattered across time and space, in many pieces—fortunately."

"Why do you say that?"

"Because with its parts separated, it cannot overwhelm us. Were it united, it could do that easily. Even so, the dangers are enormous."

"Why is it allowed, then?"

"Ask me that again, Earther, after your own people have been to consult with it. Do not risk a weak one, though. Send your strongest will."

Wyckoff had met that remark with a gulp. It didn't sound like the sort of creature he wanted Arlene to be around. Fable or not, he wouldn't risk such an encounter. He would protect her. He would go, or Verity; not Arlene.

It occurred to him he didn't know where to find it. "You said a part of it was here? Where will I find it? Will you take me there?"

"I cannot take you, Earther. The Chartmaster is accessed only through portals in the Guild Section, from which I am barred."

Wyckoff did not ask him why that was—the reason appeared obvious. Having learned basically what he had wished from the encounter, Wyckoff felt a strong urge to get away before his companion passed out.

He started to rise, without explaining, hoping the creature would simply rave on and not notice it was alone. He was to be allowed no such luxury.

Suddenly a scrawny arm lashed out, swifter than a man could have moved his arm and with greater deliberation than Wyckoff would have believed, and its fingers curled tightly around his wrist. At first, Wyckoff struggled, believing the derelict intended this to hurt.

But that was not its objective. It intended to make a plea, and Wyckoff suddenly realized that had he been able to read the expressions on its face and recognize the tones of its speech, his own first impulse would have been not anger, but pity.

Even through the machine, its words were plaintive:

"Help me, Earther. Help me pass." It struggled across the bench in an effort to be nearer.

Wyckoff shivered at contact with the coarse, dirty fur, but he did not try to pull away from it—not now, not when he knew what was really happening to it. It was not simply about to pass out, it was about to die. "The bottle!" he shouted.

"A soporific, mixed with a slow poison," the creature answered weakly. "It is expensive. But for your kindness I could not have afforded it—I would have been forced to suffer out my time. I did the same for the first temporal, long ago. As it was with him, there is no cure for the disease which afflicts me."

"You're sick?"

"Yes, and as I told you—in the biological as well as the chronological sense. You, I think, are young in both ways—is that correct?"

Wyckoff responded by nodding his head, then remembered the machine translated only what was audible. "Yes."

"And your acquaintance with temporal travel is also recent? Perhaps you were subjects of a temporal which you overthrew?"

"Yes," Wyckoff admitted, allowing his companion to assume the answer applied to both its questions.

"I guessed as much when first I saw you," the creature replied, sounding ever weaker. "Listen to me; learn from me. Do not repeat the mistakes so many others make—that I made—and search in vain for what is now forever lost. Find a place, in some obscure corner of space, in some safe era, in one timestream or another, it matters not which. There, destroy your ship, and build yourself a home." These last words it fairly gasped, and its grip on Wyckoff's arm slackened.

"What do you mean? One timestream or another? How many are there?"

No answer ever came. The creature's grip lapsed, both from his arm and from the bottle, which fell to the decking and rolled into one of the sensor-controlled gutters at the corridor's edge.

Wyckoff did not know what to do next. Others passing by attended their own business, perhaps assuming he was attending to his, more likely reluctant to get involved, a habit common in more than one human city.

Finally, he rose and summoned a city constable as he was flitting past on some kind of gravity-insulated scooter, and learned that for a price, the Guild would also provide dignified interment for the mortal remains of its departed subjects.

Chapter Thirty-Two

"You mean, you lied to the captain, Wyckoff? Why?"

Wyckoff had just finished telling Verity the story of the alien geezer—a tale he intended to keep to himself from then on, and which he cautioned the engineer not to repeat. "Because he warned me not to let her near the thing, that's why, and because he made sense."

"And you bribed the guild resident to back you up? That's even harder to take, Wyckoff. Also, it sounds dangerous."

"Not hardly, Verity. Bribery's a way of life with these people. It's business, and they'll do business with anybody, any time. That's just the way things are for them. Besides, how many times have I heard her say you're a better astrogator than she is, anyhow?"

"She's just being modest. You don't think for a minute she really believes that?"

Wyckoff didn't answer. He stepped out of the elevator and led the engineer skillfully through the crowd to the next cross-connector.

As soon as they were inside, cheek to jowl with dozens of assorted aliens, and couldn't retreat, Verity started on him again. "Why'd you have to tell her it was because she's a girl."

"I just couldn't think of anything else. Will you quit screaming at me, Verity—people are looking at us."

"Let them. They can't understand us, and we don't look any funnier than they do, especially not that guy over in the corner with the tulip growing out of his head."

"That's a woman, Verity, and that's not a tulip—it's an antenna. There's a bunch of her people here."

"Whatever. I'm just glad the captain's your wife and not mine."

"For whatever it's worth, so am I. Look, you haven't answered the question I asked you when we started out."

"What was it? I forgot."

"What do you think the alien meant by 'one timestream or another'?"

"I don't know. Are you sure that's what he really said? You know how these translator programs can scramble things."

"That wasn't it. I was careful. I tested this guy, and I can tell you, the robot had both languages down pat."

"Maybe checking out made him nutty. You said it was some sort of painkiller?"

"Let's ask the Chartmaster."

"If it appears to be propitious, Wyckoff."

"I don't know what that means."

"If it seems like a good idea when we get there. Maybe it wouldn't be."

"The old guy says they sell information and they don't care who to, Verity. Anyway, we'll know in a couple of minutes. We're almost there."

The elevator stopped. They got out and took a walkway to the opposite side of the core complex, then mounted a moving stairway that led into Guild territory. There was no guard, but the machine stopped in front of an interior hatch and would go no farther until Wyckoff displayed his masterchip.

Inside at last, they found that it was all anticlimactic. What Wyckoff expected, a giant pile of hardware sitting in a darkened room, surrounded by pulsing lights, turned out to be fantasy. All they got was an ordinary computer terminal tuned to the English translation mode, and even that was dark until the masterchip caressed its electronic palm.

"I don't know why," Verity complained, "we couldn't have done this through our own system."

"I do. I didn't want Arlene in on it. I like her just the way she is, Verity. You'd better remember that. Now, let's get on with it." He jabbed the chip into the receptacle.

Immediately, a synthesized voice responded. "Thank you for your patronage. How may Chartmaster be of assistance?"

"What services can you perform?" Verity asked cautiously.

"I am capable of answering inquiries on points of astrogation, among other subjects, of buying and selling routing chips on behalf of the Temporal Guild, and of serving as broker for chips belonging to individuals. You have now expended one credit unit."

"One credit," Wyckoff screamed at the terminal. "Why? You didn't do anything."

"Each response to a question is billable. There is a flat charge of ten credits for each individual who asks questions. I perceive that you are not the same individual I previously answered?"

"That's right," Wyckoff replied sarcastically, knowing it was wasted.

"In that case, I shall bill the necessary additional charges, plus an additional credit for the last answer."

"What?"

"Is that a new question or do you wish me to repeat?"

"Is there a charge for repeating?"

"No. However, you have asked for a positive response, which I now answer. You have now expended twenty-three credit units."

"Verity, I'm getting ripped. They should call this

thing 'Cheatmaster.' Why don't you take over, before I put my foot through its screen."

"There is no impediment," Chartmaster replied. "You have now expended twenty-four credit units."

"Not you, Chartmaster, you dummy! I was talking to him, not you. You're not getting any money for that one."

"The fee has been deducted. The error is regrettable; however, I am not authorized to adjust accounts."

Wyckoff almost made the mistake of asking it who it was, but caught himself just in time. It seemed to him they could spend ten credits getting one back. Undoubtedly, both the Guild and Chartmaster figured it the same way.

Verity did take over, and was careful, but still he went through over 500 credit units before he found out, quite by accident, that Chartmaster had a printer mode which was much cheaper. From then on they used it, though it meant sifting through a great mass of extraneous information, which consumed time—for which, of course, Chartmaster billed steeply.

Now Wyckoff understood the expiring alien's admonition. He thought perhaps the creature spoke from personal experience—that perhaps the pursuit of the dream of returning home was all-consuming to some, as was the impulse of compulsive gamblers. He knew that in her present state of mind Arlene could not have stood the strain. She would have been both vulnerable and gullible, and would have clung tenaciously to each obscurity the Chartmaster uttered, craving facts but receiving platitudes instead until their treasure was gone.

He was grateful that he possessed the ability to protect her; that he had himself no such vulnerability. He had not so much lost the Earth as gained the universe.

All things considered, though, what he and Verity learned was worthwhile. They discovered, for instance, that stored within Chartmaster, in this and various other data bases, was an almost endless number of temporal charts—most the property of some individual temporal, whose account would be credited whenever a copy was purchased. Surprisingly, Lylard had had quite a number of these for sale. They realized by now, of course, that this did not mean he had personally ever been to these places.

The same facilities existed in other parts of the galaxy, not just here on Bubawawa; and there was, of course, plenty of traffic between the bases when you took into consideration the enormous spans of time and space the temporals crossed.

But to get at them threatened to cost more credit than the humans had to waste, and ended, for the moment, their ruinous dealings with Chartmaster.

Back on *Corona* they began a search through the temporal module, looking for Lylard's horde of chips.

After what seemed an eternity of carefully scanning, and after partially dismantling Lylard's console within the module, a number of carefully packaged chips were found. Not all of them, according to Lady Bane, belonged to Lylard. Some of them were the chips that he had taken from the other temporals who had been aboard.

"So, now what?" Arlene was not accustomed to making decisions of this magnitude by herself anymore. Whenever her duties as captain overlapped those of human leader in this part of the galaxy, she threw them out to democratic discussion. "What do we do with these now that we've got them?"

"We use whatever can help us get home," Verity suggested.

"Even if they get us in trouble?"

"There must be a way to do it, Captain. Otherwise, why would Lylard have kept them? If he thought they were worthless why not simply get rid of them? Why go through all the trouble to hide them? And why would he kill the others and yet leave witnesses alive to talk about it? Lady Bane knew all about that. Evidently, Lylard wasn't worried about her talking."

"A good point. I suggest we ask the princess for her opinion."

It was Verity who called Lady Bane on the intercom and requested an audience. Besides Wyckoff, who was attending to ship's business in the guild section, he was the only human officer she was on good terms with. The first mate had been charged with enforcing her restriction to the ship and, of course, Arlene had ordered the restriction in the first place.

Arlene, Mason, and Verity went armed with stunners, though these were discreetly concealed. Arlene hoped they would not have to use them but she wanted to be ready. She had noticed a distinct change in Bane's behavior since they had been at the temporal base and that her own influence over the Kruj'jan woman appeared to be slipping. Perhaps the proximity of so many millions of other creatures within the temporal sphere, and the fact that she now had an alternative to refuge aboard *Corona*, were responsible.

Entering Bane's cabin between Verity and Mason, she immediately provoked the alien woman's indignation, though not enough, it seemed, for Bane to rise out of her imperial pose. She was startled enough by the captain's brazen behavior to lose her poise for a moment.

"You are an offal worm, Mr. Verity. You have deceived me. Why did you bring *her* here?"

"I ordered him to do it, Lady Bane," Arlene replied, in his stead. Her purpose was to reinforce the alien's belief that any female who bossed the men around was too rough a customer for her. "I am the mistress of this vessel and my orders are obeyed," she continued, keeping a careful eye on her hostess.

Lady Bane moved not a muscle. She reclined motionless on her right side, sprawled in what she must conceive as regal splendor across her bunk. The bunk very obviously had been pulled out from the bulkhead for no other purpose than to serve her as a sort of throne.

"Why have you come here?" Bane demanded.

Arlene noted with satisfaction that she had not been called an offal worm, as Verity had been. She relaxed enough to take note for the first time of Lady Bane's gown, struggled valiantly first to choke back a guffaw, and then to maintain a straight face. From the human viewpoint, everything about the ensemble was wrong— the colors, the patterns, the texture of the fabrics. It was like a crazy quilt. Yet Lady Bane clearly considered it elegant. "I have come to discuss Lylard's effects," she said finally, careful to turn toward the translator robot.

"Lylard has no effects, Captain. He is dead, and the dead can own nothing. Whatever he had is now rightfully mine. I include in that this vessel, and all it contains."

Bravado? Arlene, and most of the rest of the human crew, now had some insight into the meaning of alien expressions, at least those with bare faces, having been around so many of them of late. *She's still trying to push me.* "Well, Princess, like it or not, I'm still your only way home, and it so happens we're not making much progress in that direction."

"We are not still lost? Surely, Captain, you are not suggesting that no one here knows the way?"

"Not at all. I'm confident they do, though we may well go broke before we find a way to ask. Besides, we may already have the answer."

"More riddles, Captain. If you have it, what need is there to bother me?"

"You were the one who killed Lylard, Lady Bane . . ."

"And I have no regrets, Captain—none, except that I killed him too cleanly. It was my birthright."

"I understand that part, Lady Bane. You have made the customs of your people plain enough. But we wonder about Lylard's people. How would they regard his conduct, and yours?"

"I am unconcerned with what the temporals think, Captain."

"It's important, Lady Bane. We know the guild has means to test those routing chips, and to identify their destinations and remove the defensive routines that are embedded in them. We know that if that is done we can find Lylard's base, at least, and perhaps your home as well."

"So? Why do you hesitate?"

"Because we'll probably have to reveal how we got them, and we don't dare do that until we know how the rest of the temporals will react. We thought perhaps you could help."

There was a long pause, during which Lady Bane was obviously deliberating her answer. When she did finally speak, it was with what for her was uncommon civility. But even in translation her voice sounded grim. "I'm sorry, Captain. I knew only the temporals aboard Lylard's ship—no others. I am unacquainted with the morals of other temporals, assuming they have any more than Lylard did, and I doubt they do."

"Even a guess would help, Princess."

"A guess? If I had to guess, Captain, then I would say that Lylard was arrogant enough to dare anything—that he would not have considered whether others approved. He perceived himself as too shrewd ever to get caught, and he probably would not have been discovered for a very long time. Unlike ourselves, he was very well acquainted with temporal matters."

The humans left the alien woman's quarters having accomplished something—cordial relations with her had been restored. Otherwise, the effort was a failure. They knew no more about her former master than before. By this time, however, Wyckoff, who had been below supervising the sale of the last of the artifacts, had returned to the ship.

"Why didn't somebody ask me about that," he complained. "I could have told you. The temporals don't boss each other around—at least, not that way. The leaders don't much care who gets hurt, as long as it's not them. Don't you understand how the mob operates?"

"The mob?"

"Sure, what'd you think the temporals were, anyhow?"

"This looks like a regular government to me, Wyckoff."

"Yeah, well, maybe—depending on what you call government. But it ain't. What you see here is the same basic arrangement the boys with the blue jaws had back home. Sure, it's a little bigger, and so far as I can tell there's no real competition, but that's about the only difference I see."

"A galactic mafia?"

"Something like that—it works on muscle. The ones with the most muscle run the show; the ones with the least do the dirty work. Guys like Lylard play the game by the big guy's rules, or else they get stepped on. That's how it is here, Arlene; it's no different than anyplace else."

"But this enormous base—it runs so smoothly. There are rules, and police, and public services, and all kinds of things it takes a government to run."

"Sure. Arlene, I know what it looks like, but I also know how it works. The government and the mob are the same thing—it's still a mob, because it acts like one. Look, you're worried about what they'll do about Lylard. Don't. Lylard was a small-timer—a punk. He was a soldier; all he was worth to Mr. Big was the dues he paid. Nobody'll miss him. Nobody'll miss the guys he killed, either, except maybe their own people. They'll come out fighting as soon as they find out their bosses are gone. They don't know it yet, is all."

"You mean, they'll be after us?"

"Naw, I meant, with one another. I don't think this sort of thing is any big deal. I think it probably goes on all the time, and if it works here like it did with the gangs on the streets, what'll happen is when we try to cash in, Mr. Big'll come down on us for his cut. The local hoods are already asking questions about who we are and where we came from."

"I knew it," Arlene groaned. "We have to get out of here right away."

"Why? What's that going to hurt? Let them ask. We can feed them any line they'll swallow and be gone before they can check it out. That kind of stuff takes time, even here. It's only natural they're curious. After all, we show up with a great big ship stuffed full of loot, people are gonna talk—to us and about us."

"And *what* have *you* been telling *them*?"

"That we're the New York mob."

"Wyckoff, that's insane."

"No, it isn't. They don't know any better. There's too much going on for them to keep track of everything. For all they know, there is a New York Boss. By the time they do get wise we'll be long gone, believe me. I know how this stuff works."

"And when we get caught again?"

"We'll think of something else. Arlene, these people are in business for themselves. They're working separately, in spite of how things look. All they got is this guild thing, and that's just a bunch of the big temporals who got together and pooled their muscle so they could push the little ones around. Long as we don't get too many of them mad at us, we'll be all right."

In the end, Wyckoff, being the only human with a claim to such expertise, prevailed in his arguments, and the others delegated to him the task of converting Lylard's credit.

That could, it seemed, be done, though it would take a while to accomplish. To do it he engaged a "fixer," who functioned much the same as human lawyers did, although her methods were based not on some common, traditional-style legal system, but upon her knowledge of the guild of temporals and the power of its individual members.

Her name was Mabakka. To the humans, she immediately became Ma Barker, with a chuckle, which the translator robot recognized as a communicative vocal sound. She was an affable being, big and hairy, centauroid, with two manipulative appendages, always in motion at something or other, and four massively cross-sectioned walking legs.

So constituted, she did not sit, but crouched behind

a massive combination desk and computer console gazing out wisely at Arlene and Wyckoff, for whom she had provided chairs. "Now then," she purred, "your problem, as I understand it, is to dispose of certain goods acquired in the course of, uh, a trading venture into the hinterland."

"Yeah," Wyckoff assured her, his voice reverberating his own conviction.

"And there was some trouble with hostile primitives, I see, and there were some casualties."

"You got it, Ma." The translator made a curious burping noise. Wyckoff found it amusing. He turned to Arlene and smiled.

"And your problem, as I understand it, is that your fief, New York, is not a guild registrant, is that about right?"

"Yeah. So we want to register and get square with everybody."

"You do understand, don't you, that there's bound to be a problem over your entry—you didn't tell the Guild Resident you were nonmembers?"

"He didn't ask us, Ma."

"Please use my full name, Wyckoff. It confuses the machine when you do not."

"Sorry, Ma Barker."

"Thank you. Now then, I'm not certain I'll be able to do anything about the increase in commissions you'll have to pay because you traded illegally, but I think we can stop worrying about penalties."

"Fine, Ma Barker," Arlene said. There was apprehension in her voice despite the words. "How much is it going to amount to? We aren't wealthy, you know."

The fixer's digits punched keys, and she glanced at her terminal screen. "I'm looking at your trade balance now, and I'm inclined to disagree—you may not be wealthy by New York standards, but you appear to have done very well, particularly in your consolidation operations. You can afford it."

Arlene gave a sigh of relief. She didn't ask what "consolidation operations" meant.

"The first step," Ma explained, "is getting you admitted to membership. Once you have that, you get a call sign and a guild responder or," she added, "you can continue to use any acquired from the—the former member." She glanced again at the terminal screen. "Oh my," the machine burped, "former members, I should say. This is most extraordinary."

The humans did not respond to that, except that Wyckoff blinked noticeably.

But the machine did not translate such things and Ma treated the pause as ordinary. She continued. "As I said, the first step is membership in the guild, in order to establish guild jurisdiction. Actually," she added hastily, "it sounds more complicated than it is. All it really means is you pay an initiation fee based on the worth of your vessel and cargo, and on whatever credits devolve to the human lord who took them. I assume it was one of you? Uh, we do *have* a lord temporal, don't we?"

"Uh, yeah, Ma. Uh, Ma Barker," Wyckoff stammered out, simultaneously clearing his throat.

"It has to be an individual, of course, except in the case of plural personalities."

"We held an election, Ma Barker. I won, so it'll be me." Actually, that wasn't entirely true. The vote had been among humans only, and only officers at that, and as far as they were concerned, the office was collective, with the nominal lord's behavior subject to group control.

"Excellent," Ma replied. She rubbed her hands together briskly, then lunged at her keyboard. The process of fixing then began.

It turned out to be brutally simple. First, those temporals who had been killed were identified, and their fiefs placed under guild trusteeship, except for Lylard's, which was theirs by right of direct conquest. As for the others, their lieutenants were to be appreciated by guild valuers, who would determine the value of the succession, after which the lieutenants were invited to bid on it.

Obviously, few would be able to afford to do that, but they also had the option of challenging the authority of the new lord. If that happened, the guild would simply back the winner and take its cut off the top.

"This is all formality, you understand?" Ma explained. "It doesn't mean a thing in ninety-nine cases out of a hundred. But it sounds fair."

To the humans, it didn't. To them it sounded like what it really was—extortion. The idea behind it all was for the establishment to be able to make out. "Cut" was the operative word.

"I recommend you waive assimilation, and refuse the challenge," Ma said. "It's more trouble than it's worth anyhow. Then, the lieutenants will have to bid, and the guild will whack them instead of you."

"Why would they have to? And what if they can't? You said most couldn't afford to." Wyckoff wanted to cover all possibilities.

"Because otherwise, the guild would declare the fief vacant, open to challenge by all comers, theoretically. There again, it's mostly for show. Typically, what happens is that the lieutenants' bids are deferred. The bidder becomes indebted to the guild and pays more for the privilege. Some are sold over and over again if a succession of bidders fails to pay."

"Juice," Wyckoff erupted, with a chuckle.

"That does not translate."

"Sorry, Ma Barker," Arlene explained, "it's a colloquialism."

"In any event, you would do well to do it that way. You may, perhaps, even emerge with a small profit."

"I've gotta give you credit, Ma Barker; you know what you're doing, and you make it all sound easy."

"I am flattered, Wyckoff. The illusion of ease is the mark of the master. I shall be negotiating furiously, and for some time, even on this minor affair. You should see what goes on when a Major Temporal falls."

"I've been meaning to ask you about that, Ma. I mean, Ma Barker. Where are all the big boys?"

"But you have met one, Wyckoff—the guild resident."

"HE's a major? But he's like . . ."

"Like anybody else? Hardly, Wyckoff. It is concealed, but he has power beyond imagination, safeguards you cannot even begin to contemplate. You would never be able to defeat him as you did the minor lord whom you succeed.

"It is a fact that no great lord has ever yet been overthrown by outside forces."

"Outside forces? Does that mean it does happen?"

"Occasionally a great lord is overthrown from within, by coup and assassination. Occasionally, the actual physical assassin is an outsider with allies in the lord's household. Such things take long periods of time to settle, because the great lords have far-flung interests and many followers, each of whom may have ambitions.

"In any succession the survivors are inclined to look upon such events as fortuitous. Though the contenders may endure long struggles among themselves, the guild protects them from the rest of its membership until a clear winner emerges."

"That's probably how it all got started."

"What, Captain?"

"All this; the entire temporal system."

"Who can say?" the fixer replied. She became tense, as though she might have confronted the question before.

And perhaps she had. The captain didn't know, and didn't greatly care, but she made it obvious she would have liked an explanation if she could get one.

The silence that followed must have persuaded Ma to give in. "Certainly," she conceded, "and relatively speaking, we can all conceive a time when no temporals existed. That is to say, nontemporals such as myself can easily do this. I myself think that from time to time the temporal secret is independently discovered and temporals find their way here. This, if true at all, must be a rare event."

"How many great lords are there, Ma Barker?"

"I do not know. Perhaps no one does. They do not publish such information. Perhaps they fear to have it known. I can only tell you that as far as I can determine there is only one here, and no doubt one at each of many other comparable installations. It is my feeling that they need vast amounts of resources and great multitudes of people in order to maintain the temporal lifestyle."

"And the lesser temporals, Ma Barker?"

"There the problem is that the numbers are greater than are conveniently counted, though in terms of power, these together are less than the least of the great ones. The lesser lords are lords only because they possess ships, and then only to those who do not possess them. The major temporals are lords to all, because they built the ships.

"Do you see how it works, Captain?"

"Not entirely."

"Perhaps that is the norm, Captain—the best any of us can ever hope to do." She paused, then added, "Perhaps you will be one of the lucky ones, and find the way."

Mabakka did not explain what she meant by that remark, and Arlene did not ask.

Chapter Thirty-Three

The work toward Guild registration went on, and progressed fairly smoothly. Wyckoff was authorized to assimilate Lylard's fief. In most cases, when a minor fief became vacant, there was assimilation by somebody. Assimilation was the most common way a temporal could increase his domain, and if new holdings were not constantly being created, there would soon have been only a very few, very large holdings. There were some immense ones already—so large that only the inability to build temporal vessels distinguished them from the great estates.

There would be assimilation with substitution in Lylard's case. Lylard's estate was insignificant, and the only thing about the substitution that was somewhat unusual was that nobody could identify the New York boss for whom the humans had supposedly once worked, and upon whom they apparently had turned and mutinied.

That didn't matter to the great lords, because the New York boss wasn't registered with the guild, either. The guild took the position that if the boss had a gripe about what they did he'd holler, and they'd take care of it when he did, supporting whatever side was most propitious for the guild. Meanwhile, they'd divvy Lylard's

estate up and take their cut, leaving the new lord to
deal with any organization Lylard had had.

The operation took time, but eventually Wyckoff, as
the new lord temporal, received guild authorization to
proceed to Lylard's estate and take it over, if he could.
That was all there was to it, and when it was over, the
humans were left wondering if it had all been worth it.
What they had now was a license to steal, the endurance and validity of which depended on a consensus of
their fellow thieves, plus the guild's blessing of any
efforts they made to enforce their claim. And getting it
had cost them a great deal of credit—almost everything
Lylard had had standing to his account with the guild
when Bane had killed him.

There was one thing that came out of this for which
they could all be thankful—all the routing keys they
possessed were now guild bonded, free of any traps and
deadfalls, and now readily usable or salable. Unfortunately, none of these contained the course to Earth.

Upon learning of the arrangements that had been
made through the fixer, Bane immediately declared her
unhappiness. She complained that the humans had no
right to elect one of their own to be temporal when it
was she who had killed Lylard.

They assured her that the office was to be shared,
and Wyckoff would merely be a figurehead, but that
did not seem to help.

She then demanded a way to her home world be
found and that she be taken there at once. All who
heard her tirade would have been happy to oblige.
Lady Bane was becoming a nuisance.

Still, the idea of haste was not wholly without merit
for other reasons. They had yet to get into Lylard's
home-station data base and find out where Bane's home
was, if the information was there. If it wasn't, then, of
course, the Kruj'jan joined the ranks of other lost races;
they would have to hunt space and time for her home
planet as they would all the rest. Being in control, and
mindful always of the cost, the humans regarded the

path to Earth, if they could find it, the most promising route home for the others. This made sense to everybody, including the Dorians. Earth's resources exceeded those of the Dorian home planet and of Kruj, particularly as Kruj, in the era from which Bane had come, was still backward in many ways. Earth, in contrast, had the resources with which an immediate search could be mounted, so it was the logical choice as their first effort.

They all thought the language would be the key, so the investigation concentrated on finding out how it had made its way into Lylard's translator system. Unfortunately, there was no easy way to do this unless they knew the intended route a user would take if he wanted to visit Earth. All languages were keyed into these routing programs, as was natural, since languages are useless where they are not spoken. But there appeared to be no central index, at least not on this base.

Assuming Lylard would have retained copies of any maps he might have offered for sale through the Chartmaster, as plots on the master computer, they had searched this data base and tried to find them. Many such plots were found, but they represented the gross record of exploratory voyages, not the finely defined essence of the astro-temporal touchpoints. Naturally, they tested some of these against Chartmaster memory, but as they learned more and more about the use of that system, it became painfully apparent that without great expense they could not tell which were which. Another approach would have to be tried.

Fortified with this new insight, the humans next bought additional diagnostic equipment, then ran tests, over and over again, on all the routing programs in Lylard's little hoard. These included not only places Lylard had already been, but areas he might have planned to explore in the future. They succeeded in identifying the locations of many planets to which the languages in the main computer were keyed. Yet despite these efforts, they found nothing in the module's data base that explained why the translator had English language capability.

"There was absolutely no reason for him to have had the thing, Captain," the drive engineer lamented, "unless he had some immediate use for it. Certainly, he couldn't have known we'd be coming along."

Arlene looked up from the holo-tank and sighed. She had been watching Verity run course after course for most of her watch. She was tired of it. "Then we'll have to risk a visit to his stronghold. I had hoped to avoid that, and go straight to Earth, but it isn't going to happen, is it?"

"No, Captain, I don't think so. We'd still be searching blind. On the other hand, he may well have the information we need squirreled away there. It could be that he used his English on some other trip and forgot to clear it from his computer afterwards.

"What's discouraging is the complete absence of any record on Chartmaster. If Lylard ever had a routing key to a human planet, you'd think he'd have made copies to sell. He certainly never hesitated to turn a credit on any of the others."

"I'll call a staff meeting and we'll all discuss it," Arlene said with a sigh.

"I'll make it short and sweet," Arlene advised the grim-faced officers. "We've spent a lot of time here and even more money, and we still don't have the slightest notion how to get back where we came from.

"As I see it, we have three choices—well, actually, it's four, if you count going back to Home with our tails between our legs." She paused, and added her own grim look to theirs.

"First of all, we can continue to hunt blind and trust to luck, like we have been up until now. Second, we can mix it up with other temporals, ask a lot of dumb questions, and maybe accidentally sic the nasties on our people. Ma says some of them are not above that. Third, there are a lot of other Chartmaster branches we could hit. Who knows, we could get lucky there, too, and find one that's up-to-date before our credit runs out. Fourth, and maybe least attractive, is to try taking possession of Lylard's keep, which is defended both by automatic systems and Lylard's henchmen. *Corona* could very well be damaged, and without *Corona* there is no hope for us at all."

She paused again. "I'm sure none of this is news to any of you, but you might not have thought of it in terms of what could happen to human civilization if somebody else finds it before we do. I might add that while I don't favor giving Dorians a say in what we do, I do know how they feel. They favor going into Lylard's base." She paused again. "I'll now open the question for discussion."

A short silent wait revealed that there would not be any, so she asked the next logical question. "Is everybody ready for a vote? Anybody need time to think?"

Again, nothing.

"Okay. Let's see the hands," she said with a sigh.

One by one she went through the alternatives again. The first three were greeted by both silence and immobility. Everyone, it seemed, was ready to fight. It was resolved that Lylard's base would be *Corona's* next port of call. *Corona* was ready for the task. She had been refueled and her hull had been further strengthened, so she did not have to rely entirely on the gravitational balance. That could be important during maneuvers against hostile vessels, as could the jury-rigged controls. This system, with manual controls in two locations, had proven awkward to operate, so it was automated and all control was consolidated on *Corona's* bridge.

She had just been taken out of the repair bay, and the humans intended that she would leave immediately—a sensible decision in view of the fact that so long as she stayed, dockage fees continued, and steadily consumed credit better spent on other things.

On reflection, though, there was one more thing the

new lord temporal wished to add to her, this on the advice of Ma Barker, whom all had learned to like and to trust—more and better weaponry.

What finally sold the others was the fact that this could be done outside the repair bay in a relatively short time, and so when *Corona* finally departed, six new missile blasters decorated her formerly smooth hull, and three of her lifeboats sported the long, needlelike antennae of blast cannon on their noses.

This was regarded as fairly heavy armament for a temporal ship, which ordinarily depended on agility through time for its defense. But as the fixer had explained, taking possession of a newly acquired fief sometimes required planning of the most prudent kind. When at last the tugs towed *Corona* clear of the temporal base, and Arlene set her on course for the nearest star so that she could reenter stasis, she was the envy of every temporal she passed.

Chapter Thirty-Four

The cracking of a temporal stronghold, even with access to the temporal's own computer, was not something to be undertaken lightly. The fixer had warned the humans of that. Every lord had to face the possibility that such a thing would someday be attempted, and it was only prudent that he take some precautions.

The humans had one advantage besides possession of Lylard's module: Jerry. Near the end of the last leg of their journey to Lylard's star they met with him, in the captain's quarters, to discuss the assault.

"You've been there, Jerry. Tell us what it's like. What can we expect to find in the way of defenses?"

Jerry was enjoying a cup of the bitter brew, and sipped from a mug that was really too large for his hands. He took one last contemplative gulp, rearranged himself on the too-large chair, which had been fortified with cushions, and reached up to place the cup on the corner of the table.

"Outside the sphere, almost nothing, Captain, except at the lock, where there are short-range beam weapons whose main purpose is to repel entry. These can probably be disabled from the module, if you can figure out how to do it. When you see the sphere you will understand why Lylard didn't need anything more. Any

weapon powerful enough to penetrate its shell and all
the compartments inside would also destroy it. There
would be no point in an attacker doing that."

"I see. How big is this thing?"

"Let me see if I can convert." His little brow wrin-
kled during the short pause. "I would say fifteen kilometers, maximum outside diameter. Perhaps one kilo-
meter thick at the equator. The outside is covered with
photosensitive panels. These supply the keep's power.
The sphere rotates periodically. Again, conversion of
units is difficult, but in the absence of an internal field,
this supplies the weight."

"There's no generator?"

"No, but the difference should not be very noticeable.
Only a two-kilometer-thick slice at the sphere's equator
is used as living quarters. The rest of the space inside is
occupied by plants which supply nutrients, dispose of
waste, and generate oxygen. The sphere is stabilized by
pumping, using its water for ballast."

"How can we get in? Where are the locks?"

"There is a lock at the north pole large enough to
accommodate the vessel Lylard had. The *Corona*, of
course, could not enter it. We will have to shuttle in."

"I see," Arlene grunted. "Well, one lifeboat should
be adequate. Any other entrances?"

"None that I would recommend, Captain. There are
a couple of smaller locks, none large enough for a boat
to enter. The landing force would have to disembark in
armor. Also, these are far away from the important
sections of the sphere and it would be easy for those
inside to seal them off. It would be completely imprac-
tical to use them, especially since there will be a better
way."

"A better way?" The human had been slumping in
her own chair, her posture reflecting the general mood
of the bridge crew—moderate tension, extreme fatigue.
They had been watching screens for hours on end as
Corona crept closer to the base. At this comment,
Arlene snapped herself erect.

Jerry was startled. He recoiled, and paused before he answered, as if he needed to gather his wits again. "Yes. There are 51 Dorians inside, and Dorians will be in control of the main lock. If we can inform them of our presence without alerting the others, and if we can get some arms to them right away, I can take the rest of the station with that force alone."

"You expect resistance?" The captain's gaze was fixed and piercing. She now perched on the edge of her chair like a bird of prey.

"Unfortunately," the Dorian replied, his voice apprehensive as she hovered over him, "resistance cannot be discounted, since all the occupants are not Dorians. There are 16 Kruj'jans, and these, as you know, are a stubborn people. There are a couple of Chagi engineers, perhaps a dozen Hapicsh agriculturists, as many Thang animal handlers, and some Lupinakans—about 60 of these latter.

"The Lupinakans do all the housekeeping chores. They are not very bright people and we may expect the most trouble from them. Lylard used a drug, to which they are all addicted, as a means of controlling them. If we are careful, and time our return well, as I anticipate we shall, none of them will be in withdrawal. If we miscalculate, particularly by a long interval, they may very well equate his failure to return as a threat to their continued supply of the drug. In that state they could become very dangerous."

The captain slid back and reclined against her chair's backrest. She gazed up at the overhead and cradled the back of her head in her hands as she answered. "As you say, then, we'll just have to see that it doesn't happen." She paused, noted the Dorian's cup was empty, and motioned Wyckoff to pour him some more "coffee."

The Dorian muttered his thanks as Wyckoff topped it off and retired to his own chair over in the corner.

"What worries me most, I think," Arlene continued, "is the number of people. It sounds like an awful lot of them, Jerry, both for Lylard to have handled and for us to tangle with. How did he manage them all without any help? How did he avoid rebellion? Surely, he didn't use drugs on everybody."

Back in his corner, Wyckoff watched, puzzled. Arlene seemed to be giving Jerry the third degree. He noted the Dorian's growing apprehension, but still he hesitated to interfere. For one thing, he was certain Arlene would resent it. She was very defensive, even against him, where questions of ship handling were concerned, and at the moment she was understandably edgy, since she was about to place *Corona* at risk. Nothing seemed to come before her ship. He continued to observe in silence.

Even on the pan, Jerry could hold up his end. He seemed always to have an answer, and it always sounded reasonable. "To use an archaic English slang term I came across in the library recently, Captain, Lylard knew how to put the arm on people. Every unwilling member of his household wanted something he could only get from Lylard, and that Lylard withheld. Generally, this was a promise to someday allow them to go home. Even the three females of his own race were not free to leave him."

"That included you Dorians?" The captain's words seemed especially sharp.

"Including us, Captain," Jerry answered resolutely. "That is why we must take the central pod before anyone else can interfere."

"The central pod? Tell me about that. Why is that so important? What's in there?"

"This was Lylard's personal residence. Somewhere inside it is his treasure trove—his station computer—all the routing keys we captive races want, Earth's perhaps among them. It will be locked, but the temporal module's computer can be used to generate keys if we can discover how. We must try to do that, so that we may enter quickly. We must not allow the other races to get control of it."

The captain's voice reflected astonishment. "But you just said it was locked."

"The danger is, Captain, that there are tools aboard the sphere which could be used to break in if the party doing it had sufficient time. That is why we must not delay taking control of the sphere."

"I see," Arlene grunted in reply. It was as though she conceded Jerry the point only grudgingly. Her next question revealed her own lack of reflection. "What prevents somebody from doing that while Lylard's away?"

The Dorian paused again, gazing back at her as if to say she should have known better than to ask it.

And perhaps she should have. Certainly, sitting calmly in the corner, admittedly under no pressure, Wyckoff could see the answer coming. It was then that he realized how tired Arlene really was.

"There isn't time, Captain," the Dorian answered pedantically. "Lylard was very careful about that. He always arranged to reappear within microseconds after his departure. The people who remained back at the base while he was gone didn't have time to think about doing anything in an interval that short, much less take any overt action. Besides, everybody thought he took their routing chips with him wherever he went. He told everybody he did."

"But he didn't, did he?"

"Perhaps he did on some occasions, but not this time, Captain. You'd have found them, and you haven't."

"No," Arlene answered with a sigh. "We haven't."

Jerry picked the mug up again and took a drink from it. Evidently, it had cooled. He made a face and gulped the rest of it down nevertheless. He didn't like it when it was cold.

Up until then he hadn't really volunteered information. He had simply answered Arlene's questions. Now he offered an unsolicited opinion. "There's another problem in getting to Lylard's apartment."

"What's that?"

"Animals. Besides people, he collected exotic animals. Some of these are big and dangerous. They run loose in the enclosure around the central capsule."

"How does he get back in then?"

"There's a special vehicle, also controlled with a key generated by the module's computer. But I don't have any idea how. However, with the weapons we'll have, we can handle them, too."

The discussion continued for a short while longer, then gradually degenerated, as all such discussions seem to do after major questions are out of the way, into a morass of detail. All the information thus gained would be useful, of course, but getting it became boring. Finally, when everybody was worn out, the session broke up.

Wyckoff dropped off to sleep almost immediately after the others left, and snored loudly.

Arlene was not so fortunate. She lay awake beside him, somewhat envious of his ability to put morpheus before all the other mythical forces that torment man, and tried to figure out what seemed so wrong with their situation.

She was convinced something was, although there was no logic to support such a fantastic conclusion. But though she had learned to live with the Dorian's presence, tolerate his involvement in the operation of her ship, and even on occasions such as this one, to seek out his advice, she had never really learned to like him or any of his less obtrusive countrymen. Now, as she reflected carefully and in depth about the relationship, she decided she didn't like him any better now than she had when she'd emerged from the shower and found herself under his gun.

Accordingly, she resolved to check his story out independently, as far as was possible, and to be very, very careful to see that Wyckoff didn't know it. Her reason was the same one that had bothered her from the moment she'd first set eyes on Jerry—the Dorians were attracted to Wyckoff as they were to no other human, and seemed to perceive his very thoughts. And while Arlene doubted that could really happen, she was convinced that what he didn't know he couldn't tell anybody.

It was this resolution, made so casually in the foggy twilight of consciousness that precedes sleep, that changed the lives of all of them.

Chapter Thirty-Five

Subjectively, the voyage to the new lord temporal's base had required six months. Objectively, Lylard's personal stronghold was probably as old as the universe itself, since he had hidden it in the midst of the debris of proto-planets in orbit around a sun so youthful it had not yet achieved full brilliance.

That had been a wise choice, most agreed. Such a star would eventually go on the main sequence and stay there for billions of years, and that was the sort of thing that could be important to a temporal.

Wyckoff had little understanding of these technicalities, though his exposure to their effects had been as great as anybody's. There were facets to his character, however, that were quite as valuable as the engineering skills Verity had or those of spatial command that Arlene and Mason enjoyed. Wyckoff had street savvy, and street savvy worked as well without streets as it did with them. He had a feeling for predicting reactions that was unmatched by anybody aboard.

Corona cruised downwhen of Lylard's base, hanging in stasis until the module's instruments detected the temporal eddies created by Lylard's vessel as it rose from his keep. The instant was suitably marked on the temporal plotter, then *Corona* leapt backwards a full century. Immediately, she leapt forward again, that interval plus a full minute, just to be safe, and hung in parallel solar orbit next to the glistening sphere.

An expanded asteroid like the trading base, this tiny worldlet glistened from a surface studded with gleaming collectors, which gathered power from the young sun for use in maintaining the life support system within it.

From the depths of the temporal module, Verity continued to broadcast Lylard's personal recognition code, but no immediate reply came from the sphere.

On the bridge, Arlene looked to Jerry for an explanation. "You've been out with him before. Is this customary?"

"Not at all, Captain," he replied in his high-pitched English. "But not only have we deviated from Lylard's standard approach, the vessel is different, and its configuration will not match what the computer below has in storage. There should be all kinds of alarms going off within the keep, and eventually a living creature will take charge. I would suggest we anticipate hostility and remain alert until some reply has been received."

They already were fully alert. Also, they knew they were relatively safe. They were beyond the useful range of blast cannon, and the ship's instruments would see any missiles coming up from the sphere in plenty of time for them to dodge by retreating into stasis. The possibility of an attack did not worry them.

It was easy to see what Mabakka meant when she said the temporals didn't often bother one another. Getting in either destroyed what the attackers wanted in to take, or was too bloody to be worth it. Heavily armed as *Corona* was, she would have been hard put to penetrate the worldlet's shell, and the locks on its surface would have been difficult and costly to breach. Jerry was quick to remind the humans that they were fortunate to have an alternative.

It did, he said, occasionally happen that one temporal, for reasons of vengeance, would attack another but the guild frowned upon this. Only a very powerful lord could get away with it. Violence was for use against barbarians. Temporals were expected to cut each other's throats in a more civilized fashion.

A voice rang out through the speakers, high-pitched though guttural, and obviously Dorian. It filtered through the translator and emerged as flat, toneless English. "Lord, we are on manual control, weapons systems on standby. Please confirm your identity visually."

Arlene looked first at the others, then at Jerry. "He's one of yours, Jerry. You were right. What will he do when he finds out Lylard's dead?"

"Nothing, I hope." He took the microphone from the captain and pressed the key.

He spoke in Dorian, of course. The translator ran it together badly, since the computer could not tell which speaker was which when it had two using the same language. It was confusing, but the humans managed to follow it well enough to understand that the Dorians below were relieved.

Once those on the sphere understood, the pace of events slackened. At this point, Jerry interrupted. "Captain, I apologize for the echoes the machine causes, but my colleague at the other end does not speak your language. I could talk to him in English, of course, at the risk of confusing him further—the situation there has become very chaotic. But if you have no objection, I think the best way would be to turn the robot off. I can translate for you humans, of course."

Stationed as he was, in his familiar corner, again left out of most of the decisive process, Wyckoff was mildly surprised when Arlene agreed to the suggestion without either hesitation or argument. Indeed, he seemed to detect more apprehension in Jerry's demeanor than he did in hers. At this thought he suddenly realized how much she had grown since he'd first met her. She had really toughened up.

The interval of distraction was a short one. His attention flashed back to the crisis.

A long conversation ensued between Jerry and the

Dorians within the stronghold. In the course of this, Jerry appeared harried, and translated little of what either said. As a result, the humans on the bridge began to grow very nervous, though no one felt justified in interrupting.

Finally, Jerry paused, turned to Arlene, and said, "It was necessary that I tell those in the lock what is happening, and give them reassurance. There is much apprehension within, Captain. Dorians are in control of the main lock, but the other species are scattered throughout the keep and we do not have any way of controlling them except with force. Some of these are very astute people. We think most suspect something out of the ordinary is happening because of the alarms and because Lylard did not return immediately, as he has always done before. To those used to thinking in microseconds, a full minute can seem like a very long time. We must get arms to the Dorians immediately."

Arlene nodded and then turned to her console. She pressed her intercom key. "Verity?"

"Yes, Captain."

"Ready in the launch bay?"

"Ready, Captain."

She turned to Jerry. "You'd better get down there now, then."

Jerry put the microphone down and waddled to the elevator.

"Now," Arlene said nervously, after the Dorian was gone, "let's see what they really talked about. She flipped a switch and started the recorder, tying it into the translator device. The flat, toneless, English translation poured out.

"Khar! Listen carefully. We have a chance. Lylard has been overthrown. He is dead. The seven of us aboard this ship are about to take it. These fool humans are arming us. We will bring you weapons to use against the others."

"We have the main lock. We are ready. But we cannot reach the maintenance sections or their locks."

"Seal them, then. They will not be approached. The humans believe we will cooperate, and that this will not be necessary."

A pause followed, then the voice resumed. "They are sealed."

"Now then, we simply wait. Presently, a shuttle will approach. We will be in control. Do not fire upon it."

"Understood. We wait."

All of this had happened before Wyckoff could do much thinking about it. He stood with his mouth hanging open and listened. When the tape was finished, he gasped. "That was Jerry? Jerry said that?"

"Very devastating to your image of him, I'd guess."

"What's he up to?"

"He wasn't what you thought he was, Wyckoff. He had most of us fooled, but I never quite trusted him."

She stopped and listened. "I suspect you're about to get another shock, Wyckoff. Be careful; say nothing. I'll handle it."

The elevator door opened and Verity stepped out. Jerry was behind him, waving a plazer. He walked over to where the other humans waited. A change came over him as soon as he glanced over at Wyckoff—the note of supreme confidence in his voice suddenly vanished. Thereafter, from time to time it quivered, as though he was about to lose his nerve.

He managed to hang on. "Now, Captain," he said, pointing his weapon directly at Arlene, "we have a few more details to attend to. Move away from the controls."

Arlene did not move.

Jerry raised the plazer menacingly. "I have no time for peaceful persuasion, Captain. This will hurt."

"Shoot!"

Wyckoff had been watching, pensive but fascinated. He had a natural impulse to act, of course; to rescue Arlene. Then suddenly it left him, replaced by a decidedly unnatural feeling—the urge to rescue Jerry from her. Somehow, he perceived Jerry's need as greater, Arlene as the aggressor, and himself as the pivotal power. But he just couldn't make up his mind what to do on such short notice. He needed time to think about it some more.

When it appeared that Wyckoff was too apathetic to intervene, Jerry tried to save himself by pressing the firing stud on his plazer, but nothing happened.

"Discharged," Arlene said, smiling wickedly at the Dorian. She drew a plazer of her own from conceal-ment. "This one's charged. I'm not certain what it'd do to somebody your size, but we could find out easy enough." She turned to Wyckoff. "Cover the elevator, Wyckoff."

Wyckoff suddenly found he had made up his mind. He would stick with Arlene. He went over and stood in front of the door. Enough time had elapsed that he had thought about the situation, and he was thoroughly confused by what was going on. "What was he doing to me, Arlene? And why? We were supposed to be friends."

"I don't know for sure what, Wyckoff. All I know is what Lady Bane told me about the Dorians—they've got some sort of empathic sensitivity to one another, and occasionally to particularly sensitive individuals of other races. In humans, at least on this ship, you were it. When they first started plotting together and Jerry was anxious to gain her cooperation, he mentioned he had an influence over you.

"As for why, he did it because he wanted your job, Wyckoff. He wanted to become the lord temporal. He wasn't Lylard's slave—none of the Dorians are. They were junior partners—isn't that right, Jerry?"

Jerry said nothing. He stood silently, casting glances around, looking for an avenue of escape.

"Never mind. I already know most of it." Arlene backed over to her chair, turned it on its pivot, and plopped down in it, the wrist of the hand holding the plazer carelessly drooping.

She's the one who rescued me, Wyckoff realized suddenly. Belatedly, he added, *Of course, he ain't really all that ferocious*. This last impression had a strangeness about it, as though it might have come from outside. The difference was subtle.

He shook it from his mind and listened to Arlene, who wasn't through talking yet. "We should have been suspicious from the very start, when you first came to us.

"But you did pretty well, considering. Too well for us to swallow your story that Lylard held you against your will. You didn't complain about coming here, like Bane did. That could have been because you already knew we didn't have the routing key for Dorr aboard, but it wasn't, was it?"

Again, he didn't answer.

"There was something else you knew that I didn't realize for a long time—you knew exactly how we'd react to the sight of you. You took advantage of it, and it worked. You also had enough familiarity with our language to identify us to Lylard when we first met him. Of course, that could also have been the result of your association with us on Home, but I don't think that was it. I think you had some previous contact with humans."

She didn't bother with an accusation this time. She simply went on. "You were far more curious about us and our ship than Lylard was. You, not he, were listening on that bug. I should have realized it then—it wasn't Lylard's style, it was yours. He was direct, you're devious, and it was the way you hedged on things that got me suspicious, Jerry.

"For instance, when you were talking about the beam weapons at the locks, you said 'probably.' You'd been out with Lylard many times before, according to your own words. You'd know for certain, not just probably, that Lylard could turn them off, and if he couldn't he'd be pretty stupid to leave your people in the lock. Besides, you went out of your way to persuade us not to try the other entrances, despite the fact, as we now know, that those can be sealed by your people in the main lock.

"I was onto you a long time before now, Jerry, but I had to let you hang yourself in front of your pet human, or he never would have believed how nasty and scheming you are. That's why I didn't tell him. I'll have to admit, I was disappointed when he didn't catch on by himself, but that could have been your influence at work, couldn't it? You could have made it hard for him to want to."

Good girl! Wyckoff silently added. Disappointed or not, she proved she cared enough to cover up for him.

"You might have done better to put more polish on your own act. For instance, I thought it was pretty sloppy of you to leave the translator on English when your friends in the lock were supposed to think they would be talking to Lylard. A real star performer would have done that, then made a show of switching." She paused, and smiled proudly.

"Anyway, it's all over for you now, Jerry. After what I learned from the little alien child, I seriously doubt that anyone else on the sphere will give us any trouble." She grinned wolfishly at Wyckoff as she said that, but when it didn't seem to register, she turned her attention back to her narrative.

"You tried your best to make us think they would, didn't you?" she said with a sigh. "We'll find out soon enough, when our men get down there with real weapons and take over that lock from yours. Your wives, by the way, are sitting helplessly in a lifeboat in the launch bay. The outer door is open, the inner one closed and, of course, the boat has no more fuel than the plazers they carry have charges. I must say, it was reckless of you to think you could take the *Corona* alone. You've got real courage, for your size, but you must have figured it would be easy, the way we swallowed all your other stories."

Two phrases she uttered had caught, and now held,

Wyckoff's undivided attention—the reference to the alien child and to Jerry's wives. He was burning with curiosity to know what she meant, but it seemed destined to be delayed. There was an interruption.

"Captain?"

The speaker on the radio blared.

"Yes, Rick?"

"We have the lock, Captain. No casualties. Almost no resistance. We're moving out into the rest of the station."

They had it all before the next watch was over. It wasn't nearly the job that Jerry had said it would be. Except for the Dorians, most of the other people confined there submitted docilely to human authority. The Kruj'jans threatened some resistance, until informed that a Princess Royal was aboard, and friendly to the humans. Mason gave them charge of guarding the captive Dorians, and they were not gentle about it.

Then, at last, Wyckoff understood what Arlene had meant when she called Lady Bane a child. Though she was as large as an adult human female, next to these brutes she *was* tiny. The Kruj'jan warriors were the biggest, meanest looking, most thoroughly and disgustingly ugly creatures he had ever seen. They had been bred for this throughout the race's history, which accounted for the emphasis that was placed on selecting the proper genes.

Wyckoff found himself admiring the creature now that he understood her circumstances. He had previously regarded her as a nuisance, good only for getting in the way, and consequently had had little to do with her.

Arlene had approached her differently, with a firm hand but with genuine interest, and learned the truth— that Bane was just doing her best to survive, all alone as she was, and that her pretense of being an adult was rational. While Wyckoff had been spending much of his leisure time with the Dorian, Arlene had done the same with Bane, had gained her confidence and her

friendship, and had become a sort of substitute parent
for her.

Bane had needed that. Though bright enough, and in
her own way precocious, she was, after all, a royal
adolescent who knew that great things were expected of
her when she reached breeding age. *A tough fate to
face alone,* Wyckoff remembered remarking to himself,
when you consider what the Kruj'jan male looks like.
She'd fooled all the humans, except Arlene, and Jerry
had shrewdly kept his mouth shut.

The Kruj'jan warriors reminded Wyckoff of the creatures that haunted the TV screen on Saturday mornings
when he was a boy, though after seeing them in the
flesh, Wyckoff would have put his money on them and
not the cartoon heroes. They *looked* invincible, even
when they weren't moving, and in motion they were
the stuff that made nightmares.

That very fact, Wyckoff believed, was the reason
Jerry finally talked. He had managed to maintain his
silence for a respectable length of time before he did,
though. Long enough for the humans to get into Lylard's
central capsule and crash his computer. Long enough
for them to determine that while the temporal had had
routing chips to many other places—that he could have
taken almost any other species on the keep to its home
planet—his computer did not contain the information
necessary to find human-occupied space.

Lylard's apartment had been carefully searched.
Wyckoff, himself, had taken part in this. With his own
hands he had pawed through mountains of baubles,
fingered thousands of alien curios, cataloged hundreds
of computer data cubes.

In the course of the search he took part in the inter-
rogation sessions with Lylard's consorts, and discovered
that in their cases, too, attendance at his manorial court
had been involuntary.

By the time the humans were finished, they did not
wonder why those beings around him hated him, or
why Lady Bane had risked perpetual separation from

her own kind just to kill him. The real mystery was, why had he lasted as long as he had?

But thorough as it had been, the search of the inner pod turned up not one single artifact that could have come from Earth, and nothing to explain how English got into Lylard's computer. The humans combed the rest of the sphere and questioned every individual in it, including most of the Dorians. From the Dorians they did learn one useful thing—Jerry was a latecomer. He had not been in Lylard's service very long, having been acquired by Lylard from another temporal shortly before that temporal's last voyage. But he had taken charge of them because of the special relationship he enjoyed. They revealed this with some reluctance, denying it all until confronted with the fact the human captain knew already, but finally admitted the Dorian Zhe-rhe' was the first and only male Dorian any of them had ever seen.

They now knew for certain that the Dorians' relationship with Lylard had been unusual, but they did not yet know why. And there appeared to be no other way to find out short of turning Jerry over to the Kruj'jan persuaders.

In the meantime, Wyckoff had been doing a little rooting on his own—in Jerry's quarters aboard the sphere.

Chapter Thirty-Six

"I always liked you, Jerry, despite what you did."

The Dorian had been napping. He had not been expecting any visitors and he jumped up when Wyckoff spoke.

"You startled me, Wyckoff. You walk quietly. Have you been taking lessons?"

"You're pretty smart, aren't you, Jerry—for a jailbird."

The Dorian abandoned sarcasm, in order to satisfy his curiosity a little sooner. "Why did you come, Wyckoff?"

"I don't know. Maybe I thought we could talk like we used to, that's all. But you have to be a smart alec, don't you?"

"It was an interesting way to pass the time, Wyckoff. I found your naivete amusing. You really can be a clod, you know."

Wyckoff hit Jerry viciously in the mouth, knocking him off his little stool, and sending him crashing into the corner. "I don't like anybody well enough to take that, Jerry. The rest of them want to let the Kruj'jans work you over. I'm a whole lot nicer. I'll trade."

Jerry had risen. He did not get back on the stool, afraid Wyckoff might swing again. Instead, he stood shakily behind it. He must have known that talking beat getting hit, and so he talked. "What? What will you trade?"

"I can keep you alive, Jerry. I can save you some pain, maybe even fix it so you can escape."

"The others wouldn't like that."

"They don't have to like it. They don't even have to know we've got a deal. Besides, I'm the lord temporal."

"That, Wyckoff, is laughable."

"Want some more?"

Jerry cringed at the words. He didn't.

"You'd better lay off that kind of talk, Jerry. Right now, I'm about the only friend you've got."

"Why should I trust you?"

"What choice have you got? Either you tell me what I want to know, and I help you, or the Kruj'jans beat it out of you sooner or later anyhow."

"What makes you think I know anything?"

"Because I found this in your rooms." He held out the torn I.D. photo. "The man's name was Luddington."

"We never knew who he was, Wyckoff. When we found him he was near death. He was also quite mad. He had been adrift a long time even then, and the isolation had shattered his mind. He seemed to be expecting us. He thought we were humans, come to rescue him."

"And that's how your computer got the language?"

"Yes."

"Then how come Lylard didn't have the location where Luddington was found?"

"Because Lylard wasn't there. I was with another temporal then. He only picked the human up to get the boat he was in, and there was no reason to record the location. It was just another touchpoint to him. I was traded to Lylard some time later. The trade included some other things. The data on English was part of it—a very minor part. Somehow, Lylard never got around to transferring it from the module's computer into the big one. He didn't have a location to key it to, so he just left it where it was."

"It was all just coincidence? Why didn't you tell us?"

"Why should I have done that? If I had, you would not have come here looking for your way home. You would have known the answer wasn't here."

"And you wanted to be lord temporal, didn't you, Jerry?"

"I saw the opportunity, and I took it."

"Nothing wrong with that, Jerry. I've taken a few myself in my time. How come you never tried to pull anything on Lylard?"

"We would have, eventually, when the time was ripe. We were cultivating his trust, little by little. We could see that fighting him would do us no good, so we behaved slavishly, and followed his orders precisely. That way we could learn more from him while we waited for him to make a mistake."

"And if he had?"

"Then, like you humans, we would have searched the universe for Dorr."

"We know where it is, Jerry. We can take you there. We will take you there."

"Who do you think you're kidding, Wyckoff? I know better. Your people are only interested in finding your own world, and in the process you'll ruin everything with your stupidity. There'll be causal barriers everywhere. And if in the meantime there are more raids on Dorr, what then? Some other temporal will eventually come along and claim it. As a temporal myself, I could have protected Dorr. I would have. It would have been part of my domain, just as it was Lylard's. Other members of the guild would have had to respect that. Tell me, Wyckoff, what will the humans do with my world, and those of all the others?"

"Why should we do anything to them? It seems to me we've got our own interests to look after. Finding our way back is going to be tough enough."

"The odds against that are astronomical, Wyckoff. You probably never will, unless you happen to come across some temporal who's already found it, and unless you can persuade him to tell you where it is. The universe is a much larger place than you think it is."

"Why would I have any trouble persuading him?"

"Because nine out of ten temporals are lost themselves, Wyckoff. That's how they get to be temporals in the first place. They wouldn't help you find your people, because you might share their secret."

"Why does everything have to be so complicated, Jerry?"

"That's the way things are, Wyckoff. There have to be rules. You should be the first to recognize that."

"Yeah, I know, but why these rules? Why just a few temporals with this thing? Why not whole races? Why not everybody?"

"You astound me, Wyckoff. Big as it is, the universe would be overrun in no time, if any one race were to expand in this way. That's part of the reason none of them have ever done it."

"Yeah? What's the rest of it? And I don't just mean this double timestream thing—we had that figured out a long time ago."

"You did, did you?"

"Sure. That's why the plotter flip-flopped and changed color. That's why we can go backwards in time, or why it looks like we can go backwards. Verity explained it to me when we were in those big gas clouds, and *he* had it figured out the minute you told us Lylard couldn't see the accident coming because he couldn't see into his own future."

"I see," Jerry replied. "I guess I wasn't quite as used to you humans as I am now. I should have been more careful."

"It wouldn't have helped, Jerry. Like they said, human philosophers have been thinking about stuff like this for a long time. Verity figured time had to be a two-way flow, carrying energy both ways, and that if big stars could slow it, there had to be friction. Right?"

"Crudely put, Wyckoff, but a usable analogy. And, of course, two such forces cannot exist side by side without some sort of protective barrier. Large-scale interaction between them would destroy the universe, hence stasis, the neutral zone. Fortunately, or unfortunately, depending on your viewpoint, small-scale interaction can and does occur, but as your people had no doubt concluded by now, that, and errors which erect causality barriers, do make finding your way back difficult."

"Verity had something to say about that, too, Jerry. Of course he can do something you never could, because you can't get at those manuals. This causality thing is not as big a problem as you think—provided you're careful.

"But you never did answer my question, Jerry. Why shouldn't one bunch take over everything, straighten all this out, and make it easy on everybody?"

"One did, Wyckoff—the guild. But the guild is composed of individual temporals, most of them pretty scared and pretty selfish, who don't want any single temporal to get too strong. Any temporal, or any race for that matter, who tried that would get hit hard and fast."

"Well, if it's so big, how would they ever know?"

"The effects would show. They'd have time to do something about it. Believe me, Wyckoff, there wouldn't be any way to conceal it. Besides, the fact that these effects don't show proves it never will happen. It's impossible."

Wyckoff wasn't so sure. Ever since the spindly derelict with the dirty striped fur had died in his arms he'd been wondering how long the temporals as a group had actually existed, in terms of real time. He'd never discussed the idea with anyone else; hadn't even mentioned it, except very casually, to Verity. He had never been able to make up his own mind about the answer, which in contemplation had always promised to be droll. And for a while he had lived with the fear that Verity might say something to Arlene and upset her.

That danger appeared to have passed. Verity had evidently not ascribed the same significance to the remark that he had. Somehow, though, Wyckoff knew it wasn't the sort of thing he should just forget about—that someday that answer would be very important. After all, even the universe had to have a point of origin, so why shouldn't temporal travel? He thought that over carefully, and then answered the Dorian: "Yep, I guess you're right, Jerry. You're smarter'n me."

He stood up and stepped toward the door to call the Kruj'jan warrior who stood guard.

"What are you going to tell the others?"

"About you and that picture of Luddington? Nothing much. I don't see where it'd do any good to destroy their hopes of getting home. So, I'll probably just tell everybody that I talked to you and you don't know anything."

"What about getting me out of here?"

"What's your hurry? We're not hurting you. Sooner or later, we'll take you Dorians back to Dorr—don't you worry."

"Maybe I don't want to go back, Wyckoff. Maybe I want to go with you. I've got a feeling you're up to something and it'll be exciting."

"Aw, I don't know about that, Jerry. Everybody's pretty sore at you. Besides, you said I was a clod. Why would you want to go anyplace with a clod?"

"Well, you know how it is when you get sore at somebody, Wyckoff. Sometimes you say things you don't mean."

"Yeah, I guess I do know about that, all right, and I guess my skin's thick enough to take a hit once in a while. I don't know about Arlene, though, or the rest of the crew."

"It'll pass, Wyekoff. Give it a little time. You can see why I did what I did, can't you?"

"Sure. Uh, Jerry, I guess I can forgive and forget. I'm awful sorry about smacking you."

"So will they, Wyckoff, and besides, I know lots of other things that'd help out. You're the new lord temporal, and you're going to need some help at first, learning the territory. So I figure that maybe after a while, when things cool down a little, you and I could . . ."

Wyckoff wasn't listening anymore. He was already way ahead of Jerry—and he intended to stay way ahead.

The Dorian was right about one thing—he was up to something. Wyckoff intended to be in fact what he already was in name—Lord Temporal. Thanks to Yasha Fu, he had the formula, and there wasn't any reason he could see why it couldn't be scaled up. That alone would provide plenty of excitement, such as Jerry claimed to crave, but that wasn't the end of Wyckoff's ambition.

He knew why the great temporals went to such lengths to maintain their elaborate bases—he knew the true reason for the guild.

The guild existed because it was the only way this handful of lost creatures had any hope of ever searching two complete universes for their own way home; the only way that such disparate and relatively barbaric hordes of beings could be employed as searchers. The guild existed to maintain Chartmaster, and Chartmaster, with all its mercenary guile, was programmed to do only one super-important task—to extract a maximum of information from these lesser temporals about their wanderings.

There was no profit in being only a lord temporal, Wyckoff knew now. That was a title and a station suited only to the vain; to beings like Lylard, who would leave no lasting mark of their passage.

He resolved he would—that he would one day be something that even Yasha Fu had never dared to dream about: the light and the leader of the entire universe— the greatest and noblest of the temporals. Let others search for their home civilizations if they wished, and find them if they were lucky. The humans would not. The humans, beginning with their colony of Home, would carefully follow their mystic Lord through ages of time, as once their ancestors had followed Alexander.

But unlike the ancient Macedonian lord, who had but thirty years, Wyckoff hoped for eternity itself.

He might need all this time, he knew that, and believed he had that. He would need courage, and certainly he had that. He would need able assistants, and he thought he knew where he could find them—on Kruj, and Dorr, and Thrang, and among a myriad of other less favored but resourceful races.

Assistants, he reminded himself, not friends. He must remember what he was. Friends were fine, if you could trust them, and especially if you really liked them, but a sovereign couldn't. He could trust only his consort, and rarely, his heir.

Jerry could not, therefore, ever be his friend again, though he still had many uses. Jerry was flawed in a way that many ambitious human beings were, with ambition beyond his native abilities, so that he must attempt to make up the shortcomings with glib speech.

It was a shame, Wyckoff thought. He had known a lot of good con men in his time, never met one he didn't like, and never expected to. It was a part of their character, and of their stock in trade. In Wyckoff's opinion, Jerry would have made it as a lord temporal, especially since slick talking was probably the biggest part of it. Maybe someday he would make it.

Wyckoff would watch his back carefully.

Rob a Pharaoh and you've made an enemy
not just for life . . . but for *all time.*

FRED SABERHAGEN

PYRAMIDS

Tom Scheffler knew that his great uncle,
Montgomery Chapel, had worked as an Egyptologist
during the 1930s, and after that had become a
millionaire by selling artifacts no one else could
have obtained. Scheffler also knew that the old
man, fifty years later, was still afraid of some
man—some *entity*—known only as Pilgrim. But
what did that mean to Scheffler, an impoverished
student with the chance to spend a year "house-
sitting" a multi-million-dollar condo?

What Scheffler didn't know—and would learn
the hard way—was that Pilgrim was coming back,
aboard a ship that traveled both space and time,
headed for a confrontation in a weirdly changed
past where the monstrous gods of ancient Egypt
walked the Earth. And where Pharaoh Khufu,
builder of the greatest monument the world had
ever known, lay in wait for grave robbers from
out of time . . .

JANUARY 1987 • 65609-0 • 320 pp. • $3.50

ROBERT A. HEINLEIN

"Heinlein knows more about blending provocative scientific thinking with strong human stories than any dozen other contemporary science fiction writers."
—*Chicago Sun-Times*

"Robert A. Heinlein wears imagination as though it were his private suit of clothes. What makes his work so rich is that he combines his lively, creative sense with an approach that is at once literate, informed, and exciting."
—*New York Times*

Seven of Robert A. Heinlein's best-loved titles are now available in superbly packaged new Baen editions, with embossed series-look covers by artist John Melo. Collect them all by sending in the order form below:

REVOLT IN 2100, 65589-2, $3.50 ☐

METHUSELAH'S CHILDREN, 65597-3, $3.50 ☐

THE GREEN HILLS OF EARTH, 65608-2, $3.50 ☐

THE MAN WHO SOLD THE MOON, 65623-6, $3.50 ☐

THE MENACE FROM EARTH*, 65636-8, $3.50 ☐

ASSIGNMENT IN ETERNITY**, 65637-6, $3.50 ☐

SIXTH COLUMN***, 65638-4, $3.50 ☐

*To be published May 1987. **To be published July 1987. ***To be published October 1987. Any books ordered prior to publication date will be shipped at no extra charge as soon as they are available.

Please send me the books I have checked above. I enclose a check or money order for the combined cover price for the titles I have ordered, plus 75 cents for first-class postage and handling (for any number of titles) made out to Baen Books, Dept. B, 260 Fifth Avenue, New York, N.Y. 10001.

"The crowd was noisy in the Blue Bottle, although it was early in the evening. Tavern girls squealed as customers pinched them, gaily clad waiters brought round after round of drinks, and throughout much of the room everyone was shouting merrily. The reason was not hard to find, for in one corner of the crowded room three officers of the Imperial Navy held court, buying drinks for anyone on Prince Samual's World who would sit with them and laugh at their jokes. . . ."

BY THE CO-AUTHOR OF *FOOTFALL* AND *THE MOTE IN GOD'S EYE*

"ROCK 'EM, SOCK 'EM SPACE ADVENTURE"
—*The Chicago Tribune*

"COLORFUL, FAST-PACED . . . JERRY POURNELLE AT HIS BEST!"
—Poul Anderson

"Jerry Pournelle is one of a handful of writers who can speculate knowledgeably about future worlds. His space program background, readings in science, and Ph.D.'s in psychology and political science allow him to carefully work out the logical development of a world and its societies. . . . [*King David's Spaceship*] is a fine novel."—*Amazing*

FEBRUARY 1987 • 384 pp. • 65616-3 • $2.95

To order any Baen Book by mail, send check or money order for the cover price plus 75 cents for first-class postage and handling made out to Baen Books, Dept. B, 260 Fifth Avenue, New York, N.Y. 10001.

GORDON R. DICKSON

Winner of every award science fiction and fantasy to offer, Gordon Dickson is one of the major authors of this century. He creates heroes and enemies, not just characters in books; his stories celebrate bravery and virtue and the best in all of us. Collect some of the very best of Gordon Dickson's writing by ordering the books below.

FORWARD!, 55971-0, 256 pp., $2.95 ☐

HOUR OF THE HORDE, 55905-2,
   256 pp., $2.95 ☐

INVADERS!, 55994-X, 256 pp., $2.95 ☐

THE LAST DREAM, 65559-0, 288 pp.,
   $2.95 ☐

MINDSPAN, 65580-9, 288 pp., $2.95 ☐

SURVIVAL!, 55927-3, 288 pp., $2.75 ☐

WOLFLING, 55962-1, 256 pp., $2.95 ☐

LIFESHIP (with Harry Harrison), 55981-8,
   256 pp., $2.95 ☐

Please send me the books I have checked above. I enclose a check or money order for the combined price plus 75 cents for first-class postage and handling made out to Baen Books, Dept. B, 260 Fifth Avenue, New York, N.Y. 10001.